Ali McNamara attributes her over-active imagination to one thing – being an only child. Time spent dreaming up adventures when she was young has left her with a head constantly bursting with stories waiting to be told. When stories she wrote for fun on Ronan Keating's website became so popular they were sold as a fundraising project for his cancer awareness charity, Ali realised that writing was not only something she enjoyed doing, but something others enjoyed reading too.

Ali lives in Cambridgeshire with her family and two labradors, and when she isn't writing, she enjoys watching too much reality TV, eating too much chocolate, and counteracting the results of the previous activities with plenty of exercise!

Keep in touch with Ali via her website at www.alimcnamara.co.uk or on Twitter: @AliMcNamara

Also by Ali McNamara

From Notting Hill With Love ... Actually
Breakfast at Darcy's

From Notting Hill to New York ... Actually

Ali McNamara

SPHERE

First published as a paperback original in Great Britain
in 2012 by Sphere

A CIP catalogue record for this book
is available from the British Library.

ISBN 978-0-7515-4745-0

Typeset in Caslon by M Rules
Printed and bound in Great Britain by
Clays Ltd, St Ives plc

Papers used by Sphere are from well-managed forests
and other responsible sources.

MIX
Paper from
responsible sources
FSC® C104740

Sphere
An imprint of
Little, Brown Book Group
100 Victoria Embankment
London EC4Y 0DY

An Hachette UK Company
www.hachette.co.uk

www.littlebrown.co.uk

For Oscar, who always makes me smile.
And Jake, who simply keeps me sane.

Acknowledgements

I've loved writing all about Scarlett and Sean again. It was like coming back to a lovely set of old friends and discovering what might happen to them if I set them off on a new adventure in a brand new city.

However, this book could not have been written without the help and support of a number of people, who I would like to thank now.

My editor, Rebecca, and everyone at my publishers Little, Brown. There are so many of you involved in putting my books together that listing everyone would take up the whole page! But please know how much I appreciate all your hard work and effort.

Hannah, my wonderful agent. Slowly the dream is coming true, Hannah! And it's all thanks to your original faith in me. Thank you for everything. You always know just the right words to say.

Dan Martland and Nick Dixon. I know you guys still don't know what you did to inspire me to write two characters based on you when I came to New York last summer, but inspire me you did, and also very kindly allowed me to admit to it in public! Thank you for that, and for all the help and support you've both given me during the writing of this book. Scarlett says in the story she only expected to come back from her first trip to New York with a few souvenirs. Well, so did I – I certainly didn't expect to return with the added bonus of two lovely new friends. ☺

My wonderful family; especially my children Rosie and Tom. I can never thank you enough for all your love and support. But I also can't thank you enough for allowing me to jet off on my own and discover what New York was really like for the first time last year. Because if I hadn't, I definitely wouldn't be writing this now! I love you more than you know.

And finally, to all you lovely readers; firstly for buying my books, but especially for every email, Facebook message or tweet that you've sent me telling me how much you enjoy them. It really means the world to me.

Ali x

One

'Scarlett, can you get me another glass of juice, please?'

I close the lid of my laptop and sigh, getting up from the chair in the study to go across the hall and through to the living room where a sorrowful pair of blue eyes looks up at me from the sofa.

'Sure, what do you want this time, orange or apple?'

'Apple, please.' Sean holds out his empty glass. He manages a weak smile.

'All right, you don't have to lay it on so thick,' I admonish. 'I thought you were feeling better this morning.'

'I am, but I still feel a bit wobbly when I try to get up.'

'OK, I'll get your juice. You just stay right where you are watching . . .' I glance at the TV screen, and it doesn't surprise me in the slightest to see cars racing around a track, as per usual. 'Let me guess – it wouldn't happen to be *Top Gear*, would it?'

Sean nods absent-mindedly, his attention already lost to the petrol-head world of Clarkson, The Stig and their ridiculously priced cars.

I wander through to the kitchen and fill Sean's glass with juice. He'd been off sick for a few days now, and I'd been doing my best nursing act, when I'd been at home, looking after him. I didn't mind, even though I was just beginning to think he was pushing his luck a bit with the 'I'm so ill' looks when he wanted something. But when I'd had an extremely nasty dose of the flu last December and could barely get out of bed, let alone walk to our kitchen, for over a week, Sean had taken time off work – unheard of for him – and had waited on me hand and foot. He'd even carried me to the bathroom on one occasion when I was too weak to get there myself. So I really couldn't complain about a few glasses of juice and a sandwich here and there.

I stand for a moment, admiring our new kitchen. I'd spent many a happy hour poring over designer-kitchen catalogues with my friend, Oscar, choosing just the right oven and fridge to go with the newly installed granite-covered worktops and pale wood units. Sean couldn't understand why, when I first moved in here with him, I'd wanted to refit what he considered to be a perfectly adequate kitchen. But I told him that if I was going to move into his house in Notting Hill, I would at least want to put my own stamp on the place, and as always Sean had just let me get on with it. He was very easy-going like that.

Smiling to myself, I stare out of the kitchen window into our small, recently renovated back garden. Neither Sean nor I were really into gardening, so we'd gone for the minimal amount of planting and maximum amount of 'garden architecture' as our landscaper, Murray, had called it when we'd hired him to help us out last autumn when deciding what to do with the patch of land at the back of the house. Now we have the perfect area to sit outside in on a summer's evening, with a glass of chilled wine, chatting over the day's events with each other. Except, I realise as I stand here now, we've only ever done that once, and the person I sit out there with most often is Oscar, when we're discussing the lives of the contestants in the newest reality TV show, or the latest salacious plot twist in our favourite soap opera.

I lift the glass from the counter and head back to Sean. 'Here you go,' I say, handing him the glass. 'One juice.'

'Thanks, Scarlett. You've been great at looking after me while it's been my turn for the flu.'

I look sceptically at him. I hardly think this is

anything like what I had in December: his is more of a bad cold. What I'm seeing in front of me, I think, is the common phenomenon known as 'man flu'.

'So when do you think you'll be well enough to go back to work?' I ask, slipping onto the sofa next to him. I lift up yet more car and sport magazines and drop them on the ever-growing pile on the floor.

'Maybe tomorrow,' Sean says, turning his attention from the TV for a moment. 'But definitely by Thursday. I have to fly to Brussels for a meeting.'

'Again?' I ask in astonishment. Sean takes so many business trips abroad he might as well be a bird. His ratio of air-to-ground time is certainly enough to qualify him as one of our feathered friends.

'Yes. Come on, not *this* again, Red?' he raises a sandy-coloured eyebrow at me. 'I thought we'd been over all that. You knew when you met me that my business means I have to be away a lot.'

I shrug and stare at the TV screen. Sean's right; I did know he had to travel for meetings and stay away often – that was one of the drawbacks of running your own very successful company. But it didn't mean I had to like it. It wasn't fair. *I* ran my own company. Well, I did, with my father, but I never got to travel away from home. There weren't many opportunities to go to popcorn-machine conferences, and the only people I ever seemed to meet

4

with were the managers of cinemas. It was always me here, waiting for Sean to come back from his trips.

My thoughts are distracted by the TV for a moment. *What are they doing this time, are they actually trying to sail those cars across water? Makes a change from blowing up caravans, I suppose.*

'Don't you ever get fed up watching this?' I ask, hoping to change the subject. I really didn't want an argument today. We'd had quite a few of those lately, petty things such as Sean leaving towels on the bathroom floor, clothes on the bedroom floor. In fact, floors were quite a sticky point with us right now.

'*Top Gear*? No, it's hilarious.'

'Hmm . . .'

'It *is*! The other day I watched an episode where they were actually playing a game of darts with real cars and a huge gas-powered cannon!'

I look at him doubtfully. Is this the same man I met a year ago, who had swept me off my feet on the top of the London Eye by silently declaring his love for me in movie quotes with flash cards, *Love Actually*-style?

'And,' Sean continues, 'I seem to remember you being very interested in the episode when Tom Cruise and Cameron Diaz were driving around the race track.'

'Yes, well, that was different. They don't usually have movie stars on there, do they?' I hadn't lost my love of movies altogether since moving in with Sean. It had just been diluted to a more 'manageable' level. I gesture at the TV screen. 'A programme where three middle-aged men drone on about cars for half an hour just isn't my idea of fun. It's like *Last of the Summer Wine*, but with engines and a bit more hair.'

Sean's lips twitch in amusement as he tries to remain serious. 'What *is* your idea of a good programme, then? Hmm ... let me think. I know, there needs to be the minimum of at least one crime, preferably a murder to be solved by a dour yet lovable detective. Or the actors need to be trussed up in a corset, a pair of tight breeches and live in a big mansion in the country somewhere.'

'I do watch more than police shows and costume dramas,' I reply haughtily. 'I have quite a varied taste in televisual viewing.'

Sean grins now. 'That's right, I almost forgot – we need to make sure the leading man is a bit of a handsome fella too, and then it's your perfect programme! I should call the BBC and suggest it to them: remake *Pride and Prejudice* with Colin Firth, except this time call it *Mr Darcy Investigates*. He could ride around on his horse, unravelling local mysteries. There must have been loads of unsolved murders in Jane Austen's time.'

I fold my arms and survey him disapprovingly across the sofa. Although the idea of Colin Firth striding around

Pemberley as an eighteenth-century detective is not altogether a bad idea ...

'Well, tell me I'm wrong,' Sean challenges, still grinning.

'Why would I need to lust after TV stars when I've got my own handsome hunk sitting right here on my sofa?' I answer, my frown beginning to soften into a smile. 'When you're actually *at* home, of course,' I add.

'Hmm ... I might just let you get away with that,' Sean says, reaching across the settee and pulling me towards him.

'Oi,' I pretend to complain, as I find myself on Sean's lap. 'I thought you weren't well!'

'I'm suddenly feeling much, much better,' Sean whispers as he deftly flicks off the TV with the remote control in one hand, while the other wraps itself around my waist. And I find, for once, that it's my chassis commanding his attention for the next few minutes, instead of the highly polished, overpriced ones on the TV screen.

Two

'You're going *where* with Oscar?' Sean asks me as he buttons up his shirt and deftly knots his tie in the mirror of our dressing table.

'To the gym. Well, we're calling in somewhere first to drop off one of his outfits.'

One of my best friends, Oscar, falling on his designer-shoe-clad feet, has managed to ride the tidal wave of recession hitting the independent high-street retailer and has turned his cornucopia of a boutique, where he was selling designer fashions through the decades, into a thriving costume-hire business. Now he's offering his genuine period clothing not only to private clients and businesses, but quite often these days he is asked by magazines and newspapers for one-off items for photo shoots. And recently he's had some breaks in the film and television market, too. It was with much excitement that we'd eagerly tuned in to an episode of a new BBC1 wartime drama the other night, just so we could spot one of Oscar's hats appearing on the head of Prostitute Number Two in a scene set in the East End of London.

'You and Oscar are going to the gym?' Sean asks, turning round to face me. 'So *that's* why you're dressed like that.'

I look into the full-length mirror that stands in the corner of our bedroom. 'Is it a bit over the top?' I ask, eyeing my new black and red Nike tracksuit with matching Lycra vest top. There's also a pair of coordinating cycling shorts concealed beneath the tracksuit bottoms, which may or may not be revealed this morning, depending on just how many mirrors the gym contains.

Sean moves behind me and considers my reflection, then he kisses the side of my neck. 'No one will even bat an eyelid at you when you arrive with Oscar, sweetheart. I don't even want to try to imagine what he's going to turn up in!'

Ever since I met Oscar last year, when I first came to Notting Hill, he's always had a pretty eccentric taste in clothes. Never one to blend into the background, Oscar's taste definitely leans towards the brighter end of the colour spectrum. In fact, a macaw parrot would probably feel dull and uninteresting perched next to him.

'You'll find out in a moment – he's coming round to pick me up.'

'Why this sudden interest in joining a gym?' Sean asks, moving away from the mirror to lift his jacket from the hanger.

'Oh, no reason. Oscar and I just decided we wanted to get fitter, that's all, and we thought we'd go for a little induction today to see if we like it – it's free, after all.'

'Scarlett, I know you a bit better than that by now ...' Sean thinks for a moment while he adjusts his tie in the mirror. 'Let me guess: there's a rumour that some celebrity has joined this gym you're testing out, and you're hoping to catch a glimpse of him in his shorts.'

Damn, Sean knows me a bit too well.

'You know I've been exercising a lot with my workout DVDs lately,' I say, sitting down on the bed and pulling on my new Nike trainers. 'I just thought I'd step it up a gear.' In reality, I'd bought a box set of Davina McCall workouts and done the first DVD two and half times. The half was because I'd got distracted midway through by a man outside in the street busking Beatles songs. Not unusual in London, but in a suburban street in Notting Hill definitely a stop-and-stare necessity.

Sean waits with his arms folded. He taps his foot on the carpet for added effect.

'OK, OK, yes,' I look up at him from the bed. 'There was a tiny little rumour that Jude Law has been spotted using the gym while he's in a West End play in town, but that's not the only reason we're going there today.'

'I knew it!' he announces triumphantly, a broad grin spreading across his face. 'You'll never change, Scarlett.'

'That's not true! You know I don't watch anywhere near the amount of movies I used to.'

'No, you don't,' Sean's face becomes serious. 'But you've replaced your obsession with other things.'

'Like?'

'Like TV, and that computer of yours. You're never off it.'

I finish lacing up my shoes. 'You can talk about TV, with your stupid car programmes and your sport, you watch just as much as me. And I like my laptop. It keeps me in touch with people.'

Sean snorts. 'Not real people, though. Internet people.'

'They *are* real people! Just because I can't see them in the flesh doesn't make them imaginary.'

Sean's face softens again; he walks over towards me and kisses me on the forehead. 'Scarlett, as long as you're happy I don't mind what you find yourself obsessed with

11

next. As long as it's legal, of course,' he adds with a wink. 'Now I have to go to work. Have fun with Oscar at the gym, won't you? Don't work out too hard – you're just a beginner, remember.'

'I'll keep it in mind, thanks, Sean,' I reply, trying to sound aloof. But as Sean scoops me up into his arms to kiss me goodbye properly, as always, I melt at the feeling of his lips on mine. Some things never change.

We both head downstairs, and as Sean opens the front door to leave the house Oscar is already standing on the doorstep, about to ring the bell.

'You must have sensed I was coming, darling,' Oscar announces, flamboyantly swishing past Sean into the hall.

'Yes, I thought I could feel my retinas beginning to burn,' Sean says, pretending to shield his eyes from Oscar's bright clothing. 'Much as I'd love to stay and chat, Oscar, as always, I have to go to work. Bye, Scarlett, have fun working out those noses of yours.'

Both Oscar and I grimace at him as he closes the door.

Oscar and Sean have never seen eye to eye. Mainly because, some years ago, Sean used to date Oscar's sister, and when they broke up, quite bitterly at the time, Jennifer went to live over in the States.

'Oscar, you look . . . ' I search for an appropriate word as I gaze at the abundance of neon Lycra positively throbbing before me in the hallway ' . . . resplendent,' I decide.

12

'Do you think?' Oscar says, pirouetting around on the tiled floor. 'I thought it might be a tad over the top. But as I always say, if you're going to do something, you may as well do it to the absolute limit!'

'You've certainly done that. Perhaps . . .' I hesitate as I think about the hip and trendy private gym we're going to be entering today.

'Perhaps what?' Oscar scoots over to the wall and scrutinises himself in front of the mirror. 'It's too much, isn't it?' he wails. 'I knew it. It will have to go.' He carefully removes a shocking-pink towelling headband. 'There, what do you think now – better?'

I try not to look at the rest of his ensemble – his electric-blue Lycra leggings with emerald-green leg warmers, or his matching blue singlet with a bright pink tick across the chest. 'Much better, Oscar,' I agree. 'The headband *was* a bit OTT.'

'Fabbo! Now, are you ready to get going? We've got to drop this at the TV studios on the way, you know?' Oscar holds up a zipped suit bag containing one of the vintage outfits from his shop.

'Yes, I haven't forgotten.' How could I? We were going to a real TV studio! I was so excited. But I was trying to act cool and calm, like it was an everyday occurrence. 'Will we be OK to get in looking like this, though?' I glance down at my gym gear.

13

'Are you kidding, Scarlett, this is TV! Anything goes behind the scenes. It's only onscreen that there are rules and regulations.'

'Like what?'

'Like, they don't want you wearing big stripes because it interferes with the screen, or something, and if it's morning TV there's no black, it has to be bright and breezy.'

'So if one of us accidentally ends up on air today, then you'll have no worries, Oscar.'

Oscar tosses his head. 'There's as much chance of *that* happening as one of us dating Bradley Cooper. Too much security, darling; it's like Colditz getting in and out of there.'

We set off for the TV studios in a black cab. Oscar won't allow his clothes on public transport, in case they get squashed or *tainted* by the smell of commuters. As we trail across London in the taxi, I look out at the city I now call home.

It hadn't taken me too long to get used to living here permanently. After I'd spent a month house-sitting last year in Notting Hill, and I'd fallen in love with my next-door neighbour at the time – Sean – it hadn't taken me much thought at all before upping sticks and moving in with him. We'd relocated the offices of the popcorn-machine company I continued to run with my father from Stratford-upon-Avon down to London, and our headquarters were now based in a little office in Chelsea. But it was only me and my new assistants, Tammy and Leon, that ran the offices now. Dorothy, my father's faithful secretary of many years, had decided to retire when Dad had gone over to New York to run the new US arm of the business. Which was blossoming, after Sean had purchased a chain of cinemas last year in one of his business deals, and our popcorn machines were gradually supplying the ever-growing needs of the cinema-goers of America.

I missed Dad terribly. But he'd taken to living in New York surprisingly well. I think he quite enjoyed having the chance to do something different with his life for once, and my moving in with Sean had given him the push to move on.

'What ya thinkin' about?' Oscar asks, as we suddenly pick up speed and start moving through the early-morning traffic at a pace.

'Dad.'

'You miss him, don't you?' Oscar asks, resting his hand on mine.

I nod. 'Yes, but he's having a whale of a time over in New York. Best thing that ever happened to him, going to the States. It's been like a new lease of life.'

'Doesn't mean you shouldn't miss him, though, Scarlett. It was only the two of you for twenty-three years. It's understandable you should feel the loss.'

I nod again. Oscar always knows the right thing to say. He's been like my new best friend since I've come to live in London. Maddie, my oldest friend, still isn't that far away in Stratford-upon-Avon, when she isn't off travelling around the world with her husband, Felix, but it just isn't the same.

Suddenly the taxi driver screeches to a halt.

'What's wrong?' I exclaim, peering through the glass partition to see what's caused him to brake so hard.

'Bloody joggers!' he moans, rolling his eyes. 'Shouldn't be allowed. She just stepped right out in front of that bus, and now there's a three-vehicle pile-up.'

As the taxi driver slowly pulls around the line of vehicles, I see some early-bird tourists already snapping photos of the incident, and uniformed police officers appearing on the scene, trying to grab a couple of witnesses to take a statement from as the jogger looks anxiously at her watch.

'I don't think she is a jogger,' I remark as we drive by. 'Her clothes suggest she's going to a gym, like us, not out road-running.'

Oscar laughs. 'Two sessions with Davina McCall, and you're a fitness expert now?'

'Three, actually, and I have bought some other work-out DVDs, I just haven't had time to do them yet.'

'And will you?' Oscar asks with wide eyes.

'Depends on how I get on at the gym later this morning. I could well take up a yearly membership if I like it.'

'You mean if you catch a glimpse of Jude Law in a sweat-soaked vest!'

'There is that added incentive!'

The taxi pulls to a stop outside the TV studios where we're dropping off Oscar's outfit. While Oscar pays the driver, I look up at the rather dull building we're about to enter. It doesn't look much like I've imagined a TV studio might look. It's quite drab and boring on the outside. But as we go through the security gate outside, giving our names and reason for being there, and then on into Reception where we sign our names in a book, it begins to feel a bit more exciting. I see photographs of some of the programmes that are filmed there, and some of the personalities that work on them. Oscar flashes his visitor's pass at the smiling receptionist and we're allowed further into the building.

'So where do we have to go now?' I ask, trying to act cool but feeling a sense of nervous anticipation, like a child about to visit Santa.

'This way,' Oscar says, prancing down a long corridor.

As I follow him, I try and look as if I visit TV studios every day of the week, but the reality is my head is swivelling to and fro trying to see inside rooms and offices in the hope that I might spot something exciting going on.

But it's all quite boring, really, not at all what I expected. It's just like a normal office block.

Then as we turn a corner, and Oscar hurriedly sets off down the next long corridor, I pause for a moment to glance back at a small crowd of people gathering outside one of the rooms we've just passed.

It couldn't be – could it? It had looked an awful lot like him sitting in that chair as we'd whizzed past ... But what would he be doing here at this time of the morning?

Then I see a sign above me on the wall that says *Wake Up Britain TV Studios*, and the penny drops. He must be a guest this morning on breakfast television. I'm about to call out to Oscar to wait a moment, but the corridor stretching out in front of me is empty.

I look at my two options. Chase after Oscar and his 1920s flapper dress and matching headband, or casually wander back down the corridor and possibly get the chance to speak to Colin Firth ...

It doesn't take much thinking about.

I'm about to take a step towards my date with destiny when a young man in faded jeans and a Ted Baker t-shirt taps me on the shoulder.

'Excuse me?' he enquires.

I'm almost thrusting my hands in the air in surrender and admitting that yes, I'm not supposed to be here alone when he continues, 'Are you the fitness expert?'

'I ... I'm sorry?' I ask, looking at him in bewilderment.

'The new *Wake Up Britain* fitness expert? To say there's been a bit of a panic going on down there,' he gestures down the corridor, 'is an understatement. We didn't think you were going to make it when you said you'd been in a traffic accident. I'm Rich. We spoke on the phone.'

I stare at him blankly.

'Are you OK?' he asks, looking worried. 'Are you in shock or something? You don't have concussion, do you?'

'Er, no ...'

'Good-good, then let's get you down to make-up. You're looking a bit pale.'

He grasps hold of my arm, and before I know what's happening I'm being escorted down the corridor and into a small room decorated almost entirely in white. It has large mirrors running the length of the wall, and several high seats standing in front of the mirrors.

'Hi,' says a young girl with long auburn hair and wild jewellery, gesturing at one of the seats. 'Sit right here. Won't be a mo.'

I'm just about to explain that I'm not actually an expert in fitness, and that the only time I really get out of breath is when I have to run the length of Oxford Street on the first day of the sales, and that I can judge my current strength levels on just how many shopping bags my biceps can endure in the process without becoming too overloaded … when she whips a white gown away from the person sitting in the chair next to me.

'There, all done, Mr Firth,' she says, coyly smiling at him in the mirror.

'Thank you, Michelle,' he says, a charming smile spreading across his newly made-up face. He lifts himself from the chair and glances in my direction. 'Don't worry – you're in safe hands. Probably bump into you in the green room in a few minutes,' is his parting comment, before he's suddenly surrounded by people wearing headphones and carrying clipboards. Most that gather in the gang don't actually seem to have a reason to be there, but just need to be passing by at the time because, hey, it *is* Colin Firth.

'Now,' Michelle says, securing a clean white gown around my neck so I can't escape. 'Let's have a look at you.'

I should protest. I should say, 'No, I'm not supposed to be sitting here. I'm not a fitness expert,' or whatever it is Rich thinks I am. But I can't. Colin Firth has just spoken to me. Mr Darcy has just said, 'See you in the green room in a few minutes.' I'm not going to turn down an invitation like that, am I?

Michelle spends the next few minutes making me look fit to appear on TV. This involves spraying quite a lot of very dark base on me so I look as if I've been under a sunbed a tad too long, with a sort of spraying wand that Michelle explains is specifically made for high-definition television make-up. Then she applies more eye make-up and blusher than I've ever worn on an evening out, let alone to give me the healthy glow of a fitness instructor first thing in the morning. But Michelle insists it's all necessary under the bright TV lights, so I go along with it while I try to make it sound as if I know something about exercise and fitness. I throw in a few words I've heard Davina mention in her DVDs like 'quads' and 'hamstrings', except while I'm doing all this I'm also trying to plan what I might say to Colin in the green room, and my already overwrought mind mistakenly blabs 'Cheestrings'. I hurriedly correct myself and I don't think Michelle noticed, and if she did, she's too well trained to point it out.

My plan is that once I've spent a few minutes chatting up – sorry – *conversing politely* with Colin, on subjects like where he keeps his Oscar, I'll casually sneak out of the green room (I wonder what shade of green it'll be? My skin will look awful if the room is painted the wrong tone) just before I'm called to go on air, and then I can go and find my own Oscar. I wonder if he's missed me yet . . .

Make-up done, I'm hurried along another corridor to a pretty-looking room which, thank goodness, isn't green at all, where there are delicious-looking refreshments waiting for me on a table, and a comfy sofa with a couple of other people already sitting on it. No sign of Colin.

'Just take a seat. Lucy, she's the floor manager on this morning's show, she'll be in to have a chat about your segment in a moment,' Rich says, looking at his clipboard.

I look hungrily at the croissant on the table in front of me. We hadn't had breakfast this morning because we were on our way to the gym, and my stomach is beginning to complain.

'Shame you can't have any,' Rich says, glancing over his clipboard at me. 'They're delicious, we get them from a little bakery down the road.'

'I can't?' I enquire sadly. Maybe they were for the A-list guests only.

'You can't work out on a full stomach, can you?' he says, looking at me with a puzzled expression.

'No . . . no, of course not.'

The door opens and my settee-mates are ushered through it, presumably for their five minutes of TV fame. Rich still hovers by the door.

'Will Colin be joining us?' I enquire as casually as I can. If he isn't coming back in here then I really need to think about making my escape. And soon.

Rich looks at his watch. 'Yes, he'll be along in a minute. I think he's got caught up signing autographs and stuff down the corridor.'

I glance nervously around me. There's a little monitor across the room showing exactly what's going on in the *Wake Up Britain* studio right at this very moment as they broadcast live to the nation, and suddenly I realise that this might not have been such a good idea after all – Oscar-winning actor or not.

I clamber to my feet, about to try and make some excuse about needing fresh air, when the door bursts open and in breezes a young woman wearing jeans, a tight red sweater and a polka-dot scarf tied into a cheery bow at the side of her neck. Her black hair is in a loose ponytail.

'Hi, you must be Jemma,' she says, thrusting her hand into mine. 'So sorry – got tied up back there with Colin. But who wouldn't want to, eh, given half a chance?' She winks at me.

'Hahayeahmm,' I nervously half mumble, half laugh at her joke.

'Ye-ss … Now then,' she says, sitting down next to me. 'I just want to run through what's going to happen over the next hour. You had the email I sent last week, so that's fine … now—'

'Email?'

'Yes,' Lucy looks at me oddly. 'Are you OK? I know you were involved in a bit of an accident on your way here, but Rich,' she looks over her shoulder at Rich, 'said you were fine now.'

Why do they keep mentioning an accident? Then it all falls into place. The pile-up we drove past with the jogger ... She must have been the fitness expert they were expecting in here this morning! And now, seeing me dressed like this, wandering about in the corridor earlier ...

'So, are you?' she prompts, looking worried. 'Only you're on in ...' she glances at her watch. 'Bugger, Rich, why didn't you say? Quick, Jemma, this way!' She grabs my arm and yanks me off the sofa. Before I've got time to protest, I'm dragged along a corridor and through a door with a red ON AIR sign lit up above it.

Three

I stand there, panic-stricken, with Lucy gripping my arm like a vice. I look past a bank of cameramen and see two orange sofas. Sitting on them are the two regular *Wake Up Britain* presenters, reading off an autocue and talking into one of the cameras. Lucy holds her finger to her lips. 'You need to be quiet,' she whispers. 'They're live right now.'

I look around me and try to bolt for the exit. But Lucy is surprisingly strong and blocks my way. 'Where are you going?' she hisses. 'You're on in a minute!'

'Toilet,' I squeak. 'Desperate.'

'Sorry, no time. Ad break in three ... two ... one ... now. Go!' she calls, herding me towards one of the orange sofas.

'This is Jemma, our new fitness expert,' she says by way of introduction. 'Jemma, meet Julian and Loretta.'

'Hi, Jemma.' Loretta holds out her hand and I manage to shake it. Julian just nods as he shakes my hand. I begin to lower my bottom onto the orange sofa.

'No!' Lucy cries. 'It's your routine first, then question-and-answer after the next break. You did read the running order?' she asks accusingly, grabbing my arm again and leading me towards a small area with wood laminate flooring and a large screen behind it.

'Y-yes. Of course I did.'

'Great, well, just do your thing, the music will cue up automatically, then when you've finished, make your way over to the sofa again and Loretta and Julian will interview you. Capeesh?'

I feel my head nodding as my brain bangs on the inside of it going, *No! No! Tell her, you fool. Tell her you're not the fitness expert now before it's too—*

But it is too late, because suddenly there's silence in the studio as the ad break ends and we go live again. Lucy disappears behind the row of cameramen and gestures at me to remain on the stage.

I stare wildly around me, wondering how I can escape as I hear Loretta and Julian welcome the viewers back and talk about what's coming next. As I hear them introduce the new *Wake Up Britain* fitness expert to the

26

show, I realise there *is* no escape: I'm going to have to do this.

The opening beats to The Black Eyed Peas' 'I Gotta Feeling' begin to play, and I automatically start to sway from side to side like a dad on a dance floor at a wedding, then all of their own accord my hands join in too and begin to clap in time to the music. I now look more like a nursery-school teacher taking a 'clap and sing' class than a highly trained fitness instructor appearing on breakfast TV for the first time. *Think, Scarlett*, think*! You're on live TV . . .*

Then, like a vision from above, she comes to me in my hour of need: Davina.

I quickly pull myself together and launch into a few of the moves I remember from the DVD. I 'travel' from left to right across the stage. Perform a couple of squats, and then some more daring lunges. I come a bit of a cropper on the second set of lunges, when my trainer slips on the laminate flooring and I almost end up doing the splits. But I deftly recover, turning it into a couple of press-ups in time to the music. Then at last my torment ends as the music fades and I'm left like an upturned beetle trying to demonstrate stomach crunches with my arms and legs waving madly in mid-air.

There's polite applause from around the studio as I hurriedly pull myself to my feet again and jog lightly back over to the orange sofa.

'Well, that was ... energetic,' Julian states kindly, smiling at me as I try to catch my breath. 'And can you tell us what inspired that particular routine?'

'Er ... I like to create a fusion of different types of exercise in my workouts,' I improvise. 'I take inspiration from a number of sources.'

'I can see that,' Loretta joins in. She smiles like Julian, but it's a practised smile that shows just enough of her perfect white teeth to enable it to look genuine. 'It was certainly *varied*. So what are you going to be showing us over the coming weeks, then, Jemma? What our viewers really want to know is how to tone up and lose all their excess weight ready for their summer holidays. I'm not sure there's much call for *fusion* workouts here at *Wake Up Britain* – perhaps something a little more basic?'

I bet you're the biggest expert on dieting in this studio, I think, as I smile politely back at her. Her tiny bum barely makes a dent in the bright orange fabric of the sofa as she crosses her stick-thin legs. *In fact, you probably never eat anything bigger than an hors d'œuvre just in case it bloats your pea-sized stomach.* And suddenly, I feel a wave of sympathy for the *Wake Up Britain* viewers, who have to put up with her condescending attitude.

'Actually, Loretta, I'm sure you'll find your viewers are a bit more savvy than you think when it comes to their exercise routines. Not everyone who watches *Wake Up*

Britain is a couch potato. I'm guessing your viewers would love to challenge themselves with something new, instead of the same old boring routines we see on TV all the time.'

As Loretta glowers at me across the glass coffee table between the two sofas, Julian quickly steps in.

'Quite,' he comments, forcing a smile. 'So, apart from your *inventive* exercise routines, Jemma, what about dietary advice? What can you help our viewers with there?'

I really don't know what comes over me. I find myself turning and looking straight down the nearest camera lens. And as I do, I notice a little red light pop on above it.

'Don't,' I say clearly and plainly into the lens.

'What?' I hear Loretta exclaim next to me, as though I've just blasphemed over the nation's cornflakes.

'Don't diet,' I repeat, turning towards her. 'I don't believe in it.'

'B-but,' she stammers, 'you're a fitness instructor.'

'Dieting is for fools,' I state plainly. 'Yes, by all means eat healthily and watch what you eat. But I'm a great believer in a little of what you fancy doing you good. If you eat well most of the time, then the odd bit of chocolate, bag of chips or glass of wine won't do you much harm. In fact, it will probably do you good, stop you

29

pigging out the rest of the time and turning into a food-obsessed stick insect that daren't eat anything for fear of gaining an ounce or two.'

Loretta and Julian stare at me in astonishment.

I grin back at them, and out of the corner of my eye I notice a man waving his arms in the air.

'I-it's time for a quick break,' Loretta says, jumping to attention as she hurriedly puts a finger to her ear. 'Don't forget – when we come back, Colin Firth will be joining us on the sofa.'

They both visibly relax as we go off-air again.

'You certainly have some different views, young lady,' Julian says, eyeing me up and down. 'It's quite refreshing to hear someone telling people to eat what they want for a change.'

Loretta doesn't look so sure as she has her make-up retouched. Suddenly Lucy leaps up next to us, looking far from impressed. 'What on earth was all that about?' she demands. 'That's not the approach we discussed at all. I was quite clear in my email – didn't you get it?'

'Erm . . . ' I'm trying to think of a way of getting out of it, but in the corner of my eye I can see Colin arriving in the small studio and all sensible thought – if there had been any there in the first place – evaporates from my brain.

'Lucy, Lucy!' I hear someone call from across the

studio. It's Rich, and he's clutching some sheets of paper in his hand. 'The phone lines have gone *mental*!' he cries as he runs over to us, waving the pieces of paper. 'The viewers *love* Jemma!' He reads from the top sheet.

Love your new fitness instructor – finally someone that talks sense.

Jemma is fab. Good to see someone that's not all skin and bone on TV for a change!

If a little of what you fancy does you good, then Jemma is doing me a whole lot of good right now!

'Sorry for that last one,' he apologises, looking at me. 'You get that sort of thing on Twitter. But it's still positive. Well done you!'

Lucy looks sceptical. 'Let me see those,' she says, snatching the comments pages away from Rich. She quickly thumbs them through. 'Hmm ... Well, it looks like you're doing *something* right. You'd better stay on that sofa, for the moment,' she says, looking at me suspiciously. 'But I've got my eye on you.'

I have no intention of going anywhere if, in the next few minutes, Colin Firth is coming to sit down next to me. I try and arrange myself as elegantly as I can in my gym gear as we go live again.

'Welcome back,' Loretta says, smiling into the camera. 'Now as we've been promising you all morning, in a moment we'll be talking to Colin Firth. But first, let's hear a bit more from our new fitness expert Jemma, who apparently has been causing quite a stir on the phone lines and online, too.'

I sigh. *Can't they just bring Colin on?*

'So, Jemma, other than help us all out here at *Wake Up Britain* with your wacky routines and no-nonsense advice, what do you get up to normally – do you teach classes?'

'Er, no Loretta, not any more. I like to keep my teaching on a much more personal, one-to-one basis these days.'

'Any celeb clients you'd like to share with us?' Julian asks, his eyes widening. 'Mingle with the stars on occasion, do you?'

'I can't tell a lie,' I answer, thinking of my run-ins with Johnny Depp and Kate Winslet. 'I have spoken with a couple of well-known movie stars about their dietary and fitness requirements, yes.'

Last year, when I'd been chasing all over London and then Paris looking for my long-lost mother, I'd bumped into Kate Winslet out jogging in Kensington Gardens, and Johnny Depp exiting a chocolate shop in Paris. A secret smile spreads across my lips at the memory of Johnny ...

Loretta gazes at me with a mixture of awe and jealousy.

'Then this seems like the perfect moment to introduce our own Oscar-winning guest. Ladies and gentlemen,' she says into the camera, 'may I welcome Mr Colin Firth to the *Wake Up Britain* sofa.'

Everyone applauds as Colin bounds over towards us. He kisses Loretta, shakes Julian's hand and then he turns towards me. He's about to kiss my cheek when I hear a shout from across the studio. 'Stop! She's not Jemma, I am!'

Colin, and everyone else in the studio, turns in the direction of the high-pitched wail to see a woman dressed in fitness clothes scuffling with two security guards.

'Cut to ads,' someone hisses from the floor.

'We'll be right back in a couple of minutes with more from Colin,' Julian says calmly and professionally to camera.

My kiss, my kiss! is all I can think as I'm escorted from the building by two security guards, to find Oscar waiting for me outside. Damn, I almost got a kiss from Colin Firth … *The* one and only Mr Darcy!

'Where in heaven's name have you been, Scarlett?' he asks, hurrying over to me. He casts an admiring glance at the two uniformed officers as they depart back into the building. 'I was quite worried about you. One minute you were there, and the next – *poof*! I turned around and you were gone! Did you get lost? No one noticed you wandering around alone, did they?'

I quickly explain to Oscar what's happened as we begin to walk away from the studio gates.

'You did *what*!' he exclaims when I get to the part about the fitness demo. 'On live TV?'

I nod in embarrassment. 'It all happened so fast, Oscar, I didn't really know what I was doing. Do you think anyone saw?'

Oscar's eyes open wide. 'Did anyone *see*, Scarlett? Only the few million people that watch *Wake Up Britain* every morning! But how did the real fitness woman get in, if they thought you were her?'

'Apparently she had a pass. Once she was finished with the police, she headed straight over to the studio. She got through easily enough, but when she saw me pretending to be her, she just lost it.' I lower my head. 'Oscar, I'm so embarrassed. What was I thinking?'

Oscar laughs. 'That reminds me of the old Scarlett, getting carried away with a movie star like that. You don't do enough of that kind of thing these days.'

'What, falsely impersonate someone on live television? Then it's just as well.'

'No, live for the moment! You've got stuck in your ways since you moved in with Mr Boring.'

I shake my head at him. 'Stop it, Sean's not boring and you know it. Remember David?'

David was my fiancé before I met Sean. He was …

well, quite set in his ways, and he had a particular obsession with DIY.

'True, compared to your ex he's a prize catch, even *I* have to admit that. But you've settled into this couple-dom thing far too well, in my opinion.'

'What's wrong with being part of a couple? I happen to like it.'

'Ah, but does it like you?' Oscar says knowingly, as finally a taxi comes into view and he expertly hails it down.

And as we climb into the taxi and whizz across town towards the gym, I sit and ponder just what his comment could mean.

Four

'Where are you going?' I call down the stairs.

'Things to do,' Sean calls back, as he gathers up some papers from the living room.

'This early?'

'Yes.'

I sigh. Sean has been acting very mysteriously lately. He isn't the most open of people at the best of times, especially where his business is concerned. But recently there have been phone calls that 'need to be taken outside' and times, like today, when he has had to 'dash out' for reasons he won't explain.

'When will you be back?' I ask, pulling my dressing gown protectively around me.

'Usual time, I hope. Depends on what comes up at

the office.' Sean looks up the stairs at me. 'Haven't you got the day off today?' he asks. 'I thought you were going somewhere with Oscar again?'

'Yes, we're going to a recording of the *Antiques Roadshow*,' I roll my eyes. How Oscar ever talked me into this I don't know.

Sean's eyes open wide. 'After your last dalliance with the world of television, is that wise, Scarlett? Aren't you banned from all TV studios now?'

'Ha ha, very funny,' I say as I wander halfway down the stairs so I can see Sean properly. 'One, the *Antiques Roadshow* isn't filmed in a TV studio, it's on location. We're going to Wimbledon today. And two, this is the BBC. Last time was a different channel altogether.'

Sean grins. 'And pray tell me why Oscar is dragging you out to Wimbledon today? Has he an antique tennis racket in his possession now?'

'No, he wants to get one of his jackets valued, and I think he quite fancies being on TV himself, if the truth be known.'

Sean nods. 'I can quite imagine that. What are you taking along?'

'Me?'

'Yeah, you can't go and not take something to be valued, can you?'

I think about this. 'But I don't own any antiques.'

'I bet you do. There must be something in the O'Brien closet you could take with you. You might as well if you're going, anyway.' He leaps back up the stairs and wraps his arms around me. 'Now, as much as I'd like to stay and help you search for something, I've got to dash.' Sean looks at my downcast face. 'Cheer up, it's not that bad – even if it is the *Antiques Roadshow*.'

I don't smile at his joke.

'Hmm ... What about dinner tonight, then, at that restaurant you like on Portobello Road? Would that cheer you up?'

I nod.

'Great, I'll book us a table.' He kisses me on the forehead. 'Have fun with Oscar today, ' he calls as he bounds down the stairs again. 'It's a good job he's gay, or I might get jealous. He gets to see more of you than I do these days.'

That isn't so far from the truth that Sean should be making a joke about it.

I listen to the door close behind him and sigh. *Right, well, if you can't spend time with me at this hour of the morning, then I know who can.* I turn around and head back up the stairs to our bedroom. I pick up my laptop from the dressing table, jump onto the bed and open the lid. My Wi-Fi connects to the internet and I'm away!

I smile to myself. When I first came to London last

year I'd have loved what I'd just done because it reminds me of a movie scene. Back then I'd been desperately trying to prove you could live your life like it was a movie. Creeping about, logging on to the internet as soon as my partner had left the house was a bit like Meg Ryan in *You've Got Mail*, except that I wasn't about to find a lovely, flowery email from Tom Hanks on my screen today. No, if I was lucky I might get a 140-character tweet back from the latest celebrity I was following on Twitter.

It's a new challenge I've set myself lately, seeing who I can get to reply. It isn't easy; they're a hard bunch to crack, especially celebrities with a lot of followers. And if you pick one who's male and good-looking, you have to fight your way through all the 'Aren't you wonderful!/ How about a date?/Look at how huge my breasts are in this photo' tweets they inevitably get sent every time they update their status. Actually if you spend any time nosing through people's profiles on Twitter (which of course I only do out of necessity if they follow me first and I want to know if I should follow them back . . .) it tells you a lot about the kind of people they are in real life. For example, the people that only follow and tweet celebrities, not any normal 'folk'. I was accused many a time of living in a fantasy world when I was trying to 'live my life in a movie', but at least I was actually operating in the real world while I was doing it. I often wonder if some people on Twitter live in their own little celebrity obsessed bubble, only existing to retweet the latest reply they get from some minor Z-list celebrity, like the hairdresser of the mum of one of the *X Factor* contestants.

But in among the hundred or so followers I have on Twitter, and the few hundred people I follow, I'm doing quite well with celebrity replies. I have an impressive list – I only go for the big names! – including Dermot O'Leary, Phillip Schofield, Davina McCall and Gok Wan. But what I really want are some Hollywood A-listers to add to my ever-growing list. I've tried Ashton Kutcher and Demi Moore (before the split). My tweets aren't really off-the-wall enough for Russell Brand to respond to, and I'm a little bit intimidated by his namesake, Russell Crowe, but I keep trying my old romcom buddy Tom Hanks. I feel like I know Tom; we've spent many a happy hour together in the company of Meg Ryan, Woody and Buzz Lightyear. But Tom has so many followers, I know the chances of a reply are pretty remote.

I click on my @Mentions first. Several spam tweets, trying to tempt me into the usual 'Win a New Phone' or 'Holiday' or even 'Plastic Surgery', depending on what I've mentioned previously in my own tweets. Twitter is funny like that: you only have to mention a key word and you'll suddenly find yourself being followed by all sorts of random people. I once mentioned that I had a problem with one of my teeth, and had three inventors of alternative remedies for toothache follow me. Another time I mentioned something to do with our garden – and was followed by a swarm of online garden suppliers. The worst was when, in the space of a day, four male escort agencies began following me. I never quite figured out what I'd said to encourage that!

But bypassing the spam, and a few mentions from some of my genuine fellow Twitter users, I suddenly stumble upon it, shining out like a beacon at me from the screen ... only a reply from Hugh Jackman! *Oh my God oh my God*, I think as my fingers quiver over the keyboard. What has he said in reply to my, what I considered quite hilarious, tweet about Sean shaving and leaving his razor and foam mess all over the bathroom? I'd asked Hugh if his wife had double the problems with him – meaning during the time he was Wolverine, and Hugh has replied saying his wife virtually had to bring in pest control, the hair issues were so bad!

Aw, I think, I love him all the more now for bothering with my pretty poor attempt at a joke, but I add it to the very top of my list of celebrity replies. Definitely my best one yet, and the closest I'm likely to come to an A-lister this year after the Colin Firth incident ...

I glance at the clock on my bedside cabinet. I'd better get dressed – Oscar will be here soon. Now, what should

I wear ...? I know it's pretty unlikely me or my clothes will be seen on TV, but I don't want to take any chances, so I choose a smart pair of French Connection trousers, a Topshop shirt and a belted suede jacket. I don't really know what you're supposed to wear to an Antiques Roadshow, but I hope this outfit is slightly more 'TV ready' than 'junk shop ready'. It's a mild day for March, but I have a feeling today's Roadshow is going to involve a fair bit of standing around and queueing, and I don't want to get cold, so I grab a jumper too just in case it gets chilly out on the tennis courts. Ten minutes to go before Oscar is due to arrive. What on earth am I going to take with me to be valued? Sean's right, I *should* take something ... but what?

I go on a quick wander through the house, but nothing jumps out at me. Sean's and my own tastes are quite modern; we don't really have any antiques, as such. Hmm ... I sit down on the sofa and have a think. I wonder if the necklace my great-aunt left me in her will is of any interest? It's two strings of pearls with a cameo at the end. I've never worn it – bit too old-fashioned for me. But it might be worth taking along.

I bound up the stairs and open my large wooden jewellery box sitting on the dresser. I really have far too much jewellery, I think, as I lift up a couple of layers. I must give some of the bits I never wear to the charity

42

shop down the road the next time I have a clear-out. I check some of the little drawers on the side of the box: nope, it's not in those, either. I wonder if I've put it in the drawer with some of the other items that won't fit in the box?

I pull open my underwear drawer and move my knickers and bras around until I see a little blue velvet box – aha! But on opening the box, I'm surprised to see not the serene white face of a carved cameo looking gracefully back at me, but two beady eyes belonging to a bright shiny dragonfly.

Oh, *that's* where it's gone. I'd almost forgotten I'd got this. When I'd been packing up my stuff to move out of our home in Stratford and in with Sean, I'd come across this brooch stuffed at the back of a cupboard. Dad had said to have anything from there I wanted, so I'd taken the brooch and a few other childhood bits. I'd meant to ask him about it at the time, but as always something else had cropped up and it was packed away in my moving boxes with everything else and then forgotten about until I unpacked here in Notting Hill. Jewellery isn't a topic that regularly comes up in conversation with my father, so I'd never got around to asking him about it.

The brooch is a bright green and blue enamelled dragonfly with very delicate, opalescent wings that are as wide as the dragonfly's body is long. Unusually, one of its beady eyes is black, the other navy blue, but they both stare up accusingly at me from the white satin interior of the box as if to complain about the lack of use it has been put to of late.

I wonder if this might be worth taking along? The necklace is nowhere to be found, and Oscar will be here any minute. Without thinking about it further, I shove the little blue box into my bag and hurry back downstairs to await Oscar and the black cab hooting its horn that will no doubt announce his arrival.

It's a miserable day outside as we set off together in the taxi. Apart from his issues with contaminating his clothes, the other reason Oscar rarely takes public transport is that he just loves the ambience of arriving in a black cab at the door of wherever he's travelling to, rather than slumming it on the tube or bus. I'd much rather save my money and use my Oyster card, but I'm quite happy to go along with taking cabs as long as he's paying, and today, as the rain pelts down the taxi windows, I'm glad we're not struggling with wet umbrellas along with all the other damp commuters.

'What will they do if it's raining?' I ask Oscar. 'Will it be cancelled?' Every *Antiques Roadshow* I've ever seen, the sun has always been shining on the experts, who sit happily valuing the public's knick-knacks and heirlooms while they sit under under parasols, wearing panama hats and other suitably quaint attire.

'Oh, I doubt it very much, darling. It takes ages to set these things up. They'll probably hold it indoors.'

'But then you won't get to see the courts and stuff on the show. Isn't that the whole point of holding it at Wimbledon?'

'Scarlett, I don't know, do I? I'm just here to get my jacket valued.'

I smirk. 'Oscar, you've had your hair coloured, cut and coiffed to within an inch of its life; you've had a facial, sauna, manicure and goodness knows what else at that beauty salon you go to. *And* you've been out and bought a new outfit and shoes, even underwear, knowing you. I can't believe the only reason you're going today is to get your jacket valued. *You* want to get on TV.'

Oscar cocks his head on one side. 'So what if I do? We can't *all* masquerade as fitness instructors to get our fifteen minutes of fame, now can we? Besides, I'm hoping to get a mention of my shop in if they film me.'

'You can't do that; it's the BBC. That'd be advertising.'

'Oh, Scarlett, you worry too much. It will all be fine.'

When the taxi drops us off outside the All England Lawn Tennis Club, the rain is lighter but still falling in a drizzly haze as we join the queue to get in. I spot my first panama hat as the steward on the gate doffs his and informs us where to go in order to get our items valued. He explains that, owing to the weather, the experts are all sitting at tables in a large hall for the time being, but that they hope to extend the Roadshow outside into the grounds later, once the rain has passed. Duly informed, we go through the gates and into the famous grounds of Wimbledon.

Unfortunately, jewellery and clothing valuations are taking place in different areas, so we split up. Oscar hurries off to join the long queue snaking around the hall to get to the expert dealing in antique clothing, while I take one look at the queue for jewellery and decide there's no way I'm standing in that for the next few hours, dragonfly or no dragonfly. So I set off to take a look around.

It's actually quite difficult to move, let alone wander, the people are packed in so tightly. It's not a bit like how it looks on TV, with convivial grey-haired experts languishing at big open tables, while people bearing Great-Aunt Maud's teapot in a carrier bag, a mixture of hope and pound signs in their eyes, shuffle past as slowly as they can behind them so they can get their few seconds of fame on the screen. No; this is much more cut-and-thrust.

As I try to push my way through the crowds to see

what's going on at the tables, I can hear murmurs of 'Watch her, she looks shifty', and 'I bet she tries to push in in a minute'. People are guarding their place in the queue as closely as they'll be guarding their antiques later, if they find out they're worth a few thousand. I soon get fed up of trying to see anything, and step outside again for some fresh air. It's way too stuffy and over-crowded in there.

I find some seats outside and sit down next to an eld-erly couple who are drinking tea from a flask and eating sandwiches from a Tupperware box. They look over at me as I take my seat.

'All done, dear?' the lady asks. 'You must have been quick off the mark this morning to get to the front of the queue.'

I'm about to reply when her husband interjects. 'Don't be silly, Marg, these young folk don't get up early. I expect she's one of the production crew taking a break. Is that right, duck? Do you think you could get me in to meet Fiona Bruce? I quite like her, I do. Marg here prefers that Michael Aspel, who used to present it, but not me. Fiona's the gal; fine pair of legs on her that filly has.'

'Desmond!' Marg admonishes. 'I'm sure the young lady doesn't wish to hear about your Fiona Bruce fetish.'

'Er . . .' I smile nervously, 'actually neither of you are

47

correct. I'm not a member of the production crew, and I've only just arrived myself.'

There's a sharp intake of breath from both Marg and Desmond. 'You've only just got here?' Marg looks at me suspiciously. 'Are you here to nose at other people's valuables, then? See who's worth a few pennies? I've heard about your type. Gold-diggers, we used to call them.'

'Oh no, not at all. I've brought something to be valued. Look.' I get the dragonfly out of my bag and show it to them. 'I just couldn't be bothered to queue up. It was too hot and crowded inside.'

'Very nice,' Desmond says, inspecting the brooch. 'You should get that seen. It looks like it might be worth a bob or two.'

'We were outside those gates at six o'clock this morning,' Marg says proudly. 'We'd have been the first ones here except for some madwoman and her sister who'd camped overnight with their Cliff Richard collection.'

'Cliff Richard?'

'Yes, they'd got records, posters, dolls, the lot. Mad, if you ask me. Their tent was full of the stuff. I'll bet the whole collection was barely worth the train fare from Inverness.'

'Why have they come all the way from Inverness to have it valued here? There must have been a closer Roadshow to go to.'

'It's the tennis connection, isn't it?' Desmond states, as if this explains everything.

I stare at him blankly.

'Cliff likes his tennis, doesn't he? They thought it might be a good omen.'

'Oh, remember that year when it was rained off all day, Desmond,' Marg pipes up again, 'and Cliff led the singing around the Centre Court. That was lovely, that was.'

'Almost better than the tennis itself, Marg,' Desmond agrees, and they laugh together in that way couples do who've been together a long time and don't need to explain themselves to each other.

I smile at them both, and wonder if Sean and I will be sitting eating sandwiches and drinking tea from a flask in fifty years' time. My thoughts are broken by an announcement from inside the hall. 'Now the rain has ceased falling and blue skies are ahead of us, we will shortly be moving Ceramics outside onto the courts. If you'll please follow your marshal in an orderly line outside when requested, we would be most grateful. *Please*, no pushing and shoving, and I do *not* want to see any queue-jumping or there will be trouble. Thank you.'

'Sounds like they're coming outside,' Desmond explains unnecessarily. ''Bout time; it wouldn't be a Roadshow if they had to film it all stuck indoors.'

From the hall, a burly-looking woman marches out carrying a megaphone. 'Follow me, everyone,' she calls to the bizarre line of people shuffling along behind her. They range in height, age and size, but they all carry the seemingly obligatory Roadshow accessory of a carrier bag filled with their own unique 'antique' waiting to be valued by an expert.

Over the next few minutes, I sit companionably with Marg and Desmond and watch while more queues are marched outside by Matilda (as we nickname her) and her megaphone, and we have fun guessing what her 'queueies' have in their bags as they pass by.

Suddenly Desmond goes very quiet.

'Are you OK?' I ask him as his face takes on a deathly shade of white.

Desmond lifts a bony hand and points limply into the distance. 'It's her,' he whispers so I can barely hear him.

I'm about to ask who, but as I look in the direction he's pointing I see exactly what the problem is. Fiona Bruce, presenter of the *Antiques Roadshow*, has been released from the confines of whatever VIP room she's been holed up in. She has the sun behind her as she walks across the tarmac, and she does look somewhat goddess-like as she glides towards us.

'Fiona!' I call, before I know what I'm doing.

She turns her head away from the small entourage of TV types that surround her and looks in my direction.

'This gentleman here,' I say, pointing at Desmond, 'is a huge fan of yours. I wonder if you've got a moment?'

And surprisingly, she has.

I leave Desmond sitting next to Fiona looking as red as the tomatoes in the cheese-and-tomato sandwiches that Marg is trying to tempt Fiona to take from her Tupperware tub, and wander over to the courts.

The queues are just as long now they're outside, but instead of curling around in great snakelike twists, they stretch the length of the famous grass courts as the experts position themselves at tables underneath large sunshades that will double as umbrellas, should the weather turn inclement again. I look around me, seeing the infamous Centre Court entrance through which many a hopeful player has passed over the years. Next to it stand bronze busts of some of the household names that have graced these hallowed courts. It's quite exciting just being here at Wimbledon; I don't really mind if I get my brooch valued or not after all, it's worth it just to see all this for real instead of on a TV screen.

I notice there's a ladies' toilet open next to the entrance to Centre Court. I've been busting to go since Marg and Desmond persuaded me into taking some tea from their flask, so I climb the steps leading up to it.

Incredibly, the toilet is quiet, so I select an empty cubicle and go inside. Just as I'm finishing up, I hear someone else come in and take the cubicle next to mine.

I flush the toilet and go outside to wash my hands. I'm about to dry them when I hear a shout from the cubicle.

'Damn and blast it!'

I turn and look at the door but there's no sound, so I pull a paper towel down.

'You've *got* to be kidding me.'

'Is everything all right?' I enquire politely at the door while I dry off my hands.

'Oh, is someone out there?'

'Yes, I'm just drying my hands.' I say unnecessarily. 'Are you OK?'

'Hardly, I've just gone to pull my zip up and I've only gone and bust the blasted thing.'

'Oh dear, is there anything I can do to help?'

The bolt on the door shoots back and I'm surprised to see a face I recognise staring back at me from the cubicle. I haven't seen many *Antiques Roadshow*s, but I've seen enough to recognise this lady's face. She's one of their experts, known for her slightly outlandish dress sense, and today is no exception. She's wearing a red velvet 1970s-style jumpsuit with black patent boots and a large black belt to match, and the zip in question, rather than being just a simple trouser zip like I'd imagine it to be, is one that runs the full length of the garment from her neck to just below her waist.

'See,' she says, trying to pull it. 'It won't come any farther up than my bra. I can't possibly appear on TV like this!'

'Don't they have alternative wardrobe options for you?' I ask hopefully, picturing a large truck filled with rails of garments hanging in it for the experts to choose from.

'Sweetie, this is the *Antiques Roadshow*, not *The X Factor*. The only spare wardrobe they might have here is likely to be a hundred years old and made out of wood.'

'Oh, right. What are you going to do, then?'

'I really don't know. We're miles from the nearest decent boutique here – I'm proverbially buggered.'

I think for a moment.

'What size are you?' I ask, looking her up and down.

'Twelve, on a good day – why?'

I nod. 'I thought so. That's good! And what antiques do you specialise in again?'

'All sorts, but I mainly do jewellery here on the Roadshow. Why is this relevant?'

'Because I think we might be about to do each other a very big favour.'

53

Five

I pull at the hem of my blue silk Ted Baker dress for the umpteenth time while I sit on the sofa and stare at the brooch.

As I hold it up in my hand and turn it to and fro in front of my eyes, it's as if the dragonfly has suddenly sprung to life and is swooping about in front of me.

After we'd swapped clothes, Lucinda, the *Antiques Roadshow* expert, had taken a very quick look at my brooch and said she thought it was likely to have come from America at the turn of the last century. She'd said it was definitely a fake because of the difference in eye colour, but the brooch had been created at the time to look like an original Tiffany design. Being an imitation, she didn't think it was very valuable, but that it might be worth a few hundred pounds at auction, and then she'd had to dash with a promise to return my clothes to me by courier the next day. I'd texted Oscar and found to my relief that he'd managed to get his jacket valued and that it wasn't worth very much, so he'd let me wear it on the way home over the red catsuit.

But now, as I sit in our living room twiddling the dragonfly around in my hands, I wonder just why Dad would have a piece of jewellery like this. And, more to the point, why he would keep it tucked away all these years. I knew for a fact that the dragonfly had been in that cupboard for as long as I could remember; I'd snooped in there often enough looking for my Christmas and birthday presents when I was young. I'd even wondered if it had belonged to my mother at some stage, but when I'd asked her about it she said she'd never seen it before.

It was lovely having Mum so close now, to be able to call on whenever I needed her, even for something so simple as asking her about the brooch. We'd been apart for so much of my life, until we'd been reunited last year, that even these little things meant so much now.

'Are you ready, Scarlett?' Sean calls. 'The taxi's here.'

'Yes, just coming.' I shove the brooch into my bag and hurry through to the hall.

Tonight we're going out for a meal for my twenty-sixth birthday. Sean has organised it, and I have no idea where we we're going – it's a complete surprise.

'Are you OK?' Sean asks as we travel along in the cab. 'You're awfully quiet for someone whose birthday it is today.'

'Yes, I'm fine,' I smile at him. 'I've just got a few things on my mind, that's all.'

It wasn't just the brooch. Sean was still being very secretive around me, and I didn't like it. It wasn't like him.

'Didn't you like the present I got you?' Sean asks.

'Yes, yes, of course I did. It's wonderful, thank you.' Sean had bought me a beautiful new MacBook Air for my birthday. It was tiny in comparison to the old laptop I'd been using, and so thin and light that I couldn't quite believe it could do everything a computer was supposed to.

'I was thinking of getting you an iPad, but then you wouldn't be able to do all your work stuff on it as easily. I just thought with your addiction to – sorry – *love* of all things computerised and the internet these days, you'd appreciate something a little more portable to play with.'

I lean across the back seat of the taxi and kiss him. 'And I do appreciate it, Sean, it's a lovely gift, really. Now,

56

where are you taking me for dinner? Why is it such a secret?'

Sean lightly taps the end of my nose. 'Wait and see...'

The taxi begins to head into the heart of London's West End, but when we drive straight through Covent Garden, I really start to wonder where we're going. Maybe we're going to see a show? But then it turns into West Street...

'We're not... are we?' I ask, turning to Sean in amazement.

He nods as the taxi pulls up outside the doors of The Ivy restaurant.

As Sean pays the driver, I climb out of the taxi agog and stand staring up at this Mecca of celebrity dining. It's the restaurant you always see the stars photographed outside of in *OK!* and *Hello!* Not that I buy them any more... But I still sneak a quick peek in the newsagent's every week.

'Pleased?' he asks, as he takes my hand and we walk through the doors.

'Of course I'm pleased. But how on earth did you manage to get us a table?' I whisper, as I gaze around me in wonderment. 'You have to book about six months in advance, don't you?'

'You can do it in two if you call in a few favours,' Sean winks.

This was one of the joys of Sean having so many contacts through his business. He seemed to be able to 'pull in favours' just when it was most needed.

'You've been planning my birthday for two whole months?'

'Ah-huh. Yes, table in the name of Bond, please,' Sean says to the maître d'.

'Ah, yes,' the maître d' says knowingly, giving Sean a little wink. 'Just one moment, sir.' And he glides off into the restaurant.

'But I thought . . .' I stutter as we wait to be led to our table.

'You thought what?' Sean asks, smiling at me. 'That I was up to no good?'

I blush.

'Well, you shouldn't have. You know how much I love you, Scarlett. I just wanted to do something special for you to prove it.'

'This way, sir,' the maître d' says, reappearing. He gestures with a graceful hand. 'Your table is now ready.'

As we're led to our table, I'm still in shock. I can't believe Sean has been planning all this for *over two months*. And there was me, doubting what he was up to. *I'll make it up to you when we get home*, I vow to myself, trying to look relaxed and nonchalant as we pass through the restaurant. I'm desperately wanting to appear as if I come here all the time, while surreptitiously glancing from side to side to see if I can spot any famous faces. But disappointingly, the only person I see is a failed *X Factor* contestant who I never really liked that much, being overly loud to attract attention, and two members of the *Emmerdale* cast talking quite intimately over a couple of glasses of white wine.

'Ta-da!' Sean announces, as I'm still craning my neck at 360 degrees to celeb-spot around the restaurant.

I turn to where he's gesturing, and I'm amazed to see some familiar faces already sitting at the table grinning up at me.

There's Oscar, looking resplendent as always in a purple velvet suit and bright red shirt, and he's sitting next to Sean's sister, Ursula, who I haven't seen in absolutely ages because she's been away in Paris creating a new interior for an exclusive French perfumery. Ursula, definitely sporting Parisian chic tonight, wears an exquisite-looking little black dress. On the other side of Oscar is my mother; she looks lovely this evening in a Wedgewood blue and cream silk dress, most probably borrowed from one of the designer departments in Selfridges where she now works. She'd left her job in the local cinema when she'd suddenly been offered a position in one of the ladies departments; no-one ever knew why Selfridges suddenly phoned my mother up and asked her to come in for an interview, but they did, and within a week she was there selling expensive dresses to exclusive customers. I had my suspicions, and questioned Sean about it more than once, but he said he knew nothing. But the most surprising guests of the evening are two faces I haven't seen in a very long time: my best friend Maddie and her husband, Felix.

'What are you all doing here?' I exclaim as I hug each of them one by one.

'Sean organised it all,' Maddie says excitedly. 'Felix and I have been here since yesterday – flew in last night.'

'But you're supposed to be in ... where is it right now? I've lost track.'

Maddie and Felix had lasted approximately ten months living as a 'normal' married couple, then decided to pack in their jobs for six months and travel around all the cities and countries neither of them had visited before they 'finally settled down properly'. Personally I couldn't see Maddie ever settling down completely, she had too much free spirit in her.

'We were in Prague, but we flew back just for this. Sean was most insistent.'

I turn back towards Sean; he's standing back watching in pleasure as I greet all my family and friends. He holds out a glass of champagne to me. 'Happy Birthday,

Scarlett,' he says, grinning. 'So – do you like your surprise?'

'Oh, Sean,' I say, almost knocking the glass of champagne out of his hand as I wrap my arms around his neck. 'I love it, everyone I love is here to celebrate with me.'

'I know,' Sean nods as my expression changes and I look with sadness into his pale blue eyes. 'But New York is a very long way for your father to come for one night.'

'Yes; I wouldn't have expected him to, not just for this. He did send me a lovely card and that scarf and necklace from Bloomingdale's, so I can't complain too much.' I look brightly around at everyone else. 'But at least I have all my other friends and family here – what more could I want!'

My birthday meal at The Ivy is wonderful, celebrating with everyone together again. We have rather too much wine following the champagne, and some rather expensive but absolutely delicious food. We do even spy a few celebrities during the evening, when two members of Take That are ushered swiftly past our table with three other men in suits on their way to a more secluded area of the restaurant, and both Oscar and Sean get very excited when there's a rumour that Kylie Minogue is having dinner here this evening. But after several trips to 'the little boys' room', neither of them is able to verify that rumour.

As we leave the restaurant later that evening, the waiting press lift their heads for a split second to see if we're anyone interesting, then promptly ignore us when they realise we're not. But I don't care; I just feel incredibly happy and grateful to have such lovely friends and family.

'When will I see you again?' I ask Maddie as I hug her goodbye.

'Soon, Scarlett, soon. We've only got a few more places to visit, then we'll be back home again.'

'You're so lucky doing this,' I say wistfully. 'I wish I could travel more. Sean's always away on business, but I never get to go anywhere or do anything exciting any more.'

'I thought you were quite happy these days, making a home with Sean and running the business on your own without your dad on your back all day?'

'I am. But ...'

Maddie grins. 'Don't tell me you're starting to get itchy feet again! How long did it take this time?'

'What do you mean?' I ask, looking at her suspiciously.

'Come on, I've known you since we were kids, Scarlett, and every time you get what you want in life, you're happy with it for a while before you have to start looking around for a new challenge.'

'Perhaps,' I shrug. But, deep down, I knew she was right.

'Try and be happy with the business, won't you?' Maddie continues. 'It's going great guns now. You've done a great job managing it since your dad has been in New York, and you know it. But more importantly, be happy with Sean. Look what he did for you tonight. That took masses of organisation and planning.'

I smile as I look back at the doors of The Ivy and reflect on the dinner. 'Yes, of *course* I'm happy with Sean, why wouldn't I be? He's lovely to me.'

'Good.' Maddie hugs me again. 'I'll see you soon, Scarlett. Keep enjoying life, won't you? Remember just over a year ago, how you were chasing around after a dream? Now you've got what you always wanted, you need to keep embracing it every day.'

There's a smile on my face as I watch Maddie and Felix drive away in a taxi back to their hotel. But it's a fixed smile that fades as soon as they're out of sight.

Because secretly, even though I know Maddie's right and I should be making the most of everything I've got, I also know that, whatever anyone else thinks, there's still something missing from my life.

Six

After the excitement of my birthday meal, life settles down for a while. Sean stops being all secretive now that his big surprise is out in the open, and we continue with our day-to-day lives in Notting Hill: Sean working long hours wheeling and dealing in companies – he's a bit like Richard Gere in *Pretty Woman*, but without the 1990s soundtrack and dodgy haircuts – and me managing the popcorn-machine company with the help of Tammy and Leon.

I'd been reluctant to hire anyone at first when Dad had left for the States; it had always just been me, him and Dorothy for as long as I could remember. But it had soon become clear that I couldn't manage the business on my own, so I'd advertised and Tammy and Leon had come to me from a very well-respected agency after a long application process. They were a young married couple, and had both recently lost their jobs in different companies in the City. We'd hit it off immediately when they'd mentioned at the end of their interview that they were about to go and see a movie I'd been waiting for ages for Sean to take me to. When I'd joked about this to them, they'd asked if I'd like to accompany them that night. I knew it wasn't professional, and I should have said no, but I was desperate to see the movie. It was Bradley Cooper's latest – my newest screen crush. After the movie, we'd all gone for free ice cream together at a local parlour where Leon knew the owner. And I pretty much decided over my chocolate and vanilla sundae that they were perfect for the job, and that we were all going to get on like one big happy family.

This morning, I'm madly searching around in my cupboard looking for a particular handbag to take to work with me. It's a peacock-blue Accessorize bag with sequins and embroidery, and it matches my new purple shoes that I've decided to wear today. As I rummage about at the back of the wardrobe, I hear Sean's muffled voice.

'What on earth are you looking for in there? Although I can't complain about the fine view I'm getting of you!'

I ease myself still bag-less from the cupboard. 'Stop

perving at my behind and help me find my bag or I'll be late for work.'

'Which one?' Sean says, grinning at me from the edge of the bed where he's lacing his shoes. 'You have so many!'

'The peacock-blue one, you know, with all the sequins. I can't remember when I last had it.'

'I can,' Sean says, standing up and easing his jacket over his shoulders. 'The night of your birthday. You wore your blue dress – remember?'

'You're right!' I think for a minute. 'I wonder if I put it away with the shoes I was wearing that night?'

I look around in the wardrobe again and, as if by magic, there it is, lying in a box with my blue satin shoes. I'd obviously been a bit *too* organised that evening.

'Just ask Sean,' he says, checking himself in the mirror. He doesn't need to; he always looks so handsome when he's wearing a suit.

I open the bag and quickly begin transferring the contents of yesterday's handbag into this one. But as I put my hand inside, it catches against something cold and hard. I take a look inside and discover the dragonfly brooch. I must have forgotten I'd put it in there before we went out for the meal that night, and it must have got caught inside when I emptied it upside down on the bed at the end of the night to transfer my things back to my usual day bag. Yes; as I try and retrieve the brooch now, one of its delicate wings is indeed caught on the silk lining.

'What's up?' Sean asks, coming over to see what I'm doing.

'It's Dad's brooch. I'd forgotten I'd put it in here on my birthday.' I manage to loosen the wing and free the insect again.

I stare at the piece of jewellery now sitting in the palm of my hand, its beady eyes looking right back up at me.

'You never did find out why your father had that,' Sean says, lifting the brooch from my palm and holding it up in the light from the window. 'I thought you were going to ask him about it.'

'I was, but to be honest I've been so busy at work over the last month or so it's just slipped my mind, and what with the time difference and everything, we haven't spoken to each other that often lately.'

Sean looks at me. 'Miss him, don't you?'

I nod. 'A lot.'

'Then why don't you go and see him and ask him about it yourself?'

'What do you mean?'

'Why not take a trip to New York and visit your father, and take this,' he holds up the dragonfly, 'and solve the big O'Brien brooch mystery?'

My spirits lift for a moment. 'Sounds like a great plan, but I can't just leave the business, can I?'

'Tammy and Leon would cope; you said only the other day how well they were getting on and how much you trusted them.'

'Yes, but—'

'And it's not as if you can't be in constant touch with them if you want to. Mobile phones and the internet do work over in New York, you know. And now you've got your new MacBook, you can even Skype them daily if you want and have important conference calls about the state of the popcorn industry.'

I pull a face at Sean. 'Don't tease me. New York does sound fantastic; I've always wanted to go there. But would you be able to get away from work that easily?'

Sean's keen expression suddenly changes. 'I can't go with you, Scarlett. Not at the moment, anyway. We've got so much going on at the office, and so many things coming up in the next few weeks, it would be impossible.'

'But I can't go on my own. Not to New York!'

'Why not, you're a grown woman, aren't you?'

'I don't want to go on my own, I want to go with you. Come on, Sean, we haven't been anywhere in ages. It would be lovely to have a little trip away somewhere together, and New York would be so romantic.'

'Not really,' Sean says flatly. 'I've been there loads of times. It's not romantic at all.'

'Yes, but that's because it was business you were there for, and you're hardly likely to see the city's romantic side when you're working there, are you? Well, I hope you didn't, anyway!' I say lightly, hoping to sway him, but really I know I'm wasting my time. Once Sean has decided on something, it's rare he'll change his mind.

'I'm sorry, Scarlett,' Sean says, taking me in his arms. 'I just can't right now. But you go. Go and visit your father, it will do you good. You've been ...' he hesitates '... unsettled just lately, and I think it will do you good to get away for a while and have a break from things.'

'A break from us, do you mean?' I look up at him in horror.

'No, not a break from us, you daft thing,' Sean kisses the end of my nose. 'Just a break from here.'

'OK,' I reply hesitantly, but I'm still not sure. 'If that's what you think is best.'

'It's just that Maddie mentioned—'

I pull away from him. 'Maddie mentioned what? What has she been saying?'

'Hey, Red, calm down.' Sean tries to put his arms around me again. 'Maddie hasn't been saying anything, really. Just for me to look out for some *key signs*, she described them as. I thought she was talking nonsense at

69

first. But when I sat down and thought about it, they were all already there.'

'What sort of *key signs*?' I ask, wriggling away from him. I couldn't believe this, people wanting to organise my life again. Hadn't they tried to do that last year before I came to Notting Hill? Everyone seemed to think they knew what was best for me then, and now it was happening all over again. Even Sean was getting involved this time.

'Just things like you getting bored with life and starting to become obsessed with, I mean *fascinated* with, new things.'

'And just what sort of things would these be?' I ask, my hands on my hips.

Sean looks uncomfortable. 'Well, as I've said recently, you do spend quite a lot of time on the internet, Scarlett.'

Oh my God, I can't quite believe this. Here we are *again*. 'And? What's so wrong with that? What am I supposed to do when you're away all the time on *business*.' I emphasise the word business by doing that little air-quotes thing with my fingers.

'You know I can't help that. But you still do it when I'm home. You're always on your iPhone, on Twitter or Facebook or some other social networking site.'

'So why did you buy me a MacBook then, if you don't like me using the internet so much?' I demand. 'It hardly makes sense, does it?'

'I bought you what I thought you'd like,' Sean says patiently. 'If I'd just gone out and bought jewellery or perfume or something, you'd have thought it dull and boring.'

'And a computer is supposed to be exciting?' I reply, sounding horribly ungrateful. This discussion is rapidly descending into nothing more than childish bickering. 'Do you know what?' I say, parading back and forth across the soft carpet of the bedroom a few times. 'If you are daft enough to listen to Maddie, and then stupid enough to decide that I'm presenting symptoms of some disease that's only going to be cured by a holiday abroad, then really I'd be stupid to argue with you, Dr Sean, wouldn't I?'

'Scarlett,' Sean says, trying to approach me again, 'please don't be like this.'

'I'm not being like anything. If this is what you think is best then who am I to stand in the way of your genius idea?' I hold out my arms in dramatic Hollywood fashion with a fake smile plastered across my lips. 'Start spreading the news, Sean, because guess what? Scarlett is about to hit New York City!'

Seven

As the plane gathers speed along the tarmac I sit and stare out of the tiny window next to me, wondering what kind of miracle takes place to allow this great weighty object to claw its way off the ground and soar high into the air like a grand bird of prey, carrying its cargo up into the clouds and on to another world.

I'm finally on my way to New York City.

After Sean had suggested the trip, it hadn't taken me long to book it at all. What had taken time was organising everything else. Making sure that Tammy and Leon were actually capable of looking after the business while I was away for a whole week had been my biggest worry, but Sean had said he would pop in and check on them from time to time. I doubted how often this would actually occur, knowing Sean's hectic work schedule. But what could I do? It was either that or not go at all, and now I'd decided I wanted to visit New York – boy, was I looking forward to it!

In the few weeks that had passed since booking the flights, I'd bought new clothes suitable for a week's sight-seeing, read as many guidebooks as I could and even re-watched as many of my favourite New York-based movies as I'd had time to, to get me in the mood for the trip. I'd even broken one of my rules of never watching a Christmas movie before December so I could sit through films like *Elf*, *Home Alone 2* and *Serendipity*, and now I couldn't wait to set foot in the Big Apple.

The passenger in the seat next to me wriggles for about the tenth time that minute and in frustration I turn towards him.

'Are you going to be like this for the next seven hours?' I ask an agitated-looking Oscar, who's leaning around the side of his seat peering down the aisle of the plane.

'If we have that hot air steward looking after us for the whole flight I might become more than a little agitated, darling. Did you see him when he leaned across asking us to fasten our seat belts earlier? OMG! He's to die for.'

'I wondered why you were pretending to have a

problem with yours. He's OK, I guess, but I'd rather not die on this flight, thanks; I do actually want to see New York.'

Yes: my travelling companion today, and for the next week, is Oscar, who, when he'd found out that I was going to New York, had thrown his arms in the air with such vigour, and spun around on the floor with such finesse, that he could have been auditioning for a Broadway show.

'You're going to New York!' he'd exclaimed. 'On your own? How can that be?'

When I'd explained about Sean and his work, and that I was really going to visit Dad, his eyes had lit up. 'Let's go together, darling! And I can visit Jen while I'm there!'

As fast as Oscar's arms had raised, my heart had sunk. Jen was not only Oscar's sister, but Sean's ex-girlfriend. We hadn't ever really met properly, but I'd heard her in action in a hotel room in Paris – very long story! – and she was not the sort of person I wanted to spend any time with at all.

'Yes, why not?' I'd said brightly through gritted teeth. 'It would be fantastic for you to see her again.'

And that's how it had started.

So before I knew it I had a companion who was travelling with just as much, if not more, luggage than me.

(He certainly had a bigger case of toiletries.) And as I set out on my big adventure across the Atlantic, I was very glad to have him right there beside me.

Our flight is smooth and goes past in a flash, thanks to almost a hundred movies to choose from on the in-flight entertainment system. You can start them when you want, then stop, pause and even rewind. I'm in heaven. I don't even get a chance to listen to the playlist I've made on my iPod of New York-themed songs; although to be fair, I have been playing it quite a lot before leaving home. I'd been driving Sean mad with songs like Frank Sinatra's 'New York, New York'; Alicia Keys and Jay-Z's 'Empire State of Mind' and my favourite 'Arthur's Theme' from the Dudley Moore movie of the same name. It's such a romantic tune: 'If you get caught between the moon and New York City ... the best that you can do is fall in love'.

Although Sean did raise a questioning eyebrow at me when I was singing along a bit too enthusiastically to that one ...

Our parting this morning had been quite strange. It was the first time since getting together that we were going to be away from each other for so long. Sean was always the one on business trips, but only for a few days at a time, so it seemed odd for me to be the one leaving today. When I was about to climb into the taxi to head off to the airport, I was pretty sure Sean was regretting ever suggesting the idea in the first place.

'I'll miss you,' he'd said, gazing down at me, gently stroking a stray piece of hair away from my eyes.

'I'll miss you too,' I'd said, looking up at him. 'It's not too late to change your mind, you know. You could pack and catch a flight out tomorrow.'

But Sean had shaken his head. 'No, you go. You'll have a fine time with Oscar, and you know it.'

'I'll say hi to Jen for you if I see her,' I'd said half jokingly.

'Don't bother,' Sean had screwed up his nose. 'I don't wish to be remembered to her.'

Then Oscar had called out of the taxi window that we'd miss our flight if we didn't hurry up, so Sean and I had kissed goodbye quickly and then we were off. The last I saw of him was as I waved out of the back of the taxi window to his disappearing figure.

Oscar spends most of the flight trying to catch the eye of the good-looking air steward, but after getting nowhere he finally gives up and falls asleep under the pages of *Heat* magazine, while I watch my movies in between thinking about New York and Sean. When we finally arrive at JFK Airport (even saying that is exciting), we slowly trudge along the long, winding lines with the other hundreds of travellers trying to enter the country via the immigration desks. After we've had our faces scanned and our fingerprints taken, it's with relief that our passports are finally stamped and we're allowed through to go and collect our suitcases from the baggage carousel. Where again there's more relief when we find them safely riding round and round like weary children on a never-ending merry-go-round. We spy Oscar's cases quickly; we can't exactly miss their bright pink leopard print. But luckily my slightly less bold pale blue ones arrive shortly afterwards, and we're on our way.

The heat hits me the moment I step outside the airport into the late-afternoon air. Whoa, it wasn't like this when we'd left London, a bit damp and miserable and about fifteen degrees – here, it must be well into the high twenties.

We find the taxi rank, join the queue and shuffle forward slowly as we wait to be ushered by an attendant into one of the ever-constant stream of bright yellow taxis arriving at the airport. When it's our turn, the taxi driver enquires as to our destination, then hoists our bags effortlessly into the boot of his cab while we load ourselves inside.

'First time in New York?' he asks as we set off on our journey.

'Yes, it is, for me,' I reply as I turn my head back

around from where it's been craning out of the window to take in every new sight and sound of the city we've just landed in.

'Well the forecast for Memorial Day weekend is fantastic, sunny in the high eighties. What more could you want?'

Oscar and I smile at each other across the back of the cab.

'What's Memorial Day weekend?' I ask. 'Is it one of your public holidays?'

'Yep. Boy, have you hit New York City at a great time.' He surveys me in his rear-view mirror. 'Single, are you?'

'I have a boyfriend, but I'm not married. Why?'

'Because, honey, it's Fleet Week right now.'

Oscar and I exchange blank looks.

'Fleet Week is held every year in the city,' our tour-guide taxi driver continues, speaking to me. 'It's a tribute to our good seafaring guys and gals. Huge warships sail into the harbour, and more importantly for you,' he pauses for a quick inspection of Oscar in his rear-view mirror, 'and I'm guessing by the look of it, you as well, fella, you'll be appreciating this – thousand of sailors and marines come ashore for the week, too.'

'Oh my God, oh my *God*,' Oscar squeals into my ear. 'It's like that episode of *Sex and the City*!'

'What are you talking about, Oscar?' Oscar was a huge *Sex and the City* fan. He'd already got us signed up on some bus tour of the sights à la Carrie Bradshaw and the girls while we were here.

'The episode where Carrie, Samantha and Charlotte go to the party with all the sailors, and then Carrie ends up outside with one, but turns him down and instead tells him how much she loves Manhattan.'

I shake my head. 'Oscar, you know far too much about that show. No, I haven't seen that episode, I must have missed it.'

Oscar flicks his head back in disgust and holds up a hand. 'Scarlett, you disappoint me.'

'I'm more of a movie buff, remember?'

'Movie buff, eh? Then have you seen *On the Town*?' the cab driver asks, glancing in his mirror at me again.

I stare blankly at him.

He tuts and rolls his eyes. 'Gene Kelly, Frank Sinatra and some other guy – never remember his name – dancing their way across New York dressed as sailors? No? Perhaps this will help you remember, then.' The cab driver clears his throat. 'They sing this song as the opening number to the movie . . . ' and from the front of our yellow cab, flying across the Queensboro Bridge into Manhattan, our driver launches into the song. 'New York, New York it's a helluva town / The Bronx is up, but the

Battery's down / The people ride in a hole in the groun' ...' while on the back seat Oscar and I try to stifle our giggles.

'So, have you seen it?' he asks enthusiastically when he's finished serenading us. 'It's a classic.'

'That scene does ring a bell now you mention it,' I answer politely. 'But I'm afraid I don't think I've seen the whole movie.'

'It's a classic Hollywood musical,' he huffs. 'You really haven't lived, doll. Forget all your state-of-the-art special effects and three-D nonsense. You need to watch some Bing, Frankie and Gene, them's ya guys.'

After that, the cab driver decides that with our poor taste in cinema viewing we're not worth bothering about and turns on the radio, delighting in some easy-listening show tunes for the rest of the journey to the hotel, while Oscar and I delight in trying to spot some famous New York landmarks as we get ever closer to the city centre.

Eventually we pull up outside a very nice-looking hotel, with large elegant blue canopies hanging over the windows and a uniformed doorman waiting by a revolving glass door to usher the guests in and out. He rushes over to open my cab door.

'Thank you,' I say shyly, as I climb out feeling like a celebrity. 'That's very kind.'

While Oscar pays the driver, the doorman proceeds to

unload our bags from the boot of the cab and onto a trolley before pushing them up a slope into the hotel, while we follow gazing about us in awe at the foyer of the Park Avenue hotel we are staying in.

Inside, it's very tastefully decorated in shades of purple and black, and the moment we step away from the heat of the pavement (no, make that sidewalk!) it's a calm and relaxing haven to welcome the busy, fraught traveller. As we approach the reception desk, I'm aware the doorman is still hovering. I look at Oscar and incline my head back in his direction.

'Darling, he wants tipping,' Oscar whispers as the receptionist comes over and Oscar begins dealing with her in his best Notting Hill manner.

'Ah, OK ... erm.' I delve into my bag and find some dollars. I don't know how much you tip a doorman, and I hope this will be sufficient. 'Thanks very much,' I say, thrusting them into his hand.

The doorman glances quickly at the notes, his eyes open wide. 'No problem, miss. You just let me know if there's anything you need while you're here. Anything at all ...'

'How much did you give him?' Oscar asks as I join him at the desk. 'He looked mighty happy.'

'I don't know, I just grabbed some notes from my purse.'

'Scarlett,' Oscar shakes his head. The receptionist has turned away for a moment to fetch our keys. 'It's supposed to be a dollar a bag!'

'Oh, I think I only had tens and twenties.'

Oscar rolls his eyes. 'This trip will cost you a fortune, darling, if you carry on like that. You'd better get used to tipping – everyone does it here. And get used to how much, as well!'

The receptionist hands us our keys and, deciding we can handle our bags ourselves, we make our way up to our rooms. There had been some debate before we left as to whether we should share a room, but Oscar said he was prone to snoring and didn't want to keep me awake at night. I had a feeling it was more likely that Oscar didn't want me cramping his style if he managed to score with a good-looking New Yorker, and now we knew about Fleet Week and all the sailors being in town I was doubly glad we weren't sharing. I imagine I'd have been constantly fed dollars to 'go to the cinema', like an awkward younger brother or sister you wanted out of the way for a few hours.

My room, like the rest of the hotel, is beautifully decorated; burgundy is the main colour scheme, with hints of silver, black and grey. I've got a double bed, a huge wardrobe and chest of drawers to store the many clothes I've brought with me, plus an elegant dressing table-come-desk. There's also a small high-backed armchair in the corner of the room with a tall lamp standing next to it, and a minibar. It's much bigger than I'd expected it to be: I'd been led to believe from reviews I'd read on the internet that New York hotel rooms were quite tiny, but this isn't at all, it's very roomy indeed. Oscar and I really seem to have fallen on our feet with this hotel; it's lovely.

I've just finished unpacking when there's banging on my door. I take a quick look through the peephole and see Oscar outside, hopping impatiently from one foot to the other.

'Ready yet, darling?' he asks as I open the door.

'Not quite, come in for a moment.'

I'm not surprised to find that Oscar has changed outfits as he bounds energetically into my room. He's now wearing black designer jeans with zebra-print patch pockets and a white t-shirt with a black bolt of lightning emblazoned across the chest.

'Hurry up, sweetie. We're in New York now, we've just got time to go and explore this evening! What are you going to wear?'

'Er . . .' I glance down at the jeans and Gap t-shirt I've travelled from London in. I suppose I should change, really.

'Let me look in your wardrobe.' Oscar leaps over to my newly hung wardrobe. 'These robes are simply to die for!' he says, pulling out one of the leopard-print bathrobes that the hotel has supplied for us. 'The ones in my room are zebra print!'

'They're OK, I suppose. Different to your usual white towelling numbers.'

'Different is good, Scarlett. When are you going to start believing that? Why be the same as everyone else when you can be unique!'

'Well, you certainly are!'

Oscar spins around on the carpet. 'And proud of it. Now get in this wardrobe and find a unique first-night-in-NYC outfit to wear, girlfriend. We're going Out On The Town. And I don't mean like that lame movie the cab driver was singing us the score to!'

When I've changed into what I think is an appropriate outfit – black jeans, black boots and a cowl-neck River Island top – we set off into the evening.

The doorman smiles as he holds the door open for us to leave.

'You've made a friend for life, there,' Oscar winks as we set off into the street.

Oscar, who has visited New York before to see Jennifer, leads the way down Park Avenue.

'Ooh, what's that?' I ask, looking up at a large ornate building which dominates the junction at the bottom of the road.

'That's Grand Central Station. If you think it's grand

on the outside, wait until you go inside. Train travel back in the UK will never be the same, darling, I promise you! But not now – I've got more important places to take you tonight.'

As we walk along 42nd Street – just the name alone sends a little thrill through me – with bright yellow taxis constantly swarming by us like noisy canaries flying low along the street, and an equally large number of people bustling past us on the sidewalk, the reality that I'm actually in New York suddenly hits me. In wonder, I tilt my face upwards, gazing at the soaring skyscrapers above my head that seem to stretch endlessly up into the now darkening night skies, and just as quickly snap it back down again when the rest of my body suddenly collides with something round and soft.

'I'm *so* sorry, officer,' I say as an NYC policeman retrieves his cap from the sidewalk and begins dusting it down. 'I was just looking up at the buildings.'

'Tourist?' he enquires, eyeing me warily.

'Yes, I just arrived this afternoon.'

'Well, miss,' he says, placing his hat back on top of his thinning brown hair. 'Let me give you a little tip while you're here. Keep your eyes in front of you, behind you and to the side. But definitely not up above you, because there's a lot more to worry about down here on the streets than there is up in them there skies!'

'Yes sir, thank you, sir,' I say, hurrying to catch up with Oscar, who is waiting a few paces ahead of me, grinning from ear to ear at my embarrassment.

'I don't know, Scarlett,' he says as I reach him. 'You've only been here five minutes and you've already had a run-in with the cops!'

'Stop it, Oscar. It's late and I'm getting tired. Well, it's late in the UK.' I glance at my watch and add on five hours. 'It's one in the morning back home!'

'You need to forget about that,' Oscar says, linking his arm through mine, 'or you'll never get on US time and you'll be permanently jet-lagged while you're here. Right, let's find somewhere to eat.'

We wander farther along 42nd Street and then – *so* exciting! – turn onto Fifth Avenue.

'Ahhh,' Oscar sighs, almost curtseying before the steps of a large building which has two stone lions, much like the ones in Trafalgar Square, guarding the entrance. 'The New York Public Library . . .'

I feel like I'm supposed to know what the *Aaah* is for.

'Why are you aaahing?' I ask bluntly.

Oscar looks horrified. 'Scarlett, have you watched no *Sex and the City*?'

'Not this episode, obviously.'

'You of all people should know this one. It's from the

first movie. The New York Public Library is where Big jilts Carrie on their wedding day.'

'Ah, I see.' I look up at the strikingly ornate white building. 'Can we go inside?'

'Not now,' Oscar says, looking at his watch. 'It's too late. But we will, if only to glide down the heavenly marble staircases.'

We find an Italian restaurant just off Fifth Avenue, although Oscar assures me the best Italian food is to be found in Little Italy on the Lower East Side.

'My family originally emigrated from Italy to New York many years ago,' he tells me as we tuck into our pasta and pizza.

'Did they? I never knew you were Italian.'

'On my mother's side, yes. My great-great-grandfather emigrated here in the early 1900s from Italy. It was my wild grandmother who later came to England, and brought disrepute and shame to the family by moving there with a man she wasn't married to. That's how we ended up in London with the surname St James.'

'That's your real name?' I ask in surprise. 'I always thought it was for effect.'

Oscar purses his lips. 'Darling, I cannot deny that I do many, many things for effect in my life. But my name is not one of them. I'm proud of my family. What's left of them.'

Oscar never spoke that much about his family. I knew that his house in Notting Hill had been left to him by a rich aunt, and that from the rest of her estate he'd bought and set up his shop on the King's Road. But other than having a sister, Jennifer, I knew little else about him, aside from the fact that his parents had both passed away some years ago. Oscar was one of those people who left nothing to the imagination on the outside, with his bright, bold clothes and flamboyant personality, yet kept an awful lot hidden on the inside.

'So what was your Italian name, then? Do you know?'

Oscar pushes the last of his pizza crust around his plate.

'You *do* know, don't you?' I press him. 'What was it? Come on, tell me.'

'Promise you won't laugh?' Oscar says, eyeing me across the table.

'Why would I laugh? Italian names aren't normally funny. They're usually romantic and exciting like Ferrari, or Maserati, or Lamborghini,' I suggest weakly, beginning to struggle.

'How about Fiat, if we're going for makes of Italian sports car?' Oscar laughs.

'I must have spent too much time watching *Top Gear* with Sean. Come on, *tell*, what is it?'

'De Costa,' he says, taking a sip from his glass of white wine.

'What's wrong with ... oh wait,' I clasp my hand to my mouth to try and stifle a giggle. 'So you would have been called ...' I literally have to bite my lips together now.

'Just get it over with,' Oscar says, rolling his eyes. 'Oscar de Costa, yes.'

'Oh, Oscar, I'm sorry, it's not really *that* funny,' I try to say seriously as I feel a fit of giggles begin to build inside of me. But, as we all know, the more you try and stifle laughter like that, the worse it gets, and the hand-over-mouth technique really isn't hiding anything now as I convulse, the supressed giggles erupting inside me.

'Please, miss, allow me,' I hear a calm yet forthright voice behind me say as I feel two strong arms tighten themselves around my waist. 'I know the Heimlich manoeuvre.'

I feel myself being forcefully lifted from my chair. 'No, wait!' I shout before the two arms can squeeze even tighter. 'I'm not choking!'

The arms immediately loosen their grip. 'Oh, do pardon me. I'm so sorry.'

I turn around and see a tall, grey-haired man wearing a suit and tie. He's in his mid-to-late forties, and by the feel of his grip just now, and the fit of his suit, it looks like he works out regularly.

'It's fine, really,' I say with a half-smile. 'You thought you were trying to help me.'

He still looks mortified by his mistake. 'It's just, when I saw you convulsing with your hand over your mouth, I thought . . . '

'Please, really, just forget about it. I was trying not to laugh at my friend's name, that's all.'

The man looks puzzled. I can't say I blame him; I'm not really making much sense. 'Well, as long as you're OK, I'll leave you to return to your dinner. Again, my sincerest apologies.'

I smile properly at him now as he returns to his table, and I take my seat with Oscar again.

Oscar shakes his head. 'I don't know how you do it, darling! We only arrived a few hours ago, and you've already had an encounter with the police and had a strange and,' he cocks his head on one side and ogles the table where my rescuer is now continuing with his dinner, 'rather handsome man's arms around you! What's the rest of our time going to be like in New York, if this is what you get up to on your first evening?'

Eight

The next morning after breakfast I decide to ring my father.

'Dad, how are you?' I squeal excitedly on hearing his voice.

'Scarlett, I'm well. Did you have a good flight?'

'Great, thanks. Do you know, they have over a hundred movies to choose from on the plane now, and you can stop, pause and rewind whenever you want?'

Dad laughs. 'You don't change, do you?'

'So, when can we meet up? I'm dying to see you again.'

'Ah, there's been a slight hitch there, Scarlett.'

'What do you mean, a slight hitch?' I feel my heartbeat start to quicken.

'I'm not in New York at the moment, I'm in Dallas.'

'Dallas!' A brief vision of my father wearing a Stetson floats into my mind.

'Yes, I'm afraid I've had to dash across here on business.'

'But Dad, you knew I was flying out this week. I've come all the way over here especially to see you.' The vision begins to turn from Dad wearing a simple Stetson into a full-blown image of him as J. R. Ewing, drawn from the repeats of *Dallas* Oscar and I have been watching recently on UK TV Gold.

'And you will see me, Scarlett. I'll be back in a few days, I promise. This is a very important three-day leisure conference. It will mean a lot of revenue for the US side of the business if we get the contract I'm hoping for from this visit.'

I sigh. My father was sounding more like Sean by the day.

'OK, Dad, but I do need to see you, I've got some stuff I need to talk to you about.'

There's a pause at the end of the line. 'That sounds ominous, Scarlett. What sort of stuff?'

'Don't worry about it now; it can wait until we meet up.'

As we end the phone call, for the first time in my life I feel let down by my father. I'd flown all the way over here to see him, and he couldn't even be bothered to be here when I arrived?

There's a knock at the door. I don't even need to look through the peephole to know that it's Oscar on the other side. Even his knock is unique.

'Hey, I'll just be a minute,' I say, letting him in as I look around the room for my bag. 'I've just been speaking to Dad. You'll never guess what? He's not even *in* New York, he's in Dallas!'

'I can just see your father in a Stetson,' Oscar muses, mirroring my own thoughts. 'Very J. R. Ewing.'

'He may as well *be* JR for all the affection I'm feeling for him right now. I can't believe he's not here when I've flown all this way, Oscar. I feel let down.'

'Ah,' Oscar says, twisting the toe of his bright green Kurt Geiger shoe around on the hotel carpet. 'You may be feeling much the same about me in a minute, then.'

I stare at him. 'Why, what's happened?'

'Jen just called. She's in a similar predicament to your dad, only the opposite way around. The fashion house she works for now are flying her somewhere exotic for a photo shoot in a couple of days, so if I'm to see her it's got to be sooner rather than later. I'm really sorry, but I'm going to have to pull the cord on our plans for the next couple of days, darling.'

I try not to let my disappointment show too much, but

to be ditched twice in the space of a few minutes, first for a bunch of cowboys and now for my boyfriend's ex, was almost too much to bear.

I pretend to look for my errant bag, which annoyingly immediately appears in front of me on the bed. Typical.

'Are you mad at me, darling?' Oscar asks as I feel his hand stroke the back of my hair.

'No,' I reply in a tight voice. 'Why would I be mad? You need to see your sister, like I need to see my dad.'

'Will you be OK on your own today then, sweetie?' Oscar swings himself around onto the bed now so he's looking up at me. 'What will you do?'

'Oscar, this is New York. I only have to wander down the street and I can find loads to do. You proved that to me last night.'

'And you proved that you only have to step out of the hotel room and you find trouble. Dare I leave you on your own for a whole day? Sean will skin me alive and eat me for breakfast if anything happens to you on this trip.'

'Well, Sean isn't here, is he, and it was his idea I come in the first place, so Sean will have to put up with whatever New York has to throw at me.'

Oscar stares up at my defiant attitude open-mouthed.

'Don't worry, Oscar, I'm not going out looking for trouble.'

'No, but is it out looking for you?' Oscar enquires with a knowing look in his eye.

Armed with a map and strict instructions from Oscar on what not to do and where I was definitely not to venture in the city, I set off from the hotel later that morning on my own.

The doorman swings open the door wide for me. 'Can I get you a cab, miss?' he enquires hopefully.

'That's kind, but no thank you, er … Sam,' I note, looking at his name badge. 'I'm walking today.'

'Great idea, miss. Have a nice day, won't you?'

Wow, they actually say that? 'Thanks, Sam, I intend to. See you later.'

I walk the same route Oscar led me along last night, but decide this time to walk the entire length of Fifth Avenue. I stare in awe at the shops that I pass along the way. Names I've only ever seen and heard on television and in movies, like Saks, Bergdorf Goodman and Barnes & Noble are now right in front of me, beckoning me in. They tempt me into their lair with the promise that if I spend the wad of green dollars hidden in my purse, I too can experience the same glamorous lifestyle I've seen on my cinema and TV screens. I explore FAO Schwarz, the huge toy store, and find the Big Piano; the same one Tom Hanks danced and played chopsticks on in the movie. I want to have a go myself, but it's full of children having a fun time, and when the occasional adult is brave enough to take a turn, there's always a friend or partner close by to take a souvenir snapshot of them so they don't feel like a prize idiot dancing in the middle of toyshop on a giant piano, and suddenly I feel lonely again.

I leave FAO Schwarz and debate whether to go into Central Park, but Oscar and I had said we'd go there together one day as he'd never had a chance to visit it properly before, so I turn back onto Fifth Avenue. And it's then I spot it across the street: an iconic movie moment standing elegantly right in front of me. Tiffany's.

There's the very spot where Audrey Hepburn would have pulled up in front of the store in a now vintage yellow taxi, eating her breakfast and then pausing to glance at the jewels in the window.

I'm still gazing in awe at the opulent-looking building as I cross over the road, then one by one I wander around all of Tiffany's tiny windows, each displaying an exquisite diamond in its best light. Wow! This is fantastic – I have to go inside. I mean, obviously I won't buy anything, it will all be too expensive. I just want to have a quick look ... and then there's the brooch to think about. My Roadshow buddy did say that it was a Tiffany replica; someone in there might be able to help me trace its history.

I'm about to go towards one of the doors, when a microphone is thrust under my nose.

'Excuse me, I wonder if I could ask you a question?'

My eyes run along the arm holding the microphone, up a shirt-covered body and finally, at the top, they find a pair of dark-chocolate eyes staring back at me intently.

The brown eyes then smile, as does the mouth below them.

'What sort of a question?' I ask, looking suspiciously at the microphone again.

'We're asking people just why they're here visiting Tiffany's today.'

'Why? I ask again. 'And who's we?'

Mr Brown Eyes laughs now. 'Well, that's more response than I get from most New Yorkers, even though you haven't actually answered my question. Allow me to introduce myself. We're from *Morning Sunshine*, it's a TV breakfast show over in the UK. Do you know it?'

I nod at him. I did know the show, but the truth was I usually watched their rival in the mornings. Well, I had, until I'd got myself banned ... but I thought it was perhaps best not to mention that right now.

'Good,' he says smiling. 'We, that's my cameraman here and myself, are just filming quick reactions from people to make up a small piece that will go out on tomorrow morning's show.'

I suddenly notice another man holding a camera standing a little way behind me. He's wearing a red t-shirt with a Union Jack flag that says *I ♥ London* and khaki combat shorts. He waves casually with his free hand.

'So would you be prepared to say why you're going into Tiffany's?' my questioner asks again. 'You'd be doing me a huge favour; we have loads of trouble getting people to stop for vox pops.'

'Vox pops?' I ask, looking at him with a puzzled expression. 'What's that?'

'That's what we call what we're doing here, asking people questions on the street.'

I shrug. 'Sure, go on then, why not?'

'Great! Max,' he calls out to the man with the camera. 'We've got one!'

Max moves a bit closer to us and arranges his camera on his shoulder. 'OK, Jamie, ready when you are.'

'So,' Jamie says, looking at me, 'if you can just tell me why you're here today, and why you're going into Tiffany's, that would be great. I'll nod when we're ready for you to speak. Oh, and don't look into the camera, look at me, OK? Don't worry if you dry up or stutter; we can cut it to make it look good for the final piece.'

'Sure,' I say with certainty, but I'm trying to remember when I last brushed my hair. I run my hand casually through it.

'Right, then,' Jamie says. He opens his eyes wide and looks towards Max, who nods at him from behind the camera. Then he nods pointedly at me and thrusts his microphone under my chin.

I blink a couple of times before I find my voice. 'I'm visiting Tiffany's today because for one, I absolutely adore movies, and I love the movie *Breakfast at Tiffany's*, it's just so romantic, and Audrey Hepburn is so elegant in it. I mean, she's elegant in all her films, but in this one in particular her clothes are just wonderful. And then of course there's the scene at the end where they get out of the cab to find the cat, that's just so sad, and then so joyous at the same time, it makes me cry every time I see it, and I must have watched that film over a dozen times.' Jamie nods at me, so I take this as a good sign and continue.

'And the other reason I'm here today is that I'm trying to trace the heritage of a brooch that has been in my family for years. It's a Tiffany replica from the early 1900s, a dragonfly – really pretty, but fake, apparently.' I quickly open my bag and pull out a black velvet pouch containing the brooch, then I hold the dragonfly up so the camera can see it. 'The weird thing is, I don't understand why my dad would ever have something like this. I've actually come over to New York to ask him about it, but he's not here at the moment, he's over in Dallas. We own a popcorn-machine company and—'

Out of the corner of my eye I see Max making a slit-ting action across his throat and I realise that Jamie has dropped the mic away from my mouth.

'Oops, did I go on a bit too much?'

'Just a tad,' Jamie says, but he smiles. 'Interesting story though, about the brooch.'

'Yes, it is all a bit odd.'

'Can I take a look?'

'Of course, ' I carefully place the brooch onto the palm of my hand. 'I'm going into the store in a minute to ask them about it.'

Jamie inspects the dragonfly. 'Wow, nice. Certainly looks real.'

'It does, doesn't it?'

He lifts the brooch up towards the sunlight, and the cobalt blue of its body sparkles against the sun's rays.

'And you say it's not a genuine Tiffany?'

'Yep, I had it valued on the *Antiques Roadshow* back in the UK.'

He stops examining the brooch and turns his intense gaze towards me. '*Antiques Roadshow*?' he says with a serious expression. 'You don't do things by halves, do you?'

I'm not sure if he's mocking me.

'No, actually, I don't,' I say, taking my brooch back from him and putting it carefully in its pouch.

'Stop winding her up, J,' Max says, coming over with his camera. 'I used to work on the *Antiques Roadshow*, years ago. The experts certainly know their stuff, and if they say it's a fake, it's a fake.'

'Thanks,' I say, smiling at him.

'So why do you think your dad has a fake Tiffany brooch then?' he puts his camera down on the ground.

'No idea. He's always kept it hidden away, but I knew it was there. I found it tucked in a box in his wardrobe when I was playing hide-and-seek with my friends one day.'

Max and Jamie exchange a look.

'When I was a child, *obviously*. It's really strange, not like him at all. I'm determined to get to the bottom of it, and find out something about the brooch's history.'

'Go up to the top floor when you get inside,' Max says, smiling. 'They'll help you out; they're very good in there. But when you're done, come back outside and let us know how it went. This is the most interesting thing we've heard today. Isn't it, J?'

Jamie nods. 'It is, actually. Sorry about before.'

'It's fine,' I smile at them both. 'Sure, I'll do that. Will you still be here when I come out?'

'Yeah, for sure. We've got to harass – sorry – *find* at least another five people with something interesting to say. And around here, that could take hours!'

101

I bid them farewell for now, and head inside the iconic building itself. After the hustle and bustle of Fifth Avenue, Tiffany's manages to exude a timeless elegance about its art deco interior that immediately whisks me back to a bygone era of black and white movies and film-star sophistication. I can almost feel the spirits of Audrey Hepburn and George Peppard wandering around, pausing to browse at one of the glass display stands show-casing the latest Tiffany designs.

'Can I help you, miss?' a man wearing a smart suit enquires, seeing me daydreaming wistfully across the store.

I quickly recover myself. 'I was just ... You see, I have this brooch, and I wanted some information on it, and I was wondering about the best place to go to ask.'

'Customer Services, miss, on the top floor. They'll be able to help you out with any questions. The lift is right over there on the back wall.'

'Thank you so much.' I smile at him and head towards the lifts.

The lift arrives and Harold, another dapperly dressed man in a suit, who must be in his seventies with his white hair and moustache, steps forward as the door opens. 'Going up, miss?' he enquires.

'Yes, please,' I say, walking past him into the lift. 'I'd like Customer Services.'

'Gladly, miss,' Harold says, pressing a button on the lift console.

I watch as the lift rises up through the floors, and as it pings to announce our arrival, so does Harold. 'Customer Services,' he says as the door opens. 'Enjoy your time at Tiffany's.'

'Thank you, Harold,' I say, stepping out of the lift.

'It's a pleasure, miss.'

I could seriously get used to this.

Tiffany Customer Services, unlike your usual customer-service department where you queue for half an hour to get to an unhelpful assistant at a Formica desk only to be told you're in the wrong department, is filled with long plush settees and several antique-looking desks. And from what I can overhear from the many conversations going on at those desks, it's mostly people wanting their Tiffany jewellery to be fixed or resized. I approach one of the desks with a young man sitting behind it.

'Good morning, how can I help you?' he asks, looking up.

I tell him the story about the brooch and what they'd suggested at the Roadshow. He looks surprised.

'We don't usually deal in fakes here, miss.'

'Yes, I understand that, but I just wanted to know if you had anything on the particular history of the original brooch.'

The young man looks carefully to either side of him. 'Look, miss, if I were you I'd keep your brooch inside your purse while I was in here. Tiffany's don't take too kindly to their designs being replicated in any way, however old your piece may be. If your brooch turned out to be counterfeit goods from way back when, they might be well within their rights to seize it.'

I grip my bag to my side protectively. 'I hadn't thought of that. Yes ... yes, of course. Thanks for the warning.'

'No problem, miss. I really hope you find out what you want to know.'

'Yes, I'm sure I'll get to the bottom of it somehow. Thanks again.'

I travel back down in the lift with Harold, not doing what I had originally planned – nosying around the other floors. I suddenly want to get me and my brooch as far away from here as possible. I can't risk it being taken away from me. I'm not sure why this little brooch in my bag suddenly feels very significant, but it does.

Nine

I find Jamie and Max still standing on the sidewalk as I exit the building. They're just packing up Max's camera equipment, so they must have met enough willing volunteers for one day.

'Hey, how did you get on?' Max asks.

'Not that great, actually. The guy up in Customer Services basically advised me to get out of there as quickly as I could; he said they didn't take too kindly to Tiffany fakes.'

Max pulls a face. 'Awkward.'

'So what will you do now? Jamie asks.

I look up at him. They're a funny pair, when you see them standing next to each other. Jamie is about six foot tall, slim, with short-cropped brown hair, wearing a blue shirt and smart chino-style trousers. Max is about five foot seven, stocky, with a mass of dark curls framing a smiling face.

'I don't know. Wait until I see my father, I guess. See what he has to say about it.'

'Where did you say he was right now – Dallas?' Jamie asks.

'Yeah, long story.'

'Look, we're about to go and get a coffee. Do you want to join us? We're done here for the day. You can tell us all about it. You never know, we might be able to help.'

'I don't know ...' I look at the two of them. They seem harmless enough, but they're strangers I've literally just met on the streets of New York.

'We don't bite – honest,' Jamie grins. 'Well, Max does sometimes, but that's only when I haven't fed him enough Starbucks.'

'Ha, funny,' Max says, grimacing. 'I think you'll find you're the one that has to get his caffeine fix every few hours, or he can't keep awake.' He looks across at me. 'Far too laid-back for his own good, this one,' he says, gesturing at Jamie. 'I have to give him coffee to pump him up a bit, otherwise he comes across onscreen about as lively as a giant pretzel.'

I laugh. 'OK, OK, no more bitching, you've persuaded me. I'll come for coffee.'

We walk along the street to the nearest Starbucks, and while Max gets our drinks, I sit down at a table with Jamie.

'So,' I ask, glancing across the table at him. 'Have you been doing this long?' I'm guessing Jamie is about the same age as me. He looks fairly young to be a news reporter, though. They're usually dull, grey-looking men in suits and ties when I watch TV news, which isn't often.

'Drinking coffee in Starbucks?' he asks with a half-smile.

'No ... working here in New York!'

'Yes, I know what you meant. Well . ... I've only been a correspondent here for a few months, but I've been with *Morning Sunshine* for a year now. Before that I worked in children's TV in the UK.'

'Anything I might know?'

'Why, do you watch a lot of children's television?' he teases.

I smile ruefully back at him. 'No, not that much, actually ... Why, what did you do – something embarrassing? You weren't one of the original Teletubbies, or some other children's favourite hidden inside a big suit, were you?'

'Funny! No, I worked on *Newsround*, actually, as a reporter.'

'Oh, I remember watching that when I was a child.'

'It wasn't *that* long ago . . .' he teases again, raising an eyebrow. Then he smiles.

'Hmm, quite the funny man, aren't you?' I say, folding my arms.

'Nah, not me. Max is the funny one. I'm sorry, it's just my way.'

I watch Jamie for a moment over the table. 'Do you enjoy being out here?' I ask, deciding to continue with my line of conversation. I wasn't quite sure how to take him just yet.

'Yes, I do. It's hard work, mind, but it beats standing out in the rain in the early morning reporting from the side of the road somewhere, like I did when I was a correspondent in the UK.'

'Yes, I'm sure it does. What's the difference between a reporter and a correspondent, then?'

'Nothing, just a fancier name!' Max says, returning with our drinks. 'Skinny caramel latte for you and you,' he hands both me and Jamie a cup filled with hot coffee. 'And a grande mocha Frappuccino with cream for me.'

Jamie rolls his eyes. 'It's no wonder we have to keep going into J. C. Penney's to get you new elasticated shorts to wear if you keep ingesting all these calories on a daily basis.'

'Hmm, funny man,' Max says, pulling out a chair and sitting down. 'At least I don't spend my time poncing about in Barneys' and Bergdorf Goodman's designer departments.'

I look between the two of them and smile nervously.

'Ah, don't worry about us,' Max says, sitting down and taking a sip of his Frappuccino. 'We're always like this. Hey, I've just realised we don't even know *your* name yet.'

'It's Scarlett,' I say, waiting for the inevitable.

'Cool. Like in *Gone with the Wind*?'

'Yes, my mother is a big movie fan.'

'As are you by the sounds of it,' Jamie says, looking across the table at me with interest. 'From what you were saying before about *Breakfast at Tiffany's*.'

'Yes, just a bit. I adore them. But it occasionally gets me into trouble.'

'Oh, really?' Max asks, eyeing me with a different sort of interest.

'Ha, I'm afraid it's not that exciting, and it's a very long story. I'm sure you don't want to hear about it right now. Anyway, tell me about you. Jamie was telling me how he used to work on *Newsround* back in the UK. So what have you done, Max?'

'Well,' Max smirks at Jamie and puffs his chest out a little. 'After I moved here from London, I was stationed over in LA and got to go to the Oscars a number of times.'

'Really!' I sit up in my chair with delight. 'You went to the actual Oscars ceremony?'

It's Jamie's turn to smirk now as he picks up his cup of coffee and sips on it. He raises his eyebrows at Max over the top of the mug.

Max shuffles in his chair a little. 'Not the *actual* ceremony. I filmed outside on the red carpet, with the reporter I was stationed with in LA.'

'But still, that must have been *very* exciting. I'd love to go to the Oscars.'

Max shrugs. 'Not really. Any red carpet event is a bit crap if you're the wrong side of the carpet.'

'But why? Surely it's super-glamorous, all those stars wearing lovely dresses, and the men slick and smart in their tuxedos.'

'God no, we're given an area to stand on about the size of a A4 sheet of paper, and that's for two of us, remember, with everyone pushing and shoving all around, and I'm usually balanced precariously on a stepladder with my camera so I can see over the top of everyone's head. Glamorous it is not – murderous, more like.'

Jamie nods sympathetically at him. 'He's right; I've covered a few film premieres and it's much the same at those, too. Because we're a British TV company, we don't get very high up the pecking order on the red carpet, so by the time the stars get to us they're pretty fed up answering questions. You're lucky if you can get anything out of them at all.'

'Oh.' I'm somewhat disillusioned hearing all this. I've always dreamed of going to the Oscars, and they make it sound awful. 'Maybe if you're on the right side of the carpet your experience is better,' I suggest hopefully. 'If it's your film premiere, or you're up for an award, maybe you have a lovely time.'

'Still wouldn't want to go though, even if I was the right side,' Max says, taking a large slurp of his coffee. 'Most of the celebs are so up themselves they can't see out past their own intestines into the real world.'

'Have you met many, then?' I ask, trying to keep a straight face. 'Celebs, I mean, not intestines.'

Max grins. 'Ha, I like your style, Scarlett. Yeah, a few, some are OK, others aren't. You can usually tell by the size of their entourage. The bigger the amount of people circling them, the bigger the pain in the arse they are.'

'How about you?' I ask, turning towards Jamie. 'Have you interviewed many stars?'

Jamie wrinkles his nose. '"Star" is a very overused word. Well-known people maybe, yes.'

I can't help but grin at him.

'What?' he asks.

'You're so cool about everything.'

Max almost splutters on his Frappuccino. 'J, cool? I hardly think so.'

'No, I mean chilled, relaxed, not flustered by the fact that you work in TV. Neither of you are, really.'

'Should we be, then?' Jamie asks, looking at me with that same amused expression he seems to carry most of the time.

'Well, I think it's exciting. It's more interesting than what I do; supplying popcorn machines to cinemas.'

'Are you kidding me?' Max exclaims, his eyes wide. 'My own popcorn machine, that's like my life's dream!'

'But it's not your average job, is it?' Jamie continues. 'When you were telling us about your dad and mentioned it earlier, I thought it was a bit unusual.'

'I guess it's not standard issue, no. But it's still not as great as working in television.'

'TV is not all it's cracked up to be, I guarantee you.'

I look at Jamie over the table while he studies me equally intently in return. There's something about him I can't quite put my finger on. Maybe I *have* seen him on TV before.

'But it just might come in handy for you right now,' he says mysteriously.

'How do you mean?'

'With your brooch. I think we can help you. I know

112

someone who works on the US version of the *Antiques Roadshow*. Maybe they might be able to help you trace its history.'

'There's an American version of the *Antiques Roadshow*? I never knew that.'

'Yeah, the guy that presents it used to visit the same dentist as me,' Max says, putting his empty Frappuccino cup down on the table. 'I sometimes used to see him when I was waiting for a check-up. Er ... Walberg, his name is, Mark, I think.'

'You have the same dentist as Mark Wahlberg?' I ask in astonishment. 'Wow, the *Antiques Roadshow* is way cooler over here if they have movie stars presenting it.'

Jamie and Max both laugh. 'No,' Max says. 'Not the ex-rapper, now actor and producer Mark Wahlberg. This guy is called Mark L. Walberg. Same name, different spelling.'

'Oh right,' I blush. 'Sorry.'

'It's fine,' Jamie smiles. 'I bet he gets it all the time.'

'I bet he wishes he got rapper Wahlberg's wages, though!' Max jokes. 'They're worth a lot more than anything you'll find on that Roadshow.'

'So I'll have a word with my friend about your brooch,' Jamie continues, 'and see if Harry knows anyone that might be an expert in such matters, you know, fakes rather than the real thing.'

'That's very kind of you.' I smile at them both. 'I'm so glad I came to Tiffany's today. I should have known it would help me in some way.'

'You never know,' Jamie says, 'you might be able to help us out too. This could make a good story, if you were interested in being on *Morning Sunshine*.'

Hmm ... at least it would be on a different channel, and I'd actually be appearing as myself this time. 'Of course I would. Sure, that sounds great.'

'Right, well, let's swap numbers and I'll be in touch.' Jamie gets out his iPhone. 'It seems like bumping into you today, Scarlett, could be pretty beneficial for both of us.'

Ten

That evening, to make up for 'abandoning me' during the day, Oscar takes me for dinner at Serendipity 3, the eclectically decorated restaurant made famous in the movie of the same name. This, of course, pleases me greatly.

'What are you doing on that phone, Scarlett?' Oscar asks, putting down his menu for a moment to see what I'm up to. 'For heaven's sake, you're supposed to be choosing your rather yummy, by the looks of this fabby menu, dinner.'

'I'm seeing if there's a Wi-Fi signal in here,' I say, furiously tapping at my iPhone.

'Why do you want Wi-Fi in a restaurant, darling?'

'Because I haven't tweeted today, and I want to find

out what's going on back home. I've had to switch off data roaming while I'm here, or it will cost me a fortune.'

Oscar looks amused. 'The last time I used anything called "data roaming" over the internet I met a Greek chap called Cosmo. He didn't speak much English but he had a very big—'

'Oscar!'

'I was going to say kebab shop, actually. Just off the Edgware Road.'

'Hmm ...' I narrow my eyes at him. 'Moving on ... how was Jen?' I almost say this through gritted teeth. But I manage to turn it into a smile of sorts.

'She's very well, thank you. She's working as a PA to the boss of one of New York's top fashion houses now. Oh, you should see her, Scarlett, she does look the business in all her finery. Very Carrie Bradshaw, she is. I'm so proud.'

My menu suddenly becomes infinitely absorbing. I give up on the internet and put my phone back in my bag. I'll tweet later on the hotel's free Wi-Fi. 'That's great. Good for her. Let's order, shall we?' I say with new-found enthusiasm, keen not to talk about the 'fabulous' Jen any more.

'So, darling, what did you get up to today?' Oscar asks after we've studied the sumptuous menu for a good few minutes and finally placed our order. 'Were you a tad lonely all by yourself?'

'Actually no, I had a lovely time strolling along Fifth Avenue in the morning, and then in the afternoon I met some people outside Tiffany's.'

'Oh *yes*?' Oscar pricks up his ears. 'Outside Tiffany's, eh? Were they rich and dripping with diamonds?'

'Hardly. They work in television.'

Oscar opens his eyes wide and blinks at me. 'Television, how fabulous! Are they famous American stars?'

I laugh now. 'No, they're both from the UK, actually; they work for one of our breakfast TV shows.'

'God, not the one you were banned from?'

'I wasn't banned! I was just asked to leave the building on that occasion.'

Oscar opens his eyes even wider. 'OK, OK.' He holds his hands up in submission. 'I'm not going down that U bend with you now. So who are these TV types, then?'

'They're not from *Wake Up Britain*, they're from the other one, *Morning Sunshine*, and they were filming a piece outside Tiffany's. I helped them by answering some questions.'

'Cool.' Oscar takes a first sip from his glass of Serendipity's infamous frozen hot chocolate that the waiter has just brought us both. 'Oh my days, Scarlett, this is to die for. Quick, try yours, darling, it's heavenly!'

I take a sip of my own frozen hot chocolate. An odd

combination to achieve, you'd think. But Oscar's right: it is indeed heavenly.

'So what are they like?' Oscar asks after we've enjoyed a couple of minutes of pure chocolate indulgence. 'These TV bods.'

'Really nice. They took me for coffee in Starbucks, and I told them all about the brooch and they've offered to help me.' I tell Oscar what happened in Tiffany's, and then what Jamie had said about his contact.

'That's good of them,' Oscar says, his eyes narrowing. 'What do they want in return?'

'Nothing. Well, they might want to run a story about it, if it turns out to be anything interesting, that's all.'

'Hmm, I knew there'd have to be something in it for them. You can't trust these televisual types, Scarlett; I've met them before. Especially not journalists.'

'Jamie's not a journalist, he's a correspondent, and Max is a cameraman. They're hardly tabloid hacks.'

'Oh,' Oscar says pointedly, his mouth forming a big O. 'They're both *men*, are they?'

'Yeah, and what of it?'

'Scarlett, you're a pretty girl in a foreign town . . .'

'That sounds like the tagline from a movie.' I put on a deep voice. 'She was just a pretty girl in a foreign town . . .'

'Don't mock me, darling. I'm only looking out for you.'

'Oscar, they're both harmless. Max is really down to earth and funny, and Jamie, he's, well ...' I pause. How do I describe Jamie? I stir my straw around in the remnants of my chocolate for a moment.

'He's what?' Oscar prompts.

'He's just all right, that's all. I don't know how I know this, Oscar, but I do.'

Oscar raises his eyebrows. 'Scarlett ...'

'What? Look, you can come along and meet them when they get in touch next, if you want.'

Oscar nods approvingly. 'I think I might just do that. My man radar is pretty accurate. Even with straight men. They are straight, right?' he adds as an afterthought.

'I think so. Funny, we didn't really get around to discussing our sexual preferences.'

'Didn't you?' Oscar looks shocked. 'That's usually one of the first topics of conversation when I meet a stranger in Starbucks.'

Eleven

Next morning, I'm up and out of the hotel early and heading towards the Empire State Building. As I stride happily along the streets, I think about Sean and the conversation we've just had on the phone. Sean had been very eager to hear all about my first day in New York and what I'd got up to. And I'd told him most of what I'd done, strangely skirting around the TV issue for some reason. I hadn't *not* told him, I'd just been sparing with the details after what Oscar had said about Max and Jamie both being men. Instead, I'd given him much more to worry about when I'd told him all about Fleet Week in the city and the hordes of sailors we were expecting to see while we were here. And, as I'd suspected, that subject had immediately relegated any other topic of conversation to the bottom of the 'non-urgent' pile.

As I find myself on the junction of East 34th Street and Fifth Avenue, I see the Empire State Building towering up before me in all her glory. A doyenne of the New York skyline for so long, it's odd to see her standing here squeezed in among all the shops and restaurants that line the streets below. I feel as though something as prominent and important as this should be set aside away from everything else, so that she can be admired for all her art deco beauty, not squashed at the corner of a busy street for dogs to pee on and litter to be scattered at the foot of.

I enter through the door at the foot of the building and am at once surrounded by yet more art deco wonder, immediately drawing me back to a bygone age of Hollywood splendour, of Ginger Rogers and Fred Astaire swirling around a dance floor.

'Excuse me,' a woman with a foreign accent says, barging me out of the way as she pushes past and heads for the ticket desk.

I suddenly remember why I've got up so early to get here. I need to do all the big tourist attractions in New York early, or the queues will get really long later on. I break away from waltzing with Fred and hurry along behind her, following her up to buy a ticket on the first floor. We wind our way around a long series of roped areas, reminding me very much of the queueing system at Disneyland Paris, and I'm thankful again for setting my alarm early this morning when I realise just how long the queues can get here. After I've paid for my ticket, there's yet another set of ropes and a small queue to wait for the lifts to take us up to the observation deck.

The lifts are tiny, and as we all excitedly squeeze into one and whizz up to the eighty-sixth floor, I watch in amazement as the numbers flash past on a little counter above the doors, measuring our journey to the top. When we arrive and the doors part for us to exit the lift, I'm surprised at just how small the observation deck seems. I've watched *Sleepless in Seattle* more times than I care to admit, and Meg Ryan would have whizzed around in a couple of minutes and immediately known Tom Hanks wasn't up here waiting for her.

Even though it's still early, the deck is already pretty packed with tourists. Thankfully today, unlike when I ventured to the top of the Eiffel Tower last year on my own, it's not filled with loving young couples canoodling in every corner. In fact, as I gradually make my way around each side of the observation deck, it becomes increasingly noisy and boisterous. I turn a corner onto the east side of the deck and am stunned to see a gang of young men in the process of stripping off their clothes and folding them neatly into piles on the floor.

I can't help but stop and stare at them as one by one they pull from their bags what look like big black hairy rugs. I'm not the only one: they're starting to draw a small crowd of onlookers who, for a few minutes, are distracted from gazing out at the incredible views of Manhattan and the surrounding area and are watching what's going on on the observation deck itself.

The men begin to pull on the rugs, and I realise they're not rugs at all but costumes, monkey costumes – no – as one speedy chap get his head on first, gorilla costumes.

'Do you know what they do?' an elderly oriental woman standing next to me asks.

'Yes,' I smile knowingly. 'I do, actually. They're all dressing up as King Kong.'

'But why they do that?'

'Because of the movie,' I explain. 'You know, the part where King Kong climbs to the top of the Empire State Building and then battles with all the planes?'

She looks at me with uncertainty. 'King Kong, he is a monkey?'

'No, he's a gorilla, but a really big one. Oh, I need to get photos of this. It will look great on Twitter!' I begin snapping pictures of the dozen or so men now all dressed as King Kong.

'You guys need a girl,' someone shouts from the crowd. 'To kidnap!'

The apes all beat their chests in agreement and begin lolloping around the assembled crowd in search of an appropriate victim. Thank God I don't have blond hair, I murmur to myself, thinking of Fay Wray in the original movie, and oh, who was the actress in the recent remake?

While I'm desperately trying to think of her name, I realise three gorillas are now poised in front of me, beating their chests.

I shake my head and point at my black hair.

Gorilla number one pulls a curly blond wig from behind his back.

I shake my head again. I'm not sure why I don't just speak; it's as if I think they're real gorillas, incapable of understanding English.

The crowd begins to clap, slow rhythmical claps supposed to encourage me to join in with this nonsense. 'Come on, gorgeous,' someone shouts, 'play nice and put on the wig. The guys have gone to all this trouble, they need a girl to finish the job off properly.'

What did he think they were going to do up here? Hang over the edge of the viewing platform with me dangling under one of their hairy arms, about to fall to my doom?

'All right, I'll wear the wig so you can take a photo, but that's it, OK?' I grab the blond wig from the gorilla and tuck my long black hair underneath it. Then I shove my camera at the guy that shouted out. 'Can you take a photo for me then, since you were so keen for me to do this?'

I stand with the King Kongs and have my photo taken in a traditional pose. Then one of them whispers through his mask, 'This is all for charity, ma'am. Do you think we could pick you up and make it look like we're running off with you?'

'What charity?' I whisper back into his wrinkled rubber face.

'A children's home in the Bronx.'

I sigh. 'OK then, but make it quick.'

I let the gorillas lift me up and hold me sideways across their hairy arms, like one of those bridal shots of the male wedding party all holding the bride up. Then we do a couple of photos of me pretending to run away with a pack of hairy gorillas chasing after me, and me pretending to scream while they lift me up in the air above their heads. By the end of it I'm actually quite enjoying myself, but I don't let on.

When we eventually come to the end of the photo

shoot, one of the gorillas pulls off his head and passes me back my camera. The chap I'd given it to originally had got bored after the first set of photos and moved on.

'Thank you, ma'am,' he says, smoothing his cropped blond hair. 'You've really helped us out. We were offered more sponsorship if we found a willing young lady to take on the Ann Darrow role. The guys back on the ship will have to pay up big time now.'

'The ship?' I look back at him enquiringly. Then I notice the other King Kongs are now stripping off their costumes and dressing in naval uniforms. I'd been so surprised to find men undressing at the top of the Empire State Building, let alone fit-looking ones, that I hadn't really noticed what they were undressing out of. 'Oh, you're sailors!'

'We sure are!' he gives a small salute. 'Seaman John Jefferson at your service, ma'am. We wouldn't have been allowed to do this here today if it wasn't Fleet Week, and our small stunt was for charity. The city's many fine landmarks are very accommodating to us sailors during Fleet Week.'

'That's very good of them.' I can't help breaking into a smile at his courteous manner. He's like a caricature of a movie sailor, standing in front of me and saluting like that. Now I can see the others dressed in their uniforms, I can just imagine him in his full crisp white shirt and trousers, doffed hat held in front of him, calling me ma'am. 'They certainly seem to welcome you to the city.'

'They sure do,' he says as he pushes the gorilla suit down off his torso so it sits around his waist, revealing a white vest and a pair of extremely muscular arms. 'It's my third time here in NYC for Fleet Week; we always have a whale of a time.' He regards me for a moment. 'No . . .' he says, and he shakes his head.

'What do you mean, no?'

'Well, I was just wondering something, and then I thought, John Jefferson, this ain't the sorta lady that you ask that kinda thing of.'

'Ask what kind of thing?' I just can't help but smile coyly at him. He looks so cute standing there, his top half all squeaky-clean and polished-looking with his blond hair all neat and a twinkle in his bright blue eyes, his bottom half still clothed in the hairy gorilla suit.

'There's a big party tonight at one of the bars down-town, and I wondered if you'd like to come along? I mean, you can bring your boyfriend or . . . or your hus-band, if you have one with you on holiday?'

'How do you know I'm on holiday?'

'I'm just guessing, since you talk the way you do and the fact you're at the top of the Empire State Building. Not many locals do that on a Monday morning.'

'That's true. Yes, I am on holiday. But no, I'm not married or here with my boyfriend,' I'm careful to say.

'I see ...' he replies, considering this. 'So, do you wanna come to the party? You can bring a friend?'

'Yeah, I'll come,' I say, a grin spreading across my face. 'And I know just the friend who'd like to tag along with me.'

Twelve

'Praise the Lord that is Jimmy Choo!' Oscar hails, raising his arms in the air. 'We're going to a sailors' party! I need to leave you alone more often, Scarlett.'

'We don't have to go,' I tease. 'It might not be that much fun ...'

'Are you kidding me?' Oscar looks like I've just suggested we don't eat for a fortnight. 'This is like, Season Five, Episode 67, *Anchors Away!* The one I was telling you about in the taxi, where the girls are invited to a sailors' party. Oh my God, Scarlett,' he squeals, clapping his hands manically like a performing seal. 'This is beyond my wildest dreams, I'm actually living Carrie Bradshaw's life!'

Later that evening, we arrive at the bar where the

party is being held. The place is huge, and teeming with white uniforms filled with surging male hormones. They spill out onto the sidewalk, and lean casually up against the stairway so we have to squeeze past them to make our way up to the main entrance. Oscar doesn't even try to hide his joy at this minor inconvenience.

'Hi,' I say to the sailor manning the door.

'Good evening, ma'am,' he nods at me, and raises a smile at Oscar who has come dressed tonight in his own version of naval uniform: a tight navy and white striped long-sleeved top, white trousers, braces and a bright red neckerchief tied jauntily around his neck. He'd wanted to go out and buy a peaked sailor hat this afternoon to complete his look, but I'd managed to stop him just in time by reminding him of the old adage 'less is more'.

'Seaman John Jefferson said for me to come along tonight?' I mention hopefully.

'Ma'am, you don't need no names to get in here looking like you do.' He looks appraisingly at my choice of dress; it's crimson, with a long slit up one side. 'And your friend's outfit is mighty fine too.' He winks at Oscar, and Oscar nearly passes out on the spot.

'Thank you, sir,' I beam at him. I grab hold of Oscar's arm and drag him away from the sailor and in through the doorway. Inside is a huge bar on three levels, and every level is packed to the brim with uniformed seamen of differing ranks. It's like a huge sea of white has washed over the bar. It's occasionally broken by a tiny dash of colour from a shimmering dress or a sparkly handbag decorating the women that mingle among the sailors.

'Well, kiss me Hardy, it's Christmas come early!' Oscar says, spinning around when his head can no longer spin far enough for him to take in the whole panorama. 'Scarlett, I'm diving in! Get the drinks in, darling; I'll be back in two shakes of a duck's tail. Or would that be shag, seeing as we're in a room full of men of the sea.' He turns back briefly and winks. 'And if I can't get one of those tonight, then my name's not Oscar St James, master of seamen everywhere!'

'Oscar, wait!' I call as he disappears into the sea of white. 'What am I . . .' But he's gone.

I make my way over to the bar, and try not to look too conspicuous as I stand there waiting to be served. Suddenly, coming to this party doesn't seem like such a good idea after all. The sailor standing next to me leans over in my direction.

'Buy you a drink, ma'am?'

'Er, no thanks. I'm getting them in for me and a friend.'

'I'll buy your friend's too. What's her name?' He grins at me through yellowish teeth, and I can smell the alcohol fumes wafting from his breath.

'Oscar, and he just *loves* sailors!'

This line seems to work, with not only this sailor but a few others that try their luck with me in the minutes afterwards. Eventually the barman sees me and drifts over in my direction.

'What's it to be, miss?'

'I'll get these,' a voice behind me says.

I'm about to turn around and bat back yet another unwanted advance, when I realise I recognise this voice.

'Jamie!' I say in relief as I turn around. 'What on earth are you doing here?'

'Trying to get a story, for my sins,' he says, grinning at me. 'We've been asked to do a piece on Fleet Week, and I'm looking for a different angle to just ships and sailors parading up and down in straight lines.'

'Well, this is certainly different.'

'Do you guys want serving or not?' the barman calls from behind us.

'Sorry, yes, yes we do. Two Cosmopolitans, please.' I turn back to Jamie. 'What would you like?'

'Not one of those, that's for sure. I'll just take a beer – Bud if you have it.'

The barman nods and goes off to make the cocktails.

'*Sex and the City*?' Jamie asks.

'I'm sorry?'

'Your drinks; are you ordering them because of the show? I had a friend once who was mad on it.'

'Yes, my friend is too. That's why I'm getting them. He's so excited to be here tonight too because of the show.'

'He?'

'Oscar – he's gay,' I say, as though this explains everything.

'I see. Well, I don't see, really. What's that got to do with the TV show?'

I explain to him the about the *Anchors Away!* episode.

'I must have been fortunate enough to miss that one,' Jamie says, grimacing.

I laugh. 'No, it doesn't really seem like your sort of show. I have to say, I haven't watched that many episodes either. It's Oscar who's the fan; we're even supposed to be going on a tour while we're here of the *Sex and the City* hot spots.'

'I've heard about that, sounds horrendous.'

'Again, Oscar's idea. But it keeps him happy, so I don't mind.'

'What keeps *you* happy, then, when you're not investigating antique brooches?' Jamie asks, his dark brown eyes looking directly into mine.

'Two Cosmos and a Bud!' the barman calls from behind us.

'No, my shout,' Jamie says, reaching for his wallet as I delve into my bag. He hands over a note and then passes me the two cocktail glasses. 'Shall we see if we can find a seat amid all this madness?' he asks. 'Or is a boring TV reporter cramping your style, compared to these sailor boys?'

'No, not at all. Again, I only came here tonight for Oscar.'

We wind our way across the bar and eventually find a high table and two stools tucked in a corner slightly away from the partying going on in the rest of the bar. I send Oscar a quick text to let him know where his drink is, but I don't hold out much hope of him picking it up. I predict he'll be far too busy with whatever poor sailor he's set his sights on.

'I think I might be able to help you with your brooch,' Jamie says when we've got ourselves settled at the table.

I'm trying to sit as elegantly as I can in my dress, perched on top of a high stool, but it's not easy. The dress keeps gaping open, and I try desperately to keep it together to maintain a shred of decency about myself and to conceal the colour of my knickers.

Jamie tries to be polite and force his eyes away from my dilemma, but they do keep darting back to my exposed legs.

'You can?' I ask, gripping the two pieces of red fabric tightly in one hand while, with the other, I casually try to sip my cocktail.

'Yes; if you're free sometime in the next couple of days, my friend from the US Roadshow will take a look at your dad's brooch for you.'

'Really? That would be fantastic, thanks!'

'No worries. They work at the Met when they're not doing the show. The Metropolitan Museum of Art?'

'Yes, I know what the Met is. I'm thinking of visiting it while I'm here.'

'Really?' Jamie looks surprised. 'I didn't think it would be your sort of thing.'

'Why not?'

He shrugs. 'Don't know really, you just don't strike me as the art museum type.'

'There's an art museum type?' I tease, taking a sip of my drink. 'And what do they look like, then? Studious, bead-wearing types in glasses and sandals?'

'Hmm, she thinks she's a comedian.' Jamie takes a swig of his beer. 'Certainly not sexy English women wearing dresses slit up to the thigh, that's for sure.'

I blush and take another sip of my cocktail, and find to my surprise that it's finished. I pick up Oscar's. It's not like he'll be needing it any time soon.

'I have a boyfriend,' I murmur, intensely studying the

contents of the glass as I stir the liquid around with the little plastic cocktail stick.

'Ah,' Jamie nods. 'I thought you might have. Where is he then, this boyfriend?'

'He's back in London, working.'

'Didn't he want to come with you on your trip?'

'No; we thought it was best for me to have some time away for a while.'

'We?'

I look up at Jamie now. 'Yes, we. Sean's been to New York loads of times, and this trip was supposed to be about me seeing my dad as well as the city. That's why my friend Oscar is here with me; his sister lives here.'

'Right,' Jamie says, nodding, but he doesn't look very convinced. 'So is that how you were getting rid of all the sailors earlier, by telling them you had a boyfriend?'

'Oh no, when they offered to buy me and my friend a drink, I just mentioned my friend's name and it soon got rid of most of them when I told them he was gay.'

'Most?'

'The ones it didn't I sent in his direction.'

Jamie laughs. It's a big, bold, warm laugh that instantly makes me want to laugh along with him.

'You're a bit mad, you, eh?' Jamie says, grinning at me now.

'Am I?'

'Yeah, I think so. But in a good way.'

'I'm glad it's in a good way.'

'Whoa! Look at that,' Jamie exclaims at something over my shoulder. 'Now that is a story in itself walking across the floor. Imagine coming into a room full of sailors dressed like that. He only needs a hat. Oh wait, he's wearing one now.'

I don't even need to turn around.

'That will be Oscar,' I say unblinkingly.

'That's your friend?'

I do turn around now, and see Oscar walking towards us with his arms draped around not one, but two sailors. He's wearing one of their hats at a jaunty angle and has also managed to collect a series of lipstick kisses over both his cheeks.

'Scarlett, darling!' he coos as he reaches my side. 'This is where you've got to. Meet Lewis and Dawson – they really float my boat, don't you, boys!'

The sailors give little nods of their heads.

'And who might this be?' Oscar raises his neatly plucked eyebrows at Jamie.

'This is Jamie. I told you about him, remember? He's here looking for a story.'

Jamie kicks me under the table.

'A-about bars. About bars, that's right. New York bars, and how they overcharge tourists.'

'So you're the infamous Jamie?' Oscar loosens his grip on his two bodyguards and folds his arms across his chest. He tilts his head to one side as he gives Jamie the once-over. 'Where's your partner in crime tonight then, what's his name – Mac?'

'I assume you're referring to my cameraman, Max?' Jamie regards Oscar equally coolly. 'He's probably at home watching a movie or playing on his Xbox, if I know Max. We're not glued at the hip.'

Oscar's hands rest on his hips now as he strikes a confrontational pose. 'So why are you here tonight, then, if you're supposed to be working and he's not?'

'Because I source the stories, and Max just comes along when we need to film them. Look, what is all this?' Jamie turns towards me. 'Why am I getting the third degree?'

'Oscar's just a little protective of me, that's all.' I turn my attention back to Oscar. 'Oscar, stop it. I just bumped into Jamie when I was at the bar, and he saved me from all the sailors that were bothering me.'

Oscar narrows his eyes for a moment, stares hard at me and then at Jamie, and then he grins. 'And that was a bad thing? I've been trying to get sailors to bother *me* all night!'

The rest of the evening passes without too much incident, unless you count Oscar dancing the lambada on a tabletop with one sailor, then singing the theme tune to *An Officer and a Gentleman* with a chief petty officer on a makeshift karaoke as incidents. With Oscar, I just counted them as part of everyday life.

'You won't use this in your report, will you?' I ask Jamie at one point, while we watch Oscar being helped down off a table.

'Are you kidding me? No one would believe it!' He smiles. 'Have you had enough of this floor show yet? It's a bit over the top in here for me now. Do you want to get out of here, go somewhere a bit quieter?'

I hesitate.

'It's OK, you're safe with me. Now I know you have a boyfriend back in London, I wouldn't dare put a foot wrong.' He winks. 'It's fine; honestly. I'm only trying to wind you up.'

'Oh, go on, why not?' It is getting a bit hot and claustrophobic in here now, and even though we've been in a small group for over an hour, we all keep being hit on by different sailors. Which is actually starting to be rather tiresome. Well, it is for some of us. Not for others ...

'Oscar,' I call over to him in the middle of a group of young seamen. 'I'm going to head back to the hotel. Jamie will see me there safely. I'll catch up with you in the morning.'

'Sure, darling!' Oscar waves his red neckerchief in the air with a flourish as a departing gesture. 'Don't do anything I wouldn't do!'

Was there anything?

Jamie and I exit the club and gladly breathe in the fresh air of the New York evening once again.

'Do you want to get a taxi, or take a walk?' he asks.

'Depends where we're walking to.'

'Hmm ... funny. Have you been down to the Hudson River yet? It's beautiful at night.'

We walk across town through Chelsea, and Jamie is right about two things: he doesn't put a foot wrong, and he is the perfect night-time tour guide as we walk along the lamplit streets. As we reach the piers and gaze out at the view from Manhattan over towards New Jersey and down towards the point where the Hudson meets the East River, I get my first glimpse of the Statue of Liberty. Although tiny from where we are standing, she still glows like a welcoming beacon from her viewing point in the water, dominating the New York skyline that she watches over and protects.

'I see you've spotted Lady Liberty,' Jamie says, looking over at me silently watching the statue in awe. 'She's quite something, eh? Even at this distance.'

'Yes, I can't wait to visit her properly. Oscar and I are hoping to go in the next couple of days.'

'Make sure you get off the boat at Ellis Island, too. A lot of tourists only go to the statue; it's such a waste. Ellis Island is really interesting, even if you haven't got American roots to trace.'

'That's the place where all the immigrants had to come through originally, wasn't it, to get into New York?'

'That's right. Some of their stories are fascinating.'

'Fascinating as long as you don't find out your relative is a mass murderer like Eva Mendes does when Will Smith takes her there.'

Jamie looks at me quizzically.

'In the film *Hitch*, that's where Will Smith, the Hitch character, takes Eva on their first date to impress her, but it all goes horribly wrong when they find out that her ancestor is a serial killer.'

'I know,' Jamie nods. 'I have seen the movie.'

'Have you? Sorry.' I've spent too much time with Sean. Sean hardly ever watched romcoms, or any other movies for that matter. 'I thought you didn't know it.'

'It's a good film. Just wondered why you used a movie to describe the place.'

I give him a wry smile. 'I do that a lot; you'll get used to it.'

'Will I, now?'

'So,' I hurriedly change the subject, 'why did you go over there? Did you film a report?'

'No, I actually went over to try to trace my family.'

'Do you have American roots, then?'

'My mother's family have American roots, but I didn't find anything out when I went over to Ellis.'

'What about your father?'

Jamie shrugs. 'Never knew him.'

'That's sad.' I pause for a moment, wondering whether I should tell him my tale about finding my mother after years of not knowing her. 'I never knew my mother either, until last year.'

Jamie turns towards me. 'Really?'

'Yes. It's a really long story though, if you want to hear it. Shall we find somewhere to go and I'll tell you if you like?'

We find a little coffee shop that's still open, and both decide to order milkshakes rather than coffee. Surprisingly, we both opt for banana.

'Wow, that's some tale,' Jamie says when I tell him all about how I went to Notting Hill to house-sit for a month and ended up not only leaving my then fiancé, David, but meeting Sean and finding my mother again after over twenty years.

'Yes, it was a pretty huge turning point in my life. But Mum and I are very close now.'

'How is your dad with it?'

'He was difficult at first, which is understandable. But

now it's all fine. I don't think Mum and Dad will ever be best buddies, but they tolerate each other for my sake. No, that's not fair; they get on slightly better than that. It somehow works when we're all together, which isn't too often of late since Dad's come over to New York.'

Jamie takes a long slow sip through his straw. 'You were quite lucky in the end, finding your mum like that.'

'We did a fair bit of chasing around first, and finding her wasn't just down to luck. Remember what I told you about Sean, and how he helped?'

'Yeah, he sounds like quite a guy.'

'He is.'

We both drink from our milkshakes.

'I don't think I'll ever be that lucky,' Jamie says. 'With finding my own dad, I mean.'

'Doesn't your mum have any idea where he is?'

'Not now. Apparently he was some actor with a fake name, you know, one of those they change to get an Equity card. That's why I can't trace him. Mum got pregnant with me, and by the time she realised, the guy was long gone.'

'That's terrible.'

Jamie shrugs. 'It's no big deal. I've lived with it most of my life, why should I let it start bothering me now?'

'I felt like that until I started looking for my mum. But

143

don't you feel as though there's something not quite right all the time?'

Jamie nods. 'I guess. It feels a bit like—'

'A piece of the jigsaw is missing,' we both say at the same time.

'That's exactly it!' I say, excitedly pointing my finger at Jamie. 'That's how I'd felt my whole life, and then when I found her it was like it all fitted together.'

Jamie sits backs resignedly in his seat. 'You're one of the lucky ones then, aren't you? That sort of thing doesn't happen for me, or the many other thousands of people trying to trace lost relatives.'

I feel a strange sensation pulling around my heart. For a moment I can almost liken it to the feeling I used to have when I first met Sean. I used to say it felt like gymnasts leaping all over my heart doing backflips and somersaults. But this is odd, this feels like ... oh, what does it feel like? It's just different, somehow.

'Anyway, on to happier topics,' Jamie says, keen to change the subject. 'When do you want me to arrange a meeting with Harry about your brooch?'

'Any time. I don't have any definite plans while I'm here. Oscar and I were going to Central Park tomorrow. But I'm really keen to visit the Statue of Liberty now I've seen her all lit up.'

'By the look of your friend when we left the bar, I

don't think he'll be in any sort of state to get up early tomorrow to board a boat to Liberty Island, do you?'

'Good point. Maybe a nice quiet day in Central Park might be just what the hangover doctor ordered.'

Jamie smiles.

'What?'

'Scarlett, I've only known you five minutes, and it appears to me that a day spent with you is *never* going to turn out to be a "nice quiet day".'

Thirteen

It turns out Jamie is right: Oscar is in no state when I knock on his door at eight a.m., our usual meeting time for breakfast, to be heading off to the Statue of Liberty ferry down at Battery Park.

'Unnhhh,' he grunts, standing in front of me in his black and white silk polka-dot pyjamas with a pink fluffy sleep mask pushed up onto his forehead. 'What time is it?'

'It's breakfast time, Oscar,' I reply brightly.

'Don't even mention that word to me.' He waves his hand in my face and staggers back into his room. I follow him and close the door.

'What time did you get in last night?' I ask, picking up a pair of abandoned braces off the carpet. I'm almost

146

expecting to see a half-naked sailor come staggering out of the bathroom, but it seems Oscar is alone.

'Oh, I don't know, three, maybe four . . . ' Oscar sits on the edge of his bed with his head in his hands.

'Alone?'

'Er . . . no.'

'So where . . . ?' I look around the room: in addition to the braces, the rest of Oscar's clothes from last night are strewn all over the floor too, so I know he must have been pretty worse for wear when he came in. He's always so fastidious about hanging and folding things.

'They have a curfew on the ship. Got to be back by morning. He didn't stay long.' Oscar manages to look up at me and wink. 'Long enough, though.'

'Oscar!' I screw my face up. 'Please, I don't wish to know the details, thanks. Look, are you getting up now, or what? I need to get breakfast even if you don't.'

'Oscar just needs a little bit more beauty sleep and then he'll be raring to do whatever you see fit for us today, darling.' Oscar's whole body tips to the side in one swift movement and he's back under the duvet with his mask down over his eyes before I can blink. 'Come back and wake me when you've had your lovely breakfast . . . '

'Don't you worry, I'll be back. You're not letting me down again today, Oscar St James!'

After I've breakfasted alone and passed a few more minutes on my daily phone call to Sean, I'm about to head up to see Oscar again when my phone rings.

'Jamie,' I say, surprised to hear from him so soon. We'd exchanged numbers last night so that he could contact me when he'd arranged a meeting with Harry at the museum.

'Hi Scarlett, sorry to call so early but I've spoken to my friend this morning and Harry has a free appointment at ten-thirty, if you can make it uptown to the Met by then?'

'Erm . . . ' I glance at my watch.

'Sorry it's such short notice, but Harry's off to Paris tomorrow for a few days to do some work at the Louvre. Can you rearrange your plans at all? I know you were thinking of heading into Central Park today. The Met is right next door.'

'It just so happens . . . ' I begin thinking of Oscar, still sleeping off his hangover in his bed across the hall. 'That could fit in perfectly with my plans this morning.'

I climb the vast wide stairs outside the Metropolitan Museum of Art and enter through the doors, avoiding getting involved with the queue to buy tickets. Now, where had Jamie said I should meet him? Oh yes, over here by these big Grecian-looking pillars. There's no sign of him, so I stand next to them and wait. It's nice and cool in the museum, unlike outside where the temperature is already rising into the eighties even this early in the morning. And although it's already beginning to fill with eager tourists, there's an air of calm and tranquillity inside its great walls, which I like.

'Hey,' Jamie says, as I gaze up at the ornate building's wide ceilings. 'How are you?'

My head drops back down. 'Hi again. I'm good, thanks.'

'You found it OK, then?'

I smile at him. 'A building this size? I couldn't exactly miss it.'

'Yes, that's true.' Jamie is wearing black jeans and a white Calvin Klein t-shirt. I'm glad to see he's dressed casually, because I'm not exactly overdressed this morning. I've walked all the way uptown to get here, so I'm wearing trainers, cut-off denim shorts and my Take That tour t-shirt from last year. 'So,' he says, looking around him. 'Now we just have to find Harry. Ah, there she is.'

She? I turn to where Jamie is looking to see a tall, attractive blond woman walking gracefully towards us.

'Jamie,' she says in greeting, kissing him on both cheeks. 'How lovely to see you again.' Then she waits politely to be introduced to me.

'Harry, meet Scarlett,' Jamie says, smiling at us both. We shake hands.

'Lovely to meet you, Scarlett. I can't wait to see this brooch of yours. Jamie has told me all about it.'

Harry, or Harriet I now realise, leads us through some security doors and up the stairs to her office. Then we take a seat at her very ornate and clutter-free desk. In fact, her whole office is pretty much clutter-free, as is Harriet herself. She cuts a very elegant figure in her no doubt designer, powder-blue sleeveless dress and shoes. I feel very drab and scruffy sitting opposite her.

'So,' Harriet says, pulling up her own chair after she's offered us refreshments. 'Let's take a look at this brooch.'

I take the brooch out of my bag and hand it over to her.

'Mmm,' she says, examining the dragonfly carefully. 'It's a very good copy.' She takes one of those magnifying eyeglasses that experts often use and inserts it into her right eye. 'A very good copy indeed.' She allows the glass to fall from her eye and catches it in her hand. 'Where did you say you got it from?'

'It's my father's. I don't know where he got it from, I'm afraid. I'm going to ask him about it while I'm over here, but I haven't had the chance yet.'

Harriet nods, still inspecting the brooch. 'Well, I can tell you it definitely is a fake, like you were informed back in the UK. No Tiffany original would have unmatched eyes like this. But it's a very good one. I would go so far as to say that it may even have been made by one of the same craftsmen who worked for Tiffany at the time, it's that good.'

'Really?'

She nods. 'Whoever owned this may have thought it actually was genuine.'

'Wow, so it's definitely old then. They thought it was, back in the UK.'

'Yes, it would have been made at the turn of the century alongside the other genuine Tiffany brooches of the time, then sold on the black market and possibly traded back into the mainstream. It's difficult to know exactly with fakes like this. But I can tell you, even though it's fake, it's worth several thousand dollars.'

'Wow,' I say again. 'I never thought about it being worth anything, I was just interested to know more about it.'

'It could be worth more if you had some history with it. Anything with a proven history always sells well at auction.' She hands me back the dragonfly brooch.

'Thanks, Harry,' Jamie says. 'We really appreciate this.'

'Anything for you, J,' Harriet says, smiling coyly at him. 'Give me a call sometime, yes? And we'll have that drink you keep promising.'

'Sure,' Jamie says, smiling warmly back at her. 'I've got your number.'

I feel a bit awkward, sitting in the middle of this flirt-off. So I glance around the room and spy a familiar couple hanging on the wall next to me. It's a photo of Meg Ryan and Billy Crystal.

Harriet sees me looking at it. 'Are you a fan?' she asks. 'It's signed, take a look.'

I get up and walk over to the photo, and see it's a still from *When Harry Met Sally*, the scene set in the museum when Harry insists they talk in funny voices for the rest of the day. Of course, that scene must be set in the Met, I'd never thought about it before. I love that film; it's one of my favourite New York movies, and I see that yes, it is signed at the bottom by each actor.

'My predecessor was a huge movie fan,' Harry explains. 'She was here when they filmed that scene in the museum. She managed to get a couple of stills signed and left me with one as a parting gift.'

'How lovely of her. I absolutely adore that movie.'

'Do you? I can't bear it myself. Meg Ryan is so irritating in any movie she's in. As far as I'm concerned, that's a reason to stay away from the cinema if I see she's the lead actress.'

Perhaps Harriet wasn't so perfect after all. But then she redeems herself.

'Would you like it? The photo. I've been looking for a worthy person to donate it to since I moved into this office. But everyone who works here is either too old to care or too young to remember the film.'

'Are you sure? Won't they want to keep it at the museum?'

'No, she gave it to me. I'd like it to go to a good home. And any friend of Jamie's is a friend of mine.' She smiles at him again – and is she actually fluttering her eyelashes now? Yes, I think she is.

Oh, so that was it. She was trying to curry favour with Jamie. But if it meant I was going to get the photo . . .

'If you're sure, then of course I'd love to take it off your hands; thank you so much, it's very kind of you.'

As we leave the Met Museum with a promise to keep Harriet updated on the brooch's progress, and an added bonus from my visit clutched tightly in my hand in a Met Museum paper bag, we walk towards Central Park and I grin at Jamie.

'What?' he asks.

'She likes you.'

'Who, Harry?'

'Knew who I meant then!' I tease, pointing my finger at him.

'Ha, you got me. Yes, I knew who you meant. I know. She's been trying to get me to take her out for ages.'

'Why don't you then?'

'She's a fair bit older than me, for one.'

'Is she? How old are you?'

'Twenty-four.'

I'm surprised at this; I thought Jamie was at least my age, if not a bit older. He seems very mature for his age.

'Did that surprise you?' he asks. 'It does most people.'

'A bit, yes; I thought you were about my age or older, even. I've just turned twenty-six.'

'Good of you to admit that,' Jamie grins. 'Most women don't like to. But seriously, I think the age thing comes from being an only child and living with my mother. I had to grow up fast.'

'Yes, I know that feeling, remember.'

'And I am one of *Morning Sunshine*'s younger reporters.'

'So that's why you won't take Harriet out, because of the age gap?' We've entered Central Park now, and everywhere you look there are people biking, walking, roller-blading or just sitting quietly, basking in the New York City sunshine. It's just like you see on the TV or in a movie, but I'm too intrigued at this moment by Jamie to take it all in fully.

'That, and the fact that she's not really my type. Shall we go this way?' Jamie asks, changing the subject and pointing in the direction of a path. 'Where are you meeting Oscar again?'

'Strawberry Fields.' I take a quick glance at my watch. 'But not for ages yet.' I'd given Oscar plenty of time to get over his hangover before insisting he brave the bright sun of the day.

'Great, I'll take you for a quick tour. You'll love Central Park. So many movies have been set here, you wouldn't believe.'

While Jamie and I walk through Central Park, he shows me all the places that I recognise instantly from the many movies I've watched over the years. From classics like *Breakfast at Tiffany's* and *Kramer vs. Kramer*, to romantic comedies such as *You've Got Mail* and *When Harry met Sally*. Then there are children's movies like *Stuart Little*, *Home Alone 2* and *Enchanted* (although I've always had quite a soft spot for this film – and for Patrick Dempsey) to comedies such as *Three Men and a Baby*, *Crocodile Dundee* and *Elf*. As we walk through the park the list is never-ending, as is Jamie's quite incredible cinematic knowledge. We pause at what appears to be an old-style funfair and look down at the brightly coloured rides twirling their passengers around in the brilliant sunshine.

'In the winter months this is the Wollman Rink,' Jamie informs me. 'You'll remember it from movies like *Love Story*, *Kate & Leopold*, *Maid in Manhattan* ...'

'And *Serendipity*,' I add, staring wistfully down at the bustling area which at the moment it is hard to imagine ever being anything so cool and graceful as a skating rink. 'It's one of my favourite New York movies.'

'Of course, how could I forget *Serendipity*.'

'Everything happens for a reason,' we both say at the same time, and then we look at each other.

I grin at Jamie. 'Don't tell me you believe that too? It's one of my favourite sayings.'

He shrugs. 'Not really, but it's a good one to choose if you're going to believe in that kind of stuff.'

'So how come you know so much about movies?' I ask. 'I've been impressed with your very extensive knowledge while we've been walking around the park.'

'Are you taking the Michael, Miss O'Brien?' Jamie asks, looking at me suspiciously.

'No, not at all. I think you probably know more than I do about them, and that's saying a lot, I can tell you!'

'I don't know; I've always liked movies, I guess, since I was small. When I was growing up I spent quite a bit of time alone because Mum would be working at night, so movies were my thing. Kept me company, I suppose. Does that sound weird?'

'No.' I shake my head knowingly. 'No, it doesn't sound weird at all. Oh!' I look at my watch. 'Oscar ... I'm late!' I'm about to get my phone out of my bag to text him to say I'm on my way, when I hear my name being called.

'Scarlett, wherefore art thou, my darling Scarlett!'

What on earth?

Jamie and I both turn in the direction the voice is coming from. It's slightly distorted, and sounds like it's being projected over a loudspeaker.

'This way,' Jamie says, grabbing my hand and pulling me towards the main road that encircles the whole of the park.

As we stand watching cyclists coming towards us along the one-way system that operates around the perimeter, they are joined by joggers, roller-bladers and some of the many horse-drawn carriages that take tourists for sightseeing trips around the park. And it's from aboard one of these carriages that we hear my name being called again.

'Scarlett, wherefore art thou?'

It couldn't just be one of the plainer carriages that my name was being hollered from. Oh no, it had to be one of the really fancy white ones, the type that honeymoon couples hire, or that people propose to each other in. And as it approaches, dramatically hanging off the side with a megaphone in his hand is Oscar.

'Scarlett, darling, when I'm calling *yooouuu*-oooh-ooooh,' he sings down the megaphone.

'Oscar!' I wave furiously at him from the side of the road, my face flushing like a tomato.

'*Darling*, there you are,' he calls, still talking into the megaphone. 'Whoa, Pedro! We've found our damsel in distress.'

The horses are brought to a halt, and as Oscar climbs down from the carriage we walk across to him on the other side of the road.

'What are you doing?' I demand. 'I thought I was meeting you at Strawberry Fields. Why didn't you just call me?'

'I couldn't,' Oscar booms, still talking into the megaphone. 'Oops!' he grins sheepishly, reaching for the off-switch and lowering the megaphone. 'I couldn't,' he begins again. 'I came out without my phone, then when I'd sat and waited for a while I thought, in my hungover state, that maybe I'd misheard you and got the wrong place, so I decided to try and find you like this.'

'By hiring a horse and carriage?' I exclaim, gesturing up at the ornate contraption behind us. 'There must be easier ways.'

'Oh, I didn't hire it, darling. I met Pedro in the bar last night, didn't I, Peds?'

Pedro lifts his hat and waves from the driver's seat of the carriage.

'He said if I was ever by the park to pop by and he'd give me a free ride. You know I never turn down a free ride, Scarlett.'

I hear Jamie cough from behind me.

'Hmm … and the megaphone?' I enquire, looking down at it still clutched in Oscar's hand.

'There were a group of cheerleaders having a break as we trotted around, and when I told them what I was doing they said I could borrow it as long as I got it back to them as soon as.'

'And you think *I* live a mad life?' I remark, turning back to Jamie. 'You wanna try being with this one for a few days.'

'Ah, the infamous Jamie again,' Oscar says, fixing Jamie with a steely gaze. 'I should have known you'd be hanging around somewhere in the bushes.'

'At least I'm not singing my way around Central Park in some sort of Cinderella-meets-Judy-Garland night-mare.'

'To be compared to the fabulous Judy is the highest of compliments!' Oscar exclaims with a flourish of his hand. 'I thank you. Now, who wants a ride before my carriage turns into a pumpkin?'

'Tempting though that is,' Jamie says flatly, 'I need to get to work.' He turns to me now. 'I'm supposed to be meeting Max in a few minutes to edit our piece on Fleet Week.'

'Sure, well, thanks again for all your help this morning, Jamie. It was really kind of you to introduce me to

Harry and then show me around the park with a guided movie tour like that.'

'No worries, any time. Let me know when you find out some more about that brooch of yours, yes?'

'Sure, I have your number now.'

'Great, I'll see you guys later then. Have fun in your pumpkin, Cinders,' he says with a wave up to Oscar, who is now arranging himself back in the seat of the carriage.

'I will, Buttons!' Oscar waves gaily from the seat.

I roll my eyes.

'Seriously, give me a call,' Jamie whispers into my ear. 'I'd like to see you again while you're here.'

'Sure, that would be fun,' I reply, trying to sound casual. But as I climb up to sit beside Oscar, I feel that pull inside me. Because I know I really want to see Jamie again too. And soon.

Fourteen

After our carriage tour around Central Park, Oscar and I
take a wander along to Bloomingdale's on 59th and
Lexington, and come away with more than our fair share
of their infamous Little, Medium and Large Brown bags.
Then we take a walk back down Fifth Avenue, stopping
off at all the stores we've not had a chance to visit yet.
After the heat of Central Park, going into those cool, air-
conditioned spaces is an absolute joy, and we don't want
to leave them in a hurry.

'So,' Oscar asks while we're browsing around Saks,
'what's going on with you and Buttons?'

'What do you mean, what's going on? Nothing is going
on.' I hurriedly begin examining a pair of jeans in a size
that's clearly far too small for me.

'*Scarlett*?' Oscar says, drumming his fingers impatiently on his folded arms.

'What?' I hang the jeans back on the rail. A year doing 'carb-free' wouldn't get me into those. Actually, even a year doing 'food-free' wouldn't have the desired effect.

'I know you better than that by now. And even though you know I'm not Sean's greatest fan, I wouldn't want to see him getting hurt.'

I turn to face Oscar. 'What are you talking about? Why would I hurt Sean?'

Oscar raises his eyebrows. 'What was all the whispering before Buttons left us today, then?'

'Nothing.'

Oscar's eyebrows get even higher.

'Really, nothing is going on. We just have a lot in common, that's all.'

'Such as?'

I explain to Oscar all about Jamie's father.

'So, you're both from single-parent families,' Oscar says with a shrug. 'There are hundreds of thousands of you out there in the world; doesn't make him anything special.'

'He's also a big movie fan like me. In fact, he's probably an even bigger fan, if anything.'

'Not possible,' Oscar says, resting his hands on his hips.

'Well, he knows enough about them. He was telling

me this afternoon in great detail about the many movies that have been filmed in Central Park.'

'And so, where is all this going to lead?'

'It's leading nowhere. I like him, that's it. Isn't that allowed?'

'Depends.'

'On?'

'On whether you fancy him, too.' Oscar fixes me with one of his penetrating looks that have struck fear into grown men and rude shop assistants many a time.

'Oscar!' I tut, and begin walking away from him.

'Scarlett,' Oscar catches up with me and spins me round. 'Do you?'

'No.' I look directly into his eyes. 'I don't. Yes, he's good-looking, but no, I can honestly say I don't fancy him. There's just something about him I like, and I can't quite put my finger on it. It feels like we've … got a connection.'

'Hmm.' Oscar's eyes narrow as he considers my explanation. 'Well, darling, as long as you continue *not* to put your finger on it, and you stay *un*connected from each other, then I guess it's OK …'

'Oscar! We don't all think like you, you know.'

Oscar shrugs merrily. 'Life would be a lot simpler if people did sometimes! At least I know what I want and just go out and get it.'

'Even if that something doesn't know it wants to be

had! Come on you,' I say, linking my arm through his. 'Let's go get that coffee, I could do with a drink.'

'In this heat, darling, better make it iced,' he winks. 'We both need to cool off.'

As we continue our wander back along Fifth, my eyes are drawn, not for the first time, to a huge cathedral standing quite at odds, yet very elegantly, amid the modern architecture of the shops and offices.

'That's St Patrick's,' Oscar says, seeing me looking over towards it. 'It's New York's, I think in fact America's, largest Catholic cathedral.'

'How odd that something as regal and splendid as that is squeezed in amid all the tackiness and flamboyance of the Fifth Avenue shops.'

'That's very poetic of you, darling.' Oscar grins at me.

'Yes, I suppose it is. Shall we go in and take a look?'

'You want to go into a cathedral?' Oscar says with a look of horror. 'Why?'

'I don't know, I'd just like to, that's all. You don't have to come if you don't want to.'

'But I thought we were heading over to the Rockefeller Center now, and going for a drink up in the Rainbow Room?'

'I just found out the other day it's closed at the moment. Jamie told me.'

Oscar pouts.

'But we can find somewhere else to go just as exciting after?'

'Oh, all right then.' Oscar rearranges the many carrier bags on his arm. 'If you insist, darling; I shall put my best holier-than-thou face on and accompany you into the cathedral.'

As we enter through two great bronze doors adorned with religious figures, we find the inside of St Patrick's Cathedral to be a calm haven away from the hustle and bustle of Fifth Avenue. Great neo-gothic archways line the whole length of the aisle, finally forming a huge dome above the altar. While Oscar takes a look around at the tiny individual chapels that adorn the edges of the cathedral, I take a seat in one of the many long pews that spread down the length of the nave.

As I sit in the peaceful surroundings, I feel immediately calm and comforted by the great building. I look up at the vast yet intricate architecture and then around at my fellow 'worshippers', most of whom are tourists, like me, sitting down for a few minutes' break away from life, allowing this wonderful building to soothe their tired bodies and busy minds.

The man sitting in front of me is deep in prayer right now. Well, I assume that's what he's doing; his head is bent and his suited body is very still. He's been like that since I sat down. I'm just beginning to wonder if he's OK when the grey hair on his head moves a little and his head lifts.

Phew, thank goodness for that, I think, he is actually alive.

The man turns his head a little to the side, distracted from his thoughts by a child being scolded by his mother for running down the aisle of the cathedral, and suddenly he looks familiar. Where have I seen him before?

Oh yes . . . As he stands up to leave the cathedral, and I can see his whole face now, I realise it's the same man who tried to give me the Heimlich manoeuvre in the restaurant the first night we were here.

He notices me staring up at him, and the same look of half recognition crosses his face too.

'The restaurant,' he says, pointing at me.

'Yes, that's right. Small world.'

'Isn't it?' He looks around him. 'Getting some peace and quiet, are you, away from the madness outside?'

'Yes, something like that. It's very beautiful in here, I've never visited before.'

'I try to drop in as often as I can after work. It calms me down after a stressful day at the office.'

'What do you do?' I ask, to be polite. I immediately regret it, as the man now walks around the end of the pew and slides into the seat next to me.

'Do you mind?' he asks. 'It seems disrespectful to remain standing, both to you and to the cathedral.'

'No; you're in a free country, aren't you?'

He laughs. 'Yes, we sure are. Are you here on holiday?'

I notice he hasn't actually told me what he does. 'Yes, I am. My friend is just over there looking at the chapels,' I add, in case he's a weirdo trying to latch onto me.

'Ah, yes, you were in the restaurant with him the other night.'

'That's right.'

'Having a good time so far?'

'Yes I am. Very good, thanks.'

'Good. That's good.' He stands up again. 'Well, it was nice meeting you again . . .'

'Scarlett, my name is Scarlett,' I offer without thinking.

'And I'm Peter. Well, Scarlett, maybe we'll meet again. They say everything happens in threes.'

'Yes, that's true, they do. I prefer "Everything happens for a reason", though.' I could kick myself. *Just why am I telling him this?*

'Well,' Peter says, smiling. 'If you believe everything happens for a reason, and I believe everything happens in threes, we'll definitely be seeing each other again very soon.'

'Perhaps . . .' I whisper as I turn and watch him walk away down the aisle. 'But in a city this size, what are the chances of that happening?'

Fifteen

'I cannot believe you have dragged me out of my bed at this time of the morning on holiday,' Oscar says as we walk towards Grand Central Station to catch the subway down to Battery Park.

'We have to leave early, Oscar. We're going to visit just about *the* biggest tourist attraction New York has to offer. If we don't get one of the early ferries, the queues are horrendous later on.'

We're finally off to visit the Statue of Liberty and Ellis Island, and I'm really excited. Partly because I've been looking forward to visiting Lady Liberty since I saw her for the first time with Jamie; and partly because I hope today I might be able to find out something about my family history at the Ellis Island Immigration

Museum, and at last begin to trace the history of the brooch.

Dad was in Chicago now. Infuriatingly, he'd flown there from Dallas as a result of some business he'd picked up at the conference, with a promise he'd be back in the next couple of days. I never thought I'd say it, but my father was starting to remind me of Sean. When we lived in Stratford-upon-Avon, running our business together, I couldn't get him out of the house. Now it seemed I couldn't stop him jetting all over the country just when I wanted him with me in one place. So I still hadn't had a chance to ask him anything about the dragonfly, or to surprise him with my news about the brooch and its history.

As we walk into Grand Central Station, I gasp.

'Wow, this can't be real, can it?' I ask, spinning around me as I gaze in amazement at the chandeliers hanging above my head, and at the intricately painted green and gold ceiling.

'Yep, this is Grand Central. Pretty amazing, isn't it?' Oscar says, taking an admiring glance around him too.

'For a subway station, it's incredible.'

'It's a train station, too.'

'But it's so ornate.'

'I know, and you're here when it's pretty quiet, so you're seeing it at its best.'

We're standing on a central concourse by a large gold clock, and on either side of us two vast cream staircases stretch up to a mezzanine that encircles the entire station.

'It's like something out of a movie,' I gasp again.

'I think Grand Central has been in quite a few movies,' Oscar says, thinking. 'You should know, darling, you're the expert.'

'Yes, I'm pretty sure it has.' But I'm so taken aback by the beauty of this utilitarian building that, for once, all movie thoughts have been erased from my mind.

'Come along; we need to get a move on if you want to catch this ferry and be the first to step onto Liberty Island this morning,' Oscar says, grabbing hold of my arm and leading me towards the subway.

'Yes, you're right. I'm just so stunned by this interior, Oscar.'

'Told you you would be. I remember when Ursula came here for the first time, she was stunned by it too.'

Ursula was an interior designer, Sean's sister and Oscar's best friend. But Oscar didn't see her as much these days since she'd started travelling a lot with her work.

'You miss Ursula, don't you?' I ask him as we walk towards the subway.

'Oh, I do!' Oscar says as he pops his ticket into the

barrier and skips through. I push mine in too, then follow him. 'Much like you miss mad Maddie,' he continues. 'But it means we've got to spend lots of fab time together, darling, since the two of them have been jetting off around the globe on their adventures. And you know what they say; every cloud has a Scarlett lining!'

I slip my arm through his as we make our way down into the New York subway, knowing that as long as Oscar is by my side there can never be too much wrong in life.

When we reach Battery Park there is a very short queue just starting to form to buy tickets for the ferry, but it doesn't take us long before we're down by the water-side going through the very stringent security checks before we can board the boat.

We manage to get a seat on the right-hand side of the upper deck. I'd done my research, and knew that this was the best side to get a great view of Lady Liberty as we sailed across the bay towards Liberty and Ellis Islands. As we wait for the boat to fill up and set sail, I leave my seat for a moment to take a look around at the view of Lower Manhattan. What is it about this place, I wonder, as I look across at the skyscrapers and buildings all huddled together across the water? What makes it so special?

Before I'd come here, everyone had said, 'You'll love New York so much'. Not one person had had a bad word to say about it, but now I am here I realise they're right;

I am falling in love with this city of extremes and opposites. The streets are filled with the tallest, most contemporary skyscrapers you can find anywhere. They dominate their older siblings; the smaller, almost antiquarian buildings that really don't seem to fit in with the city's plan at all. One minute you see someone running in a pair of high heels or a suit because they're late for work, and the next, you see someone doing exactly the same thing in more appropriate attire, just for fun. And everywhere you go there are people – diverse, unique, individual people living their own lives, each with their own problems, but all living here crammed into this wonderful city together.

'What are you looking at?' Oscar calls from his bench.

'The Staten Island ferry,' I reply, seeing the bright orange ferry sail across the water next to us. 'It's the same one Melanie Griffith rode every day in *Working Girl*.'

'Trust you to find a movie,' Oscar says as I sit down again next to him.

'Can't help it here, can I? They're everywhere.'

'It's such a fab city.' Oscars claps his hands in excitement as the ship's horn sounds and we finally set sail for the islands. 'I wonder what thrills Lady Liberty will bring us today.'

Our first stop is Liberty Island, where most of the passengers including Oscar and I alight to go and visit the great lady herself. We'd had our first glimpses of the statue as we sailed over from Manhattan. It was breathtaking then, but standing beneath her now looking up, both Oscar and I are open-mouthed at her feet.

'Wow,' I whisper in awe.

'You can say that again, darling. The folds on her gown are simply gorgeous.'

I drag my face down from Liberty to look at Oscar. 'Trust you to notice that. I expect you'll be wanting a crown like hers, too.'

Oscar tilts his head to one side as he observes Liberty's crown. 'I could sell something similar to certain members of my clientele, I won't deny it.'

'You could sell anything to anyone, you.'

'In the garment line, yes, I have to agree that matching the right outfit to the right person is definitely my forte.'

'Maybe it's in your blood. Maybe generations of De Costas have been dressing people for years.'

Oscar laughs. Then he looks serious. 'Do you really think so, Scarlett?'

I shrug. 'Don't know, but we could find out today, couldn't we, when we go over to Ellis Island. We could try and trace your history as well as my brooch's.' I'm trying to spark Oscar's interest; I know he isn't particularly enthralled by the second part of today's excursion.

'It might be fun to take a look, I guess. What harm could it do?'

We spend the next hour or so wandering around the statue, having our photo taken in front of Lady Liberty and visiting the island gift shop. Basically, just being your average overexcited tourists. Oscar does indeed buy a crown, but one of those green-foam joke ones, which he immediately places on his head. I buy a t-shirt and a small statue to put on my desk at work. Somehow I think I'm going to miss this place when I'm back at the office day in, day out, and this will remind me of being here.

We head back to the ferry to travel across to Ellis Island. The immigration museum is housed in the original station building where the immigrants would have arrived when they set foot on US soil for the first time. On the outside it's a huge red and cream brick building, and when we venture inside we find a great hall lined with Stars and Stripes flags, and an exhibition showing photos and items of luggage from some of the original immigrants.

We take a wander around. 'Look, there's a movie,' I say, seeing a board advertising a short information film with a showing every forty-five minutes.

'That'll be exciting,' Oscar says flatly, continuing to walk on. 'Do you think we get popcorn?'

I look at my watch. *Damn: we've just missed it.* 'We'll come back in half an hour. I think it might be good.'

'Darling, you and your movies, we don't have to see *every* one, do we? It's not compulsory.'

'I'll tell you what, we'll go and look at the records for now, then we can come back for the film in a bit.'

'Sure, whatever,' Oscar says, inspecting a large carpet bag in one of the displays. 'Ooh, I do like that bag. I wonder if Harvey Nicks does something similar?'

We head for the part of the building where visitors can try tracing family members that might have travelled through Ellis Island before fully entering the 'promised land' of America.

It all looks a bit complicated to me, so I ask for help.

'Yes, ma'am,' one of the hovering stewards says. 'How can I help?'

'It's kind of complicated,' I explain. 'I'm trying to trace the history of this brooch.' I pull the dragonfly from my bag and show the man. 'And I think it's possible one of my relatives might have made it here to New York at the turn of the century. I just wondered if it might be possible to see if any O'Briens came over here then?'

The man smiles at me. 'Do you have anything else to go on besides that? A year, or a boat they might have travelled on? A first name, maybe?'

'Er . . . no.'

'Ma'am, do you know how many O'Briens we're likely to have listed on our books as immigrants at the turn of the century? The Irish community were one of the biggest populations to come here at that time.'

'Ah, I hadn't thought of that.'

'I'm sorry, but if you can find out a bit more information about your family, then you could always come back or maybe go online to trace them. We have a very comprehensive website. What about your friend here, does he have someone he'd like to trace?'

'Oscar,' I prompt, nudging him. 'What about your family?'

Oscar turns his head from his examination of the room and back towards us. 'You really think you could trace my great-great-grandfather?' he asks sceptically.

'If he came through Ellis on his way into New York, we can, yes, sir. I just need a few details from you.'

We spend the next few minutes at a computer with the man inputting details and pulling up old records, and sure enough, a short while later, Oscar has all he needs to know.

'I can't believe it, Scarlett,' he says, staring in awe at a piece of printed paper. 'This is actually my great-great-grandfather's signature on this document.'

'I know, it's wonderful what they can trace these days, isn't it?'

'And to think he came over here with his brother, and then the rest of his family joined him from Italy later. I never knew that. I thought it was just him.'

Oscar stares in wonder at the sheet of paper. I've never seen him like this.

'Shall we go and watch that film now, Oscar?' I ask gently. 'Then we can learn a bit more about how they came to be over here in the first place.'

'Absolutely,' Oscar says keenly. He looks at his bright pink Gucci watch. 'There's one starting in a few minutes.'

As we take our seats in a large theatre that's already packed with people, an Ellis Island tour guide appears and spends a few minutes talking us through the film we're about to see. She spends time giving us lots of background information about what the immigrants went through on their way over to Ellis, and what happened to them once they arrived. Then it's time for the film to begin.

It's a black and white film about the immigrants, told in their own words. The voices are unbelievably chilling as they recount the tales of what they had to go through to get to Ellis Island: leaving their own countries in northern Europe, then being processed by ticket onto the ships that took weeks to get to New York.

According to the film, they were packed onto the ships like sardines in a can, and not treated much better, it seems. 'We could see no sky, only water,' one of the women says, speaking of her time below deck in steerage. 'If you were lucky enough to have a blanket, you went up on deck to get some fresh air. But the waves crashed over the deck and the seasickness was so bad that some nights I would pray the ship would go down.'

It's quite shocking to watch, and as I glance over at Oscar I see he's obviously moved by the film too. I put my hand out to him. And as he turns his head towards mine for a split second to acknowledge my touch, I see tears glistening in his eyes. I wrap my hand tightly around his.

As the film continues, we see the huge entrance hall we've stood in just a short while before looking at photos and the exhibition with all the other tourists, as it would have been many years ago, filled with immigrants trying to gain their freedom from the cruel dictatorships and oppressive regimes of their own countries. And what a few moments ago seemed like part of a dusty old museum, now seems incredibly real.

We watch the people having health checks for trachoma and mental health issues, and the unfortunate ones that didn't make the grade being marked with white chalk and set aside to face the cruellest punishment – a return trip on the boat they'd just made the interminable crossing over in.

'If I'm made to return, I'll throw myself off the side into the sea rather than go back to Russia,' one of the men says hauntingly.

Usually during information films like this at parks and museums there's a certain amount of fidgeting and noise when people who have just come in for a rest or to pass a few minutes start to become bored. But I can't help noticing the intense hush that fills the auditorium while the film is being shown. I don't know if it's the people's stories, or the fact that we're actually sitting in the very building where everything took place, or a mixture of the two, but all I know is that what we are watching and hearing is deeply affecting every single person sitting in this room with us.

And none more so than Oscar.

'Oh, Scarlett,' he says, tears streaming down his face as the film finishes and dimmed lighting shows us the way to the exit. 'I can't believe what my family had to go through to come here. The conditions on those ships were just horrendous.'

'I know, I was shocked too.' I reach into my bag and find Oscar a tissue.

He dabs at his eyes. 'I get seasick, Scarlett, and the thought of being on one of those ships for weeks going up and down, up and down.' Oscar actually starts to look a bit green.

'Shall we get some fresh air?' I suggest.

Oscar nods and blows his nose noisily on my tissue.

We take a walk outside. I'm surprised at how the film has affected Oscar; I've really never seen him like this before. I'd found it moving, yes, but Oscar is in bits.

He pulls a pair of big dark glasses from his satchel and takes gulps of air while he puts them on. Then I know he's beginning to return to the old Oscar when he looks down at the crumpled tissue still clutched in his hand.

'Oh my, why am I using this?' he exclaims. Holding it disdainfully away from him between his thumb and fore-finger, he tosses it into a nearby bin as if he's disposing of a dirty nappy. 'I have my own monogrammed silk hand-kerchiefs for just such an occasion.' With a flourish, he now pulls a square of bright purple silk from his pocket and begins dabbing at his forehead like a nurse mopping a patient's brow.

'Drama queen,' I tut, rolling my eyes. 'You don't have to put it on for me, you know.'

'I'm not putting it on,' Oscar says, lifting his glasses up. 'Look how red and puffy my eyes are; it will take hours for these to go down. I wonder if they have any cucumber in that café over there.' He glances in the direction of the island's restaurant.

'Stop worrying about your appearance, for once. Let's talk about why you were so upset in the theatre.'

Through his glasses Oscar stares at me. 'I don't know exactly. It took me by surprise too. It was just the thought of my own family going through all that just to come here to start a new life, a better life. If they hadn't I probably wouldn't be here now.'

'That's true.' I think for a moment. 'There's something about discovering more of your family roots, isn't there? Whether it's living family or long-lost relatives you never knew.'

Oscar nods. 'It makes you feel like you belong, somehow. Like you know where you came from.'

I think about Jamie.

'Come on,' I say briskly. 'Do you feel like you can handle some more yet? We've still got the rest of the exhibition to look around.'

'On one condition,' Oscar says, nodding earnestly.

'What's that?'

'I get to keep my glasses on. I can't possibly have people seeing me looking like some cartoon mutation of Betty Boo and a little green alien from *Toy Story*.'

I shake my head. 'Whatever makes you happy, Oscar.'

We go back inside the museum and take a look around the other floors of displays tracing more of the immigrants' stories through photos and memorabilia. In one room we find cases of clothes and possessions that belonged to families that were processed through Ellis

Island, and once more it all becomes overpoweringly real again.

'Oscar,' I try to say in a steady voice as I stand in front of a large glass cabinet. 'I think you'd better come over here and look at this.'

'Why?' Oscar asks, wandering over to stand beside me. 'What is it?'

The display inside the cabinet contains a large trunk, a long dress on a mannequin, fabric, some shoes, photos, pens and other family effects.

'Look at the name, Oscar,' I say, pointing up at the information board at the back of the cabinet. 'Look at the name.'

Oscar looks to where I'm pointing. 'But that says … De Costa.'

'I know, and keep reading. It also says your great-great-grandmother was a seamstress, and when your grandfather couldn't make a living as an electrician he learned the trade from her. He then went on to run and then own a factory that made dresses, and then …' but Oscar isn't listening to me any more – he's already engrossed in reading the board for himself.

I stand silently waiting for him to finish, and when he does, I watch him start at the top of the board and read through it all one more time, as if he can't quite believe it. Then he turns to me.

'This says my family went on not only to own a dress factory, but that they designed and made their own dresses – ball gowns and evening gowns, Scarlett, not just any old daywear. My great-aunt did monogramming and another did pattern-cutting, and one of my great-uncles owned a shoe and boot store. At one stage they even supplied the theatre trade, too.'

I smile at him.

'You know what this means, don't you, darling?'

I nod. 'It's in the genes, Oscar. Your love of clothes, the fact that you run a successful clothes shop and now supply to television, too – it's all in your family genes.'

Oscar shakes his head and stares into the cabinet again. 'And to think that these are their actual things.' He places his hand up against the glass like you see prisoners do in movies when their beloved is on the other side of a partition. It's such a touching sight, I half expect one of the ladies' gloves lying over the big wooden trunk to jump up and position itself against his palm. 'My family's things.'

I put my hand gently on his shoulder, fearing a teary episode like before. But Oscar simply turns towards me.

'I've got you to thank for this, Scarlett,' he says, wrapping his arms around me. 'If you hadn't insisted we come here today I would never have discovered any of this.'

'Don't be silly, Oscar. We were always going to visit the Statue of Liberty together, you know that.'

'The statue, yes,' Oscar says, leaning back from our hug to look at me. 'But you were the one that wanted to come here to Ellis Island. I would have just stayed on the ferry and been back in Manhattan shopping or doing something equally frivolous by now. I've found my family, thanks to you.' He looks back into the cabinet again. 'I've found where I come from, and now I feel like I belong.'

We sail back to Manhattan later that afternoon, armed with more souvenirs and photos of Oscar standing in front of the cabinet and outside the Ellis Island Great Hall. Both Oscar and I are very quiet as we watch the Statue of Liberty getting smaller and smaller in the distance.

While Oscar is trying to come to terms with all that he's learned during our visit, my mind is filled with two thoughts: first, that I'll never, ever complain about queueing or being delayed when I'm travelling again, after seeing what those poor people were prepared to endure to begin a new life here in the US. And second, after seeing the effect that tracing his family has had on Oscar, and remembering how I felt after finding my own mother, there's absolutely no doubt in my mind now.

I must try and help Jamie find his father.

Sixteen

After we've disembarked from the ferry, we head into Battery Park.

'Shall we get an ice cream?' Oscar asks, looking around him.

We've eaten lunch at Ellis Island, but it's so hot now in the burning afternoon sunshine that a nice cold ice cream sounds just perfect.

'Can you get such a thing here?' I ask jokingly. 'Isn't it all hot dogs and bagels at these stands?'

'Let's take a look around, shall we?' Oscar says. 'In New York you never know quite what you'll find.'

As we walk around Battery Park, Oscar becomes increasingly distracted in his search for an ice cream by the many marines that seem to be filling the park this afternoon.

'Oh my,' Oscar says, fanning himself as we come

across a display of marines doing pull-ups on a high bar, press-ups on a mat and various other physical activities. 'It's getting even hotter now.'

They do put on a pretty impressive display in their white vests and khaki camouflage combats, and the muscles on some of them would put Hugh Jackman's Wolverine to shame.

'Having a quick perv, are you?' a voice over my shoulder says.

I turn around. 'Max! Hi!'

He grins at me. 'That's nothing,' he nods in the direction of the marines. 'I do that twice over every morning before I go to work.'

I grin. 'Well, they are asking for volunteers for the pull-up bar, if you want to have a go.'

'Nah,' he shakes his head. 'Wouldn't want to show them up. So what are you doing here, apart from admiring the view?'

'We've just been over to see the Statue of Liberty and Ellis Island.'

'Fantastic, did you enjoy it?'

'Yes, it was great, Oscar found out loads about his family while we were over there. Didn't you, Oscar?'

'Hmm?' Oscar mumbles, still drooling over the marines. He turns towards us now. 'I do apologise, I was somewhat distracted there for a moment.'

'So I see,' Max says, a smile twitching on his lips. 'You must be the Oscar Jamie has been telling me all about.'

Oscar eyes him dubiously. 'What's he been saying, and who might you be?'

'I'm Max. I work with Jamie as his cameraman.'

'So you're the other half of the gruesome twosome.'

'What did you just say?' Max asks in surprise.

'Oh, don't mind me, sweetie,' Oscar says with a dismissive wave of his hand. 'I've been out in the hot sun too long today. I'm sure you're lovely really, and any friend of Scarlett's is a friend of mine!' He swivels on his heel and looks keenly around him. 'Now, I'm off to find ice cream! What is it about this place; sixty-nines I can find no problem, but where's a cool, fluffy Mr Whippy Ninety-nine when you want one? I shall return forth-with!'

Max watches Oscar skip merrily away along the path with a mixture of horror and disbelief.

'Is he for real?' he asks me in amazement.

'Incredibly, yes he is. But his heart is in the right place, even if his morals aren't always.' I turn from Oscar's departing figure back to Max. 'So what brings you to Battery Park today?'

'I'm meeting Jamie in a while, more vox pops.' He pulls a face. 'I doubt he'll be here too early though, he was on a live this morning to the UK and he won't have had much sleep.'

I look blankly at Max.

'A live link to the *Morning Sunshine* studios. Because of the time difference, when it's early morning over there it's *very* early morning here. Between you and me, I don't know how he does it sometimes; he keeps some very odd hours.'

'Ah, right, I see.'

'He told me about bumping into you at the sailors' party the other night.'

'Did he?'

Max nods. 'And about your trip to Central Park.'

'That's right, it was after we'd been to see his friend Harry at the museum,' I hurriedly insist, as though I need a reason to have been with Jamie.

'So you've met *Harry*, have you?' Max raises his eyebrows deliberately.

'Yes . . . ' I wonder what he's insinuating.

'And how is she? Still trying to get her claws into Jamie?'

I shrug. 'Can't say I noticed, really, I was too interested in finding out about my brooch.'

Max raises his eyebrows in mock surprise this time. He has quite bushy black eyebrows, and they almost perform on their own without assistance from the rest of his face.

'You didn't notice Harry when she was in full swing? Either she's toned it down a lot in recent times, or Jamie is losing his touch with the ladies.'

'What do you mean?'

'Come on, Scarlett, you must have noticed the effect my young companion has on the female members of the population. God, you only have to look at his followers on Twitter to know that.'

'Jamie is on Twitter?'

'Yeah, he's got loads of followers, tons more than me.' He rolls his eyes. 'Us guys behind the scenes don't get any recognition, only the pretty boys up front.' Max pulls out his iPhone. 'Look.' He taps in a few digits and there is the familiar face of Jamie grinning back at me from his Twitter profile.

'Twelve thousand and four followers!' I exclaim in surprise. 'How'd he manage that?'

'Smiling a bit on TV and holding a mic under people's noses, generally.'

'That's ridiculous.'

'Tell me about it! I bet three-quarters of them are women, too.'

'Really?'

'Yeah, because they're the ones watching the most breakfast TV, aren't they? Sorry if that sounds sexist, but it's true. Generally they're getting the kids ready for school in the morning before they go to work, or they're stay-at-home mums.'

'I guess.'

'And the other quarter of those followers are likely to be gay.'

'You can't say that!' I give him a reproving look.

'Just did. Never been that politically correct, me. And I bet it's true. Come on, Scarlett, it can't have escaped your notice that my microphone-wielding friend is quite easy on the eye?'

I can feel myself blushing. 'Well, no ... I suppose he's quite attractive if you go for that type.'

'What type?' I jump as I hear Jamie's voice behind us. 'What are you two gossiping about? And, more to the point, we meet again, Scarlett!' He smiles.

'Ice cream!' I improvise, seeing Oscar coming up the path towards us carrying two great ice-cream cones. 'I was just talking about the type of ice cream I hoped Oscar would bring me.'

Oscar rolls his eyes as he sees not only Max, but now Jamie as well, standing by my side. He thrusts a cone into my hand. 'I suppose you two will be wanting one of my Mr Whippy specials now?' He rolls his tongue around the ice cream melting down the side of the cone. Then he winks. 'I can recommend them, they're very tasty.'

'Suddenly I've gone off the thought of ice cream,'

Max says hurriedly. 'Hadn't we better get on, Jamie, lots to do and all that?'

'Nah, what's the hurry?' Jamie says casually. 'I've only just got here.' He looks with disdain at Oscar.

'What are the two of you filming today, then?' Oscar asks. 'The life cycle of a slug, or something equally enthralling?'

'Almost,' Jamie says, not taking the bait. 'We're interviewing women on why they find men in uniform so attractive. That's why we're down here today, so we can catch the women's reactions to the marines doing their stuff.'

'Why only the women?' Oscar asks, looking affronted. 'What about the men?'

Jamie looks at Max. 'It would be a different angle, I guess. What do you reckon?'

'Put this guy in front of the camera and we're making TV gold right before our eyes,' Max says, grinning.

After Oscar has complained that he isn't wearing the right outfit for TV and that his hair is too frizzy from the boat ride earlier, that Max is holding the camera too close and they aren't filming him from his best side, finally Oscar gets his moment of fame. And boy, does he milk it.

I sit down on a nearby bench and watch him overact for the camera, gesticulating like the conductor at the

191

Last Night of the Proms while Max tries to keep the camera trained on him and Jamie the microphone in front of his mouth.

That was strange, what Max said about Jamie earlier. About the effect he had on women. I'd noticed it, of course, when we were with Harry the other day, and I couldn't deny that, with his dark chestnut hair and chocolate-brown eyes, he's an attractive guy. But I didn't feel like that about him – did I?

I'd told Oscar I didn't fancy Jamie, and that was the truth, I was sure of it. Yet I did feel an attraction of sorts towards him, I couldn't deny it. But it was different, somehow. Different to anything I'd ever felt before. Different even to how I felt about Sean.

'All done,' Jamie says, wandering over to join me at the bench. 'He sure can talk.'

'Oscar, oh yes. If talking ever becomes an Olympic sport, he's a gold-medal winner for sure.'

I look over at Oscar. Max is showing him a playback of what they've just recorded, and Oscar is looking non-chalant as though he does this all the time, when I know inside he's squealing with delight that he's going to be on TV.

'I was wondering if the two of you would like to come to a party tomorrow evening,' Jamie says. 'The American TV station we share our office with is hosting it. It's their big annual fundraising bash for charity, and I've got a couple of spare tickets. There might be the odd celebrity there too, if you're into that sort of thing.'

Jamie didn't know me very well, did he? Really, was I into that sort of thing?

'Yes, I think we're free,' I try to sound casual. 'Is there a dress code?'

'Black tie, I'm afraid,' Jamie says, as though that's a bad thing. 'Could you and Oscar manage that at short notice? It's a bit of a pain, I know.'

I smile. Was he *kidding*? We were in New York, shopping capital of the world. This would be heaven …

'He only said black tie, darling, he didn't say anything about the rest of the outfit.'

Oscar is standing in the middle of Saks Fifth Avenue men's department in a purple velvet lounge suit. To be fair, he has got a black tie on, barely visible against his black shirt, and he does look good in it. It's very Oscar. But will the executives at TVA think it acceptable attire?

'I know, and you know that isn't what black tie actually means.'

Oscar sighs. 'It's so unfair, you girlies get to go out and buy something new and sparkly, and us dudes are all expected to wear the same boring thing.'

'My apologies for the interruption, but is that the TVA ball you're going to?' the young male assistant hovering nearby pipes up.

'Yes it is, why?' I reply.

'Because it may say black tie on the invitation, but you get all kinds going to that. It's TV, isn't it? They're very . . . how can I put it . . . *creative* with their outfits. Let me assure you, you won't look out of place at all if you turn up wearing that.'

Oscar claps his hands in delight. 'In that case, my good fellow, did I spy the shimmer of gold lamé over there?'

Thankfully Oscar sticks with his original choice of purple, and I manage to find a beautiful dress in a deep-green, gleaming silk after exploring womenswear for a relatively short time. It's long and sleeveless, with a low-cut cowl neck, and for me it's very fitted. I'm just glad we haven't been in New York longer; otherwise some of the delicious yet highly calorific meals we've been indulging in would have prevented me from even look-ing at a dress like this, let alone purchasing it.

Luckily the dress is displayed with coordinating silk court shoes, and I find a small black beaded bag in Women's Accessories. I know I have some black dangly earrings with me that will match perfectly, so my look is complete.

We're both pretty exhausted after our day on the islands, and then trying to find emergency outfits to wear for tomorrow night, so it's pretty late when we finally head back to our hotel. We grab a quick pizza en route and each go our separate ways as soon as the lift reaches our floor, desperate for a shower and the comfort of our beds.

'Ahh,' I sigh about half an hour later as I flop onto my bed wrapped in my leopard-print bathrobe. 'What a day – New York, you never fail to surprise and amaze, do you?'

My phone rings in my bag.

'What now!' I grumble, rolling back up off the bed to get it. I reach into my bag and look at the screen. 'Dad, hi.'

'Hi Scarlett, sorry to call so late, but I thought you'd like to know I'm back in NY now.'

I smile to myself at my father calling it NY.

'That's great, Dad,' I yawn.

'Have you been burning the candle at both ends since you've been here, Scarlett? Is that why you're so tired at nine-thirty on a Wednesday night?'

'No, not at all. It's just been really hectic. You've no idea what's been going on.'

'Really, what? I thought you were coming over for a spot of sightseeing and some shopping? What else could there be?' He pauses for a moment. 'Actually, I take that back – it's you, Scarlett. Whenever you're involved in something, there's always a drama going on.'

I feel myself stifling another yawn. 'Tell you what, Dad, let's meet up in the morning and I'll tell you all about it.'

'Breakfast? Lunch?' Dad asks.

'Better make it brunch. It might take the equivalent of two mealtimes to explain everything.'

Seventeen

I'm on my way over to a little restaurant Dad has suggested not far from his apartment, that he says serves great breakfasts. I suspect he knows this because he's sampled one too many of them, but I don't care. I'm just glad to be seeing him again after so long, even if I do feel pretty apprehensive about the whole brooch thing now. Suddenly, taking something that Dad has had hidden away for so long and trying to investigate its history doesn't seem like such a good idea. What if there was a reason he'd kept it under wraps all this time? What if Dad knew it was a fake? Or worse, what if it *was* dodgy counterfeit goods, and I could get us both into all sorts of trouble just by having it here in America again?

Stop it, Scarlet, I reprimand myself. *You're simply letting your overactive imagination run riot again. Dad will have a perfectly good explanation, I'm sure, and then that will be that.*

I arrive at the King's Arms, more what we'd call a pub in the UK than a restaurant, and look around for Dad. Then I spy his dark brown hair poking over the top of the *New York Times*.

He looks up as I come in and smiles.

'Scarlett!' he says, standing and wrapping his arms around me in a huge bear hug as I get to his table. 'How's my girl?'

'Dad, it's good to see you again.'

We both sit down and quickly choose from the menu so that we can begin to talk properly without being interrupted.

'So,' Dad says when the waitress has taken our order. 'How's everybody back home? How's Sean?'

'He's good, thanks. Yes, very well.'

'And your mother?'

'Yes, she's good too, getting on well at Selfridges now.'

'Oscar?' Dad asks in a hopeful tone.

I nod. 'Oscar is just Oscar, as always.'

'And you've had fun while you've been here, the two of you?'

'Yes, when we've been together we have. Oscar was off seeing his sister Jennifer for the first couple of days, so I was pretty much on my own then.'

'And what have you been getting up to all on your own in the big city?' Dad says almost jokingly. But behind his deep brown eyes I sense concern.

'Ah,' I fiddle with my paper napkin. 'That's what I need to talk to you about.'

First I tell Dad all about the *Antiques Roadshow* and the brooch, and the moment I mention the dragonfly he visibly stiffens. Then I tell him about coming here to New York, bumping into Jamie and Max and visiting Harry, and then finally all about Ellis Island, including what happened to Oscar. By the time I've done all that, our breakfasts are just being served.

Dad is having waffles with maple syrup, which he insists he doesn't eat regularly and is just having as a treat today. And by looking at him I have to believe that. He doesn't look like he's gained any weight since he's been here. I am having a sort of granola with yogurt and bananas. I'm thinking of my green dress for tonight.

'So,' I ask as Dad pours the syrup over his waffles. 'Aren't you going to say anything?'

My father puts the jug of syrup carefully on the table and looks up at me. 'What do you want me to say?'

'You could start by telling me why you've kept a fake Tiffany brooch hidden away in the house all these years.'

Dad sits back in his chair and clasps his hands together in front of him on the table. He twiddles his thumbs around for a moment as if he's considering something.

'It was given to me many years ago by ... by a friend.'

'And?'

'*And* that's it.'

'Why? It seems an odd thing for a friend to give a man, a brooch, don't you think?'

My father's eyes narrow as he gazes across at me, then he shakes his head. 'It's no good, is it? You won't rest until I tell you the full story, so I may as well give in now while my waffles are still hot enough to remain edible.'

I shrug my shoulders. 'You know me, Dad.'

'Don't I just? If you can follow a trail halfway around the country and to Paris and back to try and find your mother, this isn't going to faze you one bit.'

'So what *is* the story then?'

Dad sighs. 'The dragonfly was given to me by a friend of mine who I met not long after we moved to Stratford-upon-Avon. She was having money problems at the time, so I lent her some cash and in return she gave me the brooch as a sort of security on the loan. But then she disappeared, and when I went to have the brooch valued I found out it was a fake.'

I think about this for a moment while I spoon some of my yogurt into my mouth. Dad does the same and begins cutting into his waffles.

'But why would you keep it all this time if you thought it was fake? We moved to Stratford over twenty years ago.'

Dad finishes his mouthful of waffle before replying. 'Sentimental reasons.'

'What do you mean, sentimental reasons?'

'Do I have to spell it out for you, Scarlett?'

I stare at my father over the breakfast table. 'You mean, you and this woman were ... but you and Mum hadn't split up long then, had you?'

Dad looks down at the table. 'Actually your mother had been gone eighteen months when we moved to Stratford. She left me, remember. I was lonely and I met this woman, she was just there for the summer, she was with a touring company doing *A Midsummer Night's Dream* ...' His voice trails off as he thinks back.

'What happened?' I prompt gently.

Dad stares at me in surprise as though for a moment he's forgotten I'm even there. 'We got to know each other pretty well that summer. Of course, I always knew she was going to move on with the company eventually, that was her job. But when she left she went very suddenly.'

'Why?'

'I don't know. I never heard from her again; it was all very unexpected.'

'But she left you the brooch?'

'Yes, I lent her the money and she left me the brooch, but I never, ever saw her again.' Dad picks up his cutlery again and begins to eat. But by the look on his face he's no longer enjoying his waffles.

'Did you try and trace her?' I ask. 'Through the touring company she was with?'

'Of course I did. But they said she'd left them in the lurch too, and they had no idea where she was.'

We both go quiet for a bit while we eat our breakfast and ponder our own thoughts.

'I have to ask this, Dad,' I say after a bit, 'but do you think she was just after your money?'

Again, Dad purposefully finishes his mouthful of food before answering. He shakes his head. 'No, she wasn't like that. She wouldn't.'

'But why would she just up and leave like that without saying goodbye?'

'I don't know, Scarlett and I really don't want to talk about it any more. It's past history.'

'I bet this dragonfly is something to do with this woman's history,' I say, my mind still racing. 'Maybe it was an heirloom in her family. Maybe it was passed down through generations from mother to daughter—'

'Scarlett ...' my father warns. 'What did I just say?'

'Sorry.'

'Do you have the brooch with you now?' he asks.

'Of course,' I reach into my bag. 'I carry it with me all the time at the moment.' I pass the dragonfly carefully to my father, and watch him while he places it gently in the palm of his hand. He simply looks at it as if he's absorbing a multitude of memories from its many colours. Then he quickly passes it back to me.

'Like I said – past history. You keep the brooch if you like, Scarlett. Someone might as well have some enjoyment out of it.'

'The expert Jamie took me to see said it might be worth several thousand dollars now.'

'Even better, then. Put the money to good use if you want to sell it.'

'Don't be silly, Dad. I'm not going to sell this brooch if it's got sentimental value for you.'

'Old memories fade fast, Scarlett. It was a very long time ago now. Do what you want with the brooch.' He waves it away with his fork. 'Now, tell me about these Jamie and Max fellows you've been mentioning. Is Sean OK with you spending time with other men while you're here?'

'Oh, Dad, not you as well!'

Eighteen

'Wow,' I gasp as we enter the huge hotel ballroom the TVA party is being held in that night. 'It's amazing.'

The room has been decorated entirely in gold and white. White lilies are draped elegantly along the centre of all the tables in long glass vases, and even bigger arrangements of lilies, roses and orchids fill every corner of the room. There are huge swags of gold fabric swooping from one side of the room to the other, and everywhere I look handsome waiters wearing white shirts, gold waistcoats and tight black trousers bustle about with trays of champagne and canapés.

'I think I've died and gone to heaven,' Oscar coos, eyeing the waiters. 'Either that, or I'm having a wonderfully inventive dream.'

'Champagne, sir, madam?' one of the waiters asks, hovering next to us with a tray.

'Ooh, yes please,' Oscar says, grabbing two glasses while managing to give the waiter the eye at the same time. 'There you go, darling, get that down you. Enjoy your first taste of New York high life.'

It's extremely good champagne, and we polish our first glass off pretty quickly while we surreptitiously peruse the New York glitterati milling around us. Then we swiftly move on to our second when another waiter passes by with a tray full of topped-up glasses.

'There you are,' a familiar voice says, arriving next to us. 'I was wondering where the two of you had got to.'

'Jamie, hi.'

Jamie looks pretty smart in his black tux tonight. Actually, he looks more than that, he looks really gorgeous, and I can't help but notice all the admiring glances he receives from female guests as they pass by, and the occasional male one too. Max hadn't been too far off the mark.

'You look wonderful, Scarlett,' he says, looking me up and down appraisingly. 'Green really suits you. And the brooch looks great with that dress.'

I'd decided to wear the dragonfly at the last minute. My black earrings just hadn't been enough to complement the simple cut of the dress, and it had looked a bit plain. It was Oscar's idea to add the brooch. And as usual where clothes are concerned, he was spot on.

'Thanks. I wasn't too sure about wearing it, but it's good for it to be out on show again after all this time. Hey, guess what, I actually got to see my dad today at last.'

'Cool, what did he say?'

I tell Jamie all about what Dad had said earlier. Oscar becomes bored during my tale and wanders off to find a waiter to harass, or something equally Oscar-like, to amuse himself.

'Hmm,' is Jamie's non-committal response when I've finished my story.

'What do you mean, *hmm*?'

'Sounds like there's more to it.'

'How can there be more to it? The brooch belonged to a woman Dad met who had money troubles, and she ran off and left him with the debt. Sounds like she saw him coming, if you ask me.'

'Possibly,' Jamie screws up his nose. 'But my journalistic senses are twitching.'

I can't help but laugh. 'You're a breakfast-TV reporter, Jamie. You're hardly Donal MacIntyre undercover.'

Jamie gives me a disapproving look. 'Ha, ha, funny, and it's *correspondent*, actually. You wait. I bet there's something more to all this than he's letting on.'

'More to what?' I feel a hand on my shoulder as Max drapes his arms around Jamie and me and energetically jumps in between the two of us. 'Isn't this great? Free drink *and* free food all night? And check out some of the birds … I mean *women* here. Man, they're fit.'

I smile at Max. He looks slightly more dishevelled in his tux than Jamie does, and his bow tie is already hanging loose around his neck.

'And just how many glasses of free champagne have you had already, Max?' Jamie asks, removing Max's arm from his shoulder.

'Dunno, lost count after the sixth. But I tell you something, it must be strong stuff: when I was coming out of the gents' just now I thought I saw Bradley Cooper walking towards me. Now what the hell would he be doing here tonight?'

I look down at my glass; it must be good stuff. I wouldn't mind having lovely visions like that. I'd better get some more down me.

'It probably was Bradley Cooper,' Jamie says casually. 'The owner of the station has some pretty big celebrity friends. He usually tries to get an odd one or two of them to come along to help boost funds for the charities, so I've heard.'

Max and I turn to each other in amazement, and then back to Jamie.

'How can you sound so casual about it?' I ask. 'Are you actually saying that *the* Bradley Cooper might be at this party?'

Jamie shrugs. 'Yeah, and?'

I open my eyes wide and my mouth even wider.

'How can you even *say* that?'

'Yeah, man?' Max agrees. 'How can you? I'm sure I'm not hyperventilating about it for the same reasons Scarlett is, but *Bradley Cooper*, star of the *Hangover* movies! You know how much I love those films.'

Jamie looks at us both like we're mad. 'I like them too, but I'm not going to drool all over him just because he's at the same party as me.'

'We're not going to drool over him,' Max says. 'Maybe just say a little hi and how's your monkey?'

'That sounds like something Oscar would say,' I laugh. Then I have a thought. 'Speaking of Oscar, has anyone seen him? If he knows Bradley Cooper is here we'll never keep him away from the poor guy.'

'Oh,' Max says, suddenly looking worried.

'What's wrong?'

'Shortly after I thought I saw Bradley coming towards me, I saw Oscar heading towards the men's toilet too.'

The same thought strikes us all at exactly the same moment, and we look at each other in utter panic, then head off in the same direction in hot pursuit of Max as he shoots across the ballroom. But as we hurtle down a corridor and around a corner, we almost crash headlong into Oscar as he floats dreamily towards us.

'Oscar?' I ask him, as we pull ourselves abruptly to a halt. 'Where have you been?'

Oscar simply points back towards the gents' toilet.

'And did you see anyone you knew in there?' I hardly dare ask.

He nods again, a glazed expression still covering his face.

I look anxiously at Jamie and Max.

'Do you want to tell us about it?'

'Scarlett,' Oscar says, holding up his hand. 'I shall say only this. What happens in Manhattan stays in Manhattan. But for as long as I live, I will *never, ever* take a pee in a public urinal that will be as enjoyable as the one I've just taken in that one back there.'

And with that, he skips merrily back into the ballroom, leaving the three of us all staring at each other open-mouthed.

'Oscar, what really went on in that toilet?' I ask him a bit later when it's just the two of us again. I still haven't seen Bradley Cooper. I know he's here because there's always a crowd of women floating around certain parts of the room, and wherever you see a big gaggle of peroxide and heels and you hear giggly voices, you know Bradley isn't too far away. But trying to get anywhere near him is virtually impossible, and I'm not prepared to fight with the queens of silicone to get close to him.

'Nothing,' Oscar says, dropping a crab canapé into his mouth. He chews quickly on it for a moment, then swallows. 'I just took a very good look, that's all.'

'Oscar!'

'Well, I'm never going to get another chance like that again, am I?'

'I suppose not. And?'

'Scarlett!' Oscar pretends to looks shocked. 'What would Sean say?'

'Sean's not here, is he?' I take a sip of my champagne. This stuff is good. How many glasses have I had now? Even I'm starting to lose count.

'True . . .' Oscar looks to both sides of him, then leans in towards me. 'Just between the two of us . . . Let's just say the monkey didn't disappoint.'

I knew it.

'Scarlett, what a lovely surprise to see you here!'

I turn around to see the now familiar face of the chap who'd tried to give me the Heimlich manoeuvre in the Italian restaurant, and whom I'd met again in St Patrick's Cathedral. 'Hi, it's . . . erm.'

'Peter,' he reminds me.

'Yes, of course, Peter. How are you?'

'I'm very well thank you. And yourself?'

'Good thanks, yes. Oh, this is my friend Oscar.'

'Enchanted,' Oscar says, dangling his hand in front of Peter.

'Indeed,' Peter smiles at him and turns Oscar's hand over so he can shake it in a more manly fashion.

'So what brings you here tonight?' Peter asks again.

'I have a couple of friends working for British TV who had spare invites, which they gave to Oscar and me. I hope that's all right?'

'Of course, I can't see anyone complaining, can you? It's good to see you again, Scarlett.' He inclines his head towards Oscar. 'And to meet your friend. So what do you both think so far?'

'It's just fabulous, darling!' Oscar enthuses. 'The food, the wine, the fact I just saw parts of Bradley Cooper I've only ever dreamed about.'

Peter stares at Oscar. Then he looks to me for verification.

'He just bumped into Bradley Cooper a few minutes ago,' I hurriedly explain. 'It's a long story.'

'Ain't that the truth,' Oscar says, grabbing another glass of champagne from a passing waiter.

'Ah, yes, Mr Cooper, our star guest this evening. He

211

seems to be quite a hit with the ladies. And some of the men.'

'From what I've seen of him, yes,' I grumble.

'Haven't you met him yet then, Scarlett?'

'No, you can't get close to him, can you, with all the gold-digging stick insects hanging off him all night. God, I bet they don't even know half the movies he's been in, they're too busy having their Botox topped up to have time to go to the cinema.'

A loud guffaw escapes Peter's mouth. 'I like your style, Scarlett.' He thinks for a moment. 'Do you mind if I borrow your friend for a while, Oscar?'

'As long as you make sure she's back before she needs renewing,' Oscar jests. 'It's an English library joke,' he explains when Peter doesn't laugh.

'Ah ... of course.'

'Hmmph ... Americans!' I hear Oscar moan as Peter guides me across the ballroom floor.

'Where are we going?' I ask him.

'You'll see in a minute,' he says mysteriously as two burly-looking security guards step aside to let us through a door. 'Now, wait here for a moment. I'll be right back.'

It's a good job I've had a few glasses of champagne. Under normal circumstances I wouldn't let a strange man drag me into an empty room in a hotel. But my brain is suitably warm and fuzzy right now to allow it to happen and not care too much about the consequences.

I take a look around the room; there are a couple of comfy red velvet sofas, a glass table with three single orchids standing elegantly in a long vase. Some more champagne and canapés occupy another table covered in a white cloth, and here's me standing like Mrs Awkward in the middle of it all. I'm about to head over to the champagne when a door on the other side of the room opens a little way and a head pops though the gap.

'Is it safe?' he asks.

I can feel my mouth opening, but there's no sound coming out. *Work, damn you! Now is not the time to malfunction; you won't shut up normally.*

'Safe from . . . ?' I manage to whisper to a head that looks remarkably like Bradley Cooper's.

'Er . . . how can I put it politely?' He opens the door a tiny bit further and I'm allowed a glimpse of some more of the Cooper physique. 'The female contingent that has been following me around all night.'

'You mean all the Silicone Samanthas hanging off your every word, in the hope you might pass them your phone number or get them a part in your next movie?' I immediately clap a hand over my mouth. Alcohol always did make me a tad too honest.

Bradley laughs. 'Is that what they're doing? And there

213

was me thinking I was hilariously witty and entertaining to be attracting that many women.'

'I'm so sorry,' I say, blushing the same colour as the sofas. 'I shouldn't have said that. It just came out.'

'Don't worry about it,' Bradley says, fully opening the door now and entering the room. 'I like your honesty.'

Oh my: I'd thought when I'd bumped into Johnny Depp in Paris that time my legs had felt pretty weak, but seeing Bradley standing right in front of me like this, and in a black tux and white shirt too . . . he's even untied his bow tie so it hangs loosely around his neck . . . I really do feel the need for one of the sofas right now. *Perhaps it's all the champagne?* I wonder for a moment as I stagger back towards one of them.

'Are you all right?' Bradley asks, rushing over to me and grabbing my hand to assist me as I sit – well, it's more like fall – down on the sofa behind me. I know he means well, but that really isn't helping. I feel even more giddy now.

'Yes, really, I'll be fine.'

'Let me get you some water.' Bradley looks around the room and spies a jug on the table with the champagne and canapés. He leaps over to it, fills a glass, then comes back to the sofa and places it in my hand while he sits down next to me.

I sip on the water while trying to disguise the trembling of my hands. I don't do very well.

'You're shaking,' he says, seeing me. 'Are you dia-betic, hypoglycaemic or something like that? Should I get you something to eat?' He leaps up towards the table again.

'No! No, really I'm fine. Please sit down again.'

Bradley takes a quick glance at the canapés as though he's sizing up which one might be the sweetest should sugar be needed in a hurry, then makes his way back over to the sofa again. He waits until I've finished drinking.

'So, what are you doing in here anyway?' he asks. 'Escaping, like me?'

'I don't know really. Peter brought me in here and said he'd be back in a minute.'

'Peter … oh, you mean Pete Butler. Yeah, I think he's gathering up people ready for the auction.'

'Yes.' At least I think we're talking about the same person. 'They're having an auction?'

'Yeah, and I'm supposed to be hosting it to raise more funds. Pete can be very persuasive when he wants to be.'

'Yes, I can imagine.'

'How do you know him?'

'We've … bumped into one another a few times around New York.'

Bradley seems to accept this explanation and nods.

'Yeah, Pete gets about. He's not your usual head of a TV corporation stuck behind a desk all day. If he was, I probably wouldn't be here now.'

'Wait, Peter is the head of TVA?' I ask in astonishment.

'Yeah, why, didn't you know that?' Bradley regards me suspiciously now. 'Who are you, anyway?'

'Scarlett,' I say, holding out my hand again, this time for Bradley to shake. (Plus it seemed like a good excuse to hold his hand again.) 'I can't believe we haven't been introduced before.' *Smooth, Scarlett, smooth . . .*

'I'm sure I would have remembered if we had,' Bradley replies, adding his own layer of charm now, and enhancing the effect by locking his blue eyes onto my mine.

I can feel myself starting to come over all dizzy again, so I take another sip of water.

'So you're from England, Scarlett?' he asks, still watching me intently.

'Yes, originally Stratford-upon-Avon, but I live in London now.'

'Stratford, that's Shakespeare country. Land of the Bard.'

'Yes, something like that.'

'I'd love to do Shakespeare at Stratford someday.'

'Would you?' I ask, with a bit too much amazement. What was it with all these Hollywood stars that made

216

them feel a need to tread the boards? 'But you make such great movies.'

Bradley smiles at me, and I have to take another large gulp of water to calm myself.

'Do you think so? Which ones do you like in particular?' he asks.

'Er ...' Don't say *The Hangover*. Don't say *The Hangover*. '*The Hangover*,' I squeak, when nothing else is forthcoming.

Luckily Bradley smiles again. 'Actually that's one of my favourites too. We always had a great time when we were making them.'

Just as Bradley's entire repertoire of movies suddenly springs to mind, and I'm about to launch into a full-scale, in-depth discussion of my specialist subject with one of the hottest actors in Hollywood, the door bursts open.

'I told you this is where he'd be, Peter,' a young woman in a vibrant yellow dress insists, marching into the room. She's carrying an iPad and looks extremely harassed. 'I'm so sorry, Bradley,' she fawns. 'We seem to have misplaced you for a bit there.'

'I'm not a pair of glasses,' Bradley replies, rolling his eyes. 'Hi, Pete.' He looks over the canary's shoulder towards Peter, who has followed her into the room.

'Bradley,' Peter casually acknowledges him. 'I see you've met Scarlett.'

I suddenly realise we're still holding hands, and hastily pull mine away.

'I have, and what a refreshing change she is from all the,' he turns to me, 'what did you call them, Scarlett? *Silicone Samanthas* I seem to have spent most of my evening with.'

'Did I say that?' I begin to flush again.

'I think you did . . .' Bradley grins at me.

'We're ready for you to do the auction now, Bradley,' the canary flaps, giving me a beady, birdlike eye before scrolling through pages on her iPad. 'Otherwise the band won't start on time and then we'll overrun.'

Bradley stands up. 'Excellent! I think I'm going to enjoy this now. Especially since I have a glamorous new assistant to help me out.'

'And who would that be, Bradley?' Peter asks with a knowing smile.

'Scarlett,' I hear Bradley say at the same time as an iPad crashes to the ground.

Nineteen

'Lot Eight: this very elegant Tiffany necklace and ear-rings set,' Bradley announces from his podium, while I hold aloft the velvet case containing the jewellery.

The auction has been going incredibly well so far, and I seem to have picked up the demonstrating technique with some ease, I feel. I've watched them on the shopping channels often enough, displaying their goods, and it's not so different from that, really, as I march up and down with my wares, flourishing my hands across the various lots, tickets and promises like a weatherman predicting storms and high pressure across a map of the British Isles.

Oscar, Jamie and Max had looked a mite surprised to see me when I'd first stepped nervously onto the stage beside Bradley. In fact Oscar (after he'd stopped staring at Bradley's crotch) had mouthed the words: 'How the hell have you managed to get up there with *him*?' and proceeded to point at Bradley in what he thought was a discreet manner by masking his pointing finger with his other hand – but was in fact quite obvious to anyone standing in front of him; i.e. us up on the stage.

'Do you know that guy?' Bradley had asked when he'd seen Oscar pointing. 'Only I met him earlier in the gents' toilet. I've never seen anyone stand quite so long at a urinal and not pee.'

I'd looked casually across at Oscar. 'Never seen him before in my life. I expect you get some very odd types at these events. Act like they know you and everything.'

Bradley was about to agree when Peter had taken to the stage to introduce his star guest and his new assistant for the evening. I could actually feel the pain of all the daggers being cast in my direction with looks varying between jealousy, outrage and pure evil intent from certain members of the audience, and I'd wondered if I might need a bodyguard for the rest of the night after this appearance.

But once we'd got into the swing of it, and the bids had started coming in, I'd forgotten all about my safety and concentrated on helping Bradley raise as much money as we could.

We're just in the middle of auctioning a VIP trip for two to have dinner at the Top of the Rock when I happen to glance down in Oscar's direction. Not only do I see the familiar faces of Max and Jamie standing next to him clutching glasses of beer now instead of champagne, but I see another face I think I recognise, though I'm not immediately sure where from. Then, when I see her laughing and chatting with Oscar, I realise who it is. It's Jennifer, his sister.

I've only ever seen her properly in photos at Oscar's house, and the only time we've ever come into contact – well, you couldn't even call it that really – I was in a wardrobe and she was in a hotel room with Sean (you had to be there) and I couldn't see her face.

What is *she* doing here, I wonder, as we move on to the next lot, a pair of cut-glass crystal vases.

'Now then,' Bradley asks. 'What am I bid for this lovely pair of crystal vases donated by everyone's favourite department store, Bloomingdale's?'

As the bidding gets under way, I keep a close eye on Jennifer while I parade up and down with the vases. She appears to be chatting happily to Max, and now she's moving onto Jamie … they've all formed a little circle together.

'Scarlett, could you hold the vases up a little, please?' Bradley asks from the podium.

I nod hurriedly and thrust the vases in the air.

'Gently, Scarlett, we want them in one piece, not thousands.'

There's a ripple of laughter from around the room, and Jennifer looks up towards me. A flicker of recognition crosses her face, and then I see a different look as she fully appreciates the extent of the situation unravelling in front of her. She swivels on her heels, turns her back to me and begins talking one-to-one with Jamie. I see her flick her blond hair over her bare shoulder as she laughs artificially at whatever anecdote he's telling her.

Jamie laughs now, too, and seems to be lapping up everything she's saying to him. She even playfully rests her hand on his shoulder.

'Scarlett,' Bradley's voice jolts me back to reality from the podium, 'the vases?'

Startled by his voice, I jump, and as I do one of the vases slips from my grasp and flies through the air into the crowd. At the same time, out of the corner of my eye I spy a very agile Max dive across the floor below me like a rugby player catching a ball in mid-flight. He just manages to grab the vase and save it from smashing on the floor into a hundred mini-ashtrays.

A huge round of applause breaks out around the room as Max holds the vase aloft like a trophy, acknowledging the plaudits of the crowd. He passes it back up to me then and whispers, 'Concentrate, Scarlett, you're part of the Wolf Pack now.' Then he winks and returns to the others in his party who are all staring at me, aghast.

Jennifer looks disparagingly up at me, and I look equally disdainfully back down at her. How can you dislike someone you don't even know, I wonder? But I do: I dislike Jennifer with a passion. It can't just be because she's Sean's ex – can it?

'. . . And I think we'd better close the bidding for the vases now, before Scarlett starts juggling with them again,' Bradley jokes from the stage. 'Now to our final lot for the evening, a luxury weekend stay in one of the top Tower Suites at the Waldorf Astoria hotel. What am I bid for this fabulous prize, ladies and gentlemen?'

'Do you come with it, Bradley?' I hear someone shout from the crowd. Thankfully it's not Oscar.

'Sadly no, madam, I'm afraid not.'

The bidding goes ridiculously high for this lot, although I'm not quite sure what a weekend stay in a suite at the Waldorf Astoria would actually cost, but Bradley seems quite pleased when his gavel bangs down.

'And that concludes our auction for this evening,' he says, flashing the famous Cooper smile at those guests still lapping up his presence. 'Thank you so much for digging deeply in your pockets tonight. Sunnyside Children's Home will be extremely grateful for your generosity.'

'Wait,' I hear a shout from the crowd. 'I'd like to donate some money!'

Bradley looks out into the sea of people. 'I'm sure we won't be saying no to an offer like that. If you'd just like to see Maria here,' he gestures to the canary, 'I'm sure she'll be more than happy to accept your kind donation.'

'No, I'd like to bid on something.'

Here we go, I think. I bet it's something to do with Bradley. Watch out, Mr Cooper, or you'll be auctioned off in your underwear to someone's wife or girlfriend in minutes.

'I'd like to know if your assistant will put her dragonfly brooch up for auction. My wife has taken quite a shine to it.'

My brooch? Not Bradley ...

'Yes, I'd bid on that too,' I hear another shout from the floor. 'I'll start you at five hundred dollars, if you will, Scarlett.'

But ...

'I raise that to seven hundred.'

'Eight hundred!'

'One thousand.'

'Ladies, gentlemen,' I hear Bradley say from his

podium. 'This is a little unfair on Scarlett, maybe she doesn't want to donate her brooch!'

I look up at him in a daze. Do I want to donate it to the auction? Dad had said to do what I wanted with it ... and making money for a children's home seems like a very noble way for the dragonfly to end its time with the O'Brien family. But I have to make sure it fetches the several thousand dollars that Harry has said it's worth.

'If you offer me enough, it's yours!' I shout jubilantly up into the ballroom ceiling. 'But you haven't bid any-where near what this little insect is worth yet. Let me tell you this,' I say, leaping up to the podium and moving in on Bradley's mic. 'No, you can stay, Bradley,' I insist as he goes to step down. I wrap my arm companionably around his shoulders. 'I had this brooch valued by none other than one of your trusted experts on the *Antiques Roadshow* just this week at the Met Museum, no less, and she said it was worth in excess of several thousand dollars. So get bidding!'

I quickly unpin the brooch from my dress while the bidding begins, and then proceed to demonstrate the dragonfly's skills by swooping it along the front of the crowd back and forth so they can all get a closer look at my little blue and green buddy's beauty. And after the initial hilarity has died down, it seems to work as the bids begin to fly in, along with the dragonfly, not only from our first two bidders but from others who have joined in.

'Three thousand five hundred dollars,' Bradley calls. 'Do I hear more? Three thousand six hundred. Three thousand seven hundred, eight hundred. Do I see a nine? Thank you, sir. Now who's going to make it a cool four thousand?'

Four thousand dollars – just for my little brooch!

'Anyone? Surely someone will finish the evening off nicely for us?'

There's a sudden hush around the room as we wait to see if anyone else will bid. 'I'll give you five thousand dollars,' a voice at the back of the room calls. 'But the bidding stops now.'

You can hear the gasps from around the room as people all crane their necks to see who's bidding.

'Done!' Bradley calls, banging his gavel down on the podium with a flourish. 'The dragonfly is sold to the gentleman at the back of the hall for the final sum of five thousand dollars.'

A huge round of applause breaks out, and Bradley breathes a sigh of relief as he steps down from the podium.

'Well done,' he says, coming over to me, before the canary can start flapping her wings. 'You didn't have to do that.'

'I had great fun being your assistant,' I grin at him, still euphoric from the dragonfly's sale. 'Thanks for asking me to do it.'

'I meant sell your brooch,' Bradley smiles back. 'But if I ever find I need a vase-juggling assistant to help me auction goods again, then I'll be sure to look you up.'

'Oh, right . . . yes, of course.'

'Although I don't actually have your number . . .'

Oh. My. God. Was Bradley Cooper actually asking for my number? Don't I usually wake up at this point in the dream?

'Here's mine,' he says, reaching into his jacket pocket and pulling out a card. 'I owe you, Scarlett, after helping me out tonight, so if *you* ever need an auction-eer, or anything else while you're in New York, give me a call.'

And then the canary and her flock of feathered friends descend upon him and he's engulfed in their flapping and tweeting once again.

I look down at the card in my hand; the ink hasn't faded away to leave a blank sheet of paper like it did once before in one of my dreams about Bradley, nor has a phoenix suddenly swooped in and carried it off to its fiery cave like it did in another. No, the number is still there in simple black ink, alongside that of his agent and manager.

'Impressive,' Peter says, standing alongside me now,

looking down at the card too. 'You're a fast worker, Scarlett.'

'What, this? Oh, it's nothing.' I hurriedly grab my bag, that I've slid under the podium, and shove the card inside. 'I ... I mean, it *means* nothing.'

'I've known Bradley a fair while now, and he doesn't give his number out to just anyone, you know. Especially not his private number.'

'I guess I'm just one of the lucky ones, then,' I shrug. 'I won't be using it, anyway, not in the way you're suggesting. I already have a boyfriend.'

'Then he's a lucky fellow,' Peter says, smiling. 'I can imagine most of the women here tonight would forget all about their boyfriends, and even their husbands, if Bradley Cooper gave them his number.'

'Not me,' I throw my shoulders back defiantly. 'I love Sean, and I wouldn't swap him for anyone. Not even a movie star.'

'Good for you! There're still *some* decent people left in this world.'

'Yes, of course there are.'

'I really appreciate you giving up your brooch tonight, too. It was very kind and generous of you to do that. The children's home will be so grateful for all the donations, but that added amount will really boost our total.'

'I'm more than happy for it to go to a good cause. Who bought it in the end, do you know?'

'One of our benefactors, I believe, for his wife.'

'Ah, well, I hope she enjoys wearing it.' I hand the brooch over to Peter.

'Are you absolutely certain about this, Scarlett?' he says, taking the dragonfly and holding it up to the light to inspect it. 'It wasn't a family heirloom or anything, was it?'

'Yes and no. But really, it's fine. It will do much more good this way than gathering dust in some old jewellery box at home.'

'Then thank you again.' Peter rests his hand on my shoulder. 'You're a very generous and loyal young woman, Scarlett, and it's my pleasure to have bumped into you so randomly in my city this week. You know what they say . . . '

'*Everything happens for a reason,*' we both say in unison, laughing.

'Here's my number, Scarlett,' Peter says, handing me a card now. 'If there's anything you ever need while you're in New York, then you let me know. And just for the record, that's not a come-on, OK?' He winks. 'I know about Sean.'

I blush. 'Thank you, Peter, here's mine.' For once I remember to hand over one of the business cards I always carry with me and never remember to hand out. 'It has my mobile, sorry, cellphone number on there too.'

'Thank you.' Peter puts the card firmly inside his jacket pocket. 'I'd best let you get back down there to your friends.' He gestures to Oscar, Jamie, Max and Jennifer.

'Oh they're not *all* my friends. One of them isn't, definitely.'

'Do I sense tension?'

'No. No, it'll be fine.' I turn to him. 'Thank you again, and thanks for setting up that meeting with Bradley, earlier ... '

'You knew about that?' Peter looks surprised.

'Peter, I may look, and sometimes act, like a dippy female. But I'm not stupid.'

'You're certainly not that. You're one sharp cookie, Miss Scarlett. If you wanted, you could do anything if you put your mind to it. I don't know exactly what you do back in the UK, but if you ever want a job with me, there's a desk with your name on it.'

I smile at him again, not sure if he's joking, and then, like Bradley before him, Peter too is swept up in a throng of people needing his attention and he's gone.

I return to the others.

'Now you,' Oscar says, grabbing me and thrusting his arm through mine, 'you aren't going anywhere until you tell me exactly how you ended up onstage with Mr Sex On Legs!'

'And,' Max says, mimicking Oscar's voice and mannerisms by linking his arm through mine on the other side, 'you're not going anywhere either until you tell *me* just how you know Peter Butler, the head of TVA!'

'Jamie? Anything you want to know?' I ask, looking between him and Jennifer.

'Yes, only how on earth this lovely lady can be in any way related to the person hanging onto your left arm right now?'

Jennifer gives a high-pitched cackle. It's probably more of a squealy giggle, but to my ears she sounds like a pantomime witch screeching away as I see her wrap her bony arm around Jamie's shoulder. I suddenly feel incredibly protective and want to steer him away at once from her spells and potions.

'Of course, the two of you haven't met, have you?' Oscar suddenly realises. 'Scarlett, this is my elusive sister, Jen. Jen, this is my beautiful best buddy, Scarlett.'

The two of us smile at each other. Actually it's more of a snarl, but we disguise it as smiling for the sake of the others.

'Scarlett, we meet at last. How is Sean? Not with you in New York, I hear ... I do hope everything is OK.'

Hmm ...

'Yes, everything is just fine, thank you, Jennifer. He's very busy with work at the moment, so sadly couldn't come over with me this week. But luckily Oscar agreed to accompany me. He thought it would be a good chance to see his only sister, since he never gets to see her otherwise . . .'

Touché!

Jennifer's eyes narrow, but she still keeps the fixed smile plastered on her bright red lips. 'Well . . . I wouldn't want to keep you from your tales of how you tricked your way onto the stage with Bradley Cooper, now would I? Or indeed, how you know Peter Butler. How *do* you know him, anyway?'

She seems more keen to get this information than she is to find out about Bradley Cooper. *Interesting.*

'Long story, Jennifer. Long story.'

'Then don't let me hold you up any further, Scarlett. I'm sure Jamie here will keep me company for now. Won't you, Jamie?'

'Sure,' Jamie nods. 'If you'd like me to.'

'Hoorah!' Oscar cries. 'Right then, let's hit that bar, it's cocktails all round!'

And as I'm escorted away by Oscar and Max, I can't help but look back to see Jennifer leading Jamie towards a chaise longue in the corner of the room.

Twenty

I knock back far more cocktails than I should, given the amount of champagne I've already had, and soon the whole room starts to have a very pretty, hazy quality about it, as if I'm seeing it through one of those soft-focus lenses. So it's not only the band that's in full swing by the time they've played a few songs of the evening's set, but me too.

'Scarlett, are you OK?' Max asks me as I wrap my arm around his shoulder. 'You're not balancing too well at the moment.'

'It's these damn heels,' I say, reaching down towards my feet and pulling the green silk shoes off. I hold them above my head. 'Be free, feet!' I declare. 'Go forth and do what you're supposed to do; use your whole self for walking, not just your toes!'

I wave my shoes at a couple passing us at the bar. 'You, madam, do your feet a favour and release them from the shackles that your expensive and . . .' I take a closer look at her feet, almost falling over in the process ' . . . if I may say so, very lovely shoes are imprisoning them in.'

The couple hurry on past.

'Philistines,' I mutter, grabbing my empty glass.

'What *has* got into you this evening, darling?' Oscar asks, leaning forward on his bar stool to peer at me. 'You never drink this much. Even when we went to that wine-tasting evening at that French bistro in Notting Hill you were able to walk in a straight line on the way home. Unlike me, who found myself sitting in the lap of that exchange student outside a restaurant on the Portobello Road when I accidentally toppled into his table.'

I roll my eyes. 'There was nothing accidental about that, and you know it. And talking of laps, *she* might as well be sitting in Jamie's if she gets any closer to him.'

Max and Oscar look over to where Jamie and Jennifer are still sitting at a table together.

'Oh, don't pay any heed to them, darling.' Oscar gives a dismissive wave of his hand. 'That's just Jen's way. She's always a bit over-friendly.'

'I wish she'd be over-friendly like that with me,' Max says, gawping in their direction. 'Especially in a dress with as little fabric as the one she's wearing tonight.'

I've seen and heard enough. 'I'm going to get some fresh air,' I announce. 'I feel a bit ... I ... I just need some ... OK.'

I stagger towards the doors of the ballroom, trying to avoid colliding with the other guests, and feeling like I'm in one of those computer games where you have to jump over obstacles and collect objects to rack up the points. I gain fifty for avoiding a woman with a massive diamond tiara in her hair, and another bonus of one hundred when I swerve to prevent myself crashing into one of the waiters carrying a full tray of drinks.

Finally, I see light at the end of the game tunnel when I spy the French windows to the hotel garden. I pull them open and stagger outside onto some decking.

Luckily I don't have to stagger too far, as waiting on the decking for me there are some wooden seats, benches and one of those two-seater swing things with a canopy over it. If I'd been sober I'd have never even attempted the swing seat – even if Bradley Cooper *and* Brad Pitt had been waiting for me on it with a Scarlett-sized gap in between them. So why in the state I'm in now I think I will find it an easy task to perch myself on this constantly moving object I'm not sure, but somehow after several attempts of shuffling in and out in time with the swing, I manage to hop on.

The rhythmic movement of the seat swinging back

and forth, rather than having a negative effect on me, is actually quite soothing, and soon I'm wondering just why I was getting so het up in the ballroom back there.

What did it matter if Jamie wanted to let Jennifer slobber all over him like a lovesick puppy dog? No, she wasn't a puppy dog, she was more like a vixen from a wolf pack. Only not a nice comedy wolf pack like my new pal Bradley was in. Oh, no, a nasty, vicious vindictive one that couldn't stand it that you were going out with their ex-boyfriend and they weren't!

Was that really why I had issues with Jennifer, I wonder. Did I think she was still smarting over Sean casting her aside for me? And if that's the only reason, why was I so put out tonight when I saw her with Jamie?

I think about this for a few more minutes, my alcohol-saturated brain taking longer than usual to process my thoughts.

Oh, I suddenly think as something else occurs to me. *Oh* . . .

The situation I'm in now – removing myself to sit outside in the dark on my own when I need to collect my thoughts – is a bit too close for comfort to the same situation I found myself in at Disneyland Paris with Sean. I'd left Maddie and Felix's wedding because I was jealous of Sean spending time with another girl. Only last year,

Sean had come outside to see if I was OK, and it was then that I began to realise how I truly felt about him. At least Jamie wasn't likely to do the same tonight, so I was safe on that count.

'There you are, Scarlett,' Jamie says, his head appearing around the side of the swing canopy.

I nearly swing myself off the seat in surprise.

'Are you OK?' he asks, watching me swing manically back and forth. 'Oscar said you'd come out here for some fresh air.'

'Wha-what are you doing out here? I mean ... why?'

'Can you slow that thing down?' Jamie asks, looking like a demented spectator at a tennis match as his head tries to follow the seat as it swings rapidly back and forth. 'Or do I have to take a chance and jump on at an appropriate moment?'

I manage to put my feet down on the decking to slow the swing for a second while Jamie hops on.

'That's better! I was getting seasick watching you sway back and forth.'

I manage a weak smile.

'Are you OK with this thing still swinging? You look a bit green around the gills. That could have something to do with all the alcohol you've put away tonight, of course.' Jamie smiles, and I feel even sicker.

God, this can't be the same as Disneyland Paris? I

know I don't feel the same way about Jamie as I felt about Sean back then, *still* feel about Sean now, I remind myself ... But *could* that be why I felt the way I did when I saw Jamie with Jennifer? No: it wasn't jealousy I was feeling, I simply wanted to protect Jamie from her barbed claws. But my feelings were so strong, I'd needed to remove myself from the room ... Oh, this is such a mess. I've got myself in deep, as usual, and now I don't know what to do. Where is Sean when I need him? Actually this is probably the one time having Sean here wouldn't be such a good idea.

'Scarlett?' Jamie asks again. 'Are you sure you're all right? You're very quiet.'

Suddenly the combination of the alcohol, the emotion and everything that's happened this evening takes over and I burst into tears.

'Obviously not. Erm ...' Jamie gropes about in his pocket. 'Is this the moment where I'm supposed to produce a clean hankie?'

I nod as large teardrops roll down my face.

'No can do, I'm afraid. How about this? It's a napkin from the buffet table. It's clean.'

I take the paper napkin from him and dab at my eyes. Then I shiver.

'God, now you're cold, too. And I've only gone and left my jacket inside. I'm rubbish at this stuff. Hey,' he nudges me with his elbow. 'I'd never make a good romantic lead, would I?'

I sniff and give him a half-smile.

He holds out his arm. 'Come here,' he offers.

I slide along the seat and let Jamie wrap his arm around my bare shoulders. And it feels surprisingly comforting having him this close to me. It doesn't feel as threatening, or as exciting, as having another man's arm around me should do. It simply feels right.

Twenty-one

I roll over in my bed.

'Ohh . . .' I groan as I turn my head to the side, but my brain takes a few seconds to catch up with it, and as it does it clunks over to the side of my head like a lead weight. 'Oh, this is not good.'

I slowly open one eye, and then the other, and realise that not only am I still alive and in New York, but I desperately need to drink some water and visit the bathroom.

I manage to do the last of these things first, by rolling out of bed and staggering across the floor to the bathroom. As I catch a glimpse of my reflection in the mirror, I'm relieved to see I am at least dressed in a vest top and pyjama bottoms, but I don't look at myself too closely as I wash my hands. I feel bad enough, and seeing Morticia Addams – actually this morning it's probably more like Uncle Fester in a bad wig – reflected back at me is really not going to help. I escape as fast as I can from the bathroom, fill a glass of water from the bottle of Evian on my dressing table and slump into the purple high-backed armchair while I attempt to sip at the water.

Had I really drunk that much last night? I remember feeling fairly OK on the champagne … but what had happened after that? I try and think back to the night's events.

There were the Bradley Cooper incidents, they'd gone well as far as I could remember. Yes, he'd given me his phone number – that must count as a plus. Or did I dream that? I look around the room for my bag and see it lying on the dressing table next to me. I reach inside and find his card tucked in the pocket just where I'd left it.

I nod my head proudly at that little achievement, and place the card on the dressing table.

Then I try to remember some more.

Oh, then *she'd* turned up, I think, feeling my skin begin to crawl as I remember Jennifer. She'd been all over Jamie, and that's when I'd started to down the cocktails with a vengeance. Hmm … then what happened?

I think as hard as my pounding head will allow me to.

I was sitting outside on the swing seat on my own, and then Jamie's face had appeared around the side, and he'd sat down next to me; it had felt so comforting when he'd had his arm around me, I remember that part. But that's where it all starts to become a bit fuzzy. I drink a bit more water and try hard to recall some more of the evening, but nothing is forthcoming from my alcohol-addled brain.

I reach into my bag again and pull out my phone, to see if that will give me any hints. No new missed calls. No new dialled calls. No new received calls. Hmm ... but I have had a few new emails, so I take advantage of the hotel's free Wi-Fi to pick them up, but they're nothing exciting, so I do something I haven't done for a while: I log on to Twitter.

Nothing major on my timeline right now; a couple of mentions I reply to ... Oh, I know what I was going to look up. I find the search box and type in Jamie's name. Ah, there he is, smiling back at me from his photo. I click on his profile.

It seems odd seeing Jamie on Twitter. I don't know why it should, but I stare at his photo for a few seconds before I continue investigating the rest of his profile. *Who does he follow?* I file through the names, recognising a few celebrities. The rest must be friends, work colleagues and the usual complement of strangers everyone follows on Twitter, hoping they might turn out to be really interesting people with witty things to say.

Then I take a look at his followers, and Max is right: the vast majority of the ones I file through are women. Then I check out some of his tweets, and who's replying to them. Yep, again mostly women.

Wow, it seems Jamie *is* a bit popular with the ladies – of all ages, it appears by the look of his Twitter account. I smile; I'm not sure why this thought amuses me, but it does. Maybe it's because I don't see it myself. Of course, I can see that he's not exactly ugly, that he's a very attractive young man. But he just doesn't do anything for me. Not in that way, anyway. He's good company, and I like him. But that's as far as it goes, for sure.

Why, then, can't I remember what happened after he put his arm around me on the swing seat last night? That thought does worry me a little . . .

There's banging on my door.

I manage to drag myself over to it and take a look through the peephole. It's Oscar.

I open the door and let him in while I crawl back to my bed and pull the duvet over me again.

'Dearie, dearie me,' Oscar sings, sounding far too bright for this time of the morning. Actually that's a point, what time is it? I don't think I've even focused on a clock yet. 'We *are* looking rough this afternoon, aren't we?'

Afternoon?

'What time is it, Oscar?'

'One-fifteen. I thought I'd better come and check on you, you're not normally such a heavy sleeper. But then,' he winks, 'you don't normally drink quite as much as you did last night, do you?'

'Oh, Oscar,' I groan. 'Was I that bad?'

He nods. 'Yes, you were. It's just as well you fell asleep when you did out on that swing seat. At least you were out of harm's way then.'

'I fell asleep?'

'Ah-huh, we found you out there with your head in Jamie's lap, sleeping like a baby.'

I shoot up in the bed. 'My what! My head was where?'

'In his lap. You were both out there swinging away, he was out for the count too, and you were all curled up like a little green kitten next to him with your head resting in a rather delicate area.'

'Oh, *God*,' I say, pulling the duvet up over my head in an attempt to hide my embarrassment. 'I'm never drinking again.'

'Of course, none of us has ever said the same when we've found ourselves the worse for wear the next morning, or in a spot of trouble. Oh, I could tell you some tales ...'

'Not now, Oscar,' I uncover my face, if only because I need some proper air. 'Whatever am I going to say to Jamie when I see him?'

'I don't think you need worry about Jamie just now.'

'Don't I? Why?' I ask, hoping Oscar will say Jamie knows nothing of the incident and slept through the whole thing. Then I have another thought. 'You don't think he might be gay, do you, Oscar? It's something I've wondered a couple of times, and it would explain why I really like him but don't, if you get what I mean. A bit like you and me.'

Oscar throws back his head and screeches with laughter.

'Darling, you really are hungover, aren't you? Of course Jamie isn't gay.'

'But how do you know? He might be.' I realise I'm clutching at straws now, to get myself out of a predicament I can't even remember if I'm actually in.

'Believe me, Scarlett, I'd know if he was gay. My gaydar is one of the best in the business. That guy is as straight as that microphone he clutches, and just as dull, if you ask me.' Oscar waves his hand in the air. 'Anyway, forget about some daydream that features Boy Wonder marching in Pride this year – you've got far more important things to concern you right now.'

245

'Like what?'

Oscar tilts his head to one side and looks at me, and he appears to be reading something. 'Like, how you're going to explain to Sean why there's a heart with *I love Bradley* tattooed on your right shoulder.'

Twenty-two

Happily the tattoo turns out to be drawn in black marker pen, and after a lot of scrubbing I manage to get it off.

But what's more worrying is I still can't remember how it got there, or how I ended up falling asleep in Jamie's lap.

Oscar agrees that the best course of action is to leave me be for the afternoon to recover, and decides to take himself on his own tour of the *Sex and the City* hot spots around town. I don't feel too guilty about this; I know he'll be in seventh heaven checking out all the places the 'girls' are supposed to have hung out at in the show. When I've scrubbed and showered, I head down to the local Starbucks and order myself a large caramel latte with an extra shot of espresso. I cast a brief glance at their range of sandwiches and pastries, but my stomach decides that coffee is singularly the best option right now, so I take my cup and sit by the window to watch the New York world pass by while basking in the generous air-conditioning.

After I've sat there for a while I gradually start to feel a little more human again, as the caffeine begins to work its magic on my hangover, and when I return to the counter for a second cup, this time I take a chance on an apple and cinnamon doughnut. I'm halfway through the doughnut when my phone rings – it's Jamie.

I stare at the screen for a few seconds in panic, wondering whether to answer, but decide I've got no choice. 'Hi, Jamie.'

'Hey Scarlett, how are you feeling today?'

'I'm in a Starbucks on my second cup of coffee, and I'm only just eating my first bite of the day. Does that give you any clues?'

'That rough, eh?'

'Pretty much.'

'Listen, me and Max have a favour we'd like to ask you.'

'Yes?' I'm pleased he hasn't mentioned the 'lap' incident.

'We need to come and film your hotel towels.'

'I'm sorry, Jamie, I think the phone signal must be

breaking up because I thought you said you wanted to come and film my hotel towels just then. How odd would that be?'

'I did.'

'Why on earth would you want to do that?'

'We need to get some footage of someone stealing towels for a story we're doing about New York hotels that are tagging towels and bathrobes to prevent them being stolen.'

I take a large sip of my coffee as I try and take this on board. 'You're kidding me – right?'

'No, deadly serious.'

'And you want to come to my hotel to do it?'

'Yes, and if possible film you stealing them.'

'You're gonna make me look like a thief?' I explode into my phone, causing my fellow coffee-drinkers to look up from their laptops, smartphones and newspapers.

'No, of course not. We'll probably just film you from behind.'

And this is supposed to make me feel better, being asked to provide shots of my bum to fill people's TV screens over their Coco Pops and toast?

'You'd be doing us a huge favour, Scarlett. Pleeease . . .'

'Oh, all right then,' I sigh. 'When do you want to come and film?'

249

'This afternoon, if possible.'

I think about the state I've left my room in. 'Can you give me a while?'

'Sure, we're just doing some editing at the studio right now. It needn't be until later.'

'Great, my hotel's on Park Avenue on the corner of—'

'It's OK, I know where your hotel is,' Jamie interrupts. 'After all, how do you think you got back there last night? Look, got to go or we'll never get this edit done. Meet us outside at, say, five? We can't just roll up with all our equipment, or the hotel might get suspicious. We'll need to find a way to get inside unnoticed. Catch you later.'

'Wait, all *what* equipment?' I ask, but he's gone.

Right then, I think, as I hastily finish my coffee and doughnut. What's my biggest worry right now: how quickly I can turn my hotel room from a pigsty into a palace? Or what, exactly, happened within those four walls last night?

I tidy up my room as best I can and then, at just before five o'clock, I head downstairs to the hotel foyer.

It's Sam on the door. That's good, I think, that could come in handy . . .

'Hi, Sam,' I call. 'How are you today?'

'Good, miss, thank you. And yourself?'

'Very well.' I hover by the door.

'Off out, are we?'

'Er no, not just now. I'm waiting … for some friends.'

'That's good, miss.' He smiles at me expectantly, waiting to see what my next move will be.

I look out towards the sidewalk. 'I … think I'll just wait for them outside. It seems like a nice evening.'

'It is, miss. Warm, but pleasant all the same.' He holds the door open for me, and I escape outside.

How was I going to sneak two grown men and their 'equipment' in past Sam? Even saying that sounded dodgy. And what was all this equipment, anyway? Jamie hadn't really explained too much over the phone. Then, as a taxi pulls up a little way down from the hotel, I see just what I've let myself in for as Jamie, Max and what looks like half a TV studio begin to pile out.

'What is all this stuff?' I ask, as I find myself surrounded on the sidewalk by a camera, a big furry thing I recognise to be the top of one of those boom mics, some poles and a large spotlight.

'Our equipment,' Jamie says. 'I did warn you.'

'I know, but do you really need all this stuff?'

'We might do,' Max explains. 'It depends on what the conditions are like in your room. I might just get

251

away with the camera, but to be on the safe side, and since we were coming by taxi, we decided to bring the lot.'

'And how are we supposed to get all that through the foyer without anyone noticing?' I ask, looking back towards the hotel doors. Luckily, at the moment Sam is caught up with some new arrivals, who are just checking in to the hotel with all their cases.

'Could you create a diversion?' Max suggests.

'Such as?'

'Strip all your clothes off and run around naked in the foyer. I'm sure we could creep past then.'

I give him a disapproving look. 'You'd be too busy gawping to creep past, *and* you'd probably trip over your equipment, if not your own tongue, in the process. No, I am not stripping my clothes off in public so you two can sneak into the hotel.'

'Well, what then?' Max says. 'I'd do it, obviously, but you'd never lift this camera.'

'Is it that heavy?'

Max hands me the camera. 'Whoa,' I say as my arm is nearly pulled out of its socket. 'That's even heavier than my shopping after a day at the January sales.'

'You gotta be strong to be a cameraman,' Max says, proudly flexing his muscles. 'Not like these namby-pamby reporters.' He regards Jamie's biceps with derision. 'Only thing they're capable of holding up is a microphone, and then not for too long.'

Jamie opens his mouth to respond but I hold up my hands. 'Boys, boys, now is not the time for bickering. We need to find a way of getting you inside, remember?'

The three of us stand on the pavement for a few seconds thinking, then as I watch Sam in his doorman's uniform ushering people in and out of the building, I have an idea.

'How are you at tipping doormen?' I ask Jamie.

'Not bad,' he replies, looking at me suspiciously. 'Why?'

'How about maids?'

'Quick,' I call out of the back door. 'Hurry up, we don't have long.'

Jamie and Max appear from around the side of a huge rubbish cart carrying their equipment. They stare at me as they see me standing at the back door.

'Suits you,' Jamie winks.

Max looks me up and down. 'The dress is nice and short and I'd have preferred some heels, but you don't do too bad as a French maid.'

'I'm not a French maid!' I insist as I pull at the hem of my dress. It's just my luck that the only maid to be coming off duty at the hotel right now is four foot eleven and a size eight. This dress is practically indecent.

We'd tipped, OK *bribed* Sam on the front door to find a maid who was likely to take another 'tip' to let us borrow her uniform and a dirty laundry trolley for a few minutes. This would allow the boys to stash their equipment under the cover of some of the hotel's sheets and towels, so that I could push them up to the hotel room in disguise.

This had all worked well until the maid Sam had produced was Adriana, a tiny Portuguese girl. She hardly spoke a word of English, but was grateful to earn a few extra dollars. I barely fitted into her doll-sized dress, but I was only going to be wearing it for a few minutes, I reminded myself, and Jamie had been very good at helping me with my brooch. This was the least I could do to help him get his towel story.

'Just stick your equipment in there and let's get going!' I say, shoving the trolley at them.

'My God, she even talks dirty as well!' Max grins as he places his camera carefully in the trolley, while Jamie lifts in the lighting and sound bits.

'Max, I'm warning you!' I growl.

'Sorry! I'll be good, gorgeous. Just be careful with my camera.'

'Right, I'll meet you guys upstairs in a few minutes,'

254

I say, pulling the trolley back towards me. God, this thing was awkward to control, probably because it was carrying a fair bit more weight than it was used to with just dirty laundry inside.

'OK,' Jamie says. 'What room number?'

'Five-one-O.'

'See you in a bit then. Oh, Scarlett,' he calls to me just as I'm pushing the errant trolley off into the distance. 'Jennifer Lopez has got nothing on you, you know.'

'What?' I ask turning back.

'*Maid in Manhattan*,' Jamie grins. 'I thought you'd like the movie reference.'

'Of course, yes, thanks.' But living my life like a movie didn't really matter right now, and controlling this damn trolley and getting up to room 510 without anyone seeing me did.

I manage to – I can only call it wobble – the trolley towards the lift and wait while the lift seems to take an absolute age to descend to the ground floor. When it finally arrives, I'm overjoyed to see that it's empty, so I push my trolley inside and select the fifth floor.

I wonder while the lift ascends and I watch the numbers tick by whether I should have tried to find a service lift instead of using the public one? But it seems pretty quiet; it looks like I've got away with it. One, two, three, uh-*oh*, it's stopping on three. The doors slide open and a young couple get in. They barely glance at me as I stand with my head bent in the corner, having eyes only for each other. Hopefully that's it, I think, as we begin to move again, but no: the lift stops on the fourth floor as well.

'Going down?' a refined English voice enquires as an elderly gentleman peers into our lift.

The young couple, who are now playing tonsil hockey in the corner, are too obsessed with each other to answer. I'm forced to reply. 'No, going up.' I hope this will prevent him climbing in, but it doesn't.

'Well, it has to go down eventually. The more the merrier!'

He eyes me as the doors close. 'Which rooms do *you* clean?' he asks, lowering his gold spectacles so he can check out my dress more clearly. 'I haven't noticed you on *my* floor. I'll have to put in a special request with the management.'

'Staff only!' I insist as I hurriedly push my trolley out of the doors at floor five, yanking on the hem of my dress as I leave.

I'm pleased to see that Jamie and Max are already waiting for me in my room. I'd given Jamie a key so he could let himself in.

'How'd it go?' he asks, as he helps me through the door with the trolley. 'Did anyone try and stop you?'

'No; I just had to put up with being perved at by some grandad, but apart from that it all went smoothly.'

'Great stuff. You're a star for doing this, Scarlett. We owe you.'

'It's the least I could do; you did help me with my brooch, after all.'

Jamie smiles. 'Ah, that was nothing, and I didn't have to dress up like a stripper to do it.'

I wince. 'Do I really look that bad?'

'I think you look great,' Max calls from where he's setting up his camera on a tripod.

Jamie shakes his head reassuringly. 'Ignore him. You look fine. We were wondering if you had a robe you could wear for the filming. We thought it might make it look more realistic if you were actually wearing hotel property.'

'Sure.' I go over to my wardrobe and pull out the leopard-print robe.

'Wow!' Max exclaims. 'That's different.'

'I know, no plain white here. Apparently you can buy them in zebra print at Reception, if you want.'

'Right, if you could slip the robe on over your maid's outfit,' Jamie suggests. 'We won't be able to see it underneath. Then we can get on with some filming. You don't mind if I help myself to some towels from your bathroom?'

'No, go ahead,' I say, slipping on the robe. 'They're clean.'

We spend the next twenty minutes or so with me pretending to steal the towels from my hotel room while Max shoots me from different angles. I have to do lots of takes – and I actually quite enjoy the whole process of being the 'star', even if all I am doing is packing the towels into my own suitcase then zipping it up with an evil look in my eye. (I add that extra bit just in case my face gets in shot, even though Max assures me they're only filming my back view and my hands doing the packing.)

Just as we're finishing up there's a knock at the door, and we all freeze.

'Who's that?' Jamie hisses.

'I don't know. Probably Oscar, coming to see where I am.'

'Make sure it is before you open the door – we can't have anyone else seeing the equipment or we'll be in trouble for filming in here without permission.'

I go over and take a look through the peephole, but I can't see anyone.

Odd.

I ease open the door just a tiny bit in case it's someone from the hotel staff who's seen something suspicious and has come to check up on us. But I still can't see anyone outside. So I open the door even further and poke my head out.

'Surprise!' calls a voice that makes my heart leap so far up into my chest with shock that I nearly decapitate myself on the half-opened door. 'I bet you weren't expecting to see *me* tonight!'

'Sean ...'

Twenty-three

'What are *you* doing here?' I ask him as I stand in the doorway, open-mouthed with shock.

'I missed you, so I thought I'd fly over and surprise you.' He comes over and kisses my wide-open mouth.

OK, that doesn't sound like Sean to begin with.

'B-but you never do things like that. Why?'

'Maybe it's time I started. Aren't you going to invite me in?'

'What? Oh, right, yes, of course.' Then I think about what's going on in the room. 'Actually, Sean, I should just explain—'

But Sean is already carrying his suitcase through and into the room. 'What the ... who are you?' He stares at Jamie and Max standing in the corner. 'And why have you got a camera?' He looks between the three of us, and then back at me in my robe. 'And why are you dressed like that, Scarlett? What the hell is going on here?'

'Sean, it's fine, really, calm down. These are my friends Jamie and Max from breakfast TV. I told you about them, remember? I'm helping them out with some filming. And it's not like I'm naked or anything, I've got this on.' As I say these words and open up the robe, I realise I've made a mistake, but it's too late to tie it up again as Sean's eyes are open as wide as my mouth was a few moments ago.

'Just what sort of film is it you're making?' he demands.

'Scarlett, maybe we'd better go,' Jamie suggests quietly. 'I think we've got everything we need here now, and you obviously have things you need to sort out.'

'It's fine, Jamie. You don't have to,' I say, glaring at Sean.

'No, really,' Max joins in. 'I've got all the shots I need. We'll quickly pack up our stuff and be out of your way.'

While Max and Jamie hastily gather all their stuff together, Sean and I stand in silence, watching them. I'm pretty sure this isn't quite what Sean had in mind when he imagined jetting over here to surprise me.

'I'll let you know when I've edited the piece

together,' Jamie says as he leaves. 'And you can pop over to the studio to have a look if you like.'

'Thanks, Jamie, yes I'd like that; I'll give you a call. It's been fun this afternoon, thanks.'

'No prob, it's us that should be thanking you. Anyway,' he says when he feels Sean's eyes boring into him, 'we'll leave you to it. Nice to meet you, Sean. I've heard a lot about you from Scarlett.'

'Have you?' Sean says with a steely expression. 'That's good.'

'Good luck, kiddo,' Max winks. 'Catch you soon.'

And they're gone.

I turn to Sean. 'What was all that about? Those people are my friends, and you burst in here unannounced and behave like this?'

'Looks like I got here just in time. What have you got yourself into, Scarlett? Two men in your room with a camera, and you dressed like some cheap hooker?'

I've never felt like slapping Sean before, but for one split second I nearly do just that. But luckily my sense of humour takes over and I just laugh.

'That is *so* far from the truth it's actually amusing.'

I quickly do my best to explain to him just why I'm dressed the way I am, and why Jamie and Max were in my hotel room, and Sean begins to relax a little.

'I knew I shouldn't leave you alone in New York,' he

says, shaking his head in disbelief when I've finished my tale. 'Just what else have you been up to while you've been here that you haven't told me about?'

I'm glad Sean seems to be returning to his usual relaxed self. It's really not like him to be angry. 'Just let me get changed out of this and I'll tell you all about it while we have a drink and some food downstairs. You must be hungry after your flight.'

'Yes, I am,' Sean says, looking at me as I'm reaching for the zip on the dress. 'I'm really hungry, but it's not for food at this very moment . . .' He sidles up behind me and wraps his arms around my waist. 'Don't take off that maid's dress just yet . . .'

We end up not going downstairs for food, funnily enough, but we do order up room service a bit later, and we are now sitting propped up in bed after demolishing two portions of house burgers and fries – we'd worked up quite an appetite – and drinking the champagne Sean had insisted we order. It's very romantic, and quite unlike him.

'So why did you decide to fly over all of a sudden?' I ask. This is still bothering me; Sean didn't very often do things on a whim. He always thought everything through quite carefully, and with his business, he'd have had to get cover and cancel meetings and all sorts.

'I told you, I wanted to surprise you.' Sean takes a long sip of his champagne. 'Can't I do that once in a while?'

'Yes, of course, you know I love romantic gestures like that. But it just seems odd, that's all. I only spoke to you yesterday morning, and you didn't mention it then.'

'If I had it wouldn't have been a surprise, would it?'

'I guess not. But that still doesn't explain why. It's just not like you.'

'Thanks!' Sean says, putting his champagne glass down on the cabinet next to the bed. He rolls over towards me and strokes my hair away from my face. 'Can't you just be glad I'm here?'

'Of course I'm glad. It just seems unusual, that's all.'

'Then let me distract you from your unusual thoughts,' Sean whispers as he begins kissing the side of my neck. 'I don't know, a guy books a last-minute flight at eight in the morning to visit his girlfriend halfway around the world, and all he gets are questions.'

'Wait a minute, you booked your flight at eight a.m. your time, yesterday?'

'Mmm,' Sean murmurs, his lips moving down my neck and along my shoulder.

'But you'd have been just about to go to work then. What made you decide overnight to book a flight to New York and cancel all your meetings that day just to come and see me? You could have flown out the next day and given yourself more time.'

Sean abandons my shoulder and sits up.

'Will you just let this go?' he demands.

'No, it doesn't make sense. I know you, Sean, you forget that.'

'And I thought I knew you too, Scarlett.'

'What's that supposed to mean?'

'Nothing, just forget I said anything.' Sean reaches for his champagne glass and takes a quick sip. 'If you must know, I was due to fly in in a few days' time, right at the end of your stay, so we could spend some time together in the city like you wanted us to.'

'So what made you change your mind?'

'Nothing, I just decided to come over earlier, that's all.' Sean looks away.

Hmm, this still doesn't make sense. I turn everything over in my mind while Sean drinks slowly from his glass, still not looking in my direction. Then suddenly, like fitting that last piece of a jigsaw puzzle into place, a sense of satisfaction, dismay and on this occasion fury all rush together as I realise what's happened.

'When you booked your flight, you said it was eight a.m. in the UK, right?' I ask, turning not only my face but my whole body towards him. 'That would make it about three a.m. here.'

'Yes,' Sean replies, staring into the bottom of his empty glass. 'But I don't see—'

'And tell me, Sean,' I continue like a detective who's just figured out who the murderer is in a whodunnit, 'just before you made your phone call to the airline, had you by any chance been on the phone to anyone else?'

Sean's expression tightens.

'I might have been.'

'And would that person have been your ex-girlfriend Jennifer, by any chance?'

Sean sighs. 'Yes, she may have phoned me.'

'At three o'clock in the bloody morning?'

'No,' Sean says calmly, looking at me now. 'At about two, actually, seven a.m. my time. From some party you were all at together. She had some very interesting things to tell me about what was going on that night.'

'Such as?' I pull the sheet around me protectively. I didn't like where this was heading.

'Such as you parading about on the stage with Bradley Cooper, getting extremely drunk and finishing the night with your head buried in your friend Jamie's lap!'

I turn away from Sean and look out of the window for a moment into the now darkening Manhattan sky.

'It's not like it sounds.'

'Isn't it, Scarlett? Then please explain how it is then. Because right now it doesn't *sound* too good at all.'

I haul myself up and out of the bed, taking the sheet with me. 'And that's why you changed your flight, because of what she said?' I look back at him for a moment before I head into the bathroom. 'I can't believe you would listen to her vile gossip. You know what she's like.'

'I didn't want to, Scarlett; I even put the phone down on her. But after I sat and thought about what she'd said, it kept playing on my mind. You know you weren't quite yourself when you left London. So I decided to fly over and see for myself what was going on. And after what greeted me on my arrival here today, maybe I was right to do that.'

'I can't believe this, Sean,' I reply sadly. 'I really can't believe you still think I've got some sort of problem after what Maddie said to you in London, and much worse, I can't believe you'd think I was up to anything ... anything ... *untoward* while I was here.'

Sean opens his mouth to reply, but I cut in.

'No, Sean, I'm going for a shower before one of us says something we'll *really* regret, and so I can cool down and think about all this.' I lock the bathroom door behind me, turn on the shower and sit on the toilet seat to think.

Damn. Damn. *Damn*.

Damn that cow Jennifer for phoning Sean.

Damn that I had to get so drunk last night I fell asleep in Jamie's lap.

And damn if I still couldn't remember how I got home last night.

Jamie and I hadn't had a chance to discuss it today with Max being there, so I was still none the wiser, but that didn't give Sean the right to accuse me of getting up to no good.

I let the sheet drop away from me and climb into the shower. As the hot water runs down over me I try to fathom out what to do next.

It was so unfair of Sean not to trust me, and to fly over here to see what was going on. I'd not done anything wrong. I was pretty sure I hadn't, anyway . . . Yes, I liked Jamie. Yes, I felt a connection with him. But it wasn't like that. I just knew I wouldn't have done anything out of order last night. And I was certain Jamie wouldn't have taken advantage.

Damn you, Jen! Why did you have to stick your long pointy nose into my affairs? I wince. Bad choice of word.

I finish my shower, towel myself dry, then wrap a new towel around me when I realise that my robe is still in the bedroom where I discarded it earlier. When I come out of the bathroom Sean is asleep in the bed. I look at my watch on the dressing table. It's eight o'clock. I suppose it is quite late, for him; in the UK it would be one a.m.

now. I tiptoe about the room finding my clothes, making as little noise as possible, then I pin up my hair, pull on my shoes and quietly slip out.

I need to get out of here and think for a bit.

That's one of the great things about New York; it's a bit like London in that it doesn't matter what time of day you set foot on the streets, it's always buzzing with people. The type of people changes depending on the time of day you're out and about, but there's always a crowd to disappear into, or a place that's open to go to if you want a change of scene.

I find myself walking across Madison and up Fifth Avenue. The stores are filled with late-night shoppers and tourists, but I don't really feel like any retail therapy right now. Neither do I feel like venturing somewhere quieter. I'm not stupid; I know the parks at this time of night could be dangerous. So, where to?

And then I see it beckoning to me like a beacon of calm amid the hustle and bustle of the street and my overwrought mind.

St Patrick's Cathedral.

I find the nearest crossing and wait for the signal. One of my few New York disappointments was not coming across any WALK–DON'T WALK signals at the pedestrian crossings. So far, I've only seen little flashing red and green men. These were far too much like our crossings back home, and not at all like the ones you see in the movies or on TV. But when, finally, the green man looking after my crossing lights up, I hurry across the road and pull open the big wooden door at the back of the cathedral.

I'm surprised to find that there's an adult choir singing at the front of the cathedral tonight. The women all wear long black dresses and the men black dinner suits, white shirts and bow ties. As I slip into one of the pews at the back to listen, I'm at once completely absorbed by their stunningly beautiful voices. And the sound that fills every inch of the vast auditorium I find myself in once again feels like honey soothing my soul from within.

After I've sat there listening in stunned silence for a good ten to fifteen minutes, I realise I'm feeling calm enough to return to Sean, and I'm about to get up when I feel a hand gently touch my shoulder. I turn to see Peter slipping into the pew beside me.

'Breathtaking, aren't they?' he whispers, his face still turned towards the choir.

'Yes,' I whisper back. 'They're so good, I can't believe I was lucky enough to stumble on them tonight. I feel as if they've repaired me inside.'

I blush, realising how weird that sounds.

Peter turns towards me. 'Do you need repairing, then?'

'Kind of,' I say, feeling a bit embarrassed. 'Got some stuff going on. You know.'

Peter shrugs. 'No. But you can tell me about it if you think it might help. I'm a good listener.'

The choir appears to be finishing up for the night as applause breaks out while they take a final bow, and the choirmaster thanks everyone for attending the service.

'It's complicated,' I reply, watching them.

'It always is,' Peter says. 'And that's likely what drew you in here tonight, the thought of some peace and tranquillity.'

I nod.

'Would you like me to leave you to your thoughts? It will be quiet in here once the choir have packed up. It always is at this time of night.'

'Do you come here often, then?' I ask, and when he grins I add, 'at this time of night, I mean. I thought you said you came in after work.'

'This is after work tonight.'

'Doesn't your family mind you getting home so late?' I bite my lip. This really isn't any of my business, but Peter always seems so easy to talk to I forget I don't know him that well.

'I don't have any family. Not to come home to, anyway. My wife and I split up a few years ago, and my kids live with her out in Vermont.'

Peter states these facts in a rehearsed way, as though he's repeated them a thousand times over.

'I'm sorry, I didn't realise.'

'No reason why you should, Scarlett, we barely know each other.'

I smile at him. 'That's true. But the odd thing is I find myself wanting to tell you things I wouldn't want to discuss with my own family.'

'Why don't you then, if it helps?'

'Here?' I look around the great cathedral.

'Nowhere better in Manhattan as far as I'm concerned, for pouring your troubles out and having them heal.'

'It's a long story,' I warn him.

'I'm in no hurry to go anywhere. Are you?'

I think about Sean and our argument earlier, then I shake my head and begin to tell Peter and St Patrick's Cathedral everything that's been going on.

Twenty-four

By the time I've finished, St Patrick's Cathedral is almost empty, save for a few tourists still wandering around admiring the inside of this extraordinary building.

'So, what do you think?' I ask him, when he remains silent.

Peter's grey head tilts slightly to the side as his deep blue eyes cast their knowing gaze over my face. 'I think you're very lucky to have so many people care so much about you, Scarlett. That's what I think.'

'Yes, I know I am. But everything seems so confusing at the moment.'

'It will sort itself out. Life has a habit of doing that. When I broke up with my wife I thought it was the end of the world. But now I realise it was the best thing that ever happened to us. We just weren't making each other happy any more, and we were better off apart. It was hard on the kids, but even they're happier, without us arguing all the time.'

I couldn't imagine anyone wanting to argue with Peter, he seemed so calm.

'But I don't want to split up with Sean. I love him.'

Peter smiles, 'I know you do, and I'm not suggesting for one moment that's what you should do. I'm just saying you'll find your own way through this hiccup in your life, and when you do, you'll know that it all happened for a reason.'

I have to smile at him. 'That old chestnut?'

'It's what you believe, isn't it?'

'I suppose so . . .'

'Well then, you can't stop now just because things have become a bit awkward or difficult to handle. I think you need to step back from everything. Find something to take your mind off all this.' He thinks for a moment. 'What are you doing right now?'

'Mainly talking to you.'

'Then come with me,' he says standing up.

'Where?'

'Don't ask questions. Do you trust me, Scarlett?'

'Of course,' I reply, standing up too. 'But the last time you said "come with me" I ended up in a room alone with Bradley Cooper.'

'And that was a bad thing?' he says with an amused expression.

'OK, OK, I'll come.'

Peter hails a cab outside the cathedral and we travel downtown and across the Brooklyn Bridge, eventually pulling up outside a large house in a fairly rundown part of Brooklyn. It's amazing how just driving over a bridge can change the feel and look of a city. We'd left Manhattan with all its wealthy streets, extravagant buildings and beautifully dressed people, and arrived here in what many would call the 'real' New York, with its urban sprawl of buildings and colourful, passionate people.

'What are we doing here?' I ask as Peter climbs out and holds the door open for me.

'You'll see,' he says as he pays the cab driver and asks him to wait.

He strides confidently up to a battered-looking front porch, then rattles very quietly on the doorknocker. As I follow him I notice there are a couple of rusty but well used children's bikes leaning up against it, and a discarded baseball bat and mitt abandoned on the ground outside.

After a minute or so the door is opened by a middle-aged woman wearing track pants and a t-shirt with the logo *Friends – How you doin'?*

'Peter!' she exclaims. 'What brings you here at this time of night?'

'I just thought I'd pay you all a quick visit, Kim,' Peter says. 'Is it OK to bring a friend in?'

'Sure!' Kim says with a broad smile and a wave of her hand. 'Come on in, sweetie.'

I follow Peter into the house. Inside is a large hallway with several rooms leading off it, and a wide flight of stairs with a well-worn carpet leading up to the next floor.

Two boys of about ten years old come running through the hall, chasing each other.

'Lucien, Marcus!' Kim calls in a stern voice. 'Now I've just told you it's time for bed. Please do like the others and go and get into your pyjamas now.'

The two boys stop their game for a moment, turn and look at Kim, then race up the stairs. I'm not sure if they are heeding her instructions or continuing with their game.

She shakes her head at us. 'Boys of that age; what can you do with them? Everyone else is either getting ready for bed or in bed already. Except for the older ones, that is.'

I'm beginning to wonder just how many children this poor woman has.

'Is it all right if I take Scarlett for a quick tour around?' Peter asks. 'She was very helpful at our charity ball the other night, and I wanted her to see the home in action.'

'Sure, honey,' Kim nods. 'But there's not much action at this time of night. Like I say, most have already gone to bed or are getting ready to go.'

So this is the children's home we were raising funds for at the ball.

'Do you want one of the helpers to show you around?' she asks Peter. 'Or will you be OK on your own?'

'I think I know the place pretty well by now, Kim,' Peter winks. 'Scarlett and I will be just fine.'

Peter leads me upstairs first.

'Why have you brought me here?' I ask as we climb stairs that must have hundreds of feet stampeding up and down them every day by the look of the threadbare carpet and worn handrail.

'You'll see,' Peter says mysteriously. As we reach the top of the stairs and cross a long hallway, Peter very gently pushes open a door and peeks inside, then beckons for me to come forward. 'Take a look,' he whispers.

I come up to the door and put my face to the gap. Inside the room I see six beds and two cots all with small children sleeping peacefully in them. The room is dimly lit by a teddy bear nightlight, but I can still make out a brightly coloured border going all the way around the inside of the room, and there are toys scattered over the floor and beds.

'This is the younger children's room,' Peter explains. 'That's why they're all tucked up in bed already.'

'Are they all orphans?' I whisper, still watching the children sleep.

'Some. Some are just here because their parents can't look after them any more.'

'But why?' I ask, pulling my head away from the room to look at Peter.

'Different reasons. Usually it's drugs or alcohol abuse of some sort.'

'Both their parents? How awful for them.' I peep into the room again.

'Not always both. Sometimes they're from a single-parent family that just can't cope, and they're brought here.'

'But what about the other parent? Can't they be found?'

'Not always, if they've been estranged from the family for a while.'

'But aren't there, like, government departments for that?' I look at Peter hopefully.

He smiles. 'Ever the optimist, eh? No, Scarlett, there just isn't the funding these days for that kind of thing.'

'But that's terrible.'

'Way of the world, I'm afraid. Come on – let me show you some more.' Peter leads me across the hall to another door. He knocks this time, and we hear a lot of scuffling in the room before Peter gently pushes the door open.

Eight beds are suddenly very quickly occupied as Peter and I stand in the doorway, and the room is very quiet; too quiet. Then one of the beds lets out a tiny giggle, followed by a second, and suddenly all the beds are shaking as girly laughter fills the room.

'It's all right, girls,' Peter says. 'It's not Kim, it's me.'

'Uncle Peter,' one of the beds shouts, and a girl of about ten years old leaps from it and bounds across the room.

'Uncle Peter!' Suddenly all eight beds are emptied as Peter is surrounded by females half his size all clamouring for his attention.

'Shush, girls,' Peter says, kneeling down beside them. 'Or Kim will be up here telling me off for disturbing you. Now, I want you to meet a very special guest I've brought to see you all tonight. This is Scarlett.'

'Hi, Scarlett,' some of them reply, looking up at me with awe. Feeling very out of place, I kneel down beside them too.

'Hello, I'm very pleased to meet you all.'

'I like your hair, Scarlett,' says one of the girls who has bright red hair tied up in tight plaits. 'It's very pretty.'

'Thank you.'

'How do you do it like that?'

I'd pulled my hair up quickly into a loose chignon and stuck a few clips in it before I'd snuck out of the hotel room tonight. 'It's nothing special,' I assure her. 'It's really easy to do.'

'Will you show me?' she asks, looking up at me with big green eyes.

'Not tonight, Nicole,' Peter says. 'You've got to go to bed in a minute.'

'Another time, then?' Nicole asks hopefully.

I smile back at her. 'Yes, sure, I'd like that.'

'Right, girls,' Peter instructs. 'It's bedtime. If Kim comes up here and finds you all like this she won't allow me to come visit you again, or to tell you any more bedtime stories.'

'Yey!' they shout excitedly as they all run for their beds and jump under the covers. It's almost like something out of an Enid Blyton book, as the girls snuggle under the bedclothes and wait excitedly for Peter to tell them a story. Only these are modern girls with earrings and t-shirts emblazoned with Justin Bieber and *Glee*. But a story is a story, whatever decade you're from. I watch while Peter sits patiently at the end of one of the girls' beds and makes up his own tale about a girl living in New York who's successful and famous, yet independent and modest at the same time. When he gets to the end of his tale, he stands up among moans and complaints that it's too short, and bids them all goodnight, promising to be back again soon. He beckons for me to leave.

Outside in the hallway, I smile at him. 'You're very good at that, making up stories. You've clearly done it a few times before.'

'Yes,' Peter nods. 'I've been coming here to Sunnyside for some years now, since TVA became one of their benefactors.' He smiles. 'And I was quite well practised with my own two until they got too old for Pop to be reading bedtime stories to them.' He looks back thoughtfully at the door for a moment. 'They appreciate time, you know – the kids. We can raise as much money as we like at these charity events, and that helps to keep places like this going, but it's time they need more than anything else. People who'll make them feel cared for, even if it's just for a few minutes. I come as often as I can. But I still wish I could do more.'

'It's very sad.' I look around at all the closed doors. 'How many children do they have here?'

'About thirty in this one, but Sunnyside consists of four homes across town, each with their own families of children living inside. But they're not sad houses, Scarlett, far from it – the staff try to keep them positive and happy places.' Peter looks down the hall. 'Do you want to see some more? The boys' room is just down here, it's likely to be a bit more boisterous than the girls' room though.'

'Go on then.'

We end up touring the rest of the house: the bedrooms, the downstairs living area, and end up in the kitchen with Kim again. Peter's right, it's not a sad house at all, it's a very upbeat home with a wonderfully positive vibe about it, even with all the children in bed. I can only imagine what energy and buzz there must be when they're all running about the place.

'Enjoy your tour?' Kim asks, lifting a coffee pot from the side. 'Can I get you two anything?'

'I'm fine thanks, Kim. Scarlett?' Peter enquires.

'I'm good, thanks. But don't let me stop you if you're having one. You must need it, running around after this lot all day.'

'Ah, they're a good bunch, and we have a great gang here to help me out. Most of them have gone home now, or you could have met them too. I think Janice and Zack are still about somewhere. They're my main men, so to speak.'

'Peter was telling me that some of the children are here because they're separated from their parents when there are problems at home,' I say as Kim pours her coffee. 'Or they're from single-parent families, and the other parent can't be traced when something happens.'

'That's right. It's a real shame.' Kim sits down at a large table in the middle of the kitchen. 'Excuse me while I rest my weary feet for a bit, won't you? Please take a seat yourselves.'

Peter and I pull out a wooden chair each and sit down.

'Those are the kids that really shouldn't be here,' Kim takes a sip of her coffee, then continues. 'If there's a parent about somewhere, or even another family member, as long as they're fit to look after the kid, that's who they should be with in my opinion. This is a great place and we do our best, but we can't take the place of a mom or a dad to these kids, no one can ever do that, they need a real family.'

I feel a large lump forming in my throat as Kim speaks.

'The thing is, many of us have lost a parent we've known and had a chance to love. Sadly that's the way of the world, and the Lord, he takes people from us when he sees fit, he has his reasons. But to never have a chance to get to know your mom or dad, to love them and find out what your real family is like. It just ain't right.'

'Are you OK, Scarlett?' Peter asks, looking at me with concern. 'You look a bit pale.'

I nod.

'You do look a little pasty there, honey,' Kim says,

283

peering at me too. 'Maybe you should get some fresh air. The backyard is just through that door there.'

'Yes, I think I might do that. Thank you.'

I dash over to the door and out into a backyard full of yet more toys and outdoor play equipment. As I stand looking up at the dark New York sky, I breathe in great mouthfuls of the cool night air.

I'm such a whiner. I'd been complaining earlier to Peter about all my very minor problems, when these poor kids had got nothing in their lives. At least I had people who cared about me; I had good friends, a boyfriend, a dad *and* a mum, and what had they got?

As quickly as thoughts of my problems vanish, they're replaced immediately with an intense need to help these children. It washes over me, and fills not only my heart with hope, but my whole body with determination. But I was just Scarlett. What did I know of living in a children's home, of being orphaned or living without parents? What could I do to help?

And then it hits me. Of course.

I turn around and hurry back inside the house.

'Peter, Kim,' I announce, more resolve and determination filling me than I've ever felt before in my entire life. 'I want to help. I want to help the children of Sunnyside.'

'I knew you would,' Peter smiles knowingly up at me. 'I knew you would, Scarlett.'

Twenty-five

'Tell me again why we're heading into downtown Brooklyn this afternoon, darling?' Oscar asks, checking his look in a little compact mirror he always carries. 'I thought we'd planned on hitting the shops again, then drinks in that cool bar at the top of the Flatiron Building.'

'This will be so much better, Oscar. Well, it will give you more enjoyment, anyway.'

'More enjoyment than shopping and cocktails, darling? There's only one thing that gives me more enjoyment than that, and I really don't think that's likely to be on the menu in the back of a cab with you and Seany, now is it?'

I look over towards Sean, who is sitting on the other side of Oscar staring out of the window at the passing buildings.

When I'd got back last night, he'd still been sleeping. Sean was a pretty heavy sleeper, so I'd been able to sneak in again without waking him. But my absence last night had not gone unnoticed, as I'd found out this morning.

'Where did you go last night?' he'd asked over breakfast before Oscar had joined us. 'When I woke up you weren't there.'

'I went for a walk,' I'd replied truthfully.

'With whom?' Sean had calmly poured coffee from a pot into his cup.

'On my own.'

'You were on your own, walking the streets of Manhattan, at night?'

'Yes, to begin with I was.'

'So who joined you then?'

I hated it when Sean was like this. He wasn't even looking me in the eye. He was just concentrating very hard on arranging his breakfast. 'I met a friend when I went into St Patrick's Cathedral.'

'Do I need to ask which friend? Did he have his cameraman sidekick with him this time, or does he just come along to visit hotel bedrooms?' Sean looks up at me now, a cold expression in his eyes.

I return his gaze with an equally cool look.

'Actually, it wasn't either of them. This is another friend I've met here. Peter.'

Sean nearly chokes on his cereal. 'Another man? Isn't three enough, Scarlett?'

'Three?'

'Jamie, Max and Bradley Cooper.'

And I nearly spit my toast all over the white table-cloth.

'Bradley Cooper, are you kidding? I just helped out at the charity auction with him, that's all. Oh, Sean, that's hilarious! You thought I was up to something with a Hollywood film star? I'm actually quite flattered.'

I pick up my toast and begin munching again.

But Sean is still watching me intently across the table. 'And that would be why you have a card with his telephone number propped up on the dressing table of your hotel room?'

And it's my turn to choke, as the toast goes down the wrong way. I take a sip of juice. 'That doesn't mean anything. He was just being kind. He gave it to me after the auction in case I needed anything while I was in New York.'

'Like?' Sean's eyes widen.

'I don't know, do I? He said he owed me after the auction, and that if ever I needed a favour to call him up. He seems like a really nice guy.'

Sean still looks doubtful.

'Look, Sean, I can one hundred per cent assure you

there is nothing going on between me and Bradley Cooper.'

I can't actually believe I've just said that last sentence.

'What about you and Jamie?' Sean demands.

'No. Jamie and I are just friends. The same as Max and I are.'

'The same, Scarlett?'

'OK, so I may have seen Jamie a bit more while I've been here. But that's to do with the brooch, and we've got stuff in common.'

'Such as?'

'Such as, he grew up without a parent, the same way I did.' I begin buttering more toast.

'And you've talked a lot about this?' Sean is not eating now; he's just sitting back in his chair interrogating me. That's what it feels like, anyway.

'Yes.'

'In the many hours you've spent together while you've been here.'

I slam my knife down hard on my plate. 'Sean, please stop this now. There is nothing going on between me and Jamie, I promise you.'

'But you like him.'

'Yes, I like him. Is liking someone a crime or illegal in this state? If it is, you'd better arrest me because I've liked plenty of people since I've been here.'

'Mainly men, it seems to me.'

I sigh. This really isn't going anywhere. And it is so unlike Sean. He never behaves like this. It's almost like he's jealous.

'So tell me about this Peter you met up with last night,' Sean asks now. 'Who is he, and how do you know him?

And that's how we'd ended up in the taxi this afternoon, heading downtown to Brooklyn. Sean wanted to meet Peter, and I wanted to show Sean and Oscar Sunnyside so I'd be in a better position to pitch my new idea to them.

As we reach the house, I see Peter already waiting outside to greet us.

'Scarlett,' he says, stepping forward to open the cab door. 'So glad you could come over again. And bring your friends along this time, too.'

'Peter, this is Sean, and you've already met Oscar, of course,' I say, introducing them.

'Of course, Oscar, how could I forget?' Peter says, shaking his hand. 'And Sean, it's good to meet you at last. Scarlett has told me a lot about you.'

Sean returns Peter's handshake. 'And you, Peter. And you,' he replies guardedly.

'Come on, let me show you around Sunnyside,' Peter says, leading the way inside. 'It's a bit noisier than when

289

you were here last night I'm afraid, Scarlett. Saturday mornings are always particularly hectic around here, but today you'll get more of a feel for the place in all its glory.'

A bit noisier isn't the way I'd describe the house, as we enter the hallway and find children swarming everywhere, running up and down the stairs, shouting to each other and chasing one another across the hall and through the rest of the house. Chaotic, frenzied, manic, would be more my choice of words.

Kim quickly appears from one of the rooms with an armful of washing in a laundry basket. 'Guys, you're here already! Great to see you again so soon, Scarlett.' She smiles warmly at me. 'Now, Peter, should I show these good folk around, or will you?'

'I'll do it, Kim. You look like you've got your hands full just now.'

'When haven't I, running this place?'

'Do you want to go with Kim?' Peter asks me. 'And I'll take Oscar and Sean for the full tour?'

'Sure,' I nod. 'OK with you two?' I ask them.

'Yes, darling, whatever you want,' Oscar says, already sounding bored.

Sean simply nods.

While he and Oscar follow Peter down the hall, I accompany Kim through to a large laundry room fitted with two huge washing machines, two driers and an indoor line strung across the centre with a few odd unclaimed garments hanging on it: socks, pants and a pair of red shorts. She begins to fill one of the machines from the basket.

'Is there anything I can do?' I ask, feeling a bit helpless just standing there.

'No, I'm fine, honey, I'll be done in a minute. So, how'd it go with your guy?'

'You mean Sean? I haven't asked him yet.'

'You mean *told* him,' Kim says, filling the drawer of the machine from the biggest packet of laundry detergent I've ever seen. 'From the way you were talking yesterday, Scarlett, I can't see anyone stopping you doing what you want to, not now you've got this idea in your head.'

'Maybe . . .'

'No maybe about it.' Kim starts the wash and turns around to face me. 'Darlin', if this is what you want to do, no man is gonna stop you, I could see it in your face last night.'

Just then a little girl pops her head around the corner of the laundry room. 'Kim, me and Maisie want to go down to the store to buy candy, but Zack says we can't until after we do our chores. But I need to get things at the store to finish my chores, so can't we just combine the two?' She smiles up at Kim with a set of gappy but bright white teeth. Then she notices me standing there. 'Scarlett, you came back!' The rest of her skinny little body appears from around the door and she skips over towards me, and I realise it's the little girl from last night. Her red hair is all pulled back under a baseball hat this morning, and instead of pink pyjamas she's wearing a navy-blue sweatshirt and jeans. 'Will you do my hair now?' she pleads. 'Will you, *will* you?'

'Er . . .' I look to Kim for guidance.

'What chores are you meant to be doing this morning, Nicole?' Kim asks.

'Emptying all the trashcans. But we don't have any bags. That's why we need to go down to the hardware store.'

'I could go with you if you like,' I suggest. I look at Kim. 'Would that be OK, Kim? Then when Nicole has emptied the trash, I can do her hair.'

'Sounds good to me,' Kim says in a weary voice. 'Anything for an easy life.'

Nicole and I set off for the local hardware store together, Nicole skipping happily down the path in her battered sneakers.

'So,' I ask, 'how do you find it living at Sunnyside?'

'It's OK,' Nicole says, reaching in her pocket. 'Gum?' she offers, holding out a stick.

'No thanks, but don't let me stop you.'

'Your name is very pretty,' Nicole says after she's unwrapped her gum and is happily chewing on it. 'Scarlett. I like it.'

'Thanks. I'm named after a famous film character. You probably won't have heard of the film though, it was out a long time ago. *Gone With The Wind*?'

Nicole wrinkles up her nose. 'Nah. But your name is still cool. I'm named after a film star too.'

'Really, which one? Actually, no, let me guess …' I think for a moment. 'It must be Nicole Kidman.'

'Yip,' Nicole nods. 'My mom was a big fan of her and Tom Cruise. Actually I think she was more a Tom Cruise fan, and then when I came along she wanted to name me for something to do with him, so she picked Nicole.'

'That's nice.'

'Yeah. Kinda appropriate, though, 'cos they got split up too. Just like me and my brother Tom did. Oh, here's the store.'

I stare after Nicole for a moment, then follow her into the store. We quickly buy some bin bags with the money Kim's given us and I also buy Nicole some candy, even though I'm sure I'm not supposed to, and we begin to share it on our walk back.

'Nicole, what you were saying before about your brother, doesn't he live with you at Sunnyside?'

'Nope,' Nicole says, her mouth full of candy. 'They

293

said he was difficult; too difficult for Mom to cope with. Tom was quite naughty, so they took him away from her, before they took me. He went to a different home, I think. We couldn't stay with Mom, she was ill, too ill to look after us. Well, that's what they told me. She wasn't ill, Scarlett, she just drank. She drank *a lot*.' She looks up at me with a knowing expression. Far too knowing for one so young.

'I'm so sorry to hear that,' I say, meaning it. Then I think for a moment. 'Have you seen Tom since?'

'No.'

'How long ago did all this take place, Nicole?' I ask gently. I know I'm probably asking too many questions about things I shouldn't, but this is suddenly all very relevant.

'I was seven when I came to Sunnyside, I'm ten now. Tom left about a year before me. So I guess that's four years ago.'

I nod and quickly reach for another sweet from Nicole's bag, hurriedly stuffing it into my mouth. I hope this might stem some of the emotion that I can feel wanting to burst out from inside me in response to what this little girl has been through.

This is all so unfair – and I'm going to do something about it.

*

When we get back to Sunnyside, I help Nicole empty the trashcans, and in our search for rubbish I'm surprised by some of the sights I see throughout the house.

In the girls' room I'd visited late last night with Peter, I find a new beauty salon has sprung up, with Oscar in charge handing out tips and advice to his new protégées. Not only that, he appears to be the main guinea pig for their experiments, too. Right now he's covered in a green face mask and is having the fingernails of one hand painted bright pink by one little girl, and the other electric blue by another.

'Having fun, Oscar?' I ask, trying not to laugh.

'The best, darling,' he says, meaning it. 'My girls are such angels, aren't you?'

The girls nod happily. 'Can we play hairdressers next, please, Uncle Oscar?' one of them asks, brandishing a pair of scissors in her hand.

'Er, I don't know about that, sweetie,' Oscar replies, looking nervous. 'Maybe we should just stick to beauticians for now.'

We leave them to it and head down the hall to collect the trash from one of the boys' rooms, where it's virtually impossible to see any beds this morning, as every bedsheet has been stripped off and used to form some sort of makeshift tent, making the whole room look like an Indian village of teepees.

'Halt!' we hear as we enter the room. 'Who goes there?'

'We're collecting the trash,' Nicole replies, sounding bored. 'Can you just hand us the trashcan, please?'

Sean emerges from behind the door holding a broom over his shoulder like a rifle.

I may have been able to control my laughter in the girls' room, but this is too much. 'What are you doing?' I ask after I've stopped laughing.

'Protecting the fort,' he answers in all seriousness.

'Oh, it's a fort, is it? I thought they were Indian teepees.'

'How can they be Indian teepees when they're that shape?' he says, aggrieved. 'It's quite clear it's an army camp.'

'Right . . .' I tilt my head to one side as if I'm appreciating the angle of the sheets now. 'Of course they are: how could I not have seen it before?'

One or two heads are starting to appear from the tents now.

'Hmm, I could have you court-martialled for insubordination,' Sean says, raising an eyebrow.

'Could you now, Sergeant?' I wink.

'It's Captain, actually. I've been promoted.'

'Are these women giving you trouble, Captain?' another deep voice asks from one of the tents. I turn to see Peter's head appear from under a sheet.

'I should have known you'd be involved in all this, Peter.'

'Nothing I can't handle, Colonel,' Sean says, saluting. 'I've been dealing with this one for over a year now.'

'I've only known her for a few days, Captain, and she's not easy, that's for sure. But I'm sure you have it all in hand.' Peter salutes and returns to his tent.

'Boys!' I roll my eyes. 'Come on, Nicole, you and I have a date at the hairdresser's. Have fun, Captain.' I salute Sean.

'Shame you don't take orders that easily all the time,' Sean says, grinning.

'In your dreams, buddy, in your dreams.' I grin at him. 'Have fun in your fort.'

I spend the next hour or so showing Nicole how to fix her long red hair into different styles, and slowly the beauticians and the soldiers begin to filter down from the salon and the fort back into the rest of the house. Then Kim announces it's time for lunch and invites us to stay, which we gladly accept. We're all starving. Looking after children is not only exhausting, but gives you a massive appetite.

After lunch, sadly, it's time for us to leave, but we all agree we'd like to come back again if there's time during our stay. So with a few teary goodbyes, mainly from Oscar, we depart.

Peter accompanies us outside to our cab.

'Thank you all for today,' he says, shaking Oscar and Sean's hands. 'The children really appreciate the time, and time is just what the three of you have given them this morning.' He reaches forward to hug me. 'I hope it goes well, Scarlett,' he whispers in my ear. 'Good luck.'

'Thanks,' I whisper back. Then I say in a louder voice, 'Thank you, Peter, we've all had a lovely time today.'

'Be seeing you soon, Peter,' Sean says, nodding once more to Peter, as he climbs into the cab first.

'Look after them all, won't you,' Oscar sniffs, following him. He reaches once more for his red polka-dot hankie, which was being put to good use a few minutes ago.

'I will, Oscar, don't you worry.'

I climb in next to Oscar, and Peter closes the door on us all. As the cab pulls away down the street, we bid farewell to all the faces that now line the windows and doorway of Sunnyside as they wave madly back at us. But what Sean and Oscar don't know yet is that, if I get my way, this is *definitely* not the last we'll be seeing of them.

Twenty-six

'That was just lovely,' Oscar sniffs, blowing his nose noisily into his handkerchief. 'Thank you for taking us there this morning, Scarlett; those children have made me so grateful for my own upbringing. They're just so happy and positive about life.'

'Yes, they are, Oscar,' I agree. 'That's one of the reasons I wanted you to see Sunnyside. It's such a shame for some of them that they even need to be there at all . . .' I venture, hoping to begin steering the conversation the way I want it to go.

'Oh, definitely,' Oscar agrees. 'I heard some terrible stories from some of the children about why they're in the home. But it doesn't seem to faze them in the slightest.'

I glance at Sean. He's very quiet, sitting back in the cab listening to the pair of us.

'Did you enjoy yourself, Sean?' I ask him.

'Yes, I did. I had great fun playing soldiers with the boys upstairs.'

'Good.' I smile.

'So what's next?' he asks.

'What do you mean, what's next?'

'Come on, Scarlett, I know you. You haven't dragged Oscar and I all the way down here today just to play soldiers and hairdressers for the fun of it.'

'We were beauticians, actually,' Oscar protests.

'You didn't look very beautiful to me when you came out of that room all plastered in make-up,' Sean says, grimacing at the memory. 'Scarlett, you may as well get it over with now, I know you're up to something.'

I keep forgetting how well Sean knows me.

'I wasn't going to tell you everything just yet.' I was going to butter him up with a few glasses of wine, a nice meal and me in my sexiest dress with a pair of very high heels. 'But since you ask . . .' I take a deep breath. 'I had an idea last night while I was at Sunnyside. And, I think, quite a good one, too.' I pause, but Sean just waits, his face wearing that patient yet neutral expression it does when I have one of my 'ideas'.

'I want to set up a business to help people find their lost relatives. Children, mainly, just like the ones in Sunnyside. But it will also extend to adults.'

Sean stares at me for a few seconds in surprise; this was obviously not what he was expecting. 'Run that past me again, Red?'

'I want to set up a service to help people trace their lost relatives. I think there's a need for it. Take, for instance, all those children in Sunnyside who have been unnecessarily separated from their families, just because no one has the time or the finance to help them find someone who could take care of them. I could help them do that. And it's not just children,' I continue as Sean stares at me silently across the back of the cab. 'There's people like Oscar.'

Oscar, who has been trying to push himself further and further back into the seat while I talk, opens his eyes wide in a 'don't bring me into this' fashion.

'What's Oscar got to do with this?' Sean looks at him accusingly. 'I might have known you'd be in on it!'

'Don't you look at me like that!' Oscar waggles a finger at him. 'This is the first I've heard of any of this!'

'Oscar has managed to trace his family while we've been over here, on Ellis Island. But he might need help, if he wants to continue to trace them and find out where they are today, and that's where a service like mine would come in very useful. And then there are people like Jamie.'

'I should have guessed he'd be involved somehow,' Sean says, folding his arms defensively.

'Yes, Jamie does come into it, I'm afraid, Sean. The fact of the matter is that Jamie is in a very similar situation to the one I was in a year ago. He's only ever known one parent and he wants to find the other, but wherever he's tried looking he's come up against a dead end. I want to help him, just like you helped me, remember? I want to help all the other people out there who are forever searching, always wondering what it's like to know both their parents. I know how it feels to have that one piece of your jigsaw missing, then to have it fitted back in place again. How important it is. I want to give other people, whether they're children or adults, that same feeling I'm able to have now.'

Oscar grabs his hankie from his pocket again and dabs at his eyes.

'And how do you propose to finance this business?' Sean enquires calmly, appearing unaffected by my dramatic speech.

'I'm hoping you're going to help me, Sean, at least to begin with.'

This is what Sean's company Bond Enterprises did. Set up businesses. Well, normally they bought up businesses that were in trouble, or poured money into them until they were back on their feet again, in exchange for a small cut of the profits or some shares. But this wasn't that different. I just needed help to get myself started.

Sean nods slowly. 'And where do you see yourself running this business from – London?'

I swallow hard. 'I thought maybe here, to begin with . . .'

'Here?'

It's my turn to nod now.

'You want to come and live in New York?' Sean asks in the same calm and steady voice.

'Not permanently, but I want to help at Sunnyside. I want to help the kids you've just seen this morning.'

'Hmm.' Sean gazes out of the taxi window for a moment to think. 'And how do you propose those children will finance the search for their relatives?' He turns his face back to the interior of the cab now. 'From their pocket money, or will they pay you in candy, perhaps?'

'Now you're just being silly.'

'No, *you're* being silly, Scarlett. You've dreamed up some ridiculous notion about helping everyone and his dog, and wanting all of them to have a happy ending, like you always do, and you haven't thought through the practicalities of it.'

'But this is what I want to do, Sean, and I'm going to find a way to do it, with or without you!' My joy is fast turning to anger.

Poor Oscar sitting in between us tries to shrink back

even further into the seat, and even our driver is taking the odd crafty glance in his rear-view mirror.

'I didn't say I wouldn't help you, I just said that you hadn't thought it through. You need to draw up a business plan. Some sound ideas. A strategy.'

'And you need to find a heart,' I reply coldly. 'This isn't about business plans and strategies, Sean. This is about a need. A feeling. An urge to do something to help people. And do you know what? Maybe I would be better off doing it without you, if you don't understand why I need to do this. Maybe it's time I did stand on my own two feet, for once in my life, without any help from you or Dad. I'll be the one to sort my own problems out this time. Not my knight in shining armour. Just me, Scarlett O'Brien.'

At that moment, the taxi pulls up outside the hotel and in my haste to exit the cab, I almost knock poor Sam out as I fling open my door.

I will do this, I promise myself as I storm through the foyer of the hotel. I'll do it for me, and for all the people out there just like me.

There's a very frosty atmosphere in the room when Sean enters not long after me. Considering how hot it is outside on the streets of Manhattan, the temperature inside Room 510 is decidedly chilly.

Sean is the first of the two of us prepared to thrust a

pickaxe into the thick ice, after we've stomped about in silence for a few minutes.

'Look, Scarlett, we can't carry on like this. We need to talk about this idea of yours.'

'So it's an *idea* now? I thought back in the cab it was just a silly daydream.'

'I never said that!'

'You suggested that I was trying to be some sort of fairy godmother with my head in the clouds, floating around trying to make wishes come true so that people can have a happy ending.'

Sean sits down on the edge of the bed and folds his arms. 'I never mentioned a fairy godmother. I may have said you were trying to give people a happy ending, yes, I'll accept that. But you are.'

'And what's wrong with that?' I put down the hairbrush I've been using on my hair a bit too vigorously for the past few minutes, and face him full on. 'What's wrong with trying to make people happy?'

'Nothing, nothing at all. I admire you for your constant positivity. But if you want to make a business out of your idea you need a strong business plan, some proof that it's going to work, not just some pie-in-the-sky dream like the one you have at the moment because you've visited a children's home and you want to help.' He sighs. 'I do understand your desire to help the kids,

Scarlett, I spent time there this morning too, remember? Look, how about we set up a regular donation to Sunnyside from the company?'

'*No*, Sean!' I run my hand through my hair now, and feel like ripping it out in frustration. 'You don't understand. It's not *about* the money, it's about helping people find what they're missing.'

Sean runs both his hands over his own short hair and then massages his temples. 'OK, then. Let's approach this in a different way,' he says, lifting his head. 'How are you going to go about helping people *find what they're missing*?'

'I don't know yet, but I bet I can. I did it myself, didn't I, when I found my mother last year?'

'Ahem.' Sean opens his eyes wide.

'All right, so *you* helped me find what *I* was missing. But it can be done, and you know it.'

Sean goes silent for a bit, and I know he's thinking hard because the same little furrow appears in his brow that he always gets when he's thinking deeply about something.

He gets up, walks over to the window and gazes out at the New York skyline, still deep in thought. I keep quiet. I know Sean when he's like this. This is a good sign.

Eventually he turns around from his window-gazing to face me. 'I have to hand it to you, Scarlett, it's a fine

306

and noble idea you've had. And any idea that comes from the heart is usually a good one.'

I look at him hopefully.

'And you've got the passion to carry it through, that's for sure. Anything you put your mind to usually comes to pass eventually. Even if there are a few hiccups along the way.'

I wring my hands together nervously. I really want Sean's approval on this. It's not just about the money. I'm going to do this with or without him, I've already decided that, but knowing I have his support would be wonderful.

'And you know I'll back you all the way, if this is what you really want to do. That goes without question. But if you want me to back you financially to begin with to get this business off the ground, I'm going to need to see some sort of proof that it will work. It's standard business practice,' he says almost apologetically. 'It's not just me that makes the financial decisions at Bond Enterprises; you know that. I have a board of directors that I'll have to put it to as well.'

I nod at him, wondering what he's going to say next.

'So here's the deal. You show me you can match some-one up with their long-lost relative while you're here in New York. You can extend your stay by a few days if you like, I don't mind. But prove to me and my board that you can do what you're intending to do with this company in the future. Show it to us as a viable business proposition, and then I can take it to them and try and sell it for you.'

'Really?' I ask him. 'Do you mean it?'

Sean nods. 'Of course. I'd say yes right now if it were up to me. You know I only want to see you happy.'

'Sean, thank you!' I say, running over to him and wrapping my arms around his neck. 'I knew you'd help me!'

Sean holds me in his arms, then gently away from him and says, 'Remember this is business, Scarlett – you've got to prove yourself first before you're taken seriously. This will be your business alone if it works. You won't have your dad's hand to hold on to now.'

'Oh, I'll prove it,' I reply, looking up at him happily. 'I'll prove to you and everyone else that I can do this, and I know just where I'm going to start.'

'Where, at Sunnyside?'

'No, with Jamie.'

Twenty-seven

The news that I was going to help Jamie find his father hadn't exactly gone down too well with Sean.

But when I explained the reasons I was choosing Jamie – that starting with someone I knew who had already begun searching themselves would give me a better chance of succeeding – Sean seemed to relax slightly.

As I walk over to Jamie's apartment the next morning, I think about Sean's reaction. I've never known him to be like this before. Jealousy just isn't a word I'd associate with him, yet that was the only way I could describe his odd behaviour since he'd been here in New York. Sean is so relaxed and laid-back about everything, and he never seems to stress. I often wonder how he ever gets anything done at work with an attitude like his. But he seems to, and Bond Enterprises is an incredibly successful and thriving company as a result.

I'd phoned Jamie this morning, and asked if I could meet up with him to discuss something. He'd agreed, but asked would I mind coming round to his apartment because he needed to wait in for a delivery.

So here I am, walking across town towards the address he's given me on the West Side. I know Jamie will be OK with the idea of me trying to trace his father. I don't know how I know this, I just do. So I don't feel at all nervous when I reach the red-brick apartment block and press the buzzer with his name on.

'Yep,' comes the familiar voice back through the intercom.

'It's me, Scarlett.'

'Hi, I'll just buzz you in.'

The door opens and I'm allowed access to the building. I climb the stairs to Jamie's apartment on the second floor, where I find he's already waiting for me at the door.

'Hi,' he says, opening the door wide for me to come in. 'Sorry about asking you to come here, but I'm waiting for a new sofa to be delivered this morning, and have to wait in.'

I look around the apartment. 'What's wrong with the old one?'

Jamie's apartment is surprisingly quite big. There's an open-plan kitchen and living area with a couple of doors leading off it, I presume to the bathroom and bedroom.

'Nothing really,' he shrugs. 'I just fancied a new one.'

'Oh, cool.'

'You can sit on it for now, though,' Jamie says, gesturing towards a brown leather sofa. 'It's quite safe.'

'From . . . you, you mean?' I joke, then immediately regret it. After what happened the other night at the party, and Sean's reaction to Jamie, I didn't really want to go down that road today.

'Er . . . yes,' Jamie says, his cheeks flushing slightly. 'I think we can avoid a repeat of the swing-seat incident as long as we stay off the cocktails this morning, don't you?'

'I'm so sorry about that, Jamie.' My own face reddens too. 'I don't know what happened.'

Jamie shrugs. 'You drank too much. We both did. You poured your heart out to me about many things, and then you crashed out on my lap. I wasn't far behind you, I reckon.'

'And then after we were disturbed you took me back to my hotel?' I ask hesitantly.

'Yes, but you crashed out again as soon as your face hit the bed. And I mean, hit the bed. I had to turn you

311

around to get you up the right way so I could pull the covers over you.'

A huge sigh of relief escapes from within me.

'Why, what did you think had happened?' Jamie asks quizzically.

'Nothing. I mean, I assumed that's what you'd done. You're my friend, after all.' I smile back at him.

'Yes. Your friend, that's all,' he repeats. 'Look, Scarlett, no offence. You're a very attractive woman, but I just don't feel that way about you.'

'You don't?' I exclaim, sounding a bit too pleased. 'I mean, you don't,' I lower my voice an octave.

Jamie smiles. 'You obviously feel the same way.'

I nod. 'Yes, it's weird, isn't it? I mean, I really like you and everything, but I don't fancy you, if that makes sense.'

'Perfectly. Although after I met your boyfriend the other night I think that's just as well, don't you?'

'I'm really sorry about Sean; he's not normally like that at all. I think it was just finding you in my room like that, and the camera, and me dressed the way I was.'

'No, that probably didn't help much.' Jamie grins. 'It was like something out of a movie, wasn't it?'

I roll my eyes. 'Why, just when I don't want it to, does my life choose that very moment to resemble a movie scene? Oh, it doesn't matter now,' I say, waving my hand dismissively at Jamie. 'It wasn't just finding you two in the room that day; Jen has been stirring up trouble, too.'

'Jen? Do you mean Jennifer from the other night?'

I nod. 'That's the one. She's Sean's ex. Jennifer has always had it in for me after Sean knocked back her advances after they'd broken up. She thinks it was because he wanted to be with me. It really wasn't – there was more to it.'

'Oh,' Jamie says, then he screws up his face, 'Uh-oh . . . '

'Uh-oh what?'

'I think I might have done something similar to her.'

'What? How?'

Jamie comes and sits next to me on the sofa. 'She was coming on to me really strongly, and to get away from her I told her I was going outside for some fresh air. When she wanted to come with me I told her I was going to find you.'

I screw up my own face now. Jennifer would have loved that. Not. No wonder she delighted in phoning Sean.

'Why weren't you interested in Jennifer?' I ask. 'Much as I hate to say it, she's an attractive woman. *Was* she coming on too strong for you?'

'Not my type,' Jamie says, sitting back on the sofa.

'What is your type then?' I ask, starting to wonder if Oscar might be wrong and Jamie *is* gay.

'Funnily enough, usually someone like you, Scarlett. Pretty, bright, easy-going, yet challenging too.'

I was quite enjoying his description of me until he got to the challenging part.

'I'm challenging?'

Jamie smiles. 'Come on, you know you are!'

'I prefer "interesting to be with",' I grimace, then I smile at him. 'But not your type this time, eh?'

'Nope, not this time,' Jamie grins. 'Ah, well, there's a first time for everything. I now have a proper female friend I don't fancy.'

'That's great! I think?'

'Just like in the movie *When Harry Met Sally*,' Jamie suggests helpfully.

'They end up sleeping together and getting married.'

'Yes, they do, don't they?' Jamie pulls a face. 'So not the best of examples, there. But the basic principle is the same, and until I can think of a better movie scenario it will have to do for now.'

'Deal,' I say, holding out my hand to him.

'Deal,' he says, taking hold of it.

As we shake hands, we catch each other's eye for a split second and I feel that same connection again. And by the look on Jamie's face, he feels it too.

*

Jamie returns from the kitchen a few minutes later with an ice-cold Pepsi for us both, and we settle down again on his sofa and begin to discuss the real reason I've come over here today.

'Do you really think you can find my father?' Jamie asks, after I've explained everything. He drains the last of the Pepsi from his glass. 'If I've never had any luck, why should you?'

'I really don't know, but it's my chance to prove to Sean that my idea can work.'

'Why does it matter what he thinks?' Jamie asks. 'If you want to do it just go ahead, you don't need his approval.'

'No, you're right, I don't. But I could do with some backing to help me start up, and his company could provide it.' I think about what I've just said. 'Actually, that's not fair; I do want Sean's approval on this. I want him to think I can do it, that it's not just about the money.'

'Fair enough,' Jamie shrugs. 'Then let's go for it. What do you want to know?'

I get my notepad out and begin taking notes on everything Jamie tells me about what he knows of his father so far. After about twenty minutes, his door buzzer rings.

'That will be the new sofa,' he says, leaping up. 'Back in a min.' He goes over to the intercom. 'Yes?'

'Jamie?' a female voice comes crackling through the speaker. 'Is that you?'

'Mother?'

'You don't need to be quite so formal,' the well-spoken English voice replies. 'And you might at least sound pleased to hear your mother's voice.'

'Of course I'm pleased,' Jamie says, sounding shocked. 'You ... you'd better come up.'

Jamie presses a button on the intercom and turns to face me. 'That's my mother,' he says, his face pale.

'Yes, I gathered that.'

'But she's supposed to be in Australia right now.'

'Ah, that is a bit of a shocker then. I wonder what she's doing here?'

'That's just what I'm thinking.' Jamie looks towards the door just as there's a tap on it, and he rushes over to open it.

An elegant-looking woman glides into the room. She's got long brown curly hair, tied up at the side with a bright blue butterfly clip, and she's wearing loose white trousers and a navy and white kaftan top with more colourful butterflies fluttering prettily over it. At first glance you might mistake her for someone much younger, but on closer inspection I realise from the abundance of laughter lines around her eyes and mouth that she's likely to be somewhere in her late forties to early fifties.

'Jamie, darling.' Jamie's mother wraps her arms tightly around him in a warm embrace. 'It's good to see you again.'

'Mum, it's good to see you too. But what are you doing here? You never said you were coming.'

'I thought I'd surprise you, darling.' She looks over in my direction and smiles. 'And who might this be? Oh, wait, I know who you are. You're Scarlett, aren't you?'

'Er . . . yes, that's right, I am. But how did you know?'

Jamie's mother reaches out a hand garlanded with silver bangles. 'I'm Eleanor,' she says, shaking my hand firmly, her wrist jangling as she does. 'I saw you on one of Jamie's reports. The one outside Tiffany's?'

'Of course, yes. That seems ages ago now.'

'I send Mum all my TV stuff so she can see it,' Jamie explains. 'But what it doesn't explain is why you're here, Mother.'

'I just wanted to pay you a little visit, Jamie. Nothing wrong in wanting to see my son once in a while, is there?'

'No . . . I guess not.'

'Look, I should go,' I say, gathering up my notebook and pen. 'And leave you two to it. You must have a lot to catch up on. We can finish this another time, Jamie.' I suddenly feel awkward talking about the search in front of Eleanor.

'Sure,' Jamie nods knowingly. 'Let me see you out.'

'It was nice to meet you, Eleanor. Perhaps I'll see you again while you're here.'

'Oh, I'll make sure of it, Scarlett,' she replies, fixing me with her bright blue eyes.

'Right, OK then.' I head towards the door, where Jamie is already waiting. 'Is your mother OK?' I ask him quietly as I step outside.

'She's what you'd call a creative type, if that's what you mean? She's an actress, isn't she? She's meant to be a bit unhinged. They're all a bit like that.'

'Of course she is, sorry, you've only just told me about her properly.'

Jamie nods. 'Yes, of course, I forgot. Sometimes, Scarlett, it feels like I've known you a lot longer than I actually have.' We hold each other's gaze for a brief second. 'Anyway, I'd best get back; find out the real reason she's here. Because there will be one, knowing my mother – just you wait and see.'

Twenty-eight

'This is nice – just the two of us, at last,' Sean says as we stroll hand in hand through Central Park later that afternoon. 'I wondered for a while if we were ever going to get to be alone here for any length of time. What with Oscar, your TV friends and your father earlier.'

We'd had lunch with Dad in a restaurant in Greenwich Village and, as I thought it might, the topic of my possible new business venture had cropped up over the main course.

'But who will run the business in London if you come and live over here?' Dad asked, putting his knife and fork down. 'We can't both be in New York at the same time.'

I sigh; I knew this would happen. 'It's not a permanent arrangement, Dad, it's just for a bit, to see if I can

319

make it work. Tammy and Leon have been great while I've been away – they've really come into their own, haven't they, Sean?' I ask, looking at him for back-up.

'Not that I want Scarlett to come and live here, Tom,' Sean replies, looking at my father seriously. 'But she's right; they've done a great job in the short time Scarlett's been in New York. Better than I thought they would.'

'Sometimes you just need to give people a chance to prove themselves,' I say, giving them both a meaningful look. 'So they can show what they're truly capable of.'

Dad smiles knowingly. 'The last time I did that, Scarlett, you disappeared to Notting Hill, where you proceeded to find your long-lost mother, ditch your then fiancé and ride off into the sunset with Sean, never to return.'

Sean grins now. 'So not an altogether bad result.' Then he becomes serious again. 'Tom, I really think we need to give Scarlett a chance with this one. The idea is very important to her – for many reasons. Let her at least give it a go. If it works out, the rest we can take from there.'

I reach across the table and squeeze Sean's hand. I've missed him.

'OK, then,' Dad says, nodding. He picks up his knife and fork again. 'Prove to us that you can do it, Scarlett.

Reconnect a family that has been separated for years. Just don't involve me in all the tearful reunions when you do.'

'Don't you worry, Dad,' I smile, 'the chances of you being anywhere near one of my reunions is about as likely as me declaring my undying love for Jeremy Clarkson.'

Dad looks baffled and turns to Sean for an explanation.

'*Top Gear*,' Sean states. 'Scarlett has issues with it.'

'I don't have issues, I just don't see the point.'

'There's a point to everything in life, Scarlett,' Dad says. 'Sometimes you just need to find out what it is.'

As we continue our walk though Central Park, I give Sean's hand a little squeeze. 'Yes, it's lovely to get to spend some time with you again. I've missed you.'

'Have you?' Sean asks in surprise. 'You seem to have been awfully busy while you've been here, with everything that's been going on. I bet you've not even given me a second thought.'

We stop walking and pause at the top of the Wollman Rink.

'Don't be daft, of course I have.'

Sean gazes down at the funfair and the brightly coloured rides. 'I didn't know there was a funfair in Central Park.'

'Not all year round; this is where the famous ice rink is set up in the autumn and winter. Jamie was telling me all about it when we came here.'

Sean's face snaps back towards me. 'You came here with Jamie. Why?'

'Er . . . because we'd just been to see his friend at the Met Museum about my brooch; and we came here for a bit of a wander afterwards. He was telling me about all the movies that have scenes set here. There are so many I didn't even know about. Jamie's a bit of a movie buff, like me.'

'Is he really?' Sean says with indifference.

'Sean, you've got to stop this. Jamie is just my friend, I keep telling you.'

'I know you do. But it sounds as if he's got to be quite a close friend over the last couple of weeks, and I think I'm a tiny bit jealous.'

'You know something?' I whisper, smiling up at him. 'I think you are too. But at least I know you care.'

Sean pulls me into his arms and kisses me. 'I would have hoped you knew that anyway,' he says, holding me close as he looks down into my eyes.

'I do, but a girl likes to see evidence of it from time to time.'

'Do you think I've been neglecting you then?'

'Possibly,' I shrug. 'Just a bit, maybe. But it's fine. I

know you're busy, and I knew what I was letting myself in for when we got together last year. We'll work it out, though.'

Sean pulls me even closer to him. 'I'm sorry, Scarlett, I didn't realise. Maybe you're right, maybe I have let that side of things go a little. But I'm going to make it up to you, just you wait and see.'

Later that day, I'm sitting in my hotel room trying to do some research using Google on my phone, and wishing I'd got my little MacBook with me, when my phone rings. I answer it straight away thinking it's Sean who, true to form, has managed to find 'a bit of business' to do while he's in New York, even though he's promised me he'll be back as soon as he possibly can. So I'm surprised to hear a woman's voice speaking at the other end of the line.

'Hello, is that Scarlett?' she asks.

'Yes it is. Who is this?' I ask, thinking as I speak that I recognise the voice.

'This is Eleanor, Jamie's mother. We met this morning.'

'Yes, hello again. What can I do for you?'

'I was wondering, Scarlett, if we could meet up sometime while I'm here for a little chat.'

Oh. I'm immediately on my guard. What does

Eleanor want to talk to me about? It could only be that Jamie's told her about my helping him search for his father, and she doesn't want me digging around in her past.

'Yes, that would be lovely. When were you thinking of?'

'How about breakfast tomorrow?'

Wow, she certainly doesn't mess around.

'Yes, I can do breakfast.'

'I know it sounds a little bizarre,' Eleanor explains, 'but Jamie says he's doing a live over to the UK tonight, so I know he'll be sleeping in in the morning.'

So it'll be just the two of us . . .

'Then breakfast sounds great. There's a little diner not far from Jamie's apartment that does a good breakfast.' I bite my tongue. That might sound odd, me knowing that, but it's where I went with Dad for breakfast.

'Yes, I know it,' Eleanor says, not sounding at all bothered. 'Shall we say nine?'

'Nine is great.'

'See you tomorrow, then. Bye for now. Oh, and Scarlett, not a word about this to Jamie if you speak to him before then, OK?'

'Sure, yes, that's fine.'

'Good. The morning it is, then.'

And she's gone.

The next morning I'm waiting patiently for Eleanor in the diner where I'd had brunch with my father a few days ago, although now it seems like much longer. Had I only been in New York for nine days ... really? It seemed like for ever.

I've read the menu about ten times, and know exactly what I'm going to order. Although how I'm going to eat anything when I feel this nervous I don't know. But why should I feel nervous? I haven't done anything. What's the worst that can happen? Eleanor could ask me to cease searching for Jamie's father. I think about this for a moment. There's something that has secretly been bugging me about that. Maybe she did know where Jamie's father was, but she didn't want him to find out. Maybe his long-lost father was a criminal, or a murderer or an international terrorist wanted in several countries for crimes against—

'Good morning, Scarlett,' Eleanor says, breaking into my spiralling conspiracy theories. 'I do hope I'm not late.'

'Hi ... hello,' I stutter, hurriedly standing up and dropping the menu in the process. 'I didn't see you come in. No, not late at all.'

Eleanor slides elegantly into the seat opposite me wearing another brightly coloured outfit, this time it's a dress with red and pink roses all over it. She takes a quick glance at the menu. 'Do you know what you're having?' she asks.

'Yes, yes I do.'

'Good, then let's order.' She lifts her hand and a waiter comes scuttling over.

After we've placed our orders – both for pancakes – Eleanor clasps her hands together and places them on the table in front of her.

'Now, down to business.'

I don't know whether to be intimidated by this no-nonsense approach she has to everything or whether I quite like it, but I don't have too long to dwell on the matter because she continues talking.

'You're probably wondering why I want to meet with you like this this morning.'

I nod.

'It's quite simple, Scarlett. It's to do with Jamie's father.'

I knew it. Here we go. I fiddle with the corner of my napkin.

'I think I know where he is,' she continues.

'And you don't want me to go looking for him, is that it?' I interrupt. 'You want me to back off my search and leave him alone.'

Eleanor looks puzzled. 'What are you talking about – back off your search?'

'My search to find Jamie's father. He told you about it, didn't he, last night? That's why we're here this morning. You're going to ask me to stop looking because you don't want Jamie to see him again.'

Eleanor shakes her head. 'You've lost me now, Scarlett. Why wouldn't I want Jamie to see his father again after all these years? That's why I'm here with you today.'

Eleanor and I sit and stare at each other as the waiter brings Eleanor's herbal tea and my coffee.

As he leaves the table, Eleanor speaks first.

'I don't know why you think we're here today, Scarlett, but Jamie hasn't said anything to me about you searching for his father.'

'He hasn't? Then what are you talking about?'

'I saw you on one of Jamie's clips he sent me with a brooch, a brooch shaped like a dragonfly.'

'Yes, that's right, I was taking it into Tiffany's.'

'Do you have it with you, by any chance?' Eleanor looks towards my bag hopefully.

'No, I'm afraid I don't. Why?'

'Oh, that's a shame, I wanted to take a closer look just to make sure.'

'To make sure of what?' This was getting odder by the moment.

The waiter brings our pancakes now, and sets them

down on the table with a jug of syrup for me and blueberries and cream for Eleanor.

'To make certain if it had got one blue eye and one black. It was difficult to see on the TV screen, it was only on for a few seconds, and it doesn't matter how many times I play that bit over and over, I still can't tell.'

'The dragonfly does have one blue eye and one black,' I say carefully. 'Well, it did.'

'What do you mean, *did*?' Eleanor says in an urgent voice. Her hands grip the edge of the table tightly.

'I don't have the brooch now; it was sold in a charity auction. It raised quite a bit of money.'

Eleanor releases her grip on the table as her face drops into her outstretched hands.

'What's wrong? Look, Eleanor, I'm not really following all this. What has the brooch got to do with anything, and how would you know it had got one black eye and one blue, unless . . . ' my voice trails off as I realise what I'm saying. Then, as the rest of the jigsaw begins to fall into place in my brain, my hand claps over my mouth as I suck my breath in sharply. 'You'd already seen it before up close.' My hand falls limply back down into my lap.

Eleanor looks across the table at me; her blue eyes stare back into mine.

'Did the brooch belong to you originally?' I ask. 'Were you the person who gave it to my father?'

328

Eleanor nods.

'You're the woman from Stratford?'

She nods again, and there's sadness in her eyes.

'But you left suddenly, Dad said. Why?'

'I think you've already worked all this out, Scarlett. But I'll honour you with a proper explanation. I was pregnant.'

'With Dad's baby?'

Eleanor nods.

I think about this for a moment. 'But why, why didn't you stay? You could have at least told him, even if you didn't want to stick around.'

'I was young, and I didn't know what I was doing. Your father was a very attractive man, Scarlett, but he was just out of a bad relationship, your mother had not long left and he had you. He didn't want to be lumbered with another child to look after.'

I shake my head. 'No, you're wrong. Dad would have looked after you and another baby. He wouldn't have turned you away.'

'Yes, I knew that deep down, but like I said, I was young and foolish then, and I thought I'd be trapped. So I left, and Jamie was eventually born in London after I'd travelled around for the next few months.'

'Jamie!' I shout. My hand flies up to cover my wide-open mouth.

'Yes, Scarlett,' Eleanor says calmly. 'Jamie. Who did you think I was talking about when I mentioned a baby?'

'I ... I don't know. I'd just assumed you'd had more than one child, that it was another baby. But that means that Jamie could be my brother.'

'Half-brother, yes, if it's the same brooch. Is your father's name Tom?'

I nod.

'Then it's definitely him.' She smiles. 'I knew it the first time I saw you on the TV screen. You remind me very much of Tom.'

'Do I?'

'Definitely. The way you spoke to Jamie with such passion about the brooch, and your love of the movies, it's just like your father used to be. He had a great passion for life did Tom, back then. Life had knocked it out of him a bit, and understandably so, given what he'd been through, but it was still there, lurking.'

I think about this. Then my hand covers my mouth for a third time as something else occurs to me.

'But that's just the same as it's been for me with Jamie since I met him here in New York ... he's constantly reminded me of someone too, but I couldn't think who it was. Now I know – it's *Dad*.'

Eleanor smiles.

'The two of you seem to have really hit it off. Jamie was talking about you a lot at dinner last night.'

'Was he?' I smile. Suddenly my feelings for Jamie all make sense. Now I know why it feels like we have a connection but aren't actually attracted to each other. Apart from the incredible shock at finding out I've got a half-brother, I'm also feeling a massive sense of relief about why I've been feeling the way I have.

'But telling you all this is the easy part,' Eleanor says as she picks up a fork and begins prodding at her pancakes.

'What do you mean?' I ask, realising that I haven't even touched my own food yet.

'Our next and biggest problem is how to go about telling Jamie that you're his half-sister, and your father that he has a son he knows nothing about.'

Twenty-nine

'He's your *what*?' Oscar yelps as I have lunch that same day with him and Sean on a rooftop restaurant overlooking Central Park. 'How can this possibly *be*? Details, darling, and fast!'

'Calm down, Oscar, people are looking.' Actually people were doing nothing of the sort. Oscar's antics were nothing if not normal in New York, but I wanted to see how Sean was taking this news. I glance across at him. Calm is how I'd describe his demeanour right now. So nothing new there.

'Care to explain further, Red?' Sean enquires, leaning back in his seat. 'Or is this another one of your flights of fancy, brought on by a little too much of this glorious New York sunshine?'

'No, it's not, actually. As you know, Sean,' I give him a meaningful look, 'I met up with Jamie's mother this morning and she has explained everything.'

I go on to tell them what Eleanor told me, and as I do Oscar's eyes grow wider at the same time as Sean's get narrower.

'In the name of Carrie Bradshaw, you couldn't make this stuff up!' Oscar cries at the end of my story. 'That is incredible, darling, and all because of your silly brooch.'

'I know, amazing, isn't it?' I look towards Sean.

He simply shakes his head. 'How do you do it?' he asks.

'What do you mean?'

'I send you over here for a simple break, some time away and a bit of a catch-up with your dad, and you end up with all this going on!' He shakes his head again. 'Your poor father, that's all I can say.'

'What do you mean, "my poor father"? I've found his long-lost son. He's going to be so happy when I reunite them.'

Sean opens his eyes wide now, not in amazement like Oscar's are, but in disbelief. 'Scarlett, for one, he doesn't even know he has a "long-lost son", let alone that he's even looking for him. And two, he might not want to *be* reunited.'

'Why ever not?'

'Do you remember what happened last time you tried to reunite your father with someone he hadn't seen for years?'

Sean is of course referring to the time I held a dinner party to reunite my two estranged parents after they hadn't seen each other for over twenty years. It didn't exactly go well. I seem to remember there was a lot of shouting and a fair bit of broken glass.

I shake my head. 'That was different. My parents had unresolved issues they needed to work through.'

Sean laughs. 'It was like a scene from the *Jeremy Kyle Show*, only slightly prettier.'

'Stop it. It worked out all right in the end, didn't it?'

'Yes it did, luckily for you. But this is different. You need to tread carefully; this is someone your father doesn't know exists, remember? And what of this Eleanor woman? He might not be too pleased to see her, either.'

I'd already thought of that. But I won't let Sean's sensible, practical ways win out.

'It will be fine; I'll make sure of it. We'll all pitch in and *make* it fine. You'll help me, won't you, Oscar?'

Oscar puts down the drink he's been sipping while Sean and I have been arguing our points. 'Of course I will, darling. Just name it!'

'Right,' I deliberately turn away from Sean. 'Well, first

we'll need to find a way to get everyone together without causing too much suspicion.'

'Hmm . . .' Oscar drums his fingers on the table while he thinks.

Sean sits back in his chair and folds his arms. 'On your own head be it!'

'Hush, Seany, I'm thinking!' Oscar snaps, holding his finger up to silence him. 'You've done your usual "this won't work, we shouldn't even try it" routine. Now let me take over.'

Sean opens his mouth to object but Oscar just waggles his finger in front of his face.

'Now then, something lovely and New Yorky, where everyone can meet up without being suspicious . . .' He purses his lips and twitches them back and forth. 'I know, what about the Brooklyn Bridge?'

'Why the Brooklyn Bridge?' I ask.

'Because that's where all the great reunions take place in movies and on TV.' He holds his arms out dramatically for effect. 'Lost souls spy their beloved from afar walking across the bridge towards them before they're even able to speak to each other. Then it takes them ages, usually because it's in slow motion or there's a musical interlude, before they can get to their loved one. It's always wonderful, and so very romantic.' Oscar clasps his hands together happily as he thinks about this.

'It would be perfect, Oscar, if I was reuniting two old flames, but I really don't think Dad and Jamie are looking for a romantic introduction, are they?'

'Hmm,' Oscar's hands wilt. 'No, you're probably right. Let me think again . . .' His eyes turn to the sky as if he's seeking heavenly inspiration. 'Aha! I've got it!'

'What, what?' I ask excitedly.

'You host a fabulous picnic, darling, in Central Park!'

'A picnic?'

'Yes,' Oscar says, his fingers wiggling in excitement. 'One of those wonderful American-style picnics like you see on TV and in the movies with Frisbees and baseball, and you invite us all along with the excuse that you want everybody to meet everyone else.'

I think about this.

'It could work, I guess. But how am I going to introduce Dad to Jamie? I can't just say, "Dad, this is your son, Jamie, this is your father". And I know it's been a long time, but I'm sure Dad will recognise Eleanor as soon as he sees her.'

'Ahem,' Sean interrupts from across the table. 'May I say something?'

'I thought you didn't want to be involved?' Oscar says huffily.

'No, go on Sean,' I say, nodding at him. 'I want as much input as possible on this.'

'This whole picnic scenario is again reminding me very much of the time you reunited your parents, Scarlett. You *do* remember that dinner party?'

'Yes, of *course* I remember it.' *Oh, why does Sean always have to be so* sensible *about everything?* 'And like I said before, it all worked out just fine in the end. So unless you've got a better idea, Sean, I think the picnic idea could work. A big family picnic will be a relaxed and happy environment for everyone to meet up for the first time. What could possibly go wrong?'

Sean sighs. 'Don't say I didn't warn you, Red. Just don't say I didn't warn you.'

Thirty

'A picnic,' Dad grumbles as I try and lay out a cloth on the grass of the Great Lawn in Central Park. 'Why a picnic?'

'I just thought it would be a nice way for everyone to get to know each other,' I say, trying to remain cool as I begin unpacking the contents of the picnic hamper Oscar and I collected from Dean & DeLuca, a gorgeous delicatessen in SoHo, earlier today. I'd remembered Will regularly visited there in the TV series *Will & Grace*, and now that I had a reason to use it myself I thought I'd give it a go. 'I've met some great people since I've been here in New York, you all know me, so I'd like you all to get to know each other.'

Dad sighs. 'All right, but I'm only doing this for you.

Where are the others, anyway? Why is it only us two here?'

'Sean has gone to get some champagne.' I'd decided at the last minute that if everything went well, a touch of bubbly might be nice. 'And Oscar has gone to borrow an ice bucket.'

Dad shakes his head in disbelief. 'Champagne and an ice bucket, who are we entertaining here, Scarlett, the President?'

Sean had said something similar when he'd gone off moaning a little while ago.

'No, I just want it to be special, that's all. Now stop standing around and help me unpack some of these things.'

Sean and Oscar return with their allotted scavenged items, and soon my picnic is looking very elegant all laid out on the lawn. Dean & DeLuca have certainly done us proud, with their assortment of fine foods.

Max is the first of our guests to arrive.

'Hey, Scarlett, Oscar,' he says jovially. Nice outfit,' he remarks to Oscar.

'Thank you, darling,' Oscar pirouettes on the grass in his lime-green dungaree shorts, black vest and yellow sun visor.

Max looks warily at Sean.

Sean extends his hand towards him. 'Max, welcome to

this slightly odd gathering Scarlett is insisting on holding on this very hot afternoon. Thanks for coming.'

Max shakes Sean's hand. 'No worries, I'll go anywhere if there's free food involved.'

'Help yourself, there's plenty. Beer?' Sean offers, holding out one of the ice-cold beers I've been chilling in a cool box.

'Nice one,' Max says taking it. 'I'm liking this picnic idea already.'

Well, that's one awkward greeting out of the way ...

Peter arrives shortly afterwards, bringing his own contribution to the proceedings: two bottles of rather expensive white wine.

'So who are we waiting for now, Scarlett?' Dad asks as he drinks from a glass of Peter's wine. 'Good choice, if I may say so, Peter. You certainly know your wine.'

'My friend Jamie. He's also bringing his mother. She's staying with him just now.'

'That's nice for him.'

It could be. On the other hand, the next few minutes could be very difficult ones indeed.

After another few minutes have passed – it seems like hours to me – I see Jamie approaching us across the grass.

'Hey,' he says as he reaches the picnic. 'Not late, am I?'

'No, not at all.' I look around for Eleanor. 'Isn't your mother with you?'

'No, she said she'd meet me here. She had a few things she needed to do first. She'll be along soon, I'm sure.'

Oh . . . could this be a smart move on Eleanor's part, I wonder? Let Jamie and Dad get to know each other a bit first before breaking the news?

'So, this is the infamous Jamie I've heard so much about,' Dad says, approaching Jamie across the grass. 'I've just been talking to your friend Max.'

Jamie waves casually to Max, who is tucking into one of the delicious cupcakes that Dean & DeLuca have provided us with.

'Hi,' Jamie says, extending his hand towards Dad. 'Pleased to meet you; you must be Scarlett's father.'

I don't know what I expected to happen when they shook hands. Maybe that it'd be how it was when I first met my mother; I knew at that very moment who she was. But Jamie and Dad just start up a conversation about Jamie's job and what he's been doing that morning. While Sean, Oscar and I stand there watching with a mixture of anticipation and amazement as if something magical is about to take place before our eyes.

'You do look familiar, now I come to think of it,' Dad says, standing back to view Jamie better. 'When I was in the UK I used to watch that channel in the morning, and I probably saw some of your reports.'

'Quite possibly,' Jamie says. 'I'm usually on quite early, though, if I'm doing a live report. It's the time difference.'

'I've always been an early riser, haven't I, Scarlett?' Dad says, bringing me in on the conversation.

'Hmm, what's that?' I'm just mesmerised seeing them standing there together. How had I not noticed it before? Jamie really is the spitting image of Dad. Dark hair, dark eyes, same build, they even have the same mannerisms. They both stand there with their legs slightly apart, arms folded, an occasional hand gesticulating around a point for added effect.

'I said,' Dad repeats for me as I move towards them, 'I've always been an early riser. That's why I think I must have seen some of Jamie's reports when I was back in the UK.'

'Yes, yes you have.' I nod hurriedly.

'You all right, Scarlett?' he asks. 'You look a bit flustered.'

'Yes, I'm fine. It's all fine. It's wonderful you two are getting on so well. I mean, considering you've just met and everything.'

'Scarlett,' Sean steps in. 'Peter would like a word.'

'Back in a mo,' I grin wildly at them both. 'You two

just keep *chatting*!' I sing, sounding like Bruce Forsyth on *Strictly Come Dancing*.

'What are you doing?' Sean whispers as he ushers me away out of earshot. 'Just stay calm, they're getting on fine.'

'I know. It's just so stressful, that's all.'

'Get this down you then,' Sean says, thrusting a glass of wine into my hand.

I knock it back in a few swift gulps.

'Blimey, Red, I didn't mean literally. Go steady, it's only lunchtime, you know.'

'By all means tell me it's none of my business,' Peter says, wandering over towards us. 'But is everything all right? You look very pale, Scarlett.'

'Peter, you once said that life with me never seemed to be dull. And you're about to witness one of those times when it will be anything but,' I say as I spy Eleanor coming towards us across the Great Lawn. 'Sean, you'd better fill this up.' I thrust my empty wineglass at him as I head over to intercept Eleanor.

'How's it going?' she asks as I reach her side. 'Have I left it long enough for them to get to know each other yet?'

'I thought that might be what you were doing. Jamie's not been here that long actually, but they seem to be hitting it off quite well. I can't believe I hadn't noticed how similar they are until now.'

Eleanor glances in Dad and Jamie's direction. 'Yes, aren't they? Your father hasn't changed all that much, you know. He's a bit greyer than I remember him, with a few more lines, maybe, but he's still the same Tom.'

Jamie looks over towards us.

'Uh-oh, we've been spotted,' Eleanor says. 'It's show time, Scarlett!'

The two of us walk casually towards the picnic party. Dad has his back to us as we approach.

'Mum,' Jamie says. 'You made it, then?'

Eleanor nods at Jamie as my father turns his head to see who the newcomer is to our proceedings.

His mouth drops open.

'Elle?' he says immediately. 'It is you, isn't it?'

'Hello again Tom,' Eleanor smiles. 'It's been a long time.'

'I ... I can't believe it,' Dad says, shaking his head in amazement. 'What are you doing here in New York ... in Central Park ... at this picnic, for heaven's sake?'

'Scarlett invited me, Tom,' Eleanor says calmly. 'I'm Jamie's mother.'

Dad shakes his head slightly as he looks at Jamie again, as though he's forgotten the rest of us are here. 'Why yes, yes of course you are. What an amazing coincidence, though, that our children know each other! I'm Scarlett's father.'

'Yes, I know.'

Dad's expression of astonishment now turns to confusion. 'How could you possibly know that?' he turns to me. 'What's going on here, Scarlett?'

I lick my lips nervously. Where was Sean with that wine? But I notice he's standing back with Peter a little way away from us, watching, and even Oscar and Max's impromptu game of Frisbee has come to an abrupt halt as they sense something big is unfolding nearby.

'Yes,' Jamie asks, looking at Eleanor. 'What *is* going on, Mum? How do you know Scarlett's father?'

Eleanor, always so strong and confident before, suddenly looks anxious and fragile. She puts her hand on Jamie's arm for support.

'Mum?' Jamie says, taking his mother's weight. 'What's wrong?'

'Let's get you over to the picnic, Eleanor,' I say, taking charge. 'We've some seats over there; you can rest for a moment.'

We quickly walk Eleanor over to the picnic and she sits down. Sean offers her a glass of water but she takes a glass of wine, as do I. We both take several large gulps.

Dad and Jamie both stand and watch us, then they look at each other, mystified.

345

'Will someone please tell us what's going on?' Jamie asks. 'Mum?'

'I will,' I say, taking a deep breath. Eleanor still looks a little pale. 'You remember when Sean challenged me to reunite a family, and that if I managed to do it, he would take my idea for setting up a business seriously?'

My father and Jamie both nod.

'Well, I've done just that. But not quite in the way I thought I might.' I can feel my heart beating hard against my chest as I get nearer to the moment of truth. 'Jamie, I'm pleased to tell you that I've found your father.'

'You have?' Jamie asks, looking shocked. 'Where is he?'

'At this very moment not that far away from you.' I glance at Dad.

Jamie screws up his face. 'Well, Scarlett? What do you mean?'

Dad nods slowly as though he's gradually absorbing all this information. 'I think that what my daughter, in her slightly Scarlett-like way, is trying to say is, and please correct me if I'm wrong, Eleanor, but I think I'm your father, Jamie.'

In our little part of the vast area of greenery that is Central Park, there's silence while everyone digests this piece of information they've just been given.

Oscar, surprisingly, is the first person to speak.

'Oh lordy, it's just like *Star Wars*,' he sings, clapping his hands together.

We all turn towards him.

'What?' Sean snaps. 'What are you talking about now, you rainbow-coloured lunatic?'

Oscar tosses his head back, ignoring Sean. 'This whole scenario,' he says, strutting forward with a wave of his hand. 'What you just said, Tom. It was just like when Darth Vader tells Luke Skywalker that he's his father. And of course, Scarlett, you would be Princess Leia, the sister Luke never knew he had.' He looks around at his audience, who are stunned into silence not only by my revelation but by Oscar's follow-up.

'Hmm, and who else do we have in this tale ... Oh yes, there's Peter, you would be Obi-Wan, the all-knowing wise Jedi, and Max, as Jamie's friend, you could be—'

'Han Solo,' Max says. 'Don't you stick me with one of the robots. I want a good part in all this. If anyone's going to be C-3PO, let it be you, you're the one with so much to say for himself all the time.'

'Hmmph,' Oscar tosses his head again. 'Now, Seany, who can we find for you to be? Something boring like a Storm Trooper.'

'I think you've probably said enough for now, Oscar,' Sean says sternly, nodding in our direction. 'Maybe it's time someone else spoke.'

347

'Of course, of course, my apologies one and all.' Oscar scuttles back out of the spotlight. 'I got a little carried away with myself, there.'

Dad and Jamie turn away from Oscar's performance to look at each other again. Each man regards the other for a few moments, neither of them speaking.

'Well, Darth,' Jamie says, breaking the silence. 'How does it feel to have a son you never knew you had?'

Oh God, Dad hates jokes, especially ones made at solemn moments like this. That won't go down well.

My father stares at Jamie for what in reality is only a few seconds, but which feels like hours to me, until finally he breaks the silence. 'I can tell you this for nothing – it feels like the Force is very definitely with me today, Luke.'

You can almost feel the sighs of relief as they rebound from one to the other of us like a line of dominoes toppling to the ground, except we're not falling down, we're virtually leaping with joy that Dad and Jamie both seem to have taken this momentous news so well.

As my father and Jamie immediately fire question after question at Eleanor, and she patiently tries to answer each one as best and as honestly as she can, I stand back and watch them, realising that it's now *my* legs that feel a tad wobbly after all that.

'You OK, Red?' Sean asks. 'Looks like you got away with it this time.'

I love hearing Sean use my nickname again. It makes me feel things are almost back to normal.

'I can't quite believe it myself, Sean. I actually got something right at long last.' I turn to him in excitement. 'I did. I got it right this time!'

Sean smiles down at me. 'You always get it right, Red. Sometimes the path you travel is a little bumpy, that's all.' He kisses me on the forehead. 'Shall I break into that champagne now?'

'Yes, let's! See, I told you we'd be needing it.'

Sean hands round eight glasses, then pops open the champagne cork and goes from person to person, filling each glass. Then he taps on the side of his own glass with a fork.

'I think this calls for a toast,' he says. 'Can I ask you all to raise your glasses to the person that's brought us all together today, and who has managed to reunite a father and son and prove me wrong about her ability to do just that. To Scarlett, everyone.'

'To Scarlett,' everyone echoes as I blush profusely.

'Thank you, but it wasn't just me. If Eleanor hadn't seen the brooch on Jamie's report, she would never have known about any of this.'

'So we have that old brooch to thank,' Dad says.

'What did you do with it in the end, Scarlett? Do you still have it?'

'Scarlett auctioned it, she tells me,' Eleanor says. 'Which is such a shame.'

'For charity, though,' I insist. 'A children's charity, too. It raised quite a bit, didn't it, Peter?'

Peter nods. 'Yes, Scarlett was very generous with her time and possessions that night. Sunnyside will benefit for a long time to come as result of that donation.'

'Not as long as they would have benefited had I sold it on your behalf,' Eleanor says resignedly.

'Why would that have made a difference?' Peter asks.

'Because, even though the brooch appears to be a replica due to its mismatched eye colour, I happen to have proof that it's not a fake at all. My brooch was actually a genuine, one hundred per cent Louis Comfort Tiffany dragonfly.'

Thirty-one

'I'm just looking through the records,' Peter says as we stand in his office in a very tall, very grand skyscraper in central Manhattan. 'It should be about … here. Yes: it was bought by a George Harrison, I remember now, he was buying it for his wife, umm …' Peter thinks, 'that would be Lucinda.'

'George Harrison, like The Beatles' George?' I ask in surprise.

'Except that that George Harrison is dead, Scarlett,' Sean reminds me.

'Yes, yes, of course I knew that. I meant, he has the same name.'

'Yes, Scarlett,' Peter says kindly. 'Like The Beatles' George. I'll give him a call, shall I? I know George and Lucinda fairly well.'

351

Sean and I take a seat in Peter's sumptuous office while he asks his secretary to get George on the phone.

After we'd got over Eleanor's shock announcement, she'd calmly explained that the brooch was an original passed down through her family for a number of generations. The reason all the experts thought it was fake, albeit an extremely good one, was because of the dragonfly's differing eye colour; a deliberate addition by the master craftsman at the time. He had been asked to make something unique for a wealthy businessman to give to his lover, something no one else would know was real, and they'd come up with the plan to replace one of the eyes. Eleanor still had the original documentation to prove the brooch's authenticity, along with the second matching eye, should someone ever want to replace it.

Oscar and I had both thought it so romantic and had ooh-ed and aah-ed at the story. Sean and Jamie had thought it mad that someone would go to so much trouble to give someone else a gift. I smile to myself; maybe they did have more in common than I'd thought.

'George … Peter. Yes, how are you?' Peter asks as his call gets put through and he swings himself around in his leather chair. 'Uh-huh … yep … sure, we can do that sometime … Look, the reason I'm phoning, George, is do you remember bidding on a brooch for Lucinda at the fundraiser you came to the other week at the Plaza?' Peter listens for a moment. 'Yes, that's the one, the dragonfly. You don't happen to know if Lucinda would be willing to sell it back to me, do you?'

After another minute or so of conversation, Peter puts the phone down. 'He's going to call her and check, but he can't see any problem. He doesn't think she's even worn it yet.'

Good – this sounds promising.

'So, how are you two?' Peter asks, looking at us both over his desk. 'After yesterday? I mean, that was a bit dramatic, wasn't it, at the picnic? I felt like I was in an episode of *Days of Our Lives*.'

'Peter, that's nothing,' Sean smiles wryly. 'That's what living with Scarlett is like on a daily basis.'

'Ignore him, Peter,' I shake my head. 'Things are good, thanks. Dad and Jamie spent some time together last night after the picnic, both with Eleanor and on their own. They seem to be coping with it all quite well.'

Peter nods. 'That's good. And yourself, Scarlett, how are you coping?'

'Me?'

'Well, you've just found out you've got a half-brother you never knew you had. Your father and Jamie aren't the only ones who've had to take that kind of news on board.'

Peter's right; with everything that's been going on in the last couple of days, I haven't given much thought to mine and Jamie's relationship in all this.

'I'll talk to Jamie when he's had a chance to get to know Dad a bit better. Besides, Jamie and I have known each other for a while now. It's only been hours for him and Dad.'

It's only really been a few days for Jamie and me. Even though it feels like I've known him for ever.

The phone rings on Peter's desk.

'Yes, put him through please, Jane. It's George,' Peter says, covering up the mouthpiece. 'George, thanks for getting back to me ... No, really? Oh, that's too bad ... Do you know which one?' Peter reaches for a pen and scribbles something on a piece of paper. 'Right ... yes, women indeed. Well, I wouldn't know, would I? Ha! Yes, maybe I'll do that. Have to go now, George, yes golf sometime soon. Bye for now.' Peter replaces the handset in its cradle. 'It's not good news, I'm afraid. Apparently Lucinda decided she didn't really like the brooch all that much when she got it home. She hadn't realised about the eyes not matching until she saw it up close. So she gave it away to a local thrift store.'

'What's a thrift store?' I ask.

'It's like one of our charity shops,' Sean says. 'Do you happen to know which one?'

'Yep,' Peter holds up the piece of paper. 'It's a Salvation Army store just off Broadway and Twelfth.'

'I can't believe someone would pay all that money for a brooch and just give it away a few days later,' I say in disbelief.

'I can,' Peter says. 'You don't know these women, Scarlett. The money they spend on clothes and jewellery in a week would keep a place like Sunnyside going for a year.'

'Come on,' Sean says, standing up. 'We'd better get going, see if this thrift store still has your brooch, and, more importantly, if we can get it back.'

'Good luck,' Peter calls as we leave the office. 'Let me know how you get on.'

As with most journeys across Manhattan, it's far easier and quicker for us to walk than to get a cab or the subway, so that's what we do.

'Funny this, isn't it?' Sean says as we walk along Park Avenue heading towards Broadway. 'It reminds me of just over a year ago, when we were searching for your lost mother across London. Now we're searching for a lost brooch on the streets of New York.'

'Yes, I suppose it is a bit déjà vu. In fact, a lot of what's gone on here has been very much like my adventures of last year.'

'Do you mean the reuniting of people at a big gathering, like you did the other day?'

355

'Yes, that and a few other things.' I think it best not to mention how my time with Jamie has reminded me of the first few weeks of my relationship with Sean.

'Were you happier then, Scarlett?' Sean asks suddenly, stopping in the middle of the sidewalk. He looks deep into my eyes as if he's searching for his answer before I get the chance to reply.

I think carefully before speaking.

'No, I wasn't happier. Things were different, that's all.'

'What do you mean?'

'I didn't know you so well then; we weren't together. Now I do, things are more stable, I suppose.'

Sean pulls a face. 'Stable. That's doesn't sound very exciting.'

'It's not supposed to. A year ago when we were chasing all over London and Paris, it *was* exciting. It was just what I needed at the time, something a bit different in my life.'

'And what about now? What do you need now?'

I think again. 'I guess I still yearn for that same sense of romantic excitement I felt when I was first with you, Sean. I can't help it; it's a part of who I am. That's what I've enjoyed about coming here to New York; I've had a little taste of that all over again. But I don't mind giving it up to be with you. I love you.'

'And I love you too, Scarlett, very much. But you make it sound like it has to be a choice; an exciting life, or me.'

'Don't be silly,' I say, wrapping my arms around him. 'I love my life with you, you know that.'

Sean is about to reply, but I stifle his doubts by placing my lips over his and kissing him very slowly.

'That might make it slightly better, I suppose,' Sean says when we've finished. 'But perhaps we'd better try that again, just so I'm a hundred per cent sure of your reassurance in this matter.'

We eventually find the Salvation Army thrift store and venture inside. It's much like a charity shop back in the UK, except the donations here are unwanted American items of clothing, jewellery, books and games, instead of British ones. A quick scout around the shop doesn't reveal the dragonfly brooch anywhere, so we go up to the counter to enquire.

'Can I help you guys?' a short, dark, quite round lady wearing a colourfully patterned blouse and a red head-scarf asks from behind the counter.

'Yes, please,' I say politely. 'We were wondering if you'd had a dragonfly brooch brought in here in the last few days.'

'A dragonfly, you say? Hmm...' She thinks about this

357

deeply for a moment. 'Tallulah!' she suddenly shrieks. 'Have we had any dragonfly brooches in here lately?'

Tallulah appears from behind a curtain, the complete opposite to her headscarfed colleague. She's tall and skinny with frizzy, bright red hair, which she has clipped up at the sides with large plastic flowers.

'Yuh, Dolores?'

'These folks want to know if we've had any dragonfly brooches brought in here in the last few days.'

Tallulah adopts a pained expression, which I assume is her thinking face, but which makes her look at this very moment as if she's trying to pass something rather hard.

'We had a necklace with a butterfly on it a couple days ago, that was pretty,' she eventually suggests.

'Any good?' Dolores asks us.

'Er, no,' I smile politely. 'It was specifically a dragonfly we were looking for, you see—'

'There's a hat in the window with an owl on,' Tallulah continues, still going though her list of animal-themed stock.

'No, it has to be this particular brooch because—'

'Earrings in the shape of a cow?'

'No.'

'Pig slippers?'

'No.'

'We've a full-sized stuffed bald eagle out back that can sit on your shoulder like a pirate's parrot. That would make a fine and novel accessory, I've always thought, haven't you, Dolores?'

Dolores is about to make a comment when Sean steps in to prevent any more nonsense. 'Ladies, I'm sure you've lots of fine things for sale; it's a very impressive store you're running here. But it's a unique brooch we're looking for. Do you keep a record of the items when they're donated, items that might be worth a few dollars more?'

Dolores looks at Tallulah, and they raise their eyebrows in a telling way. 'Oh my, Tallulah, I reckon we've only gone and got Prince William come into our store.' They both look eagerly at Sean. 'Say something else,' Dolores encourages.

'Like what?' Sean asks, looking bewildered.

'Like *whoat*,' Dolores repeats. 'Ah just love it!'

'Ladies,' Sean says, trying to calm them down, while I stifle my giggles. 'I can assure you I am not Prince William.'

'Well, you look awful familiar,' Tallulah says, eyeing him up and down. 'Doesn't he, Dolores?'

'You sure do,' she agrees. 'Hugh Grant, then?'

'No,' Sean says sternly.

'Jude Law?' Tallulah tries.

'No.' I can see Sean's starting to get angry now; the back of his neck is starting to flush red.

'Dolores, Tallulah,' I interrupt. 'I can assure you that if Sean here was a famous movie star, I'd be the first to know.'

'Well, you speak mighty fancy,' Dolores says huffily.

'So do you have a record book or something similar we could look at, please?' I ask hopefully.

Dolores looks to Tallulah for her approval. Tallulah gives it with a brief nod of her head, and a book is retrieved from underneath the desk. Dolores begins to thumb through it slowly.

'It would only have been in the last few days, we think,' I suggest helpfully.

'It will be in here if it was worth anything, honey, don't you fret.' She flicks through a few more pages, and then runs her finger down one column. 'Ah-hah! Here, one dragonfly brooch, brought in three days ago by a Mrs Lucinda Harrison.'

'That's the one, that's the one!' I shout excitedly. I look around the shop. 'Where is it, do you know?'

'Sold,' Dolores says, pursing her lips tightly. 'The day after it came in. It made fifty dollars, though, so it did well.'

'What! But that can't be possible, it was worth—'

Sean cuts me off. 'Does it say who it was sold to, Dolores?' he asks. 'Do you keep a record of that?'

Dolores shakes her head. 'No, we only record where they came from and how much they make, on the pricier items.'

I sigh. So much for that, then. A dead end. 'Thank you for your help anyway, we really appreciate it.'

'No problem,' Dolores says, putting the book back under the desk.

'I don't suppose it was either of you two that sold it?' Sean asks as a parting shot, as we're about to leave the shop.

The two of them shake their heads. 'No,' Dolores says. 'I work at the Seven-Eleven on a Wednesday, and Tallulah has her regulars at the massage parlour.'

'Sure,' Sean says as we back out of the door. 'Well, thank you for your time, ladies, it's been ... illuminating.'

'Now this really *does* remind me of last year,' I say as we walk dejectedly back down Park Avenue again. 'Getting nowhere with our enquiries.'

'Yes, and I'm afraid I've got no solutions for you this time,' Sean says. 'Tracing thrift-shoppers in New York is a bit out of my jurisdiction.'

'Damn, and that brooch would have been worth so much if it was a genuine Tiffany. Eleanor said we could use it to help Sunnyside if we found it again.'

'Do you think she meant it?' Sean asks. 'People say all sorts of things when they think the situation is one way, but if we did discover where the brooch was, do you think Eleanor would still be in such a hurry to give it away?'

'I don't know, but in theory it's not hers to give away, is it? It's Dad's, and Dad gave it to me to do what I liked with. So if we find it, it's really up to me what happens.'

'That's true.'

'But since finding the brooch now is looking about as likely as me becoming some sort of . . . film or television superstar, I really don't think we need worry too much.'

Sean smiles as he links his arm through mine. 'Red, knowing you, I wouldn't draw the line at anything!'

Thirty-two

'Are you sure about this?' I ask Jamie as we walk towards the building where his office and studio are located, just off Lexington Avenue. 'I'm not sure I'll be very good on camera.'

'Are you joking?' Jamie says as he unlocks the outer door to what appears to be a large block of apartments. 'We couldn't shut you up last time!'

Once inside, we climb a small staircase and unlock another door. This is not how I'd expected the studio to be at all. I'd thought it would be somewhere much more glamorous, and had I not known what was inside, I would have assumed it was simply more Manhattan housing hidden behind the plain brick walls.

'This is the office,' Jamie says, dropping his bag on the desk.

The office is made up of a very large desk housing several screens, computers and other gadgets that I don't recognise, a second smaller desk, a sofa, a couple of chairs and a bookshelf with lots of souvenirs and trinkets that obviously have special significance for the office users.

'This is where we do all our editing,' Jamie explains. 'When Max and I have made a film about something, we come here to edit it all together before it gets sent to London.'

'It's a nice little office,' I say, looking around me.

'Yeah, it's cool. Look,' he says, opening a door. 'We even have a shower through here. All the mod cons.'

I laugh. 'Excellent.'

'OK, what we'll do is take you into the studio in a minute and record you saying your piece. Then we can cut it in with some footage of you talking about the brooch from before, outside Tiffany's, so people can actually get to see the dragonfly.'

When we'd told Peter what had happened at the thrift store, he was already one step ahead of us.

'I thought that might happen,' he'd said. 'So I've come up with a plan.'

He'd then set about telling us his idea. I would record an appeal for my brooch, telling people the story behind it. 'Pull on folks' heartstrings,' Peter had suggested with a knowing nod of his head, and then he'd assured us he would have it played over his network on some of the news channels to see if we got any reaction.

And here I am with Jamie, at his office and studio, about to do just that. I'd offered Sean the chance to come along too, but he'd suggested this would be a good chance for Jamie and me to have some proper time together.

'Do you know what you're going to say?' Jamie asks while I look about the room nervously. We weren't even in the studio yet, and I could feel my heart beginning to race.

'Er . . . I thought I'd just talk about Dad, and how the brooch meant so much to him, and how it got given away by mistake.'

Jamie screws up his face. 'This is the US, Scarlett, you'll need a bit more than that to get them intrigued.'

'What do you think I should say, then?'

'Take a seat,' Jamie says, gesturing at the white sofa. 'Let's have a think. Right, let's see . . . ' He sits down next to me. 'You need to start by telling them how this brooch has reunited a family.'

'You mean Dad and you.'

Jamie nods. 'Yeah, me and your father.'

'He's your father now, too.'

365

'I know,' Jamie picks up a cushion from the sofa and twirls it around in his hand. 'I know.'

'How are you feeling about that?'

Jamie shrugs. 'OK I guess.'

'Did you get on all right yesterday, when you spent time together just the two of you?'

'Yeah, it was fine. But it's gonna take a while. We've only just met.'

'Of course. Dad's OK once you get used to him. He can be a bit brusque at times, but that's just his way. He says what he means.'

Jamie smiles. 'I'd rather he did. I prefer the no-nonsense approach, me.'

'Yes, you do, don't you? You know, I can't believe I didn't notice before how alike you are.'

'There was no reason you should, was there? Any more than we could have known we were brother and sister.'

An awkward silence sits down on the sofa between us while Jamie pretends to rearrange his cushion.

'I always knew we had a connection, though,' I say bravely, ignoring the invisible third party. 'Didn't you?'

Jamie looks up at me. He nods. 'Yeah, but I thought it might be something else for a while. That's kinda awkward now, isn't it?'

'Yes.' I screw up my face. 'But we did realise the other day that we didn't *actually* fancy each other . . .'

'That's true, I guess.'

The silence settles back in its seat again.

'I've never had a brother,' I venture this time. 'What are you supposed to do with one?'

Jamie shrugs. 'I don't know. Never had a sister, either. I guess we'll just gradually learn what it's all about as we go along.'

'Sounds good to me. Although I think we've been making a pretty good job of it already, don't you?'

Jamie grins. 'Yeah, sis, I think we have.'

'Right, are you ready?' Jamie asks a little while later, when we're all set up in the studio with a huge camera facing me, and two big white lights shining down onto my face.

The studio too wasn't at all what I was expecting. It was a tiny room, with a big screen at the rear, over which Jamie said we could add whatever backdrop we wanted after we'd finished filming, depending on what looked good. There were two small screens in front of me, one that showed Jamie the TV studio in the UK when he was broadcasting live, and the other what he looked like himself.

'How do you cope with all this?' I ask him as I sit nervously in the chair waiting for the off.

'You get used to it. You're lucky, I have an earpiece to

contend with as well, with all sorts of nonsense being babbled at me most of the time! Ready to go?' he asks again. 'I'll count down from three, and you'll see a red light, then you're on. OK?'

I nod.

'And stop looking like a rabbit in headlights,' Jamie laughs. 'I'm not going to run you over, just film you.'

'You might as well be. I'd be in less distress than I am right now.'

Jamie gives a dismissive shake of his head. 'In three, two, one,' he says. He nods again.

'Hi … er, my name is Scarlett … yes, that's right, it's Scarlett, and I would like to talk to you about my dragonfly that's gone missing.'

'Cut!' Jamie says, pushing a button on the camera. 'What was that? You sounded like you were going to talk about a pet.'

'I know, I know, I'm sorry. I'm just nervous.'

'Right, let's give it another go. In three, two, one.' He nods.

'Hi, I'm Scarlett, Scarlett O'Brien, you were probably thinking I was going to say O'Hara then, weren't you, like in the movie?' I bury my face in my hands even before Jamie has the chance to say 'cut'.

'What are you doing, Scarlett?' he asks. 'This isn't what we rehearsed.'

'I know, it's just, every time that red light comes on I forget everything and my brain goes to pieces.'

'I know it's hard, but just try and focus on what we talked about before, OK? Right, one more go then,' Jamie says hopefully, getting ready to push the button. 'In three, two, one.' He nods.

'Hi, I'm Scarlett O'Brien and I really need your help. You see, I'm looking for something, something quite unusual. It's a green and blue dragon, and it was mistakenly given to the Salvation Army thrift store ... What?' I ask Jamie as he reaches for the off-button again.

'You're looking for a dragon now?' Jamie pulls a face. 'Looper alert.'

'Is that what I said? Damn, this is hard.'

'I don't know why you're finding it so difficult. When we spoke to you that day outside Tiffany's you weren't nervous, you spoke to us really easily then.'

'It wasn't like this, though, was it? All formal, with lights and buttons and screens; it was just natural.'

Jamie considers this. 'Right, one minute.' He pulls his iPhone from his pocket and taps it a couple of times. 'Max, hi, yeah, what are you up to this afternoon? Not much? Great. Fancy doing some extra-curricular filming ...?'

*

369

'OK,' Jamie says. 'Are you ready?'

'Yep,' I nod.

'Are you ready?' he asks Max, who's standing in front of me with his camera on his shoulder, pointing in my direction.

'I'm always ready, you should know that by now,' Max says, not moving his head from behind the lens.

'Well, Lady Liberty is going nowhere, so let's go for it.'

We've come down to Battery Park, and we're standing on the water's edge with a distant view of the Statue of Liberty behind us. Max and Jamie had decided between them that this would be the ideal place to film me. 'Having the statue in the background will add to your tale and give it some good old Uncle Sam, Stars and Stripes, Pledge of Allegiance American pride. The viewers will love it.' Max had said.

'OK, here we go then, roll 'em, Maximilian,' Jamie calls.

Max rolls the one eye I can see from behind his camera. 'We're on,' he says calmly.

Jamie turns towards the camera.

'When Scarlett O'Brien came to New York to trace the history of a piece of antique jewellery, she didn't realise that that same brooch was in fact the key to bringing together a father and son who had never met.'

And so the interview unfolds, with Jamie asking me

about Dad and himself – carefully leaving out the fact that he is the son in question – and how the brooch has managed to reunite a family, and yet now, because of the selfless act of giving the brooch away at a charity auction, the one memento that the family would so dearly love to have in its possession has gone missing.

'So,' Jamie says to camera, 'if you see this brooch, please contact the TVA studios on the number at the end of this film, and help Scarlett fit the final missing piece back into her family's jigsaw.'

'And cut,' Max calls from behind the camera.

'Was that OK?' I ask in relief as the camera and microphone are both lowered. 'You don't think it was a bit over the top?'

'Are you kidding me?' Jamie asks. 'People will love it!'

'He's right,' Max says, putting down the camera. 'They really go for this family-in-turmoil kinda thing. That's how the whole Oprah and Jerry Springer phenomenon took off.'

'All right, well, I guess you know what you're doing.'

'By the time we edit this little baby together, you'll be a TV star all over the US of A, darlin',' Max drawls in a bad Texan accent.

'And this will be a good thing?'

'Of course!' Max assures me. 'How can it possibly be bad?'

Thirty-three

Max may have been joking, but after he and Jamie have
edited a short piece of the footage we shot in Battery Park
together with the piece of me outside Tiffany's, even I find
it quite a heart-wrenching couple of minutes to watch. So
when Peter arranges for it to be shown at the end of both
the local news bulletins and a couple of national ones, it's
then that things really start to go a little mad.

First, I'm asked to be interviewed by a couple of local
news stations, which involves me sitting in a studio much
like the one Jamie tried to film me in to begin with, with
an earpiece in my ear and a green screen behind my
chair. The presenters ask me questions, which I try to
answer as coherently as I can while feeling as if my
mouth is suddenly filled with cotton-wool balls and my
brain stuffed with something similar.

They want to know about my search, and how I found out I had a brother, and how we're all getting on now we've been 'reunited', and the odd thing is, the interviews seem to go fairly well. I don't make a complete fool of myself or babble on about something quite irrelevant like the movie I watched on cable last night, or the shoes I saw in the window of Saks on the way to the studio.

But even after all the news bulletins and the interviews, we still have no new leads on the dragonfly. The person who has it can't live in New York, can't watch television, or can't want to be found.

The madness really starts to take hold when calls like this begin coming in.

'Scarlett,' Sean says, holding the hotel room phone away from his face. 'It's *Marsha & Friends* – it's like a daytime chat show here, and they want you to come on their show as a guest to talk about your hunt for the brooch.'

'Me?'

'*Yes*,' Sean says slowly as if I'm a child. '*You*, Scarlett. Will you do it? Can you cope?'

'Of course I can cope.' Being a guest on *Marsha & Friends* can't be that different to the local news interviews I've done so far, can it? 'Of course I'll do it, Sean. Tell them yes.'

But I may have underestimated quite how different it is.

'So, Scarlett,' Marsha asks me from her side of the desk as I try to get comfortable on the incredibly hard sofa her guests are expected to sit on. 'Tell us how this dragonfly brooch we've all been hearing so much about brought you here to New York to search for your family.'

'Well, that's not quite how it happened, Marsha.'

'But didn't you go across to Ellis Island to try and trace them?' Marsha asks, leaning in towards me. 'That's usually what people go there for.'

How did she know about that?

'Yes, I did go to Ellis Island as a tourist, and yes, I did search for my family while I was there, but I didn't find anything out. My friend Oscar did, though, he found he was related to a long line of Italian—'

'So what made you want to begin searching for your family then, Scarlett?' Marsha cuts me short. 'Did you have a difficult childhood?'

'No, I had a very happy childhood, actually.'

'Both parents at home?'

'No, just my dad, but—'

'Aha, so you felt the need to search for a long-lost mother?'

'No, I did that last year back in the UK and I found her, and we're all quite happy now.'

Marsha opens her eyes wide and I see a glint.

'You searched for your long-lost mother and found her? Tell us about that.'

I tell Marsha, her audience and the viewing public as quickly as I can about how I'd looked for and found my mother last year.

'And this is how you met your boyfriend? How wonderful is that, ladies and gentlemen!' Marsha turns to the audience, who burst into spontaneous applause, encouraged by the floor assistant who madly waves her arms in the air at them.

'Is he here?' Marsha asks.

'Yes, he's over there.' I point to Sean sitting in the audience.

The camera swings around and pans in on Sean who, redder than I've ever seen him before, smiles – though I can tell it's more of a grimace – at the camera and half raises his hand in acknowledgement.

I grin at him, and as soon as the camera swings away from him he pulls a pained face back at me.

'So, is this what drove you to help your father to meet with his son, so they could share that same sense of joy and belonging as you'd felt?'

'No, not at all to begin with. I didn't know about Jamie when I came here to New York. We met accidentally when I was researching the dragonfly brooch, and he filmed me for a TV station over in the UK . . .'

I go on to tell Marsha the whole story while her audience sit enraptured.

'But I do know what it feels like when you don't know your whole family. You feel like you're not quite complete. A piece of your jigsaw is always missing, is the way I'd describe it. Which is why I want to set up a trust to help people find their lost relatives.'

'Yes, I've heard about this. Tell us more,' Marsha asks eagerly.

I tell her about Sunnyside and the children there, and all the other people I think I could help with my idea. And by the time I've finished, Marsha actually looks quite moved, and a couple of the women in the audience are dabbing at their eyes with tissues.

'So this would be a charitable organisation?' Marsha asks.

'In the main, yes. Obviously if someone was able to pay and wanted our help, then the fee would go towards helping others.'

'Well, Scarlett, it may all have happened accidentally for you, but it sounds absolutely fantastic, and I wish you the best of luck with everything. Oh, just one more thing: what will you call this charitable trust, if you manage to set it up? Just so our viewers can look out for it?'

Oh ... I hadn't thought of a name ...

'The Dragonfly Trust,' I announce off the top of my head.

'Of course, how perfectly apt; let's hope you manage to trace your mascot again. I'd like to thank you for being such a wonderful guest today.' She holds up her hand. 'Scarlett O'Brien, everyone. And remember, if you see that dragonfly brooch, get in touch with us!'

And that's not the only interview I'm asked to do.

Over the next week, I do three more US TV shows, all of them national, and the phone never stops ringing. Sean is constantly on his mobile, taking calls from companies and individuals offering to donate to this new venture of mine, once I get it up and running.

'Well, Red,' he says one evening when we've finally got some time alone and we're out having dinner together. 'It looks like I was wrong. Looks like this really might be a viable business. *If* you can actually trace people, that is. The success you had with your dad and Jamie was just luck, really.'

'That doesn't matter. If all these people are going to put their faith in me, I'll do it.'

Sean smiles. 'You're a very determined person, aren't you, when you put your mind to something. Scatty a lot of the time, with your head in the clouds, but your heart is in the right place, and that's what really counts in life.'

'What's made you suddenly say that?'

'I've been doing a lot of thinking lately, that's all. About us, and what it will mean if you start running this business over here.'

I put my hand across the dinner table and take hold of his. 'It doesn't have to change anything. Things will just be a bit different, that's all. I'll be here in New York some of the time, and in London the rest. A bit like you, when you're jetting off on your business trips.'

Sean nods. 'I know; it's just odd.'

'What, because it's me doing it and not you?'

'No, I don't mean that. I mean ...' He struggles, which is very unlike Sean. 'I know you had the business with your father before, but that was different. This time it will be all yours, and it sounds as if it could be big, too, from the interest we've been getting already. But if you've got all that going on in your life ... Well, you might not need me in it any more.'

I'm almost lost for words. This is *so* unlike Sean. He's usually so confident and self-assured about everything.

'Sean, don't be silly! Of course I need you, I'll always need you.'

'Really?' Sean looks across at me with genuine concern on his face.

'Yes! Absolutely I will.'

'Even if life with me isn't very exciting any more?'

'Sean, please. I love every day I spend with you, whether there's excitement involved or not.'

Sean is about to say something else, but his phone rings; he rolls his eyes. 'Better get it; it might be more investors in your scheme. We'll be needing an assistant and an office soon, if it carries on like this.' He gets up from the table and takes his phone outside.

I think about him while he's gone. I've never seen Sean like this … how would I describe it … lost, vulnerable even. The last time I'd seen him look anything like that was when we were at the top of the London Eye together last year, and he was about to declare his true feelings for me.

'Scarlett,' Sean says coming back into the restaurant. 'Good news. Peter thinks he might have found your brooch.'

Thirty-four

'Where?'

'A lady has just called the TV station and said she saw it being worn at a fashion show about a week ago.'

'A fashion show? How ever could it have ended up on a runway?'

'I don't know.' Sean throws some dollars on the table. 'But Peter has a name we can speak to at the fashion house. He's already called, and we can go round and see the chap now.'

'At this time of night?'

'Yeah, he's working late, apparently. Come on, Scarlett, look sharp. Do you want to get this brooch back, or not? Plus,' he grins, 'We're off again – it's just like old times!'

We head over to the address Peter has given us. Wave Designs, just off Fifth Avenue, is located three storeys up in one of the older buildings I'd admired, when I first came to New York, as being brave enough to hold its own against the soaring new ultra-modern skyscrapers that dominate the skyline.

We buzz the intercom outside, then take the elevator up to the third floor and Sean knocks on the appropriate door along the hall.

'Yo, it's open,' a male voice calls.

We push the door ajar to find a large open-plan office. Inside there are boards all over the walls with sketches and swatches of fabric covering them. Desks are equally as haphazardly strewn with paper, fabric, plans, old coffee cups – just about everything you might find in a fashion designer's office. Except that it's not sleek and sophisticated, as I would have expected a New York fashion house to be; it's really a bit of a pickle.

'You guys must be the Scarlett and Sean Peter was telling me about. I'm Julian, Julian Jackson, I'm the owner of Wave, how can I help you?'

In contrast, Julian is dressed a bit more how I imagine a fashion designer should look. He's wearing an eclectic mix of clothes, some new, some possibly second-hand, in an assortment of mismatched colours. His look is completed with a purple trilby sporting a brown ostrich feather. Oscar couldn't have worn it better if he'd tried.

'Yes, we are,' Sean says, walking over to shake Julian's hand. 'Our apologies for bothering you at this time of night, Julian, but Peter said you might have some information for us.'

'Yeah, he said you were looking for a brooch, right, and some lady had seen it at one of our shows?'

'Yes, that's right. I guess one of the models might have been wearing it,' I suggest hopefully.

'We showed all our new collections recently, not quite on the scale of New York Fashion Week, you understand, just a few local events,' he explains. 'We're just a small outfit. I'm only lucky enough to have an off-Fifth Avenue address to work from because my uncle owns this building and rents me these offices pretty dirt cheap.'

'I see.' *That explains a few things*. 'Well, it's a brooch in the shape of a dragonfly. It's green and blue, about this big.' I hold up my fingers to demonstrate.

'Hmm . . .' Julian thinks. 'Blue and green, you say? I wonder if we used it on the *Enchanted* collection. My assistant was in charge of gathering accessories for that one. Just one moment, she's out back.'

He goes to a door and calls down a staircase. 'Jenny, darling, could you come up here? There are some people that would like to ask you a couple of questions.'

Suddenly I get an odd feeling in the pit of my stomach. And that feeling only intensifies when 'Jenny' appears at the top of the stairs, carrying a roll of fabric that's almost as big as she is.

'What's wrong, Ju?' she asks, resting the roll on the ground so that she can see who she's talking to. And now we can see all too clearly that the person standing in front of us wearing a crimson dress is Sean's ex, Jennifer.

'What the hell are you doing here?' she asks, running her hand over her blond hair and straightening her skirt.

'I might ask you the same thing!' I demand. 'You told Oscar you worked as a PA for the boss of a high-class fashion house.'

Jennifer wrinkles her pert little nose. 'I may have exaggerated that fact slightly when I spoke to him over the phone. How the hell did I know you two were going to show up here? Anyway, it wasn't a complete lie; it's in my career plan. Sorry, Ju,' she says when Julian makes a small pained noise behind her. 'But even you know we're just small fry here. Looking good as ever, Sean,' she says, fluttering her spider-like eyelashes at Sean.

I can only shake my head at the audacity of her.

'The feeling isn't mutual, Jen, I can assure you,' Sean

replies flatly. 'We're here about a brooch. A dragonfly brooch, to be precise. Do you have it?'

'I'm sorry, you'll have to be a bit *more* precise,' Jennifer says, her blue eyes wide with innocence. 'What exactly do you mean – a dragonfly?'

'Oh, for God's sake, Jennifer, stop messing about,' I snap. 'You know exactly what Sean means. It's the brooch I auctioned off at the ball we were at the other week.'

Jennifer pretends to think. She puts a bright pink fingernail to her chin. 'Can't say it rings any bells.'

I'm about to lunge at her, but Sean holds me back. 'Don't let her wind you up, Red.'

'Oh, how very quaint, you have nicknames for each other; what does she call you, Sean, Yellow?'

'Enough, Jen,' Sean says firmly. 'Did you, or did you not, use that same brooch in a show recently?'

'I might have.' Jennifer says huffily. 'But I bought it fair and square in a thrift store. It's not like I stole it, is it? It was just there waiting to be purchased.'

'But you must have known it was the same brooch,' I ask, trying to remain calm.

'So?' Jennifer shrugs her bony shoulders. 'There's no law against me buying your old tat, is there? It was perfect for the show.'

Sean's hand is already there in front of me before I can move.

'Don't you watch TV, Jen?' he asks calmly. 'Only Scarlett's been all over it this week, appealing for help in finding that brooch.'

'Not that much, no,' Jennifer says airily. 'What's she been on? Some grotty little cable channels that no one watches, that go out in the middle of the night?'

I hope they don't have a smoke alarm in here, because the amount of steam coming out of my ears right now is bound to set it off in a minute.

'Pretty much every prime-time TV channel, talk show and news bulletin,' Sean says proudly. 'You can't have missed her.'

'Well I'm afraid I did.'

'I thought you looked familiar.' Julian, who has been perched on the edge of a desk watching in wonder at all this unfolding in his offices, suddenly pipes up. 'Weren't you on *Marsha* the other day? We watched that, don't you remember, Jenny? When we were waiting for that fabric to be delivered, we had it on in the office.'

Jennifer flushes the same colour as the burgundy velvet she's been carrying up the stairs. 'No, can't say that I do, Ju. I don't think I was really watching it.'

'Yes you were, you made a comment about how it looks like TV actually adds more like twenty pounds than ten, and ... oh my,' Julian says, realising what he's saying.

'So you did see it, then?' Sean asks. 'Why didn't you give me a ring and tell us you had the brooch?'

'Because,' Jennifer snaps, shoving her roll of fabric to the ground. 'Because of *her*.' She points viciously at me. 'She always gets everything.'

'Whatever do you mean?' I ask. 'I don't get everything. Far from it.'

'You got Sean. You took him from me.'

'No I didn't, and you know it. He wasn't yours to take by then, anyway.'

I glance at Julian, who's looking even more mystified now. 'Jennifer thinks I stole Sean away from her. The truth is he wasn't interested in getting back together with her.' I quickly explain for his benefit.

Julian nods encouragingly.

'And you took my brother away from me. It's all "Scarlett this" and "Scarlett that" when you speak to him. At least when he was friends with that other girl he had more time for me.'

'Do you mean Ursula? Oscar still is friends with her, we both are. You're just being ridiculous now, and anyway, how can he have time for you? You live on the other side of the world from him.'

Unfaltering, Jennifer tosses her hair back over her shoulders. 'And then finally you monopolised Jamie at the ball. You weren't content with having Bradley Cooper fawning over your every move onstage, and everyone telling you how wonderful you were at helping out with the auction by giving away your own stuff, no: you had to take him away from me too.'

'I did nothing of the sort! And Jamie's my brother, for God's sake.'

'But you didn't know that at the time, did you? No, Jamie wasn't interested in being with me. He kept wanting to know if you were OK, and where you were all night. Do you know what that feels like? Do you?'

I shake my head.

'No, I thought not. Because everyone wants to be Scarlett's friend, everyone wants to help Scarlett. Because Scarlett is so bloody well damn-near perfect, isn't she? Well, just this once I wanted to mess things up for you so you didn't have your fairy-tale ending. Everything *didn't* go according to the will of Scarlett. But here you are, claiming your stupid dragonfly back and making me look like the villain of the piece yet again.' She folds her arms and turns her head away from us.

There's silence in the room as we all reel a little from Jennifer's outburst, and I feel something I never thought I'd feel for Jennifer: it's pity. She must be very insecure to behave like this.

'I'm sorry to hear you feel like that about me, Jennifer,' I say in as sympathetic a voice as I can muster.

'I can assure you, I'm not perfect. Far from it. Anyone who spends any time with me can vouch for that. Few things I do ever go according to plan. But,' I glance over at Sean, 'my heart is in the right place, and everything I do, I do with the genuine intention of trying to help the people around me.' Sean smiles lovingly back at me. I turn towards Jennifer. 'So if you have a problem with my actions, I'm sorry, but it's your problem, I'm afraid. It's certainly not mine.'

Jennifer scowls at me so ferociously I'm surprised her Botox will allow such a deep furrow to appear in her forehead.

'Jen, are you going to do the right thing and give me my dragonfly back?' I ask, again surprised I'm able to remain this calm.

Casting one last vindictive look in my direction, Jennifer swivels on her heels and stomps off downstairs. She returns a few minutes later with a box, which she thrusts at me. 'Here, take it.'

'Thank you,' I say, taking it from her. I open up the box and there inside, winking up at me with its one blue eye and one black, is my dragonfly. I reach into my bag and open up my purse. 'Please have this,' I say, thrusting a fifty-dollar bill into her hand.

'What's it for?' she asks, looking at the money.

'I'm reimbursing you what you paid for the brooch at

the thrift store. I wouldn't want you to think I'd stolen something else from you, now would I?'

As we thank Julian and leave the offices, I clutch the dragonfly tightly in my hand. It feels as if I've been reunited with yet another member of my ever-growing family.

Thirty-five

'The reason I've gathered you all here today is that I have it back again,' I announce to the table as everyone sips their drinks and makes polite conversation in between courses at the lunch I've organised at the Serendipity 3 restaurant.

Everyone turns expectantly towards me.

'With help from Peter, and of course you, Jamie, and Max, Sean and I managed to locate the dragonfly a couple of days ago. We won't go into the details now, it's too complicated.' I try not to look at Oscar. I don't really want him knowing too much about Jennifer. 'Anyway, this is why I've asked you all here today, so that I can formally return the brooch to its original owner, Eleanor.'

Oscar claps excitedly as I take the dragonfly in its blue

box and walk around the table to where Eleanor is seated. She smiles as she pushes her chair back and stands up to greet me. As she takes the dragonfly from my hand, she gives me a kiss on the cheek and whispers, 'Thank you,' into my ear.

While I return to my seat, Eleanor remains standing. She looks down at the dragonfly now lying in the palm of her hand. Then she holds it up to the light so that its green and blue body shimmers and sparkles under the bright lights of the restaurant.

'Well, my friend,' she says, 'you've not changed much over the years, but countless other things have, and now it's time for you to bring some sparkle to the eyes of many others instead of being kept inside a box where no one can see you.'

She looks up at me. 'Scarlett, this brooch doesn't belong to me; I gave it to your father many, many years ago. Really, it still belongs to him. And if I'm not mistaken, he recently gave it to you to do as you wanted with it.' She turns to Dad. 'Am I correct, Tom?'

My father nods. 'You are indeed, Elle.' As he beams up at Eleanor, I see a look on Dad's face when she returns his smile that I've never noticed before, and I feel a lump in my throat as I realise the dragonfly may have reunited more than just a family.

'And so,' Eleanor continues, 'I think the best thing

my dragonfly friend here can do is to continue living with you, Scarlett, for the time being.' She walks over to me and pins the brooch on my top. 'You don't need it right now – you've already got so many investors wanting to help you out with the Dragonfly Trust – but if you ever should, this little chap will bring you plenty of dollars to help you continue your good work.'

'Are you absolutely sure, Eleanor?' I ask, looking down at the brooch.

'Scarlett, I couldn't ask for a better home for it to go to. I know you'll take good care of it. Just like your father has, all these years.'

As Eleanor and I hug, the dragonfly, so good at reuniting others, is pressed firmly between the two of us.

The rest of the lunch is a lovely, light-hearted affair with much laughter and jokes. I notice when we're finishing dessert that Sean has been missing for a while.

'Have you seen Sean?' I ask Oscar, as he scrapes the last remnants of ice-cream sundae from his bowl.

'Er … he said he had to pop out a while ago. Something about some business, I think,' Oscar replies, licking his spoon. 'Oh my days, that was the best sundae ever!' he says, checking his bowl to make sure it's all gone.

'Do you want to put that bowl down on the table and

lick it out with your tongue like a dog?' I ask. 'You look like you're going to anyway.'

'Do you think anyone would mind?' Oscar says, actually looking around him.

'Yes, I do! And when did Sean say he had to pop out? I don't remember seeing him go.'

'I think you were talking to Jamie and your dad at the time,' Oscar says, pushing his bowl away from him. 'He said he didn't want to disturb you.'

'Oh . . . oh, right.'

'Scarlett,' Peter says, walking around to my side of the table. 'Thank you so much for this fantastic lunch, but I really have to be going now.'

'So soon?' I say, standing up.

'Yes, I'm afraid so. The business won't run itself.'

'Sure. Thank you so much for coming, Peter, and for all your help in getting the dragonfly back. We couldn't have done it without you.'

'It's very beautiful,' Peter says, admiring the brooch. 'Much like its new owner. You two complement each other well.'

'You charmer,' I say, giving Peter a kiss on the cheek. 'Thank you again, for everything. Meeting you has changed my life. You know that, don't you? I don't know what might have happened if you hadn't thought I was choking in that Italian restaurant.'

'Well, you know what we always say, Scarlett, don't you?'

'*Everything happens for a reason*,' we chime in unison, grinning at each other.

'I'll be seeing you very soon, I expect!' Peter calls, as he waves goodbye and heads for the door.

'Scarlett, so sorry,' Jamie says, appearing next to me now with Max. 'But we've been called away on an urgent story. Gotta go!'

'Really? That's a shame, but thanks for coming anyway, guys, and for all your help again.'

'No worries, it's been a blast,' Max says. 'Who would have thought bumping into you while out doing vox pops would have turned into all this?'

'Yes, indeed. I thought I'd return to the UK with a few souvenirs of NY, but I didn't quite foresee a new brother being one of them.'

Jamie grins at me, and I give both him and Max a big hug.

'Scarlett.' It's Dad now, and Eleanor. 'Elle and I are going to leave you as well, if you don't mind; we've got some catching-up to do. Old times, and all that.'

Dad and Eleanor exchange the kind of knowing look only old friends who understand each other well can share.

'Sure, you two go and have fun,' I say, feeling like a

parent sending their child out on a first date. 'You both deserve it.'

I watch them leave, and turn back to Oscar. 'Looks like it's just you and me, then. More sundae?' I ask, in an attempt to keep at least one member of my party with me.

'Actually, sweetie, I might already have had a bit too much,' Oscar says, holding his stomach and pulling a face. 'I think a little afternoon siesta is in order. I'll catch you back at the hotel later, though, yes darling?'

Before I have time to respond, Oscar makes a dash for the door.

Great. I sink back down into my seat. Not only am I on my own, but I've been left with the bill, too. Some celebration.

One of the waiters comes over to me. 'Your tab, ma'am,' he says, holding out a silver tray.

'Thanks,' I say, taking the folded piece of paper from him. I hardly dare look at what it says as I open it up. But to my surprise, inside there is not a long list of food, drink and prices, but a typed note.

Are you suddenly finding yourself Home Alone*?*
Almost feeling Lost in New York*? 'Imagine' what it*
would be like to find a new friend to join your pack.
Follow the clues and you might do just that …

What on *earth*? I look up at the waiter. 'What is this?' I ask. 'I thought you were bringing me my bill?'

'I'm only doing as I was instructed, ma'am,' he says. He glances down at the piece of paper. 'What do you think it means? We've all been wondering.'

'You mean, you looked at it before you brought it over to me?' I ask disapprovingly.

He blushes. 'Well, ma'am, the gentleman was very specific about exactly when we deliver the note, and we all wondered what it was.'

'It makes no sense,' I say, looking at it again.

'Janet in the kitchen said it read like one of those cryptic crosswords, you know, the kind where you have to read between the lines?' he suggests helpfully. 'Try looking at it again.'

I reread the note. 'Hmm ... am I feeling *Home Alone*? Well, all my so-called friends and family have left me sitting all alone in your restaurant, so yes, I am a bit lonely. Almost feeling *Lost in New York* ... no, I'm not lost. Wait a minute ... ' I think about what I've just said; it sounds vaguely familiar. 'Does it mean the movie *Home Alone – Lost in New York*? Could it be that, do you think?'

The waiter shrugs. 'I don't know, ma'am, what else does it say?'

I look down at the paper again. '"Imagine" finding a new friend to join your pack ... What am I supposed to imagine about the *Home Alone* movie? That one was set in New York, in lots of places around the city ... much of it in Central Park with the Pigeon Lady, but I don't know where, exactly.'

'Excuse me for interrupting,' a lady sitting at the next table says. 'But I couldn't help overhearing. May I suggest something?'

'Yes, yes, please do,' I say gratefully, turning towards her.

'What about Strawberry Fields in Central Park? There's a memorial there to John Lennon, it's got the word *Imagine* inscribed across the centre of it.'

I reread the clue again.

Are you suddenly finding yourself Home Alone*?*
Almost feeling Lost in New York*? 'Imagine' what it*
would be like to find a new friend to join your pack.
Follow the clues and you might do just that ...

I almost go over and hug her. 'Yes, I think you could be right; it makes sense. That has to be it. Thank you, thank you so much!'

'My pleasure,' she says. 'How exciting to be involved in a real-life treasure hunt.'

Is that what this is, I wonder as I stand up to leave. 'Oh – I still need to pay you,' I say to the waiter.

'No need, ma'am, it's all been settled.'

'By the same man that left the note?' I ask.

He nods.

'Thank you, then.'

'I just need to give you one more thing.' He produces a small silver key from the pocket of his apron.

'What's this for?' I ask, looking at the key.

'Again, I don't know. Just my instructions to give you the key when you'd worked out the clue. Good luck, miss,' he calls as I thank him again and leave the restaurant. 'Let us know if you find the treasure!'

Luckily, Serendipity 3 is only a few blocks from the edge of Central Park, so it doesn't take me too long to get over there and find my way to Strawberry Fields, wondering all the time just what's going on as I clutch the piece of paper with the 'clue' on it tightly in my hand. I have a strange feeling this is something to do with Sean, but why would he be writing me a clue to get me to come to Central Park?

I arrive at the quiet area of the park dedicated to the memory of John Lennon, and find the central grey and white mosaic with the title from the late Beatle's most iconic song etched across the centre. There are a few tourists about, laying flowers on the mosaic, saying prayers and taking photos. But what is it I am supposed to find here? I look at the paper again.

Are you suddenly finding yourself Home Alone?
Almost feeling Lost in New York? *'Imagine' what it*
would be like to find a new friend to join your pack.
Follow the clues and you might do just that …

A new friend to join my pack? I look around me and notice, sitting on a bench away from everyone else, a man. He's wearing jeans, a white t-shirt, dark sunglasses and a baseball cap pulled down over his face. He casually raises his hand and waves quickly at me.

Oh boy, do I go over? It's against everything you're taught, approaching strangers in Central Park, but he looks harmless enough.

I walk over to the bench and sit down a little way away from him.

'Didn't your mom ever teach you not to talk to strangers?' a familiar voice says from under the cap.

I look hard at him from across the bench. It wasn't, was it?

'Care to join my Wolf Pack?' Bradley Cooper says, grinning at me.

'But what are you doing here?' I ask in amazement. 'I thought …'

'You thought what?' Bradley asks.

'No, no matter,' I reply, shaking my head. Maybe it wasn't Sean, after all.

'I did say if you ever needed anything while you were here in New York, remember . . .' He smiles. 'So I have a gift for you.' Reaching into his pocket, he pulls out a key. Attached to the key is another note. 'Here.' He slides it across the bench, then slides himself along next to it.

I try not to think too much about how he's actually here with me right now, or how good he smells as he sits this close. 'Why the keys?' I ask.

'I don't know,' Bradley says. 'Just read the note.'

I open up the note; it's in the same italic print as before. I read it out loud:

Prickly and not heavy at all, even though a lot of breakfast is eaten outside.

'What the hell does *that* mean?' Bradley asks. 'I've been wondering that since I got it.'

'I know exactly what it means,' I grin. 'It's Tiffany's, isn't it?'

'How did you get that to equate to Tiffany's?'

'*Prickly and not heavy at all* is Holly Golightly – Audrey Hepburn's role in the movie, and then the iconic scene at the very beginning where she eats her breakfast outside.'

Bradley shakes his head. 'You English folk sure have one strange sense of humour.'

'So it was someone English that gave you this clue, then?' I ask, pricking up my ears.

'That,' Bradley says, pulling his cap back down over his eyes, 'I am not at liberty to tell you.'

'Do you want to come to Tiffany's with me?' I ask, thinking he'll say no.

'Are you kidding?' Bradley sits up again. 'Of course! This is the most fun I've had in ages. I wanna see what's going to happen next!'

Thirty-six

We arrive at Tiffany's, and immediately I spot Max waiting outside on the sidewalk.

'Max,' I call. 'Are you my clue, by any chance?'

Max waves us over. 'I was supposed to wait inside, but it's not really my sort of place, Tiffany's. Who's your friend?'

'Max, meet clue number one, clue number one, meet Max.'

Bradley lifts up his hat for a moment, and Max nearly melts into the sidewalk.

'But you're Bradley—' he begins before we hush him.

'Sorry,' he says lowering his voice. 'You're Bradley Cooper.'

'So I've been told,' Bradley says. 'Good to meet you, Max.' He holds out his hand for Max to shake, and Max takes it like it's royalty.

'But how come you're *here*?' Max gasps, still looking with awe up at Bradley.

'Let's just say I owed Scarlett a favour, so when I got the call I couldn't refuse.'

Max is about to ask him something else when I interrupt.

'When you two have quite finished ... Max, do you have another clue for me?'

'Yep.' Max reaches into his pocket and pulls out yet another key with a note attached.

'Does anyone know what the significance of the keys is?' I ask.

They both shrug. 'No idea,' Max says. 'So we didn't lose the clues, maybe?'

'What's this one say?' Bradley asks eagerly.

I open up the note and read.

Better get your skates on, Scarlett, or you'll miss this happy coincidence.

Max and Bradley look blankly at each other.

'This is too easy,' I say laughing. 'It's the Wollman Rink from *Serendipity*.'

'You mean, we've got to go back to Central Park?' Bradley whines. 'We've only just come from there!'

'Oh, stop moaning,' I joke as I set off back in the direction we've just come from. 'What do you want, a chauffeur-driven limo to take you there?'

'Could you get us one of those, Brad?' Max asks as he hurries along behind us. 'It would be kinda cool.'

We arrive at the Wollman Rink and I look around for my next clue-bearer, but I don't immediately see anyone familiar at all. Then I see a single glove lying on a nearby bench, so I dash over and pick it up.

'I knew you'd see that,' Jamie says, appearing from behind a tree. 'Just like in the movie, eh? That little touch was my idea.'

'You're involved in this too?' I ask him. 'What's going on?'

'Can't say,' he says mysteriously. 'But look inside the glove.'

I open up the glove and there inside is another key and a clue.

Use all your spirit *to get here, but don't* bust *anything because you may find all the city girls have left the building single.*

I think about this for a moment. 'Hmm . . .'

'Hey, aren't you—' Jamie says, suddenly noticing Bradley standing next to Max.

'Yes he is,' I say quickly. 'No time to explain now. What does this mean, do you think? The words "spirit" and "bust" are highlighted, to begin with.'

'Spirit could mean alcohol, like in whiskey,' Max suggests.

'Or spirit as in ghost?' Jamie says.

'*Ghostbusters*!' Bradley shouts, then quickly lowers his voice. 'I mean, *Ghostbusters*. *Spirit* as in *ghost*, added to the *bust* part.'

'Yes, I think you're right there,' I agree. 'But what about the rest? *All the city girls have left the building single*? What building?'

'What building is in *Ghostbusters*?' Max asks, thinking out loud.

'Er ... lots,' Jamie says. 'At the beginning of the movie, the New York Public Library is haunted, and then—'

'Wait, that's it!' I shout excitedly. 'The New York Public Library is where Big jilts Carrie in the *Sex and the City* movie, Oscar told me. It makes sense – *All the city girls have left the building single*. Come on!'

As we dash back down Fifth Avenue, I'm a hundred per cent sure it will be Oscar who's waiting for me with the next clue. The venue of Carrie Bradshaw's wedding ... it has to be! But as we run up the steps and in

405

through the front doors, I see Peter waiting at the foot of one of the great long marble staircases.

He nods calmly at us as we all career towards him.

'Scarlett, Jamie, Max, Bradley,' he says, acknowledging us all; and he doesn't seem in the least bit surprised to see Bradley.

'Peter, you too?' I ask him.

'Yes, Scarlett, me too,' he smiles. 'Is this what you're looking for?' He dangles yet another key in my face. I'm getting quite a collection in my pocket now.

'Yes please.' I take the key from him and read the attached clue.

Chopsticks with his feet – is there anything this man can't do? He could probably go to infinity with his talents ...

A stony silence fills the space between the five of us as we all try and figure out the latest riddle.

'*Chopsticks* ...' Bradley ponders. 'Chinese?'

'Nah,' Max says. 'Too easy, and how would you use them with your feet, anyway?'

'*Infinity ... go to infinity ...*' Jamie repeats. 'There's something about that that rings a bell.'

'Sounds like Buzz Lightyear,' I laugh. 'Who played Buzz? No, that was just Tim Allen.'

406

'But Tom Hanks played Woody,' Peter says. 'If that helps?'

'Tom Hanks, hmm … think about Tom Hanks movies, everyone.'

We all stand in the New York Public Library foyer thinking hard about Tom Hanks, and then almost in unison shout, '*Big*!'

'Yes,' I say joyfully. 'He played chopsticks with his feet on the Big Piano in FAO Schwarz. Looks like we're off again, folks!'

Along Fifth we go again, my posse of cohorts getting ever larger now. Blimey, if I could pick up followers this quickly on Twitter, I'd be laughing, I half think to myself as we make our way together.

Into FAO Schwarz we bundle up the escalator to the first floor, where we find the 'Big' piano in full swing, with none other than Oscar himself dancing away on it.

'Oscar,' I call. 'It's me.'

'Ah, you're here at last,' Oscar says, still continuing with his dancing, his brow furrowed, deep in concentration. 'I won't keep you a minute, darling, but I've been waiting ages for my turn on this.'

We all stand impatiently while Oscar finishes his own colourful rendition of *Chopsticks*, then he takes a great, florid bow at the end before leaping energetically off the piano.

'Quite the band of merry men you've gathered around

you, eh, darling?' he says, looking admiringly at my fellow treasure-hunters all eagerly awaiting their next clue. 'I say,' he croons as his eyes rest on Bradley. 'You certainly don't mess about. We meet again, Mr Cooper.'

'The clue, Oscar, the clue?' I demand, wondering how many more of them there can be.

'Here you are,' Oscar says, pulling the key from a small satchel with a flourish. 'Good one, this.'

'You've looked?' I ask, as I open up the clue.

'Did you expect anything less of me, sweetie?' Oscar says with his hands on his hips.

'What does it say?' Bradley asks.

I glance at him; I think he's enjoying this more than any of us.

I'll have what she's having.

'*When Harry Met Sally*!' we all shout.

'The diner,' I say. 'The diner where Meg fakes it. Does anyone know where that is?'

'I do!' Max shouts, his hand in the air in a 'pick me' fashion. We're all so wound up, we're like excited schoolchildren.

'Well lead the way then, good sir!' I grin, as we all follow Max down the escalator, out of the store and back down Fifth Avenue again.

'I wish the person that put these clues together had put them in an order where we didn't have to keep passing the same places,' Bradley grumbles as we go by Tiffany's again, and then the New York Public Library, trying to hail cabs as we go.

'Do you know who's done this, then?' I ask him as we hurry along together behind Max and a sprightly Oscar, with Peter and Jamie following up the rear.

'Yep,' he says, winking at me. 'But my lips,' he makes a zipping motion across them, 'are sealed,' he says out of the corner of his mouth.

We finally arrive at Katz's Deli on the Lower East Side, the venue for the now infamous scene from *When Harry Met Sally*, and we pile inside.

'You need to pre-book for large parties,' the greeter informs us as she eyes us all standing in the doorway.

'Oh no, we don't want a table, we're looking for a clue,' I reply, forgetting that not everyone knows about our treasure hunt.

'Sounds to me more like you haven't got one,' the greeter remarks, pulling a face.

But I'm too busy looking around the diner.

'Dad!' I shout as I spot Dad and Eleanor sitting at a table. 'Look, I just need to speak to my father,' I smile sweetly at the greeter. 'He's sitting right over there.'

She sighs and shakes her head. 'Go on then. Just you, though – the rest of them stay here.'

I head into the restaurant, weaving my way in and out of the tables of diners having their sandwiches and bagels.

'You made it this far, then?' Dad asks, smiling up at me. 'We wondered if you would.'

'Of course! The clues haven't been that bad. In fact, some of them have been quite easy.'

'Well, here's your next one,' Eleanor says, opening her bag. She hands me the key with the now familiar note attached.

If this big guy had been a bit more tired and in love maybe he would have taken the elevator.

I read the clue to Dad and Eleanor. 'Any ideas?'

They shake their heads.

'I'd better go and read it to the others, then, because nothing is springing to mind for me either. Are you coming?' I ask them.

'Scarlett, we wouldn't miss it for the world,' Dad says, quickly putting some dollars on the table to cover their bill.

Outside, we all stand and debate the newest clue.

'Big guy, big guy . . .' Jamie says. 'It could be anyone; there are loads of tall actors in movies.'

410

'And why should he be tired?' Max says, pacing along the sidewalk.

'Or in love, for that matter?' Bradley adds.

'I think the clue is in the word *elevator*,' Peter says. 'What movies have elevators in them?'

'Usually disaster ones,' I say dismally.

'I know, I know!' Oscar says, jumping up and down. He's been unusually quiet up to now, while we have all been discussing the latest riddle. 'What building in New York do you need a particularly big elevator to get to the top in?'

'The Rockefeller,' Jamie says.

'No, another.'

'The Empire State Building?' Eleanor suggests, joining in.

'Exactly, Eleanor! And how do you get to be very tired? If you're *sleepless* …'

'That's it, Oscar!' I cry. '*Sleepless in Seattle*. It finishes at the top of the Empire State Building, and the big guy the clue refers to is—'

'King Kong!' Max shouts. 'He would have taken the elevator if he'd been less sleepless and in love, instead of climbing up the outside!'

'Genius, Max!' Oscar and Max high-five. 'Great minds.' Oscar goes to hug him.

'Don't push it, Oscar,' Max grumbles.

'Let me guess,' Bradley sighs. 'Back up Fifth Avenue?'

'No, let's take Fourth and Park,' Jamie says. 'It will be quicker and less busy.'

As we arrive at the Empire State Building, I'm utterly convinced I'm going to find Sean waiting at the top of it. It has to be him. Plus I don't know anyone else in New York; all my other clue-bearers have already been used up.

'Uh-oh,' Oscar says as we pile in our now customary fashion through the door. 'Look at that queue!'

Of course, when I'd visited before it had been first thing in the morning, and I'd avoided the busy times and the horrendous queueing by doing so.

'Are you the party on the treasure hunt?' a young man in an official uniform enquires.

'Yes we are, why?' I ask.

'Then come this way, please,' he says, guiding us through a different entrance. 'This will be your own private lift to the top,' he says, stopping outside a row of lift doors. 'Enjoy your time at the Empire State Building.'

'Wow, our own private lift?' Oscar gasps as we all squeeze inside. 'This is so cool.'

'I bet you do stuff like this all the time, Bradley,' Max comments as the doors close on us and we're whizzed up to the top.

'Actually no, this *is* pretty cool,' Bradley says, still wearing his baseball hat and shades. 'The whole thing, I mean, not just the private lift.'

As the lift pings to signal we've reached the top, the doors open and out we all go onto the viewing deck where, not that long ago, I'd stood with the sailors dressed as King Kong having my photo taken. I look madly around for Sean, ready to run over and embrace him for doing something so romantic. But hurrying around all four sides of the viewing platform, I can't see him anywhere.

'Hello, Scarlett,' I suddenly hear behind me.

I turn around and look at the person using one of the sets of viewing binoculars.

'Ursula! Oh my goodness, how come? What are *you* doing here?'

'Just taking in the view,' she grins. 'Actually I was wondering if you were looking for one of these,' she dangles a key in my face.

'You too?' I ask in amazement. 'But ... how did you get here? Does Oscar know?'

'No, but he will any minute ...'

'Urse! What in the name of all things Dior are you doing here?' Oscar cries, running along the viewing platform towards us.

'I'm a clue-bearer too!' Ursula squeaks in excitement.

'I thought it was going to be Sean at the top,' I say, as everyone else arrives to join us. 'Like in *Sleepless in Seattle*.'

'No, far too obvious,' Ursula says. 'He thought he'd get his sister to cover for him.'

'So it *is* Sean, then!' I say in delight.

'Ursula, you've given the game away!' Oscar moans. 'We've all kept it a secret.'

'She'd guessed anyway, hadn't you, Scarlett?'

'Yes, pretty much. Well, I secretly hoped it was him. So how many more clues?'

'We don't know,' Peter says. 'None of us knows exactly what's going on. All we know is our own little part in this. The rest is just as big a mystery to us as it is to you.'

'That's right,' Bradley adds. 'When Sean called me and said what he was doing, I was intrigued, I just couldn't say no. It's like something from a movie.'

'But how did Sean get your number? Oh, your card ...' I say, remembering Sean seeing it propped up on the dressing table.

'I don't know about anyone else, but I want to see what happens next!' Ursula encourages. 'Come on, read that next clue out.'

I look down at the paper and read.

I hope your hunt is going well so far. If there have been any problems, perhaps you should come here to retrace your history, then we can iron out any hitches …

While the others stare blankly at each other, Oscar and I smile and share a knowing look. 'Ellis Island?' I say quietly. 'Ellis Island,' he agrees.

Thirty-seven

'Please explain this clue again,' Eleanor asks as we travel in three yellow cabs down towards Battery Park.

'It's simple, Mum,' Jamie says. 'The *hitches* part of it refers to the movie *Hitch* which had a scene set here, and the *retrace your history* part refers to people tracing their families and coming over to Ellis Island.'

'I see, and we're all going to go over there now?' she asks, looking around the inside of the cab, then behind her at the one following us containing Peter, Oscar and Max.

'I hope so,' I say, wondering how we're going to get us all onto the ferry. The queues will be massive at this time of day; I just hope Sean has arranged a VIP trip over there again …

We arrive at Battery Park and, as I suspected, the queues are enormous, snaking all the way around the ticket building.

'So what now?' my father asks. 'Do we join the queue?'

'Are you kidding?' Oscar says. 'This is Scarlett, she'll be let in in no time.'

But as we hang around the end of the queue, no one appears to offer us a free pass through.

'Maybe we should ask at the booth,' Max suggests. 'Perhaps they don't know we're here.'

'Excuse me?' a voice behind us says. 'I'm sorry to bother you, but I couldn't help noticing you all standing there. Are you filming something for TV?'

Max has been randomly filming all our adventures on a small hand-held video camera while we've been travelling round New York. He stops recording for a moment. 'Not today, no,' he says. 'Why?'

'It's just, I'm from a US TV show and I couldn't help but notice that one of the members of your party is someone a little famous.' She nods in Bradley's direction.

He drops his head slightly.

'And it's a bit of a chance I'm taking here, but I was wondering if he'd like to take part in an episode we're making, over in the bay?'

417

'I very much doubt it,' Max says.

'What's the TV show?' I ask. 'Just out of interest?'

As we head across the Hudson River towards the Statue of Liberty and Ellis Island I have to pinch myself, because I'm living out one of my fantasies.

I'm standing in a speedboat next to Bradley Cooper, who is still wearing his shades, but he's removed his baseball hat for the ride, and his hair, like mine, is blowing in the fierce wind caused by the speed at which we're travelling across the water.

The programme that just happens to be being filmed in the Hudson River today is the US equivalent of *Top Gear*, and in exchange for a quick interview with Bradley about cars and a shot of him in the speedboat with the host, three speedboats in total are now racing their way across to Ellis Island, carrying my posse of clue-bearers.

As we pull up at the landing bay, I hop out.

'Are you OK to wait?' I ask my driver – a woman – just before I dash off.

'Are you kidding me?' she says. 'I have Bradley Cooper in my boat. Take as long as you like!'

I run along the wooden jetty and into the main building.

I stand in the centre of the Great Hall of Ellis Island

looking around me, wondering who on earth is going to be my clue-bearer this time. I couldn't believe Sean had flown Ursula over to New York just to do that. It was complete and utter madness, but in a very good way.

'Scarlett,' a voice says, from behind the central display of immigrants' trunks, suitcases and possessions.

'Mum?'

As I run over to my mother and hug her, here in this extraordinary building where so many people have been reunited with their ancestors, I find myself brought together yet again with a member of my own family.

'You as well?' I ask as we embrace. 'Did Sean fly you over too?'

'Explanations later, Scarlett. I have a gift for you,' she says, pulling away from me to pass me yet another key.

'But how . . . I mean, when . . . ?'

'Just read your clue,' she insists.

It shouldn't take you long to get here, should be before tomorrow or the day after . . . if you're a lucky Lady.

I pull a face.

'Oh dear,' my mother says. 'Have they all been that bad?'

'No, some have been easy. Some pretty tricky, though. Come on, we'd best go and ask the others.'

We walk back over to the boats at the jetty, and I read the clue out to everyone.

Most of the men let out loud tuttings and similar noises, to convey their disbelief.

'That's an easy one, Scarlett,' Max says, rolling his eyes. 'How could you not know that?'

'What's the answer then?' I say almost huffily. I don't like them guessing the film clues and not me.

'*The Day After Tomorrow*,' they all shout together.

'And?' I ask. 'I haven't seen that film, have I?'

'She's not keen on disaster movies, are you, Scarlett?' Dad says. 'She likes a nice love story with a happy ending.'

'Nothing wrong with that,' Bradley says, as our driver nearly melts over her steering wheel.

'So . . .' I ask, looking between each of them, 'where are we going now?'

'Liberty Island!' They all shout again as the speedboat's engines start up.

'The movie has a scene where the Statue of Liberty sinks into snow and ice,' Jamie explains as we set sail for the island. 'It gets hit by a tsunami, too, if I remember rightly.'

'Nice,' I say, as the waves begin to splash up the side of the boat again. 'Sounds like just my sort of film.'

As we sail over to Liberty Island, I'm now in a

complete daze. How are Ursula and my mother here in New York? And how long have they been here? But I hardly have time to think about it before we're mooring and I'm setting foot on solid ground again.

I hold out my hands. 'Where shall I go, to the top, around to the front?'

'Try the front,' my mother suggests.

I run to the front of Liberty Island, with Lady Liberty herself watching my every move all the way round. As I get to the most popular spot for tourists to have their photo taken, I see my next clue-bearer waiting for me. She's wearing a green foam Liberty crown, and holding a fake torch which she points at me as she sees me coming towards her.

It had to be.

'Maddie!' I cry as she runs towards me, her crown falling to the ground. 'I can't believe any of this is happening. What's going on?'

'A bit of Maddie madness right now,' she grins, placing her crown on my head. 'Here it is, kiddo, your next clue!'

Enchant me by meeting me here so we can reunite . . .
Just like so many movies that have gone before. You'll
be on one side, I'll be on the other, but for us to meet in
the middle you need to unlock your final clue . . .

'Enchant me? He sounds like a prince in a fairytale,' I laugh. Then I stop and stare at Maddie. 'In *Enchanted* the characters meet on the Brooklyn Bridge, don't they? What else did it say?' I look down at the piece of paper again. '*You'll be on one side, I'll be on the other.* Yes, it's definitely the bridge, but what's this about unlocking my final clue? Is this what all the keys have been about?'

'I don't know,' Maddie laughs. 'But you'd better get over there and find out!'

Our TV friends drop us by boat under the Brooklyn Bridge by one of the piers, and we head to the entrance of the bridge and begin to walk towards the centre.

'Scarlett, look!' Oscar shouts when we're almost in the middle.

I turn to where he's pointing and see a giant red ribbon tied in a bow. Dangling off the bow is a padlock holding shut a small box and a tag that says *To Red*.

'I bet you have to open the padlock with one of your keys,' Maddie says. 'How many do you have?'

I empty all the keys from my pocket. 'Ten.'

'Go on then,' Bradley says. 'Make a start. I've been chasing over New York all afternoon to find out what this is all about.'

'And you haven't enjoyed yourself?' I ask, grinning at him as I take hold of the padlock.

'Well, I wouldn't say that,' he smiles back. 'Come on, get going – you've got a mystery to solve!'

I begin trying each key one by one. When I get to the tenth, I look back at the others all eagerly watching me. 'I should have known it would be the last one: typical!'

But even that key won't open the lock.

'It won't work!' I cry. 'None of them works.'

'That's because I have the key . . . ' I hear a voice call as it comes towards me across the bridge.

Sean.

As he gets closer, I see he holds yet another key up in his hand.

'I have the final key,' he says, as he arrives next to me. 'Because I'm hoping it's the key to your heart, Scarlett.'

I hear Oscar gasp behind me.

I watch mesmerised as Sean opens the padlock that releases the box. Then he turns towards me.

'Did you know that it's a tradition for a couple to secure their love by locking a padlock to a bridge and then tossing the key into the river?' he asks.

Speechless, I shake my head.

'Yes, I've seen that movie,' Eleanor says. '*Tre Metri Sopra il Cielo*? It was based on an Italian novel.'

'That is correct, Eleanor, thank you,' Sean says, smiling at her. 'It is indeed an Italian tradition, and it reached New York and the Brooklyn Bridge as a result of the movie. So, Scarlett,' he asks, looking at me again, 'would you like us to secure our love?'

I look at Sean in astonishment. Yet again he was amazing me with all this, just like last year on the London Eye.

'But you've just unlocked the padlock,' I point out. 'We'd need to lock it again.'

Sean shakes his head. 'I don't mean with the padlock. I mean with this.' He drops to one knee and opens up the box, and this time I hear gasps from all the female members of the party as well as Oscar, as a diamond ring glints in the setting evening sun.

'Scarlett,' he continues, as I gaze down at him with a mixture of love and wonder in my eyes. 'I hope you have enjoyed today. I'm sorry lately if life has been a bit dull, but I want every day of your life to be just as exciting and amazing and wonderful as I hope today has been for you. And I want to be the person that makes it that exciting. I want to be there to share it all with you, every step of the way. So if you'll have me, Red, I'm asking you if you'll be my wife.' Sean takes the ring from the box and holds it up in his hand. 'Will you marry me, Scarlett?'

I open my mouth to speak, but the words won't come out. It's as if my mouth has just ceased functioning. I look at the others standing next to us, all the most important people from my life back home that Sean has gathered, along with everyone from my time here in New York, to share this moment with us.

They gaze back at me, just willing me to say the right word.

I look down at Sean again. This wonderful, incredible man . . . and suddenly I find all I need to say.

'Yes.' I nod happily. 'Yes, of course I'll marry you, Sean.'

And as the sun continues to set across the East River, everybody that's important in my world gathers around me.

And for the first time ever, my life feels truly complete.

Scarlett's Treasure Hunt

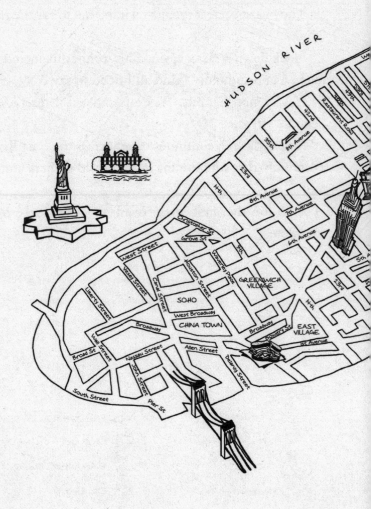

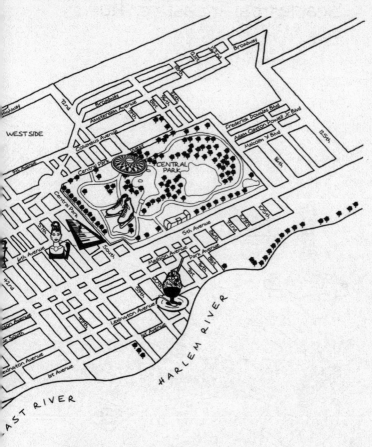

Clues:

1. Serendipity 3

2. Strawberry Fields

3. Tiffany's

4. Wollman Ice Rink

5. New York Public Library

6. FAO Schwarz

7. Katz's Deli

8. Empire State Building

9. Ellis Island

10. Statue of Liberty

Finale: Brooklyn Bridge

Ali's Guide To New York

Before you go

Best Map: *The New York Mapguide: The Essential Guide to Manhattan* (Michael Middleditch, Penguin). I lost my copy of this the last time I was there and immediately bought a new one ready for my next trip! That's how good it is!

Best App: *NewYork2Go* Shows you your exact location in NYC on a street map, gives you a map of the subway, plus a helpful guide to the city. (And most importantly no wi-fi is required to use it!)

Movies to Watch: Anything set in New York will get you in the mood! Some of my favourites: *Serendipity*, *When Harry Met Sally*, *You've Got Mail*, and *The Adjustment Bureau*. Or if you're lucky enough to visit near Christmas there's *Elf* and *Home Alone 2 – Lost In New York*.

Music to play!

In the book Scarlett has a playlist on her iPod she listens to constantly before she leaves. This is what's on it:

- New York – Paloma Faith
- Empire State of Mind – Jay-Z & Alicia Keys
- Native New Yorker – Odyssey
- Theme from New York, New York – Frank Sinatra
- Back to Manhattan – Nora Jones
- I'll Take Manhattan – Kit McClure Big Band
- Arthur's Theme – Christopher Cross
- Fairytale of New York – The Pogues & Kirsty MacColl

When you're there

Tourist stuff

You can get many books that will tell you all about the tourist attractions in more detail, but the main paid ones are:

- The Statue of Liberty and Ellis Island (sit on the right side of the boat for the best views going over!)
- The Empire State Building – do this one first thing on a clear sunny day if you can, and then 'Top of the Rock' at night (or the other way around, but the view over NYC at night is not to be missed!)
- The Met Museum – the impressionist paintings are amazing!

All these (plus some others) come under the New York City Pass – best value for seeing all the main attractions.

It will save you loads on entrance fees, plus you get to skip a lot of the queues! Talking of queues, one of my best tips would be GET UP EARLY to avoid them; all the main tourist attractions have massive queues at peak times, so go early. Your body clock is still on UK time, so getting up early is easy, as is going to bed early, you'll be exhausted from all the walking!

Places From the Movies

Again, there are loads. This is a great book if you want to do a New York 'spot the location' movie tour. *New York: The Movie Lover's Guide* (Richard Alleman, Broadway Books).

But some key 'rom-com' ones would be:

- Katz's Deli on the Lower East Side, that scene from *When Harry Met Sally* was shot there!
- Café Lallo on the Upper West Side is the café in *You've Got Mail* where Tom Hanks and Meg Ryan are on their very confused blind date.
- The top of the Empire State Building is of course featured at the end of *Sleepless in Seattle*.
- The Big Piano in FAO Schwarz is in the movie *Big*.
- Tiffany's on Fifth Avenue was made famous by Audrey Hepburn in *Breakfast at Tiffany's*.
- And from *Serendipity*, the Woolman Rink and the Serendipity3 restaurant itself (see below.)

Food

There are so many great restaurants in Manhattan that it would be impossible to list them all here, but I've picked these for the main NYC food groups: Pizza, Burgers, Coffee, and a good breakfast!

- **Best Pizza:** Johns Pizzeria, 260 West 44th Street. Great pizza in elegant surroundings.
- **Best Burgers:** Shake Shack in Madison Square Park. Get there early though, or the queues will be long . . . but it's worth it for their milkshakes alone. I had the Fair Shake – delicious!!
- **Best Coffee:** There's a Starbucks on virtually every street, but go where the locals go: Stumptown on 29th & Broadway. Hang out with the cool dudes on their laptops, or just sit and chill out with native New Yorkers!
- **Best Breakfast:** They actually claim to be the 'The Busiest & Best Breakfast in New York' and their pancakes definitely live up to that mighty statement. It's the Pershing Square Cafe just opposite Grand Central Terminal.
- And if you love the movie *Serendipity*, or even if you don't, you must go to Serendipity3 on 60th Street (between 2nd & 3rd Avenues) for their frozen hot chocolate! Heaven through a straw!

Free Stuff

A trip to New York can be expensive, there's no denying it. But there's lots of free things you can do too.

- **Central Park** – a wonderful place, and one of my favourite places to go in the city. There's so much to see here, be prepared to spend a whole day if necessary – it's so big!

But if you're in a hurry, here are some key places:

- the famous tree lined Mall – you'll recognise it straight away from numerous movies and TV shows.
- The Bethesda Fountain, with the Angel of the Waters on top, serenely watching down over Central Park.
- Strawberry Fields, the quiet area of the park dedicated to the memory of the late John Lennon.
- **The Brooklyn Bridge** – Walk the bridge to Brooklyn and back! Or walk one way and get the subway back the other. Worth it for the glorious views over the East River! Look for the Padlocks while you're on the bridge … you'll find a full explanation in the book in case you're reading this first ;-)
- **Grand Central Station** – or to give it its correct name, Grand Central Terminal. You will never look at another train station in quite the same way after you've spent time gazing around at the opulent interiors and up at the crystal chandeliers of Grand Central!

Hotels

I can only recommend the two hotels I've stayed in while in New York. They are 70 Park Avenue (which is the hotel I based Scarlett and Oscar's on) and The Grand Hyatt. Both I managed to pick up on an internet/flight and hotel deal. Definitely worth shopping around for. Both lovely places at the time of writing.

Shopping

You might be tempted to do a little bit of shopping while you're here ...

The two most famous department stores, Macy's and Bloomingdales, offer visitor discount cards, usually worth 10% off your purchases (some exclusions) – just remember to take some ID in with you, i.e. a passport, and head up to the visitor centre when you get to the stores to pick up yours.

But other than that, I suggest you either go with one pretty empty case, or travel with an airline where you can pay to take an extra case home with you rather than risk excess baggage charges, because you'll need it. New York truly is a shopper's paradise ...

Misc

Tipping

New Yorkers working in service industries rely on their tips as part of their wages; they actually get taxed up front on it! So please tip while you're there, unless the service is truly awful, which is unusual for New York; it's usually service with a smile! ☺ I've found if you're nice to people, people are usually nice in return.

And my last piece of advice would be: it's not *Sex and the City*! If you're going to New York for the first time to see the sights and shop, you will be walking – a lot! So dress appropriately. Unless of course you've got lots and lots of dollars in your Gucci purse for yellow cabs to drop you off at every doorstep!

But most importantly – enjoy, and have a great time! New York is a fantastic city and I love it.

Ali x